Fire and Rain

A Rain's Quest novel

I0686965

Dauna Grey

Gray Dragon Books

Orlando, Florida

Copyright

Fire and Rain. Copyright ©2024 by Donna Gray-Williams

979-8-9903026-0-0 (pbk.)
979-8-9903026-1-7 (ebook)

Cover illustration: Hampton Lamoureux

To

VALERIE

Never forgotten

&

SHERYL

For your encouragement

&

DARA

A continuing inspiration

Contents

Chapter 1

"Begin at the beginning," the king said very gravely, "and go on til you come to the end: then stop."

I LANDED HARD, FALLING to my already sore knees. "Thanks a lot," I grumbled sarcastically, not for the first time that morning.

At the beginning of my journey, I'd faced hundreds of miles to travel, but I didn't have a horse or a donkey. I had to travel on foot, but I didn't want to take weeks or months to get to my destination. To make my traveling faster, if not exactly easier, I'd developed a magical charm, taking inspiration from an old fairy tale about seven-league boots. A league was roughly defined as three miles. Twenty-one miles was too much at one time, but I could easily do three miles per step.

I tested this theory by beginning with short distances, steadily increasing until I had to stop completely and reconfigure the charm. It wasn't just the landings magic couldn't seem to get right. Magic tried to thrust me through any object in my way. As a person with a solid body, I couldn't go through anything more solid than I was. I had the bruises to prove it.

I'd finally had to add instructions to move or raise me around obstacles like old ruins, trees, and bodies of water. I was actually flying over treetops to avoid stationary objects, but I had no real control over the movement. It was up and down and sideways, depending on what was in the way. It was fast and literally breathtaking and had often been scary and disorienting, but I got sort of used to hurtling into and through the air covering three miles in about three minutes. I found three miles at one time was the maximum magic could handle without slamming me flat into the ground at the end of a step, no matter how much I emphasized a gentle landing. The landings were still a bit rough, but I was satisfied with three miles of hurtling instead of walking. It saved my feet if not my knees.

I'd gone the distance of about fourteen hundred miles in less than a week, but it was still exhausting. The hurtling through the air adrenaline rush was more physically grueling than I expected—or maybe it was the landings that were taking their toll. Whatever the reason, three hundred miles was my limit for a night's travel, and that's when I stopped.

I only traveled this exciting way after midnight until the wee hours of the morning, so I had the least chance of being seen. After that last harrowing step, I scooted over to the nearest tree and rested for a while, waiting for the sun to come up completely before continuing my travels on foot. I put a temporary ward of protection around myself, then I took a canteen and tasty banana-blueberry-walnut muffin out of my backpack for breakfast.

After eating, I centered myself to meditate. I did this for a few hours every day. Magic was in every living thing, but it was new to this world: young, wild, and contrary. It took ability and effort to use it. I had to tell it in detail what I wanted. The more complex the charm, the less likely magic would follow it completely, like a kid only half listening to instructions. With my consciousness, I touched the magic reserve within myself for it to become familiar with me. I needed that connection to work charms. And leaving out anything was a loophole for evasion. Misunderstandings were rampant. My meditation ritual was my "making friends with magic" time.

Magic had been saturating the Earth for almost a hundred years. That's pretty young for an entity on a planet billions of years old. It wasn't native to this planet, but it had been the catalyst to halting and reversing the effects of global warming. During the peak of the Great Warming, the ice caps had melted, and the Earth had heated to uninhabitable levels over eighty percent of its surface. Only the far north and south areas were still habitable, but with high temperatures even in winter and less than optimal rain. It took decades for the first seeding of magic to infiltrate the Earth's crust and inhabit the DNA of every living thing. It was still working its way to the center of the planet. Magic had forced many changes in the surviving people, animals, and plants. It was a few decades into the third millennia, and the human population was only a small fraction of the pre-severe-warming world of eight billion.

I don't know if there would have been any people left if magic hadn't caused the Great Warming to peak and begin to reverse. It was still too hot in the center of the world, but the temperatures had begun to creep downward from about seventy years ago. People were slowly migrating south, but not too far yet. The towns I was interested in were only forty to fifty years old and still north of the old Canadian border.

The sun was up and bright by the time I finished meditating. I stood up, stretched, dispersed my ward, then began to walk through the woods without a clear path to follow. The main road was at least twenty miles north of me. Traveling alone, I avoided main roads whenever possible to limit the opportunity for robbery, assault, or any other unpleasant occurrences that could happen to a person traveling alone. I'd been told extensively about all the hazards of travel. Duly warned, I limited my exposure to danger, because I might not be risk averse, but I wasn't stupid.

I had a charm that expanded my awareness for a few hundred yards. It was my version of radar. With that charm I could sense heat signatures, so I knew when a large animal or person was nearby. I couldn't tell by heat if they were dangerous, but for something big, I wrapped myself in a ward and waited it out. I could also create noises in the distance with another charm to move it on.

Before starting my journey, I'd practiced a variety of defensive and evasive charms to avoid dangerous confrontations—enough to sort of satisfy my Jardvari (guardians / teachers / babysitters) that I could travel safely. They thought I would be traveling to towns on the west coast, not the center of the habitable continent. Those were the towns they were most familiar with, having visited them periodically to keep me up-to-date on any significant challenges. I was heading into territory they had never vetted. I didn't know if they'd praise me for the ingenuity of my new travel method or exclaim in horror that I had ventured so far from home base. Probably both. I'm glad they weren't here to guilt me, chide me, or try to stop me. I had made promises to be careful, but I never promised to stay within a specific boundary.

After about thirty minutes, the direction I followed opened up to a very wide clearing. I was leery of clearings. They were often manmade and contained traps. I stopped still outside the clearing to look, listen, and taste the air for immediate danger.

As I listened to the quiet forest, expecting to hear insects, birds, and branches moving in the light breeze, I became aware of another small sound. I heard a faint human voice. I quietly skirted the clearing, moving toward it. I was nearly halfway around when I saw a large hole at the far end. The voice was coming from inside the hole.

"Help me. Please. Somebody help me. I'm sorry. I'm sorry. Don't leave me here," the small, childish voice pleaded repeatedly. "I'm afraid," it added in a piteous mew.

I slowly approached the hole. I kneeled down and peered over the edge, not knowing what to expect. Would I find a real child, or a creature created by magic?

A small female child, maybe nine or ten years old, sat at the bottom of the hole. It was at least ten feet deep, with steep, smooth sides. No merely human child could climb out of this hole. It was wide and rectangular, almost twice as big as a grave.

I sat down facing her, crossed my legs, and leaned over the opening. I watched and listened to her for another minute. She was sitting protectively with her knees to her chest and her arms wrapped tightly around them. I didn't see anything threatening in the hole. It seemed to be just an inescapable prison with no food or water.

It was early fall. The leaves on the trees were just beginning to turn colors because the days were shorter, not because the temperature was appreciably cooler. It was around ninety-five degrees and despite the shade from the trees, it must have been very hot in that hole. Judging by her condition, and with no water, she couldn't last longer than a few days.

"How did you get down there?" I finally asked, projecting my voice into the hole.

The child scrambled to her feet. "Help me! Get me out of here!" she demanded and stomped her foot.

"How did you get down there?" I asked again. I was in no hurry to free her until I completely understood why she was there.

She looked around, then looked up again. "I—I fell in."

I shook my head. "I don't think so. You would have broken or sprained something in that long a fall. Without food, you wouldn't have healed yet. You don't look especially hurt, just dirty, hungry, and thirsty. Try again."

Her shoulders slumped, and she dropped back to the ground. She didn't speak again for a full minute. "They put me here," she said disconsolately.

"Who did?"

She just shook her head.

"What did you do?"

She shook her head again and said nothing.

I studied her some more and sniffed the air around the hole again. I think I could guess why she was there, despite the dominant smell of urine in one corner. Sitting back in her woebegone huddle, she wasn't going to verify this without some prompting. "You're a shapeshifter—aren't you?"

She shook her head vehemently. "Girls can't shapeshift. Everyone knows that."

"It appears everyone was wrong. Apparently, they can—or at least one can. What animal are you?" I'd already guessed the Clan. My sense of smell was very good for a human.

She shook her head again.

"You might as well tell me. I'm not going to let you out until I know what you are." That was a lie. Of course I wouldn't leave a child to die alone in a hole just for being different. But it was what my Jardvari expected for this journey. They'd been insistent that I limit my risks.

"Ocelot. They said I'm an Ocelot," she whispered, but I could hear her.

"Clan Cat," I said as I studied her. The human half of a shifter only by coincidence resembled their animal counterpart, or she'd have large black spots and streaks like an ocelot. Her hair wasn't even especially streaky. It was a human short, curly brown. Her eyes were a pansy brown. Her skin was a reddish brown under the darker dirt. "So they put you in a hole when they found out."

She nodded her head. "I'm an abomination. I shouldn't exist. I must be evil."

"Someone doesn't know their history. I would expect Clan Cat to have a better education system." I studied her a long moment. My Jardvari would tell me to leave her here. In fact, they had a rule for that. Rule number thirteen: *Do not collect anomalies.* They hadn't anticipated that I would find my first anomaly in a helpless, vulnerable child. Surely they'd excuse this one rule violation.

I stood up. "Hold on, I'm going to get you out."

She scrambled to her feet as well and looked up at me with such raw hope on her face, I would have moved heaven and earth to get her out of that hole. Luckily, I wouldn't have to work that hard.

I scanned the woods surrounding us. I couldn't make this look too easy. Even my new acquaintance couldn't know exactly what I was capable of. She had to win my trust as I did hers. Just because she was a child didn't mean she wouldn't take advantage of my secrets to benefit herself or inadvertently reveal them. Rule number one was *Trust no one.* I'd heard that often enough in my childhood that they could have left it off the list of rules and I would have followed it instinctively.

I would use what nature provided to release this child. I'd need at least a sturdy, somewhat over ten-foot-long tree or branch to lower into the hole. It didn't have to be huge, just big enough to support a magical Ocelot of about sixty to seventy pounds. Ocelots were one of the smallest of the cat species, but she would shift to bigger than a real ocelot.

All shifters often shifted much larger than their animal counterparts, magic giving them more mass and weight. Magic also gave the two most dominant Clans, Wolf and Cat, some equality. While real and shifted jaguars could weigh as much as two hundred and fifty pounds and therefore dominate any Felidae or Canidae species on this continent, magic had given a boost to Wolf shifters, who now weighed as much as shifted Jaguars. Those were the two dominate shifters from Clans Wolf and Cat.

"I'll be right back," I told the girl and headed into the woods.

I entered the surrounding woods, looking at the trees until I found some likely candidates. I picked a tree and shook it, checking its sturdiness. I shifted the earth beneath the tree using an Earth charm, shaking it free. If it had been a larger tree, the root system would have been massive and probably would have affected the other trees around, pulling them free from the earth as well. I only needed a younger tree. It still had a healthy root system to reach water, but not massive.

The tree fell with a loud whoosh and thump, with me directing its fall to a space between the other trees. Using an Air charm to support most of the weight, I dragged it out into the clearing by its roots, then pulled it to the hole. I was stronger than I looked but needed to appear just as average as I seemed. *Hide what you can do* was rule number two.

I remembered to breathe heavily from my exertion and sweat a bit as I peered down over the edge of the hole again, because I didn't look strong enough to drag a heavy, dense tree far over rough ground without appearing exerted. I didn't know how observant children were, so I had to allow appearances to be deceiving.

"Stand out of the way against that far side of the hole." I pointed to where I wanted her to go for safety. "I found a small fallen tree in the woods. I'm going to push it into the hole. Don't try to climb out as a human. You'll need your claws to climb up the tree. Take your clothes off and wrap them in a bundle." I didn't think at her age she'd have enough magic to change her clothes when she shifted. She wouldn't be able to do that successfully until she was on the other side of puberty. "You'll need them when you get out. I don't have anything suitable for you to wear. I want you to shift, carry your bundle of clothes in your mouth, then climb up the tree."

I pushed the tree roots first over the hole until I was sure I could drop it at an angle. I looked down once more to make sure I wasn't dropping it on the child. She'd moved but hadn't changed yet. Instead, she just watched me as I lowered the tree.

"Go on. Change," I ordered her and stood back, waiting for her to shift and climb out. Shifting forms twice in a row with no nourishment in who knew how many days would be tiring. I didn't want her to fall asleep as a Cat afterward, so I pushed a little magic into her shift with some to spare for shifting back. I had a large magic reserve, but I gave her just enough to shift without question.

After she reached the top and sprang from the hole, I told her to change back and get dressed. While she did that, I pulled the tree back out of the hole and dragged it back into the woods. I used an Air charm to straighten it up and place it back in its hole while I used an Earth magic charm to return the dirt I'd displaced and pack it around the tree. I stood back to be certain it could stand on its own, then I used a Water charm to pull water up to feed the roots. Using basic elemental magic didn't require as much instruction to magic. It was things that didn't neatly categorize elementally that required an essay to get magic moving in the right direction.

When I returned to the hole, clapping bits of loose bark off my hands, the child was sitting down and waiting for me. She was a sorry-looking little thing, all dirty, tired, skinny, and smelly. I needed to get her something to eat and drink before she passed out.

"Why did you hide it back there?" she gestured to the woods I'd returned from. Thankfully, she couldn't see what I'd done with it from where she sat. I'd chosen one well away from her underground oubliette.

"When Clan Cat comes back, I don't want them to figure out how you got out of the hole."

"Why? Why would they come back?" Her voice betrayed her hope.

I shrugged. "If they should come back, I don't want them looking for you or your allies. Let them puzzle it out. Come on, we better get out of here before someone comes to check on you." I didn't tell her bluntly *to be sure you're dead*. She'd have to figure that out on her own.

I'd found the mound of dirt in the woods that had once filled the hole. I don't know why they moved it, but if the girl had mage magic besides shifting magic, maybe they thought she'd be able to move dirt back into the hole to give her herself a way of climbing out. If she had a lot of magic, she could have done it even if she couldn't see it or know where it was.

I decided I would charm the dirt and plants to return to their previous home once we'd left the clearing. It would hopefully look as if it had never been dug up. That should be an easy fix. The magic in the soil and plants would want to be back home and readily spring back to their former place. It would look as if the ground had never been disturbed—I hoped. I'd send a breeze through the area to mix up the scents so whoever put a child in this hole would have doubts they'd even remembered the right area.

"I can come with you?" she asked in a small, hesitant voice.

I smiled at her, then hesitated. I certainly couldn't send her back home, and she couldn't manage on her own. With this one rescue, I was breaking so many rules (at least six); my Jardvari would have a conniption fit if they knew. Of course, what they didn't know couldn't hurt them. "Sure you can. I don't have a traveling companion yet. That can be you." I started toward the opposite end of the clearing from where I'd entered, then stopped. "Which way is your village?"

She pointed ahead toward the right. Of course we couldn't go to the village that had doomed her because she was a female shifter.

"Okay. Follow me." My destination was decided. Clan Wolf it would be. I led the way out of the clearing. We walked at her slower pace. I set my charm to fill the hole as we walked farther away.

Once we entered fully into the woods, I reached into my backpack and took out my canteen and handed it to her. She gulped the water thirstily. If she was too dehydrated, she might vomit it all up again. I didn't stop her from drinking her fill. Instead, I tried a calming charm on her stomach as she drank, which seemed to work. Meeting her was a good test of my abilities. I needed real-life practice and experience.

Once she stopped drinking to breathe, I asked, "How long were you in that hole?"

"I saw two moons."

I reached into my backpack again and this time pulled out the huge hunk of bread and cheese I had wrapped up in a cloth. I handed them to her.

She started eating hungrily but paused and asked with her mouth full, "Is this *all* your food?"

"No. You can eat it all."

She continued eating, then stopped again. "We can't go this way. That way's Wolf Trap."

"Why not?"

"They'll smell me. They're my town's enemies. They'll kill us," she warned. "There's no safe place for me to go."

"We'll be fine. You're too dirty to smell like anything but dirt. Just promise me not to shift unless I give you permission."

"I don't know if I can. I never meant to shift. I just *had* to."

I needed to find a magical way to prevent her from shifting. Her need to shift would overwhelm her eventually. "Don't worry. We'll find opportunities for you to shift so you won't feel a compulsion to do it even in Wolf Trap." I was making a lot of promises and decisions, but the more I thought about it, the more I liked the idea of a traveling companion. My Jardvari had never made a rule about traveling companions. It would cause complications, but it would make the journey more interesting. I'd known no children before; I'd been the only child at home. This could be fun.

"What's your name?"

"Tara Jansen."

"I'm Rain Dare. Nice to meet you, Tara Jansen."

"Reindeer?" she asked, puzzled.

"It does sound like that, doesn't it?" My first name was given to me, but I'd chosen my last name. It was a name from history that had interested me. "It's Rain, like precipitation from the sky, and Dare, like I challenge you to do something."

She made a grunting noise in response since her mouth was full.

We walked on. I listened to her eat and drink. I wouldn't make her talk anymore with her mouth full. She might choke.

When she finished eating, she handed me back the cloth that had been wrapped around the food. Of course, she'd eaten it all. I stuffed it into my backpack and pulled out a couple of apples. What was dinner without dessert? I handed her one and kept one to eat myself. They were big, red, juicy apples.

Her eyes widened. "I've never seen an apple this big before."

I took a crunchy bite from mine. It was sweet and very juicy. "I was surprised myself. Most of the apples I've seen hereabouts are really puny."

She took a big bite of her own apple. "Mmmm," she said.

We walked and ate for a few minutes. I finished mine before she did hers. I stopped, took a small spade from my backpack and dug a hole, dropped my apple core inside, then covered it back up. I didn't need the spade to dig the hole, but it was a rule to hide my abilities.

"Why did you do that?"

"Maybe an apple tree will grow here one day."

"Can I bury mine?"

"Sure." I handed her the spade as she finished off her apple. "Give the trees some space. Dig your hole a few yards away."

Tara wiped her hands on her dirty pants and dug the hole where I showed her. She dropped in her apple core and closed it up. She didn't try to use magic to dig her hole. Since shapeshifting was magic, maybe most of her magic went to that. I would find out the more time we spent together.

We started walking again.

"Am I really going to be your companion?" She looked up at me with a sideways glance.

"Sure. Why not? How old are you, Tara?"

"Ten."

We were at least three generations into the changes brought on by magic. Ten/eleven was around the age when boys usually shifted the first time. Boys were born shifters and girls were born mages with the ability to manipulate magic. It had been that way as far as most people's memories, with no crossover of abilities—until now. No wonder Clan Cat freaked and put this child in a hole. It must have seemed completely sinister for a girl to shapeshift. It had never happened before, so it must be evil. Instead of embracing a new ability for girls, they decided to bury it. That wouldn't have been an easy decision to make. Shifters were very family oriented. Birth rates were much lower than in the past, and children were precious. It would have been difficult for anyone to cold-bloodedly kill a child. Leaving her out of sight to die was the easier choice.

"Do you have a family?"

"Not anymore," she said disconsolately.

"What family did you have?"

"Mom, dad, grandparents, aunt, and cousin."

"Was your family angry when you shifted?"

"They were afraid."

"Of you or for you?"

"I think mostly of me. Mom and Dad wouldn't touch me or look at me. They just let the soldiers take me away."

That was the reaction I would have expected from the unenlightened. Education should still be important, but the Clans could also be very xenophobic and reactionary. They only trusted their own kind. Tara was an anomaly—at least in her village. Magic wasn't finished with the changes it was making in the world. I was looking for anomalies and higher-level magic use on my fact-finding jaunt—as my Jardvari liked to call my venture into the world. But I was supposed to record them, not engage them (rules number eight and eleven). That would come much later when I had better control of my magic.

"Can you do magic as well as shapeshift?"

"Some. I can light a candle. I can move small objects. I can find water. I haven't been taught many charms yet."

Those were the three easiest tasks for a mage, and the ones they were born knowing when they were old enough to try. Everything else had to be practiced and learned over years. Mostly, domestic skills were encouraged.

I'd planned to find a place to stay for the winter among people. I was raised in fairly isolated conditions. Most of my learning and experience had come from books. In today's world, at sixteen, I would be considered an adult. I'd given my Jardvari one more year to get used to the idea, then a few months after my seventeenth birthday I set out to discover the world while I was still young enough to take risks. I couldn't wait until some undefinable time in the future when I was more powerful and magic had completed its saturation of the Earth. That could be decades from now. I needed to witness the changes, find them, and foster them. Tara was an example of people's fear and loathing of change. A lot of boys had died when the shifting ability first appeared. That shouldn't happen again.

My decision hadn't gone over very well. To appease my Jardvari, I'd taken the chains of their limiting rules and promised endlessly to be careful and to enlist their help if needed. I wasn't nearly as powerful as I would be twenty years from now, but I was tired of learning everything secondhand. I wanted to know myself what was going on in the world now.

I left home excited and hopeful. Scared and apprehensive came later, but this was what I had been born to do.

Now I had to find the perfect place to start gaining experiences. One ten-year-old wouldn't be enough. I needed a village, and it looked like a Clan Wolf village was the place for me to start.

Chapter 2

"You are old, Father William," the young man said, "And your hair
has become very white; And yet you incessantly stand on your
head—Do you think, at your age, it is right?"

WE DIDN'T TALK MUCH after Tara finished eating. I could tell she was
tired and needed to sleep as her shoulders drooped and her feet shuffled
rather than cleared the ground with each step. I pushed magic energy into
her whenever she flagged. After an hour or so, I began to scan for a good
campsite. I wanted to arrive in the village during the day, not after sunset.

I scanned the area with a charm, sensing heat and water sources. I
found a good campsite more west than north, where a small stream
trickled from a small, shallow pond supplied by an underground river.
There were no ruins especially close by. I preferred that. Ruins could be
dangerous areas of broken glass, sharp metal, deceptive flooring, animal
dens, and traps caused by the decay of long-unused buildings. I avoided
them when I could.

I guided Tara in that direction. I called a halt when I could smell the
water.

The foliage was thick around the small pond. It wasn't exactly stagnant,
but there was a dense algae bloom. I removed the algae with a charm
won easily from magic and removed the other contaminants that made
the water iffy for humans to drink. Magic had no aversion to charms
improving the quality of natural things. That was almost effortless magic,

and after we left, this would become a safer watering hole for all kinds of wildlife.

Tara had plopped down next to the pond and stared down at it instead of splashing the cooling waters on her flushed, dirty face. I didn't think she noticed my charms working.

"Go on. It's safe to drink," I assured her.

"How do you know?" she asked suspiciously.

"I can tell by look and smell." I didn't confess to having cleaned it. I was strong in all four elemental magics while most mages were strong in only two, and I wasn't sure which two magics I wanted to claim in Tara's presence. This was more *hide what you can do*, and I didn't want to limit myself yet.

She bent over the water and scooped many times, splashing as much on herself as inside.

I reached into my backpack and pulled out two canteens. I filled them and handed one to her. "Here. You can have your own canteen."

"Thank you." She took the canteen and hugged it to her chest. It had a strap that she could wear around her neck or over her shoulder. The design was based on canteens of the past, and it was made of recycled stainless steel.

I drank my fill of the water, then reached into my backpack again and pulled out a washcloth. "You can wash up. I don't have any soap with me. Just rubbing off the dirt should be good enough. Anyway, I wouldn't want to contaminate the water with soap. You can have a better wash when we reach town. I'll get you a change of clothes there, too." I gave the washcloth a little magical boost to charm away much of the grime and sweat. I'd do a more thorough cleaning charm in the morning.

As she washed, I thought about dinner. I didn't eat sentient beings, but Tara, as a predator, would benefit from some meat. Fortunately, I didn't need to hunt for dinner. I could pull almost anything out of my backpack because it was connected to my home base. But I wasn't making something out of nothing. The food and everything else I pulled out was real. It just traveled a very long distance in the blink of an eye. If one day I couldn't pull whatever I wanted out of my backpack, I'd know something was wrong at home. Eventually Tara would catch on that it wasn't an ordinary backpack, but since its extraordinary abilities only worked for me, she'd have to puzzle on it.

"We'll camp over there," I announced. I pointed to a small glade nearby.

"So soon? There's still a lot of daylight left." Her words held disagreement, but her impassive voice and general lethargy suggested otherwise.

"You're too tired to travel farther today."

I instructed Tara to relieve herself away from the camp and the water and to watch out for snakes, and did the same myself.

When Tara returned, I was seated in the center of the glade, and she came to sit next to me.

I pulled a reusable bag of beef stew out of my backpack and handed it to Tara. Her eyes lit up when she accepted it. She wouldn't mind eating it cold, but I warmed it with a Fire charm. I didn't have to produce fire to warm food. My charm could heat without burning if I was explicit in what I required. I pulled out another bag for myself of vegetables, tofu, rice, and mushroom stew. I'd have to remember to keep rice out of her meals or I'd have some explaining to do. In these times of heat and lesser quantities of rain, rice was scarce here, but it was plentiful at home.

After dinner, I handed Tara a blanket from my backpack and told her to make her bed where we sat. Then I walked a circular path around the outside perimeter. I placed stones strategically around the area to activate as a ward. I carried the stones with me. Each had a drop of my blood stored inside. Any bodily fluid would do, but blood was the best catalyst because it carried more of my essence. By infusing the stones, I could reuse them for years without having to recharge them with more blood. I'd prepared these stones before my journey. I had enough stones to ward a large building if necessary. I always used them for my unconscious nighttime protection. They lasted longer than any other type of ward.

I placed thirteen stones around us. Magic liked prime numbers. They were harder to break through because they didn't fit a pattern. I liked the number thirteen because it was still considered unlucky even today. I was contrary that way.

"What are you doing?"

She couldn't see exactly what I was doing through the foliage. "Walking the perimeter of our camp. I'm placing a ward of protection."

"What's that?"

"It's something new I learned recently. It will keep us safe while we sleep." New to her and new in the sense that I only started using it when I began my travels. If she were a human lie detector, she might detect the evasions. Luckily for me, that was a higher-level magic that no one possessed yet—not even me. When I finished laying out the stones, I charmed them with a complex protection charm, warding our camp to hide us completely to all senses. We could see and hear anyone or thing outside the circle, but they couldn't see or hear us. The air we breathed in and out would come from the top of the ward and disperse our scent far above us. Made with my blood, I would feel if it failed. So far, this type of ward lasted from setup to takedown. I could make wards of just water, fire, air, or earth, but with no anchors like the stones, they didn't last as long.

"You can go to sleep now. I'll know if someone or something comes near. Remember, if you need to pee in the night, do it in the farthest corner. Don't leave this clearing for any reason."

"I'll just rest my eyes a little," she muttered and closed her eyes. She dropped into a deep sleep, as I'd hoped she would.

I pulled another blanket from my backpack and sat down near Tara. It was too early for me to sleep. The sun was low in the sky but hadn't yet set. My own sleep would be lighter with short bursts of deep sleep, and I would be completely refreshed after four uninterrupted hours, meditating when I awoke. I only needed a longer sleep every few days.

I thought about my day's adventures and then my immediate plans for the future.

I didn't want to just hibernate on my own all winter. I wanted to stay around people. And I needed to find some kind of work so I could appear to afford shelter in town. I had access to money, but producing too much money without work would draw attention. I didn't know what kind of job opportunities Wolf Trap held, but there must be something I could do. Although inexperienced, I had book knowledge and was a fast learner. I should be able to find employment to support us. My Jardvari would prefer I didn't stay in any one place for long, but I couldn't learn enough if I didn't hang around. Rule number eight (*Interact without engaging*) was a stupid rule I always planned to disregard. Weren't interact and engage synonyms? How could I do one without the other? I could surely do both, revealing nothing vital.

That was the plan for now. I couldn't anticipate everything. I was making it up as I went along. I finally stilled my mind and went to sleep when dark fully descended.

I heard some animals approach our little camp during the night, but they steered around it and headed for the newly improved watering hole.

After gifting myself five hours of sleep, I sat up, crossed my legs, placed my hands face up on my knees, and began my morning meditations. I had hours until Tara awoke, considering how exhausted she'd been. Clearing my mind and reaching deep within myself was the only way to communicate successfully with magic. It was more approachable when I wasn't reaching out trying to use it. Eventually, when I needed it, it would recognize me and come easily.

A couple hours after dawn, I stopped my meditation when I sensed Tara stir. I felt energized and rejuvenated. I always did after a long session. The magic felt closer to me, eager to be used. If I needed to do something huge with magic, I'd definitely do it right after a meditation session.

Once Tara was fully awake, I pulled two large blueberry and walnut muffins from my backpack. Many fruits were making a comeback. I had to be sure to choose fruit with which she was familiar.

"This is *so* good," she mumbled around a mouthful of moist, sweet muffin.

"Muffins. Haven't you had them before?"

"Not like this."

"It's an old recipe—modernized, of course. It's sweetened with honey."

"Honey. I *love* honey." Of course she did. It was the only sweetener available these days besides the syrup from ripe fruit.

We finished our breakfast, drank more water from the pond, made sure our canteens were topped off, and left.

I'd already gathered my stones when Tara was finding a place to pee and then wash her face. I stowed the blankets, too. I'd also swept her clothes and person with a gentle cleaning charm before she awoke. She probably wouldn't even realize her hair was cleaner now than when she went to bed. That had been a tricky charm to perfect. I had to work on making it gentle and remove only dirt, sweat, stains, and dead skin cells without taking other things—important things like living skin, hair, and nails, or the dye of the material. But it was worth it. I could manage without enough water to clean myself for a long time.

We headed northwest toward Wolf Trap. We carefully crossed the main road after two miles of walking. There were no significant heat signatures nearby. I estimated we had about ten miles to go. We should reach Wolf Trap in the afternoon at yesterday's pace. That would give me time to look around and get the lay of the land before finding a place to sleep for the night.

I'd allowed the awareness charm to relax, except for our immediate surroundings, as I fought the jungle, the downside of not taking the main road. At some points, I could have used a machete, but instead used magic to hold back branches and make a path. It was still intense work.

I was as startled as Tara when we heard a voice calling for help.

Sending my awareness out with a charm, I sensed one human adult-sized stationary heat source. They were close enough that it was curious I hadn't sensed them before. A weak, sick, sleeping, or hurt person gave off fainter heat signatures, but they were lively now. This could be my second rescue in two days. I wondered who or what I would find this time.

"It doesn't sound like a kid," Tara whispered.

"No. It sounds like a grown man," I agreed.

"Is it a trick?"

"Good question. I don't know. Follow me quietly and we'll find out."

I used my quiet charm for us both, though it wasn't as necessary for Tara. Being a shifter and predator, Tara was naturally a quiet walker.

The call was intermittent. We stopped and started reflexively whenever we heard it. My senses were on high alert now, and the only person I sensed was ahead of us. When at last I thought we were almost on top of the sound, we'd come to an enormous tree with a wide canopy. Fallen leaves were layered beneath its branches. I scanned the ground but saw no traps.

We crept around to the other side and there he was. We came fully around when I thought it was safe, giving the tree a wide berth, and stood to see a man hanging by one ankle about eight feet off the ground.

He had his other leg resting across the caught leg. His arms were crossed over his chest. His long silver hair hung straight down. His silver beard was braided and fell over his left ear. His eyes were closed. On the ground below him were a bedroll, a backpack, and a knife. He looked like the picture of the hanged man on the old tarot card of the same name.

As we silently approached, he inhaled a breath and called in a long, loud voice, "*Help!*"

"How did you get caught in that trap?" I asked when he closed his mouth once more.

His eyes flew open. They were an unusual silvery-blue shade. He looked around sharply for a clear view of who was standing around him. He seemed to relax a little when his eyes returned to just the two of us. "Mornin', ladies. I hope you can help me." His upside-down smile looked benign, not angry. His teeth looked clean and very white. I would have expected bad teeth from an old man in old, rough clothes. From this angle, I assumed he was old by the color of his hair and wrinkles around his eyes.

"Shifters don't need snares like that for prey. How and why did you get caught?"

"It's a trap for a human right enough. I don't know what it's doin' here. There ain't nothin' here to protect. I was travelin' last night. I do a lot of my travelin' after dark. It's cooler. I got pretty good eyesight, but not good enough to see a well-set trap like this in the dark. It's hard talkin' upside down. Would you mind gettin' me down now?"

I looked at the tree. There weren't any low-hanging branches, but I could see that someone had carved hand- and footholds in the bark. I could shimmy up there and release him without using obvious magic. I went over, picked up his knife, and put it in the sheath with my own.

"Tara, open that bedroll and place it under him. That might help soften his fall. I'll go up and cut the rope."

I chanted a charm that would make my climb sure and successful. The climb was easy and probably would have been even without a charm, but I liked hedging my bets. I quickly reached the branch where the rope holding the man's ankle was tied. I took out his knife and sawed the rope.

"Better protect your head. This won't take long, but you could break your neck in the fall," I called down.

He wrapped his arms tightly around his neck and head.

"Any second now," I called down as I began to saw the last half. I didn't have to cut it completely before the rope gave under the man's weight and dropped him solidly on the bedroll Tara had spread beneath him.

He rolled onto his side and kicked his legs out and in again and again. "Ow! Ow!" he groaned.

"Pins and needles?" Tara asked.

"More like knives and more knives," he groaned, continuing to move his legs to bring back the circulation.

I quickly climbed back down the tree. I went to Tara and put my arm in front of her to back us up even more from the man. Just because he'd been unwittingly caught in a trap didn't mean he didn't deserve to be. I wouldn't take any chances that he wouldn't suddenly jump up and attack us. I had the knife he'd dropped, but he could have other weapons, or he could shift.

"Who are you?" I asked.

"The name's Qzyx. I'm what you might call a scavenger. I sell the stuff I find in abandoned old towns to new towns. I don't steal from folks. I just scavenge in the forgotten places. I won't hurt you. I don't hurt people lessin' they hurt me first."

"Qzyx? That's an unusual name. Is it a nickname or your real name?"

"Mebbe. That was a long time ago. I don't remember that far back." He sat up and tentatively stretched his legs fully out, continuing to move them back and forth while he freed himself from the rope still tied to his ankle.

I breathed in the air around him. I couldn't smell anything but sweat and urine.

"What kind of shifter are you?"

"Same answer. It's been a long time. I don't rightly remember."

I narrowed my eyes at him, but he just looked innocently at me with those strangely silverish eyes.

"How can you not remember?"

"Mebbe I ain't shifted in so long the memory don't come so easy anymore."

That was an excellent nonanswer. This old man was slippery. I moved on.

"What are you doing out here? You're too close to a settlement to scavenge."

"Yessum. That's right. I've got a few things to trade."

"What do you trade for?"

"Room and board for some days. Clothes. Campin' supplies. I stay 'til my money's gone, then head back out."

"That's not much of a life—and it's probably dangerous."

"I'm careful. Don't usually fall for this kind of trap. I must be gettin' old."

"How old are you?"

He scratched his head. His silver hair looked clean, even if the rest of him appeared a little grungy.

"That there is another thing I don't right remember. When the days get shorter, I come into town. I can see my hair's turned gray by its color, but I don't look in mirrors. I don't shave when I'm travelin'. I don't use any count of days when I work. Just notice the change in weather."

"It looks silver, not gray," Tara said admiringly. "It's a pretty color."

"Is that so? That's still an old color. Say, since you two saved me, you deserve a reward. I've got just the thing." He scooted over and reached for his backpack.

I backed Tara and me up a few more feet, just in case. "I don't need anything. I would have done it for anyone." Maybe.

He rifled through his bag. "I found some good stuff this last time. Mebbe the little lady would like a reward. What would you like? A ring? A bracelet? A necklace?" He pulled out two handfuls of jewelry. "Ladies like a bit of sparkle. I'll be able to rest for weeks on this stuff."

He sorted through his booty and pulled out a thin gold chain. At the end was a gold filigree butterfly.

"How did you get it so polished? It must have been considerably tarnished after more than a hundred years of neglect." I held on to Tara. The shine mesmerized her.

"I have my ways. I been doin' this a long time. When I get this kinda stuff, I take it to the Wolves. The Wolves are more generous than the Cats. Here, you can have this one. It ain't got a stone. The Wolves like the pretty stones." He held out the butterfly necklace.

When we didn't rush over to take it, he tossed it toward us. Tara reached forward and grabbed it before it hit the ground.

"Are you sure you don't want somethin', too? I got a pretty little bracelet you might like," he offered. He sounded very much like a salesman trying to make a deal. I didn't understand why it would be important to him for us to take something.

"Why would you give us something of value you could sell for more supplies?"

"You did save my life. I like to pay my debts."

"There's no debt involved. You are free to go where you will." As I said that, I helped Tara put on the necklace and watched her admire it around her neck. It was long enough that she could hold it out and still get a glimpse. She might never have seen any jewelry in her life. It wasn't made anymore, just found. There weren't enough people in the world to need jewelers yet. Only practical skills were needed today. There wasn't enough leisure time for the arts.

"Keep that under your shirt, Tara. We don't want to attract thieves," I warned.

She gave a disappointed sigh and hid the necklace.

I picked up my backpack prepared to leave.

"Where are you two ladies headed?"

"To the nearest Wolf town." There was no point in hiding it. It was the only settlement in the direction we were headed.

"Wolf Trap. I'll come with you if you don't mind." He stood up and began gathering his possessions.

"Are you sure you can walk?"

He wiggled one leg, then the other. "They're good to go."

"We have nothing to steal."

He turned his silvery eyes on me, made a sad face, and sighed. "I told you I don't steal. I scavenge. I also don't murder, kidnap, rape, or torture. I can be a good friend or a better enemy. I just thought you wouldn't mind a little company. I can tell you stories of my adventures."

"Stories?" Tara looked at me hopefully.

It was my turn to sigh. "Fine. But I'm watching you."

"Who could mind bein' watched by a pretty girl?" He grinned and fell into step with Tara while I walked behind.

He was an odd mixture. He seemed to be just what he appeared—a scrappy old man—but I thought he'd already lied to me. Who couldn't remember their real name? Who couldn't remember the animal they used to shift to? I didn't realize you could lose the ability to shift.

Were some people losing their magic? That shouldn't happen. Was he another anomaly? If he'd lost his shifting ability, did he know other magic?

He was amusing Tara. He was an excellent storyteller. She was talking to him, asking questions and responding happily to his over-the-top tales, and forgetting her own sad story.

I continued to watch him but relaxed my pondering about him and his motivations. He was just a temporary companion. Nothing more. I wasn't collecting him. And we'd be shed of him once we reached Wolf Trap.

Chapter 3

Alice had begun to think that very few things indeed were really impossible.

I ESTIMATED WE WERE about an hour away from Wolf Trap when I called a halt to our leisurely pace. It was a little after noon. I didn't want to arrive tired and hungry. I wanted my wits about me when I faced a town full of Wolves and other Canidae shifters.

"Why're we stoppin'? Wolf Trap's not far now," Qzyx asked, puzzled.

"Let's rest a little and eat. We can finish the supplies I'm carrying." I reached into my backpack and pulled out bread and cheese. I had plenty to go around. Tara still didn't question the way I pulled whatever I needed out of my backpack. The questions would come once she felt more secure.

There wasn't a convenient stream nearby, but we had our canteens. Qzyx had a waterskin. Primitive ones were usually made of animal skin or bladders. I must have made a grimace of distaste because he immediately defended himself.

"It's not animal skin. It's some kind of old-world material. I found it in one of the old-world towns," he explained.

"I'm surprised you find anything intact. I would think time, weather, and bacteria ate most things up."

"Not so. You'd be surprised what I can find that's still useful. A lotta people didn't just leave their homes willy-nilly. They stored their stuff with care. It's just a matter of findin' it."

"Interesting." I would have thought everything would have been scavenged a long time ago before the heat drove people to the Poles. The towns existing now were of fairly recent vintage. Ruined, abandoned cities were a better source of reusable resources than the far northern or southern areas, which had previously been covered in ice. The Great Warming didn't happen overnight. It took centuries. But during the last few decades before it peaked, it accelerated and ravaged the most populous areas with heat, drought, and rising oceans. Heat, hunger, stubbornness, and fear killed off much of the population. Survival at all costs killed off more. It was a terrible time for all living creatures.

He grinned. "Yeah, and lucky for me."

After a few minutes filled mostly with the sounds of chewing, Qzyx asked, "Tara told me her name. What's yours?"

"Rain."

"No last name like me?"

"Dare. Rain Dare."

"That sounds like reindeer," he remarked thoughtfully, with an arch of one eyebrow.

Tara giggled.

I sighed. "So, I've been told. I didn't expect anyone to know about reindeer when I chose it."

"You made fun of my name, but yours ain't real neither?"

"I chose my last name, not my first. I picked a last name from history that I liked."

He nodded his head. "Virginia Dare and the lost colony."

"How do you know that?"

"I read. People in the past took really good care of books. They cached a lot of things for future use. I think every settlement today benefits from a stored library. Nobody would know how to work any of the old tech without 'em. I find caches of books that can still be read. I like history books. We shouldn't forget our history."

"I agree. I've read a lot of history, too. 'Those who fail to learn from history are condemned to repeat it,' " I showed off. I liked good quotes.

"'Those who cannot remember the past are condemned to repeat it',' " he countered.

I looked at him with more interest. He really wasn't just some ignorant old man grabbing up valuables from the past. Maybe he wasn't just telling me what he thought I wanted to hear. "Winston Churchill said mine. Who said yours?"

"George Santayana."

"I think my guy was more well-known." I knew both names but had come across the first one more often in the history books I'd read.

"Mine said it first."

"How do you know that?"

He shrugged. "I found a book of quotes once. It had dates. I read through it and memorized the good ones. I still got a good memory."

If he did, he didn't show it off with a remembrance of personal details. "I wouldn't think you'd have a lot of time to read."

"It's too hot to explore in the middle of the day, but it's not too hot to read if you can't sleep."

"Are you carrying any books with you now?"

"I got one I think the Wolf Alpha will like."

"What's that?"

"*The Art of War.*"

I frowned. "Why would you give him a book like that?"

"Clan Wolf and Clan Cat are always fightin'. He wants an advantage."

Tara spoke up for the first time during our lunchtime conversation. She was still eating as if it would be her last meal. "Why would you help *him* over Clan Cat? Are you a Wolf then?"

"I don't know what I am, little lady, but I help them both equally. I don't smell like either Clan, so I'm accepted wherever I want to be. I'll give the Cat Alpha *The Art of War*, too."

"You'll give them both the same one?"

He grinned. "Same title. Different books. One's by Machiavelli and one's by Sun Tzu."

"Which one is best?" I'd read them both, but I thought Sun Tzu more practical.

He shrugged. "Who knows? We ain't had a real all-out shapeshifter war yet anyplace I traveled. There weren't any shifters in the past. Old-world strategies may not work in modern warfare. I guess we might find out."

"They shouldn't fight at all. They should be allies," I said disapprovingly. I had a lot to say on that subject, but now wasn't the time, and Qzyx wasn't the vessel for my views. It should be someone in power, but nobody would listen to someone with only seventeen years under her belt and female besides, even if she'd read more old books than anyone on the planet. Females weren't powerful enough yet. They had more trouble accessing their magic than shifters. That would change as magic matured, but for now, shifters ruled.

"That I'd give money to see. Cats and Wolves are natural enemies."

"Why?" Tara asked.

He shrugged. "Dunno. From what I hear, they never got along from the start. I wasn't born then, so I can't say for sure, but I heard in the beginnin' Wolves and Cats could be born into the same family and the family would split up 'cause of it."

"Are there only Cats and Wolves?" Tara asked.

"Well, there are a few other types that live with Wolves like Coyotes and Foxes, but only types of cat live with Cats. All cats are Cats, but not all Wolves are wolves."

Tara frowned. "That doesn't make sense."

"It's the old classification system that groups animals by family," I explained. "All cat species are from the Felidae family. Wolves belong to the Canidae family, but so do other species, like coyotes and foxes. Shifters somehow seem to recognize that they belong to the same old family category." Tara still looked puzzled. It was difficult to explain orally with Cat and cat, and Wolf and wolf meaning somewhat different things.

"It would be interestin' to see other types of shifters pop up," Qzyx idly mused.

"Like what?" Tara asked.

His eyes lit up. "I'd sure like to see a dragon."

I frowned at this bit of whimsy. Other types of shifters were a real possibility, but I hoped dragons weren't one of them. "I don't think you would," I told him. "Dragons would rule the world, creating chaos." And they would probably not be shifters, but monsters we would have to fight.

"Mebbe. It might depend on what kind of dragons they be."

"What do you mean?"

"I read about dragons in some books I found, but they ain't real. Everythin' I've read about 'em is made up. Way, way back hundreds of years ago, people thought the world was flat and at the ends there be fierce, scary dragons. What if the real thing is completely different? What if they ain't the monsters people thought they were?"

"How would you know it was a dragon if it wasn't like in the books?" I asked skeptically.

"Mebbe, they look the same, but act different. I'm jest sayin'. People made up dragons. They made 'em huge, dangerous, breathin' fire, flyin', eatin' everythin' that moved. What if they ain't like that at all? What if they only ate vegetables and liked to read good books?" Qzyx said with a humorous gleam in his eyes.

"What's a dragon look like?" Tara interrupted curiously.

"It's like a giant lizard with wings, sharp teeth, and long sharp claws. They hoard stuff—gold and jewels, mostly. They eat people along with everythin' else," Qzyx told her. I noticed he didn't mention the eating virgins thing. That wasn't something I would want to explain to a ten-year-old.

Tara's eyes had gotten wide, and her mouth hung open as she listened. Qzyx was too damned good a storyteller. As a fantasy, dragons were interesting, but I wouldn't want to meet them in reality. I wasn't sure what magic could or would produce. Thinking too hard about them might just make them real—and I doubted they'd be as benevolent as Qzyx proposed.

"You're going to scare Tara," I said sharply. "Dragons are a myth of the past. They should stay in the past."

Qzyx gave Tara an apologetic smile. "Sorry. My imagination gets away from me from time to time. Sometimes I like to think of as many as six impossible things before breakfast."

"That's almost another quote. I have that book," I told him. "The proper quote is 'Why, sometimes I've believed as many as six impossible things before breakfast.' "

He grinned. "It's a good book. Impossible things make better stories than real things."

Tara looked at me. "You have that book? Can I read it?"

"Sure. I have it in my backpack. For now, I think it's time for us to move on," I said, standing up. I reached into my backpack again. "Here. Everyone have an apple for dessert. We can eat them while we walk."

They took the apples, and we started walking. I let Qzyx and Tara lead the way again while I walked behind. He continued to entertain Tara on the last leg of our journey, this time with stories about elves and fairies—other creatures I wasn't sure I wanted to exist. He even had me smiling at some of his tales. For someone who spent most of his time alone, he had an easy way about him and a facile tongue. He was an interesting puzzle, but I wouldn't try to solve him this time around. Adding Tara to my fact-finding jaunt was enough of a deviation to the script my Jardvari had worked out with their rules. I shouldn't bend any more rules this early in my exploration. In Wolf Trap, he would go his way and we would go ours. In a village I knew to hold over five thousand people that should be an easy thing to do—right?

We reached Wolf Trap less than an hour after lunch, arriving at the main gate. It looked large enough to house five thousand people. It had high walls of mismatched stones, wooden gates, and two burly guards barring the entrance. Qzyx assured me everyone in town knew him.

If I'd been traveling alone, I would have stayed outside the town and watched it for a while. I might have waited for other travelers and followed them in. That could have taken anywhere from a few hours to a few days to a few weeks. Caravans traveled from town to town but sometimes months apart. Despite my caution, I was more than willing to speed things along by following Qzyx's lead.

Qzyx hadn't lied about being well-known. The guards greeted him immediately.

"Hey, Q-man, how ya doin?"

"Fine as the hair on a frog."

The guards laughed. "You kill me with those weird expressions."

"They ain't weird. They're old. That's how people talked a few centuries ago."

"Ha, ha. Yeah, ya probably are that old."

Qzyx just grinned good-naturedly at the ribbing.

"Who have ya got there with you?" One guard scrutinized Tara and me. He immediately shifted to a wolf to take a sniff of us because his olfactory receptors were much sharper in that form than his human form.

Tara stood stiff and scared, expecting at any moment to be exposed as the wolf sniffed over her. I put a reassuring hand on her shoulder. I don't know what they expected to find from sniffing us, but I knew what they might find. I'd already stirred the air and made sure the scent of wolf was all over us, and I obscured the faint cat musk she might still carry with the scent of garlic. I'd picked that scent up coming from someplace within the town. I had one moment of fear when he spent more time sniffing Tara than me, but he finally stopped and stepped back.

The guards examined the contents of my and Qzyx's backpacks, one still wolf while the other had us turn out our pockets for sniffing. My backpack appeared to only hold the blankets we'd used and a change of clothes. Once the smelling portion of the inspection was over, both guards spent more time poring over Qzyx's treasures. He was carrying a lot of jewelry, metal utensils, and the books he told us about, besides his waterskin, a knife, change of clothes, and bedroll.

"What brings you to Wolf Trap?" the guard still human asked me when he'd finished with Qzyx's treasures.

"They're with me," Qzyx announced.

"That's nice, but why? Are they relatives? Is this your girlfriend? Even the older one's a little young for you, Q-man."

Both guards laughed again. It was odd seeing a wolf laugh. The human one slapped Qzyx on the back. He stood his ground with little trouble, still grinning pleasantly.

I spoke up. "My cousin and I lost our family in a fire. We're looking for a new place to stay. Qzyx thought we'd like Wolf Trap," I told them. I'd been working on a back story as we walked.

They eyed me thoughtfully. "How old are you?"

"Seventeen." I couldn't decide whether it was better to lie or tell the truth, so I told the truth. I could always claim to be lying later if that was the best choice.

"Are you a good mage?"

This was an odd question to ask. I didn't think there was any sort of ranking yet of mages like there was of shifters. "I think so," I said again cautiously.

"Then you came to the right place."

"Why is that?"

"We've got a special job for mages here. You'll see when you report to the Administration building in the next two days."

"What will I see?"

"If you're plannin' to stick around, you'll need a job. This job is for any qualified mage. That's alls I'm sayin'. You'll find out more at the Administration building. Don't forget to report, 'cause we'll report you. Now I'm gonna tag ya as a stranger."

"How will you do that?"

He brought out a stamp pad. "I'm gonna stamp your hand. This ink'll stay visible for thirty days, no matter how much ya try to wash it off. Everything ya do can be reported to the Alpha. If ya do something we don't like, we can banish you from town. If we find you acceptable, you'll get the solvent to remove the mark. If ya don't get the solvent, the mark will burn into your hand. It'll hurt for a long time and maybe scar."

That was pretty harsh, and I doubted it was true. I didn't think mages were capable of that kind of magic yet. It was a pretty good threat, though. No one would know it wasn't true until the thirty days had passed, and they'd worry the whole time. I let him stamp our hands with a big black *S*. Qzyx asked for the *S* instead of *T* for trader. He said he was staying for a few weeks this time.

When we were stamped, I asked the guard, "Tell me, is there a good place we can stay for the night?"

He looked both of us over this time. "Q-man knows all the cheap places. How good are ya lookin' for?"

"Just good enough," I told him. He knew the extent of my fortune from opening my money pouch and hadn't demanded any tribute. Maybe because I was with Qzyx.

"Try the Tooth and Claw. It ain't fancy, but the food's good. It's not too expensive, but it's a little rough. The owner's okay though. He's good at keepin' the rough from becoming the maimed or the dead. Q-man knows the way."

What an awful recommendation, but I wasn't worried. I thought I could steer any trouble away.

"Thanks. We'll try there."

"I've been there. What he said's true enough. I may as well stay there, too," Qzyx said and led the way.

Tara stuck close to me. I knew she wasn't comfortable here. She'd been raised to dislike all shifters from the Canidae family. That wouldn't change anytime soon. I frowned at her when I saw her wrinkling her nose at the wolf smells, baring her teeth, and snarling softly. I nudged her shoulder and shook my head. She stopped her angry Cat behavior immediately and looked wary again.

The Tooth and Claw was located in a ramshackle building of wood and stone. It had long skinny windows on the ground floor. The look of the place didn't exactly give me the secure feeling I wanted in a place I'd be unconscious for a few hours. I'd have to be on my guard here as much as when camping in the forest.

The tavern had no lobby as such. The stairs leading to the upstairs guestrooms were at the front of the main room. At a front counter, a young woman took our silver and registered me and Tara for one of the ten small rooms. She told us checkout was before noon the next day and that meals were extra if we ate at the inn. We examined our small but adequate room, then left to explore. Qzyx told us he had business in town, and he'd meet us back at the inn for dinner. He then took off after registering. I thought I'd be done with him by now, but as our only acquaintance, I wouldn't shun him yet. He could still prove useful. I'd ask him questions about Wolf Trap.

We headed out to get a look at the town.

"What will I do when you get a job?" Tara asked in a worried voice as we walked down Mart Street toward the main town square near the center of town. The street was appropriately named because it contained all the usual shops: baker, butcher, candle, clothing, dry goods, and so on, all the necessary commodities for civilized existence. The world was far from reaching twenty-first century levels, but some technologies had been revived. Solar and wind power were providing some electricity, but not enough for everyone.

"If there are no good options, then we'll leave and find somewhere else to stay. I won't desert you."

Tara still wasn't mollified. She'd only known me for a day. She didn't know if she could trust me. She didn't know who to trust. If I hadn't come along, she'd be dead. Even if she'd escaped that hole on her own, she'd have had trouble surviving. I was her lifeline.

"Try to trust me, Tara. I didn't rescue you just to abandon you. Stop playing with that necklace Qzyx gave you. Someone might see it and try to steal it."

She obediently lowered her hands. She hadn't had it for half a day and already she'd taken to patting and touching it. It was a pretty little piece of delicate jewelry. If everyone had one, it would be safe to expose it. Instead, Qzyx—and I by allowing him to give it to her—had made her a target. I hope I didn't live to regret our little indulgence.

We checked out every store but purchased nothing, despite Tara's soft exclamations over all the merchandise. I didn't want to lug around a lot of extra stuff until we were permanently settled. We wouldn't stay at the Tooth and Claw any longer than we had to.

The sun was just setting by the time we made our way back to the inn for dinner.

The bartender was a craggy, grizzled, middle-aged man. He had a patch over one eye, and old scars on his face and arms. I fished a silver coin from my pocket, placed it on the bar, and said, "I'd like two meals. We already have a room for the night."

He took the coin and eyed it carefully. Coins were minted by both Clans. They were mixed alloys of gold, silver, or copper from small, medium, to large. The smallest, mostly gold coin was the most valuable. I had access to many different coins, but to be safe, I used one that appeared to be Wolf made.

He handed me some copper coins in change. "We've got deer stew. I can add extra vegetables if you want. There's brown bread, too. You can have beer or boiled water."

"We'll both take water. I'd like just raw vegetables and nuts, no meat, but my cousin will have the stew with the extra vegetables." I led the way to a table near the front exit and the closest escape. I didn't see any sign of Qzyx yet.

The bartender brought us our meals instead of sending a server. Before he turned away, I asked, "Sir, are there any jobs available in town?" Maybe I could learn more about the special mage job from someone else.

He looked me over. I didn't look like anything special. I had made sure of that.

"What can you do?"

"I can do many things. What I choose to do is another question."

He grinned suddenly. "Fair enough. There are lists of job openings at the Administration building but ask around at any store and you'll find a job. There's also farm work outside the town."

"The guard at the gate implied there were special mage jobs available."

"Are you any good?"

"What do you mean by good?"

"Do you have strong defensive or offensive magic?"

"Are you talking about fighting magic? Do you have a military force?" The much bigger towns on the west coast did. It wouldn't be surprising if Wolf Trap had one as well.

"We don't have a standing army doing just military things. Every shifter has a ranking and can be called to serve if necessary, but we haven't deployed significantly yet. We have top brass in place, but most working soldiers patrol, guard, hunt, and recon. The others work regular jobs. The Alpha wants to improve the effectiveness of his army. He's starting a new squad of battle mages. If you have decent magic, he might take you on if you pass the tests."

"You're going to war?" This wasn't good news.

"Maybe. We don't like how close Cat's Paw is to Wolf Trap. It's time something permanent was done about it," he said darkly.

"You look like you've already been to war."

He narrowed his eyes but answered. "I lost my good looks to Clan Cat 'bout ten years ago. We had a little dispute over who had hunting rights to the forest down the road."

"Who won?"

"We did," he growled and with that, he stomped back to the bar.

"We won," Tara said in a low voice.

"Forget about that. The only 'we' in your life now are you and me."

"Are we going to stay here in this town?" Tara asked glumly, not yet eating.

"We need to stay somewhere for the winter. I don't want to be caught out in the open during the stormy season. Why not here?" The bread looked good. I cut off two pieces from our small loaf and gave one to Tara.

Five guys who looked like they worked in dirt and muck all day walked in and sat down at a front table. Another group walked in and sat two tables away from the first group. They all ordered boilermakers. I was curious to see the effects of alcohol on shifters.

"Eat up. I don't like the looks of the shifters coming in now."

"Am I safe here?" Tara asked, eyeing the newcomers suspiciously.

"With me you are."

Qzyx showed up suddenly with his own bowl of stew, a beer, and more bread. He slid into the chair opposite us. For some reason, I felt safer now. I frowned at that thought. *I* would make us safe, not some male I hardly knew.

"I hope you ladies had a lovely day. What have you two been up to?"

Tara's gloom disappeared as she told him about everything we'd seen. He listened intently, asking diverting questions. She talked with her mouth full and often spewed out water, bursting into laughter at his ill-timed silly remarks. I didn't correct her table manners. I thought about it. I should do it. But she was only a day away from dying of hunger, thirst, and neglect. Now wasn't the time to worry about etiquette.

"You'd best eat up. Things are going to get lively soon," Qzyx said suddenly and turned his chair around to face the room.

We ate more quickly and watched the shifters get louder and angrier. This must be a regular routine for these customers because they started sniping at one another even before their second round of drinks were served by the curvy barmaids. Not even their attempts to flirt while keeping away from wandering hands held the shifters' attention for long.

Before I could eat my last carrot, a fight broke out. Tara huddled in fear beside me. I put my arm around her as I watched. Tables and chairs were knocked over. Metal mugs and plates hit the floor. Suddenly, a chair went flying into the air. I froze, staring blankly as it arced toward us.

Chapter 4

"You will observe the Rules of Battle, of course?" the White Knight remarked.

QZYX REACHED OUT AND snatched the chair out of the air. His arm swung back with the chair hanging over our heads a moment before he threw it back into the fray. I quickly straightened from my hunch around Tara when the danger was past.

I was angry with myself. Why hadn't I reacted to the situation with magic instead of doing what any helpless female would do? I'd had plenty of training and practice in self-defense while growing up, just no real-time experience. I had to think and react immediately when faced with a dangerous situation. Ducking and hiding wasn't an adequate response.

When I stopped berating myself for all of twenty seconds, I put a protection charm between our table and the rest of the room, which I should have done the instant I'd realized the anger levels in the room were rising. Anything thrown our way should be deflected now by my magic wall, and no one would get any closer than a foot before Qzyx. It wasn't as good as my stone ward, but it should save us from any further embroilment in the fight.

"Finish your meal," I told Tara quietly. "And stay beside me. They won't bother us anymore over here."

She did as she was told, gobbling down the last slice of bread. She kept her shoulders hunched and her head down as we watched the shifters assault one another with punches, shoves, kicks, and more flying objects.

It didn't take long before the bartender and a few other shifters with clubs broke up the fight with some choicely placed swings. I noticed they were careful not to land lethal blows. Shifters naturally healed faster than mages and both much faster than pre-magic humans, but not fast enough to continue fighting easily with broken arms or legs—unless their pain threshold or anger was huge.

I quickly removed my wall during the winddown before Qzyx could jump up to help. I didn't want him to feel the ward's resistance when he tried to exit. I'd done it on the fly, and it wouldn't allow for anything to enter or leave.

After the rowdy shifters were chased out, there were only four shifters left and us. The remaining four turned over their clubs and helped right tables and unbroken chairs. The two barmaids came back, picked up metal mugs and plates, dented but not broken, and cleaned up thrown food. Qzyx helped gather up the broken chairs and took them behind the bar.

"Thanks for the save," I told Qzyx when he finally returned to our table. "I didn't see that chair coming until the last second."

"No problem. I seen a lot of brawls. I know what to expect. Flyin' furniture's just one problem. Fights move around. This one broke up right quick with few shifters involved. I seen fights with as many as fifty dukin' it out."

When most of the cleanup was finished, the bartender headed back to our table. He'd seemed surprised when he noticed us sitting peacefully in our little corner of the room, apparently untouched by the chaos only moments before.

He eyed us with interest. "Sorry about the ruckus. It surely happens when those two groups are off the same night and in a mood. Then it doesn't take much to set 'em off. I'm glad to see you weren't involved in the fighting. When they come in here looking for trouble, they don't care who's in the way."

"Good job breakin' up that rumpus," Qzyx told him. "We were lucky to be sittin' up here away from their end of the room."

"We're used to it. That kind of fight is why I keep more benches than chairs in this place. The benches are nailed down and don't come up easy."

"The guards at the gate warned us there'd be a rough crowd here," I remarked. "If we decide to stay in Wolf Trap for a while, I think we need a safer place to call home."

The bartender studied Tara and me for a minute, then he nodded his head as if he'd come to a decision. "My sisters run a boardinghouse on Oak Street if you want a safe place to stay. Number 25. Tell them Stone sent you."

"Thanks. I'll check it out."

He nodded his head again, turned, and headed back to the bar with the promise of some dessert before we went upstairs.

The dessert was fruit and nuts wrapped in a honey-sweet pancake. Tara and Qzyx both ate theirs as if they thought someone would snatch it away. I was more sedate, having never starved or worried about where my next bite of food would come from.

We finished eating, then went upstairs. Qzyx went to his room several doors down, and we went off to ours. There were two bathrooms for ten rooms. Tara and I used the one closest to our room together. She was a little embarrassed to share a bathroom, but I explained it might not be safe to separate, and she settled down.

I had access to changes of clothes through my backpack. I couldn't produce her size without question, so I only gave her one of my other shirts to sleep in. I washed hers out in the sink with a little magic help while she showered. We went to our room afterward and hung her clothes around the room to dry. I charmed a steady breeze to move around the clothes to hurry their drying. I didn't need to add any heat. The night was quite warm, as usual.

We still had a lot of night left, but I could tell Tara was tired. She'd had an exciting day, and she still seemed too tense for sleep. I said a little charm to help her fall asleep and another for it to be dreamless. They were minor magics that should work.

With Tara unconscious, I could do my bigger magic work—setting wards on our room.

I'd spent a long time practicing protection charms. Stationary wards were the most reliable and powerful. I'd never had much luck with moving wards. My blood-infused stones weren't magic-intensive to set up but worked best by enclosing an area of protection. For this room, I would only ward the doors and windows. I didn't think anyone would try to come in another way.

In the bar, I had only used air to protect us because it was a good deflector. Here, I would use layers of each element of magic to create my wards. They would be impregnable except to a strong mage with abilities in all four elements: Fire, Air, Water, and Earth. With today's mages only adept in two of the four, there shouldn't be a problem.

It takes a lot of time and magic to make layered wards, and they weren't exactly permanent. Magic had trouble maintaining charms for long periods of time. Permanency was not in its vocabulary. I didn't have an anchor like the blood stones for this ward, but it should last at least through my shorter night's sleep.

It took me an hour, a complex charm, and a lot of magic to set my wards of protection. I had to whip each element up individually and contain its power to protection, not destruction, in a small area. I wouldn't say it was like herding cats, but it was close enough to leave me spent. I'd probably sleep a little longer tonight.

I wasn't ready to sleep when I finished, so I thought about the evening's events. I'd stopped being angry with myself, but I had to think about what I'd do the next time danger reared its head. I couldn't anticipate every situation I'd find myself in, but I should have been able to grab that chair or at least deflect it with magic with no one noticing. But this was my first experience with a fight. I could surely be as quickly reactive as Qzyx, a nonmage. I promised myself that I'd do better next time.

Before I finally settled down, I watched Tara sleep. She was a quiet sleeper. That was important when sharing a room. I thought my charms were working because she looked peaceful. I wanted to keep her that way.

After almost twelve hours of sleep, Tara finally awoke. She had a relaxed smile on her face at first. I could see when the memories of her situation suddenly returned, and she jerked up with a panicked, strained screech.

"Hush. It's okay. You're safe," I reassured her.

She shut up abruptly and stared at me with her big, pansy-brown eyes. She was thoroughly clean now, but still looked a little raw—nothing that more rest and food couldn't cure. I could charm the nightmares away to help, but I couldn't stop the tears she'd yet to shed. Once she felt more secure, they were bound to come. Crying was supposed to be cathartic.

Was I a bad person to hope she did her crying while I wasn't there? It would make me feel helpless because I couldn't fix it. I didn't want to feel that.

"Your clothes are dry. We'll get you some more today. I'll stay outside to guard the bathroom door while you get dressed." I'd already washed up and dressed. With all the meditation time this morning and six hours of sleep, I felt strong and ready to face whatever the day threw at me—even another chair.

She gathered up her clothes. "Shouldn't you come in with me? Is it safe for you to be out there alone?"

"I'll be careful." I followed her out to the bathroom, carrying my backpack. Everything we owned was in our hands. I didn't plan to stay another night.

I heard Tara take another shower. She probably missed the feeling of being clean after her days in a dirty hole. I couldn't fault her for that. I didn't mind waiting. Plumbing was useful technology up to a point. Large water treatment plants could be managed magically once mages became stronger.

"I'm ready," she announced when she came out. "Where are we going?"

"We'll eat breakfast, buy you a change of clothes, and check out that boardinghouse the bartender told us about. If we're going to stay here a while, we might as well find safer lodgings. I don't know about you, but I'd rather not risk another meal here among angry shifters."

"Me, too. Okay. I'm hungry."

"I bet you are. That was a long sleep you had."

She smiled shyly. "It was the best sleep I had in forever."

"I can believe it," I agreed.

We made our way downstairs. Qzyx was chatting with one of the tavern staff when we entered the bar and main room. I turned over my key at the bar before we left. If the boardinghouse didn't work out, we'd stay at a less unruly inn.

"I thought you two would never wake up."

"You don't have to hang around with us. You seem to have a lot of friends here," I said pointedly. I wasn't sure why he was sticking with us. Maybe he was just a friendly old guy who wanted to help two orphans get settled.

"I don't have any family or particular friends here. I just try to get along with everyone. There's a good bakery down the street I can show you. Tooth and Claw doesn't serve much of a breakfast."

"Sounds good. Lead on."

The bakery was called the Bread Basket. They served breakfast bread full of nuts and fruit. They had fresh butter and milk as well. Many types of animals had survived the Great Warming by heading to the Poles, just as humans did. Once magic took hold, they were thriving better than before. Adaptation had accelerated with a magical boost.

I could tell the milk was pasteurized, not raw—another bit of useful technology. Few people would know that feces regularly leaked into milk during the milking process, but I did. I could charm away impurities in my food, but I wasn't sure how well anyone else could.

We were served our own small loaf with a crock of butter and glasses of milk. I was surprised that Qzyx had the milk as well. It didn't seem a manly choice.

"This is very good," I said after eating a buttered slice.

"Mmmm," Tara agreed.

"Yeah, I miss this when I'm travelin'. I can eat fruit and nuts when I'm on the road, but I can't easily find milk, eggs, honey, salt, and flour. And who wants to cook in the middle of summer in the hottest part of the country, anyway?"

"Why not travel in the winter and rest in the summer?"

"'Cause nobody else is fool enough to do it. I've got the best scavengin' spots to myself and I can take the heat."

After a long pause for eating, I remarked, "That was quick work catching that chair last night. You have good reflexes."

He shrugged. "I was watchin' for it is all."

"Why didn't any of those guys shift? I thought that would be instinctive. I expected everyone to go all fur and fang." When I'd had time to think about it, that had puzzled me.

He chuckled. "Fur and fang. That's a good one. It's part of the laws here and in most other towns. You don't shift to fight unless your life is in danger. If you let the animal take over, you might lose control and kill someone you shouldn't. Nobody wants to suffer those consequences. A bar brawl ain't a just cause for shiftin'."

Interesting. Keeping their animal side in check would be important to accepting it. Shifting had not been a simple change for people to accept in the beginning. A lot of boys had been killed when they'd first shifted—before it was discovered that this was the new norm.

"Nobody dies in a bar fight?"

He shrugged. "It happens sometimes, but it's not deliberate. They fight to let off steam, not kill anyone. There are grudges and rivalries that deepen when they drink. But if you can't follow the rules, you can't stay in town. You could be permanently banned."

"The fight seemed real to me."

"Naw. There was hardly any bloodshed. A real fight's a regular blood-bath."

"Do they have those often?"

"There are public fights several times a year with individual and group combats. Anyone can enter. Everybody needs to practice their fightin' skills. Sometimes people are attacked by rovin' bands of outlaws between the town and farms. Or there's a skirmish with a group from Clan Cat and a huntin' party. Good huntin' land is always a good excuse for a domain fight."

"I think there's plenty of land for everyone," I said disapprovingly.

He shrugged. "The grass is always greener on the other side," he said.

"The quote I remember is 'The harvest is always more fruitful in another man's fields.' Ovid, I believe."

He grinned. "You and your quotes. However you say it, somethin' always looks better when it belongs to someone else."

I sighed. "Too true." I'd read plenty of psychology books to know something of what to expect from human behavior. How the advent of magic had changed behavior was unwritten yet.

When we finished eating, I asked Qzyx, "I need to get Tara some more clothes. Do you know a place?"

"'Course I do. This is one of the best towns for clothes and such. The bigger towns are already makin' things on the cheap. I bought a pair of boots in Wolf's Edge once that barely lasted the summer—and they cost me twice as much, too. That's why I don't travel much to them big cities on the coast anymore."

Qzyx led the way to a clothing store, and I bought Tara some pants, tunics, underwear, a sleep shirt, socks, and a pair of boots. I also bought her a backpack to carry her booty in. She immediately perked up a bit with the new clothes and stopped looking so weighed down by her past. Children were supposed to be resilient. I hoped that was true.

The boardinghouse was a couple of blocks off Mart Street. Qzyx led the way, saying he'd stayed there before. Stone's sisters had named their boardinghouse Acorn's Rest, which was apt for a place on Oak Street.

I knocked on the door and waited, with Tara and Qzyx standing behind me.

The women who answered the door seemed to be in their early forties. The one in front was short, plump, and smiling. She had soft brown eyes in a round, medium-tanned face surrounded by short, curly, light brown hair. The woman who appeared at her shoulder was almost the opposite. She was tall, thin, and frowning. She also had brown eyes, and brown hair and skin, but all in darker shades. Her hair was longer and pulled into a ponytail high on the back of her head. They both wore beige tunics and brown pants. Neither one said a word to me at first. They zeroed in on my companion.

"Qzyx! How nice to see you!"

"Did you bring back something interesting from your travels?"

"I did." He stepped forward, clasped his hands, and bowed his head, then he turned and looked at Tara and me. "These two are young friends of mine, Rain Dare and Tara Jensen. Stone told them they might find a room here."

"They might," the tall one acknowledged curtly.

"Audrey! Let me handle this. If Stone sent you, you're welcome," the short one said. "What about you, Qzyx? Would you like to stay here, too?" she asked flirtatiously and fluttered her eyelashes.

"No, ma'am. I'll stay at the Tooth and Claw. It's more my style. But I'll check in on my two young friends from time to time, if you don't mind."

"Of course not. We love hearing your stories and would be delighted to have you. We've only Luther staying here right now. He's not very sociable. The whole point of having a boardinghouse is having people to talk to."

Before this could go on any further, I interrupted, "My cousin and I would like a room we can share."

"We might have a room," the tall one said.

"Can I see it?"

"*You* won't find a *better* room anywhere," she said, affronted.

"Don't mind Audrey; of course you can see it," the short, smiling one said. "Come in. You come, too, Qzyx. You owe us the tale of your recent travels."

"Dorrie," the tall woman growled.

"We've got three empty rooms, Audrey. I'd like to have them filled, even if we don't need the money."

"Fine." She stepped aside and let us in.

"Upstairs, there are three available bedrooms, two with two single beds each, and one room with one large bed. One bathroom is shared between two rooms. Which would you prefer?"

"I'd like to see a room with two single beds."

"Front or back of the house?"

"Which one doesn't share a bathroom yet?"

"The front one."

"That one."

They led us up the stairs and immediately to the left of the long hallway. The room was big. Besides the two single beds, it held a bedside table, a dresser, and a small round table with two chairs.

"We'll provide the sheets and towels, but you'll have to keep them clean yourselves. There's a laundry down the street where you can have everything washed. You're responsible for cleaning your room and bathroom. We may inspect your rooms at any time."

The bathroom was small, the only access from the hallway. It had a shower, a toilet, and a sink.

I asked about the rent, and it seemed reasonable. We had the option to pay by the week or month, payment in advance. By the month was a little cheaper, so I chose that.

"The ground floor is off-limits unless invited. That's where we live. That's why you come in right at the stairs."

"How do I store food?"

The sisters exchanged a look.

"Our refrigerator is on the electrical grid. We can allow you some storage space for perishables, but you need closed containers for anything you store in your room. Nothing lasts long in this climate. We only purchase food a few days at a time. You should do likewise. You must take out your trash every day, and always keep your food well covered or you'll attract bugs. We don't want any more bugs than normal."

I agreed with that. "Do you often have a full house of boarders?"

"Not so much in the winter. Sudden storms discourage travel. Spring brings more people looking for work or visiting," Audrey said. "Nobody but Luther has stayed here permanently."

I looked at Tara. She'd been quiet during our tour. She probably felt she had no voice in the decision since I was supporting her. "What do you think, Tara?"

She nodded her head. "It's nice."

"What do you think?" I asked Audrey and Dorrie.

"If Stone sent you here, he must think you're trustworthy," Dorrie said, looking at her sister.

"I vouch for them, too," Qzyx added.

"Fine," Audrey agreed grudgingly.

The short one smiled at her sister. "We're Dorrie and Audrey Novak. You can call us Dorrie and Audrey."

"I'm Rain and this is Tara. Is there a school Tara can attend if we're here for a few months?"

"Yes, but school's only in session from October through March. The boys have martial arts and survival training during the spring and summer. The girls have magic training at the same time."

"That's only a few weeks away. Do I need to register her?"

"Yes. In the Administration building. It's at the end of Mart Street. You may see a lot of soldiers milling around the area. The military has its offices there, and the training camp is at the back."

"Good to know. I was told I could find a job there. Maybe sign up for a special mage job." I wasn't sure I should, but it would be as good a chance to interact with other mages as my list of rules allowed.

"You plan to apply?" Dorrie clapped her hands. "This will be the first time the Alpha has instituted a Mage Corps. Imagine battle mages. How exciting!"

"Will there be a battle?"

"Oh, yes. The Alpha is tired of chasing Cats out of the woods. They're encroaching on our land."

"Why is that? Surely, they must have plenty of woods near them." I couldn't help questioning this war idea with anyone who voiced it. I had to spread doubt wherever I could. Cats and Wolves needed to be allies, not enemies.

"There's something wrong in the woods off the lake between us. The trees are warped or something," Audrey said. "They go around—closer to us."

"That's right. I forgot about that," Qzyx said, scratching his head.

"Have you been there?" Dorrie asked. "Stone won't say much about it."

"Yeah. I been there. There is somethin' creepy about 'em," Qzyx agreed.

"That sounds dangerous. Come downstairs and tell us all about it," Dorrie suggested.

"Wait. Please. I have to go to the Administration building tomorrow to check in, register Tara for school, and look for a job. When I get a job, is there somewhere safe I can leave Tara?" That was the one thing that had me worried. What would Tara do while I was at work?

"I could get a job, too," she announced.

Both sisters turned their brown eyes to her. She was short, skinny, young, and obviously inexperienced. She hunched her shoulders as they stared. The sisters exchanged a look and a nod from Audrey.

"She could help us. We could use an extra pair of hands," Audrey finally offered.

"That's right. We can watch and feed her while you're at work," Dorrie said. "When school starts, she'll be there all day."

I looked at Tara. She looked scared. She was afraid she'd shift. I wasn't worried about that. I was worried that she'd decide to confide in someone she shouldn't. These women seemed nice enough—at least Dorrie did—but that didn't mean they wouldn't turn on us if they found out Tara was a Cat.

"Thank you. I appreciate that," I said, and I hoped I didn't sound as doubtful as I felt.

Chapter 5

Down the Rabbit Hole

WE ALL WENT DOWNSTAIRS, and our new landladies showed us how to access the kitchen without entering the rest of their living area. There was a workroom on the other side of the staircase that led to the kitchen. There was a loom and a lot of undyed yarn. Hemp and flax were the most widely used plants for cloth today. Cotton took too much water to grow. Apparently, the ladies knitted and weaved, besides running a boardinghouse.

"Most folks don't have any electrical source in their home. We were lucky to get one. Only businesses qualify right now until we can get a stronger electrical grid up and running," Audrey explained proudly. "The Alpha has been encouraging the learning of all sorts of old technology. Our other boarder, Luther, is a master plumber."

I thought about the technology needed to operate an old-time refrigerator. Besides electricity, those old refrigerators used hydrofluorocarbons—chemical compounds that were harmful to the environment. It would be a shame if people returned to using destructive chemicals and burning fossil fuels. Magic should now be the fuel of choice. It was plentiful, renewable, environmentally sound, and could replace all old power sources with good charms.

"There are plenty of stores where you can buy cooked food every day. They receive preference for food and electricity. They can feed us all. But sometimes it's nice to cook for oneself," Dorrie added. "I *love* to cook."

"If you can make sure Tara eats during the days when I'm gone, I don't think I need to store any food here. She needs more protein than I do. She's still growing." She also needed it because she was a predator.

"Of course. Meat is abundant with plenty of hunters eager to bring it in. She can earn her food by helping us during the day," Dorrie smiled at Tara.

I didn't sense any sinister undertones in that statement, but I'd be sure that Tara was honest with me about her chores. I didn't want her abused or taken advantage of under my watch.

Qzyx stayed downstairs with the sisters, chatting with them about his latest adventures while Tara and I went back up to our new room. I could hear him use dramatic pauses as his voice rose and fell with the excitement of his story. He had his audience enthralled.

"I don't like leaving you here alone while I'm out all day," I told Tara once we were in our new room with some expectation of privacy.

"I don't mind," she lied and failed to meet my eyes.

"I mind. I'm supposed to take care of you. I saved your life, so I'm responsible for you."

"Really?" She perked up at that.

"That's the idea anyway. I won't leave you anyplace you're not comfortable—not for long, at least. But I have to get a job of some kind. We need money to live here." I didn't need money, but I needed to interact with people. Working would be a good way to do that.

"Okay. I'll try to get along here. Dorrie seems nice."

As opposed to Audrey. I felt the same way, but I think Audrey was just more suspicious of strangers, which was probably a good thing. She had to take in boarders, but she let them see she didn't trust them any more than she had to. I was sure both would try to pump Tara for information in their own ways. I had to do something about that.

Once again, to protect our secrets, I planned to stifle another of Tara's urges. "Lie down for a minute. Close your eyes. I want to try something," I told her.

"What something?"

"It's something to help you keep our secrets."

"Okay." She did as I asked without further question or demur. She was very trusting in some ways. I had to be careful with her.

In my studies, I'd learned about hypnosis. It was not a foolproof method of modifying behavior, but I could use those ideas about planting suggestions combined with magic and hopefully give her a false background, combining it with the suppression of her need to shift. It was the only solution I could think of that could work without totally suppressing her personality.

"Keep your eyes closed. Now shake out your arms and legs. Imagine your worry and stress being shaken out. That's right. Keep going until you feel free of your stress."

I waited. She giggled as she jiggled, but finally settled to a limp stop. "Now, I want you to relax by tensing your body first, then letting go. Do that a few times to feel really relaxed."

When she seemed finished, I spoke again. This time I used magic to reinforce my words.

"You feel much lighter now. Your tension is all gone. Imagine that you're lying in a beautiful field with lots of pretty, colorful flowers. The sun is shining but it feels cool, like an early midwinter morning. You see butterflies flitting over the flowers. You hear the breeze rustling leaves on the tree branches. You hear birds and bees. You feel very relaxed. Not sleepy—you're still alert and aware of your surroundings. But you feel calm and peaceful." I paused after each sentence and spoke softly, my words and magic easing her into a hypnotic state.

"You are a child of nature. You belong to the world, and it belongs to you. No one can hurt you now. No one wants to hurt you. But you have a secret that no one else must know. This secret is not a burden to you; it makes you special. You must treasure it quietly. It will hurt if it is taken from you. Trust no one but Rain Dare with your secret. You must wait until she alone tells you it is safe to reveal your secret." I infused this idea with more magic, setting up an imaginary wall in her head that guarded the secret.

Now I would give her a false past that would come to her mind instead of her real past. "When you're asked about your past, you must think of this story only. You and Rain Dare are cousins from a small Clan Wolf village hundreds of miles northeast of here. It's called Fort Howl. You are Tara Jansen, traveling with your cousin. You have different last names because your mothers were sisters and took different names when they married. Your house caught fire and all your family died except the two of you. You had no other relatives. The village gave you supplies, and you left to find another home. You traveled a long time living off the land. This was possible because in your small village everyone was taught survival skills. You had fewer luxuries than Wolf Trap. You had no plumbers, no electricity, no trade, few books. Everyone worked. You know very little about Clan Cat. You've never met a Cat. You only know Clan Wolf."

I repeated this false past a few times, then had her repeat it to me. I would reinforce it every few days. If she slipped up when I wasn't here, it would be bad for us, but worse for her. I don't think Clan Wolf would take pity on her just because she was a child. Her own village couldn't find tolerance for a female shifter, and Clan Wolf had a double reason to want her dead. I had to protect her. I had to trust my magic was good enough for this crucial purpose.

"You can leave the peaceful field now, but you'll still feel at peace. Open your eyes, Tara," I said when I'd finished.

She slowly opened her eyes, looked at me, and smiled.

"How do you feel?"

She sat up and stretched. "I feel good," she said in surprise. The peace and calm of the trance were still with her. "What did you do?"

"I just told you a story. It made you fall asleep for a few minutes. That's all."

She frowned. "I don't remember."

"That's okay. I'll tell you the story again sometime." I stood up. "Why don't we go for a walk? We can walk to the end of Mart Street so I can see where I have to go tomorrow," I suggested. "We didn't walk down that far on our first exploration."

"Okay."

We went downstairs. I could still hear Qzyx talking. I didn't owe him anything. He wasn't really a member of our party, but I went back into the kitchen and told them where we were going.

"You don't need to report to us on your every move," Audrey said grumpily. "As long as you pay your rent and don't cause trouble, that's all we need to know."

"I think it's very considerate of her to tell us she's going out. Oh, we forgot to give you your keys." Dorrie stood up and went through a door to the left of where we stood. There were four doors in the kitchen: the one we entered through the workroom, the one that led to their living quarters, the back door, and the door Dorrie went through. She left it ajar, and I could see shelves lining the walls of the small room. It must be a storage area.

Dorrie returned with two keys. "The big one is to the front and back doors, and the smaller one is for your room. Locking one's door isn't necessary. It's really very safe here in Wolf Trap, but having a key gives one a sense of privacy. I only have one set of keys per room I can give out. It's costly to have new keys made. Of course, I keep a master set."

She had warned me she could enter our rooms. "That's fine. We'll manage." I took the keys. Tara wouldn't need much privacy. I would find time and a safe place for her to shift once a week.

"If I'm not here when you get back, I'll probably see you around," Qzyx said.

"I expect I'll be involved most of the time with a job—maybe the mage corps if I decide to sign up."

"Sure. The Alpha's given me a part-time job. I'm to help with the mage corps."

"Is that so?" Why hadn't he mentioned that before?

He shrugged. "I need to stay out of the wilds for a while. I'm not as sharp as I used to be. Wolf Trap will see me through the winter."

"Okay. I'll see you when I see you."

Should I be suspicious that Qzyx, a stranger until a day ago, was suddenly becoming a regular part of my life? I wasn't sure. I couldn't sense anything guileful about him, but my abilities were still untested. Only real-life experience would let me know for certain. Unfortunately, I had to be lied to, betrayed, and conned to begin to recognize that behavior in others.

I led the way down Oak Street to Third Street to Mart Street. We'd seen about half of the main street that ran through the center of town to the Administration building. It had to be at least a mile long. Maybe more. Yesterday, Tara had wanted to stop and look at every store. She'd found everything fascinating. Today she limited herself to looking in windows without pause or comment.

The Administration building was enormous compared to the other buildings I'd seen so far in Wolf Trap, but only one level. Its width made up for that. It seemed to span several blocks of Alpha's Way, which ran perpendicular to Mart Street. Its windows were large and barred, and the doorway was open. There were trees planted in front of the building.

I'd noticed a lot of greenery in the town, mostly trees and shrubs. The roads were just dirt and gravel. There was no need for fancy roads and walkways in this day with no automobiles or trucks needing level surfaces. The sidewalks and crosswalks were differentiated by the use of staggered paving stones.

There were guards on either side of the front doors here, and each had solid red armbands. I didn't remember seeing any armbands on the shifters at Tooth and Claw. Although Stone had said all shifters had a rank, maybe they only wore their rank identification when they were called to duty. Therefore, the ones with armbands were the working soldiers.

We went inside and found a lobby. There were bulletin boards along the inside walls before reaching the long counter at the back of the room. There were wanted posters, informational postings, and job postings. Each of the postings had dates that still followed a revived Gregorian calendar. Tracking time was a human tendency, and every human civilization throughout history had had some system of measurement. I imagined the new calendar might not be completely accurate—years had been lost during the height of the Great Warming when technology couldn't be maintained—but it was close enough.

There were several people milling about. A few young women were together looking at the job postings. A couple of men were in line at the counter, taking care of some business. For a town of this size, the town administration center wasn't as busy as I'd expected. I guessed the wheels of this bureaucracy ran smoothly.

I made my way down to the back counter by looking over the postings. I was waiting for a chance to ask questions without having to stand in line.

At the top of the center postings was the Alpha's undated job post:

Mages of Superior Ability Wanted For Elite Mage Corps
Ages 16 to 21
Apply at the Resources Office

Should I or shouldn't I apply? The age range meant I could interact with many mages close to my age. This would be a better opportunity to observe mages than clerking in a store or whatever other job I could find. I could also observe what passed for superior magic ability in Wolf Trap. It would be the best way to evaluate the power development of mages. If I didn't like it, I could always quit. If I couldn't quit, Tara and I could run away to another town. My Jardvari wouldn't like this at all, but this was a perfect setup for my fact-finding jaunt. Surely they'd understand that.

I didn't have to wait until tomorrow to apply. I could do it today, before I could let the rules that bound me give me doubts. I could do all my business today instead of waiting until tomorrow. I was here. It wasn't exactly crowded. Why wait? I looked around. I didn't see anything called a Resources Office.

I motioned for Tara to follow me, which wasn't exactly necessary because she never moved far from my side, and walked down to the counter at the far end of the atrium. The last man had just left, and it was free of supplicants. There was no better time.

There were two women in their late thirties or early forties sitting behind the counter. They were similar in appearance, with short, dark hair and dark blue tunics, but no military insignia. One had more symmetrical facial features than the other. I supposed she would be considered the prettier one. With no one else in front of them, they were looking at each other and talking. Neither one looked up as I approached the counter.

"*Excuse me*," I projected loudly to them.

They looked up in surprise. I knew I appeared to be an average young female, but I wasn't invisible. Did that make me easy to ignore?

"Where is the Resources Office?" I asked when I had their attention.

After looking back at each other, the plainer one asked, "Why do you want the Resources Office?"

"I want to apply for the Mage Corps."

She gave me a squinty look. "Are you sixteen or older?"

"Yes."

She looked at me doubtfully now. "You don't even look sixteen. Can you prove it?"

"How do I do that?"

"Do you have a birth certificate?"

"I'm from a small town. We didn't have birth certificates. I know my birth date and year." I recited them for her. I followed their Gregorian calendar to set my birth year.

"Just a minute." She quietly conferred with the other woman. The prettier one left the room through a door to the left behind the counter. The remaining woman sat back and watched me. I returned her gaze. She stopped looking directly into my eyes but continued to watch me. A seventeen-year-old just didn't have the maturity to disconcert her. I could put a little magic into it but saw no reason at this point to intimidate the older woman.

"What's happening?" Tara whispered.

"I'm not certain, but I suspect we're waiting for someone."

In a few minutes, the other woman came back with an older man. He had a red armband with one thick white and one thin white bar. He came right over to me.

"You want to apply for the Mage Corps?"

"Yes."

"You're over sixteen?"

"Yes."

"This is rigorous training. If you're not at least sixteen, you may have trouble."

"I'm old enough. I'm seventeen."

He looked me over a minute then said, "Come with me." He opened the pass-through on the far left side of the counter to let me into the back area. Tara stuck with me.

"Wait. No children allowed back here." He stopped and held up his hand.

"She's with me," I told him firmly.

"Send her home."

I shook my head. "No. We're new here. I can't allow her to go alone. I'll come back another time."

"Wait." He paused a moment. "She can wait behind the counter. Find her a chair," he ordered the two women. "You follow me."

I patted Tara and told her to wait quietly for me before following the man.

He led me out the door where he'd come from. We walked down a long corridor. There were doors on each side, a room's length apart. The few open ones looked like offices. He led me almost to the end of the hallway, which ended at another door. He turned to the door on the left. The sign on the wall beside that doorway said "Delta Ritchie." He rapped his knuckles sharply on the door.

"Enter."

The man with me opened the door, entered, then stood at attention, chin up, shoulders back, with arms and hands held stiffly at his sides. "Sir, I have a new recruit for the Mage Corps." He stepped aside to allow me to be seen behind him. He said Mage Corps as if it were an official name, not just a descriptive one.

"Seriously, Kappa?" The man at the desk behind the door appeared a little younger than the man before him. He had no gray in his short brown hair like the first one did. The bars on his armband were two thin black bars surrounding a thicker yellow bar.

"Yes, sir. Here she is."

The man came out from behind the desk. He appeared taller sitting down because his shoulders were broad, but his legs seemed too short for his torso. He was still taller than me at my average five foot six by a couple of inches.

I wasn't intimidated, but I think they wanted me to be. They both stood too close for me to look up easily into their eyes. I would have to bare my neck. Maybe that was a shifter thing. Or maybe it was a military thing. I held my ground and looked straight ahead.

"You're over the age of sixteen?"

"I'm seventeen." I hadn't realized I looked young for my age.

"Kappa, inform Gamma Cabello."

"Yes, sir." He turned sharply and left the room.

"You use Greek letters for rank," I said, finally figuring it out. I had puzzled a moment about a man named Delta.

"Yes. You know the Greek alphabet?"

"Yes."

"Good. That's one less thing you'll have to learn."

"Why don't you use the old rank designations?"

"Because the Cats do that. We don't want to be anything like the Cats."

The Delta leaned back against his desk while we waited. "I see you've been stamped *Stranger*."

I looked at my hand. "Yes. We arrived yesterday. I was told of the Mage Corps by the gate guards."

Before he could ask more questions, the Kappa returned with another man. He was older and had very little hair. He carried himself as if he were powerful. To have the rank of Gamma—two ranks away from Alpha—he had to be powerful. Cronyism would not allow shifters to hold the higher ranks unless they were powerful enough to do so. Friendship could only get you so far when power was the measurement of a shifter. Hierarchy was important.

"Is it true? It's four months until the next birthday," the new man asked.

"It's true. Here she is. Number fifty-two."

They stood for a moment and looked at me. I wondered why that number was significant. Was I really the fifty-second applicant? What did that mean?

"We must inform the Alpha immediately."

"This is the perfect time of year for this training."

"He'll want to begin straight away."

"Kappa, prepare to dispatch information to the new recruits. I'll inform the Beta." The Gamma ordered and nodded to the Delta.

"Right away, sir." Both men left at a brisk pace.

Delta Ritchie sat back down behind his desk. He pulled out a sheet of paper and a pencil. "Give me your name and address."

"Rain Iris Dare." I decided to add a middle name to mine. I was tired of explaining that I wasn't named reindeer. "I prefer being called Rain," I added.

"You'll be called Dare."

"Yes, sir." That should end the reindeer problem.

"Address?"

"25 Oak Street."

"A boardinghouse?"

"Yes, sir." I thought I'd better get used to addressing officers as sir.

"You can move to the barracks we've set up once you begin training."

"I can't do that. I can't stay away overnight."

"Why not?"

"I have my young cousin with me. It's just the two of us. She's only ten. I can't leave her alone all day and night."

"Well, for now, I think we can make accommodation for that. There are three other recruits that need to be home at night. However, living together develops camaraderie. You'll have to work harder to get to know the other recruits." He gave me a sharp look.

"Fifty-two is a large number for camaraderie, sir," I ventured.

"It will be whittled down to something more manageable once the trials begin. Each element will be tested. You must pass two to be accepted into the Mage Corps. We only want the best mages for this new corps. Are you a good mage?"

"I think so, sir."

"You'll be able to prove that soon." He stood up. "I have all the information I need for now. You'll be informed of the date you need to return. Be ready. It will be soon. Now I'll take you back to the lobby."

"What will my rank designation be, sir?"

"You'll be Omega Dare if you pass training."

"Is that the bottom rank?"

"Not quite. Once you've finished basic training, you'll be ranked above a Rho, our lowest rank. We haven't yet determined what other rankings will be available in the Mage Corps, but they should be equivalent to the shifters' rankings."

"Yes, sir." I didn't ask about the armbands, but I was curious. Omega was the last letter of the Greek alphabet. The Rhos had plain red armbands. If we were above them, would we have stripes or a different color?

He stood and led me down the hall to the end doorway, which led back to the counter area. The two women stood up at attention when he entered. He gave us all a nod, turned on his heel, and left.

Before I collected Tara, I asked the two women about registration for school. They helped me with that as well. I also pointed out our hand stamps. She wrote down our names and address and told me the solvent would be forthcoming at the end of the month. Now all my tasks at the Administration building were successfully accomplished.

We finally left the building under the curious gaze of the two women. They hadn't stopped eyeing me since the Delta left. I was certain they'd be talking about me once I was out of earshot. I was number fifty-two, which seemed to be important.

"Are you going to be in the Mage Corps?" Tara asked me solemnly once we were far enough away from curious eyes and ears.

"I still have tests to take, but it seems likely."

"Will you fight my Clan?"

"I want to find out what the Mage Corps is all about, but I don't intend to fight. We'll leave Wolf Trap before that happens." I had decided that much in the short time I'd given myself to consider this step. It seemed perfect for my purpose here. Was it too perfect?

"Good," she said decidedly.

We walked back to the boardinghouse, eating a late lunch along the way. I wondered how long *soon* would be to start the Mage Corps (I thought of it in capital letters now). Had they been waiting for candidate fifty-two or did everyone have the jump on me? I'd rather start on a level playing field, but as someone new to Wolf Trap, everything would be new to me.

Not knowing what to expect in this new Corps, I had no way of anticipating trouble. I could think of several rules that I might be violating here. The first three rules came to mind: *Trust no one*; *Hide what you can do*; and *Take only smart risks*. Was this a risk? Was it smart or dumb? Who knew? All I knew was that I felt excited and anticipatory, and those weren't at all the controlled reactions my Jardvari would prefer.

Chapter 6

Down, down, down. There was nothing else to do.

THE SUMMONS CAME IN the morning as a written order before I'd even had breakfast. I had to be at the Administration building within the hour. I wasn't expecting it so soon. I thought I'd have at least another day to explore the town. I wanted to get my bearings thoroughly in case I needed an unobtrusive escape. The Alpha must be eager to get his Mage Corps launched.

I'd had some second thoughts about this course of action. There were many reasons this could be a bad idea. It might draw too much attention to me. It might put me in situations where I would use too much magic. It might cause me to share too much with these mages. I might relax my guard as I engaged. But these second thoughts didn't outweigh the idea that this was the ideal opportunity to enact most of rule number eleven: *Observe, study, catalog, record (only)*. If I disregarded the *only*, I had fifty-one specimens gathered together in one place to do it all. How could my Jardvari really object?

Audrey and Dorrie promised again to take care of Tara. They were more excited than I was at the prospect of a Mage Corps. They made me promise to tell them everything that happened. Since I didn't know yet what could be shared, I only promised to share what I was allowed. I was good at keeping secrets.

I bought some fruit from a vendor for breakfast and ate it on the way.

I had my backpack with me. I wouldn't leave it behind. Its magic was important to my survival. I had protective spells on it that made it seem worthless and unnoticeable. If Tara had noticed it when I left, she would have been alarmed. It was my only tie to the boardinghouse except for her.

I was glad that yesterday I'd made time to reinforce against Tara's instinct to shift. Shifting didn't follow the old stories. A full moon didn't force a change. Silver wasn't deadly to a shifter. Shifting was just magic with a specific purpose, and it wanted to be used. Any semblance of control came with practice and maturity. Never using it didn't work. That must be why Wolf Trap had scheduled hunts and fights. And that was why I had to find time for Tara to shift even on a Mage Corps schedule.

I reached the Administration building after fifteen minutes of rapid walking. There were people milling around outside, grumbling discontentedly. Nobody tried to stop me when I went up to the door. It was closed now, with two guards standing on either side. A posted sign hung in the middle that read "Closed until Tomorrow."

I went up to the guards. They weren't the same guards as yesterday. They wore red armbands with one thin white stripe.

"Are you a candidate?" one asked.

"Yes." I held out the order I'd received.

One guard looked it over, handed it back to me, then said, "You may enter." The other one opened the door for me.

The lobby was filled with, I assumed, young women ages sixteen to twenty-one. I wasn't the last of the fifty-two expected because a quick count told me there were forty-five before me. Some were obviously friends or acquaintances, huddling together and whispering among themselves while eyeing the others. I was given several once-overs, presumably because I was a stranger. There were three others that stood out as either loners or strangers. I was glad I wasn't the only odd one out, but only I had an *S* stamped on my hand.

It took about ten minutes for the last six candidates to arrive. All eyes turned every time the door opened, and the whispers grew louder. Three of those six later arrivals were leaders of some kind and seemed to have their own cliques because a small cluster of girls moved toward each of them.

The last girl to enter did so with a confident flourish, pausing in the doorway until she was noticed, then striding boldly through the group to the front. She held her head high and only looked toward the counter. She had long, curly dark hair tied back with a red ribbon, almond-shaped eyes with long lashes, full rosy lips, and tawny-brown skin. She was about my height, but her figure was fuller. I suspected that she'd been waiting until everyone else was present to make her entrance. Several girls made their way to her side, exclaiming excitedly.

Once all fifty-two of us were present, it only took a moment for Delta Ritchie to appear behind the counter.

"Quiet!" he called in a loud, commanding voice.

The whispering died down almost immediately.

"Recruits, you will follow the Kappa—that's the man wearing the red armband with the one thick and one thin white bar. He will lead you to the mess hall behind this building where you will be seated—*quietly*—and await further instructions. Kappa, the recruits are yours."

We all turned toward the right side of the lobby. There was a door in the right wall. The Kappa opened it. A shifter with the same armband as the door guards stood there.

"Recruits, follow me, single file. Nu Patel, the man with the red armband with the thin white stripe, will bring up the rear," the Kappa stated and walked through the doorway, turning left, expecting us to follow quietly.

Soft chatter started up again as the girls awaited their turn to follow the Kappa.

I was last except for Nu Patel.

The outside hallway had a less-finished appearance and was partially exposed with only a slatted wooden half gate covering its back end. Once outside the gate, I saw a vast open space. I looked back at the Administration building and was surprised to see that from this side the building was smaller than it appeared from the street side. The rest was a façade—a long wall level with the building walls and spanning Alpha's Way. I could think of no reason for this except to block the view and contain the area.

I turned back around and surveyed the rest of the area. The ground was covered with some durable greenery I thought might be a version of pachysandra adapted by magic to resist the heat. In the distance, I could see some basic buildings with a few trees providing shade. We seemed to be headed for those.

We walked for at least fifteen minutes before we reached those three buildings. The Kappa led us into the third and farthest building, which I assumed was the mess hall.

Inside, tables were shoved against the walls. In the center, toward the back of the room, were thirty benches in four rows. The Kappa led our group to the first set of benches and seated us two people per bench. I was the last of what I thought to be the four outsiders in the last row.

In front of us was a platform that ran the length of the back of the room. On it was a higher backed central chair with two smaller chairs flanking each side. A man sat in each chair, except for the last one. The men in the chairs were maybe in their late forties or early fifties. There were two men each standing behind them, who were much younger but older than me—I'd guess anywhere from eighteen to twenty-five.

When we were all seated, we quieted down after the Kappa barked at us again. He then stepped up to the platform and took the empty seat. Once he was settled, the man in the important-looking middle chair stood up. He had thick, dark blond, slightly graying hair. He was shorter and a little stouter than the young men standing behind him. He had a strong, handsome face. His firm but generous mouth formed a warm, welcoming smile. He had a huge helping of charisma that would make him an easy-to-follow leader.

"Those of you who have lived your life in Wolf Trap know me. I am Alpha Allyn Saltwyck. I am the leader of Wolf Trap and the head of the army. You will call me Alpha whether you remain in the Corps or stay a civilian. You are the first recruits in what I hope will be an important arm of our military—the Mage Corps.

"I have long wanted to utilize our mages' special abilities in protecting our town. We shifters have taken our protective instincts to an extreme that hasn't been fair. You were not all meant to only serve domestic duties. Caring for children, husbands, and elderly parents is important, and mages have those skills, but I have seen mage power grow over the years, from simple workings to larger flares. I think you have an important role to play in our defenses. To that end, I want to explore your effectiveness in this newly formed Mage Corps. If it is successful, you will be the first and the pioneers of what I hope to be the advent of many Mage units to come." He paused to look us over, meeting the eyes of several girls in the front. He had sharp green eyes. Not everyone would have been able to tell from this distance, but I had excellent vision—as good as any shifter.

The Alpha continued. "There are fifty-two of you present today, but not all of you will successfully complete the trials or training. It will be grueling, but necessary for your safety. I require strong, capable mages. We can train your bodies to be strong, but you must train your magic. I believe if you are physically strong, then you can become mentally strong. In our belief that shifters were the best protection, we have not offered you the opportunities to become all that you can be. I intend to remedy that by taking the strongest of you and proving that you can stand with the shifters in protecting our town."

So far, I had no objections to what he'd said. He was on the right track. He wasn't the first person in history to believe *mens sana in corpore sano*—a healthy mind in a healthy body. But he might be the first in this new magic age to apply it to magic. When I eventually explored other towns, I'd find out.

"Together you will achieve a complete mastery over your magic, but in the meantime, the four men stationed in front of you will be your instructors in martial arts training. All of them are Kappas. They are the instructors of training for all our military units. The other soldiers of rank attending your training will be Zetas and Nus. For those of you unfamiliar with military ranks, Zetas are the sixth highest rank, just above Kappas. The Zetas will observe and sometimes aid in your training. Mostly you will practice your martial arts skills against the Nus. Nus are the rank below Kappas."

"You will not be unique in this training. It is the training given to every recruit. Just because a man can shift into a large predator doesn't mean he has to always shift before fighting. His strength, agility, and defensive knowledge as a man will be just as useful when he shifts. It is best to allow the man to guide the fight, not the beast." That philosophy spoke to the shifter's fear that the animal would take over. If a shift took place under the conditions of powerful emotions—anger, fear, grief, etc.—then the animal did claim the driver's seat and steered by that emotion. That's why they taught discipline and control from the age of ten, their first shifting year.

That's what my Jardvari had learned in their forays into the world to glean information. My knowledge of people today came from their observations.

"The challenge for you these first days will be a test of your magic. Ultimately, you will be assigned to the elemental group of your strongest magic. We will discover this through magic trials, and you will be grouped accordingly. I'm given to understand a mage usually has two skills stronger than the others, but one dominant. We want to discover your dominant magic skill."

"While you strengthen your body with exercise and martial arts training in the mornings, in the afternoons you will work to build the strength of your magic through individual mastery of your element. Power and control are your goals in this training. This Mage Corps could be the edge we need to beat back the Cats." He beamed at us with a fanatical gleam in his eyes. He was definitely set on this fight with Clan Cat.

"When your training is completed, your rank will be Omega and your armband will be blue. Be advised some of you will achieve leadership positions in your squad, moving up in rank based on your skills and achievements. I have great hopes for this Corps. Make me proud, future Omegas."

He stopped and waited for applause, which quickly came. The surrounding soldiers clapped, and we followed suit. He gave us all a huge paternal smile, waved a hand, and left the dais. He was joined by Delta Ritchie at the door, and the men left together without a backward glance.

The two young men who'd been standing directly behind the Alpha's chair remained. I hadn't given them more than a glance until the Alpha had gone. He was a dynamic personality who sucked up all the attention in the room. With him gone, the others could capture my notice.

What surprised me the most was that the two young men who had stood behind the Alpha were identical twins. Successful multiple births were a rarity because medicine was no longer cutting edge. Only the first twin usually survived.

These two young men couldn't be more than a few years older than me. They were definitely identical in height and breadth. Their muscle tone was the same. Their skin coloring was the same warm tan. Their hair was the same dark blond. Their nose, chin, and cheekbones were the same handsome shape. Their facial expressions were the same stoic, bland military. But the eyes were different. The one on the right had two green eyes. The one on the left had one hazel eye and one green eye. That made them easily identifiable from one another. There would be no jokes, pranks, or mix-ups with these two.

I noticed that most of the mages watched the one with the same-colored eyes, which made me think he might have other attributes besides good looks that were significant to the girls watching. While they watched him, his eyes roamed the group, finally alternating between several girls in the two front rows. I glanced at his brother to see if they had caught his interest as well and found him watching me and only me. When I looked away and back again several times, his gaze was still on me alone.

My heart leaped in sudden apprehension. He should not be looking at me. Nobody should look at me with fifty-one other girls surrounding me, and some of them quite good-looking. I had deliberately altered my appearance so that I didn't stand out. I had practiced the use of glamour since I was young. My hair was ordinarily honey colored, but I toned down the golden glow to ordinary brown. My eyes were a golden brown and my skin tone was a golden tan, which I again dulled to average tones. Without interference, I gave the impression of a golden aura surrounding me, which would be much too distinctive to retain. My facial features were pleasing enough, but not dramatic or exotic. I thought of myself as average in every noticeable way. Yet here he was, looking at me. What did he see that I hadn't hidden? Before I could puzzle it out, one of the older men stood up to address us.

"I am Kappa Idris. There were many manuals for martial arts preserved by our ancestors. We have taken these and produced a training course that combines different styles of fighting hand to hand and with weapons. You will receive the same physical training as any shifter. You need strength and endurance. You need to be able to protect yourself with or without magic. You can't rely on one skill for survival. Let me introduce you to the other men who will be your instructors." Each man stood up as his name was called.

"Kappa Jōtarō, Kappa Wójcik, Kappa Benjamin, and I will, in turn, oversee your training. Learning these fighting skills is vital to your survival under battle conditions. You will take your physical training as seriously as you will your magic training." He paused to cast a stern eye over the group.

"Keep in mind, anyone not meeting the physical requirements of train-ing cannot continue in the Mage Corps. You must give every instruction your all." He paused to give us another stern look. "We will begin today with your first magic trial. These trials will be accomplished in the morn-ings, and you will be free the rest of the day. Now, for your initial trial groups, I want you to count off from one to four. Stand up. Begin count off."

We stood up and began our count off from the front. As the last of the entire complement of mages, I was a four because the magical number fifty-two was divisible by four. Was that the reason they wanted fifty-two? Had they been waiting simply to have an even number for the groups? Was it as simple as that?

We filed into our groups. My group was simply called Group Four. Kappa Benjamin took the lead of my group. He was the Kappa from my sign-up day.

We followed Kappa Benjamin outside as quietly as a group of girls who had friends close at hand to whisper with could. We watched the other three groups march off in different directions while we were led between and behind the three one-story buildings of barracks and mess hall. Two young men with the armbands of Nus walked beside our line of thirteen mages.

I was at the end of the line as usual and should have been last, but I felt eyes on my back. I turned my head and found the different-color-eyed twin following behind me, watching. He had one yellow and one white bar on his armband. He must be one of the Zetas we were told would help with our training. I decided my best option was to ignore him as much as possible, and maybe he'd start looking at someone else.

Kappa Benjamin led us to a field with a selection of large objects. I finally noticed that two of the Nus had backpacks that they now removed. One brought out a stiff board with paper attached. The other removed some colored spikes. The one with the pencil and paper asked each of us to spell out our names as he wrote them down. The Kappa began his instructions when this was finished.

"We are testing your Air ability today. On each of the next three days, you will be tested on each of the other elements. There will only be one trial per day because we want you well rested and up to full strength for each trial. This will help determine your strongest elemental magic. As the Alpha told you, you will ultimately be grouped on the strength of your dominant magic element."

"As you can see, recruits, there are five objects in this field. The largest one weighs approximately five hundred pounds, the next one four hundred pounds, and so on until the last one of one hundred pounds. You will use Air magic alone to move one of these objects as far as you can without stopping and starting your magic. Line up behind the object you think you can move with your magic."

I watched the others choose first. Nobody stood behind either five hundred or four hundred pounds. Three girls stood behind three hundred pounds. Four girls stood behind two hundred pounds. Five stood behind one hundred pounds.

I was proficient in all the elements, but I'd decided Air wouldn't be one of my strengths. I joined the one-hundred-pound group.

Kappa Benjamin watched us choose, then he said, "Now I know what you think of yourselves. I think you're better than that. Move up one place."

We all shifted positions.

"Now everyone back up and sit down to give the active candidate room. We'll begin with the four-hundred-pound group. When it's your turn, come forward, state your last name loudly, and stand as close as you feel comfortable. When you're ready, raise your left hand. I will tell you when to begin. When you're finished, raise your right hand."

The first girl stepped within five feet of the object that looked like a large, old, metal barrel, and shouted "Costa!" She then raised her left hand. When the Kappa called "Begin!" she held both hands out toward the barrel and mumbled her charm in a low, indistinguishable voice.

Costa continued to mutter, move her arms and hands, strain forward, and stare intensely at the object. After a full minute—which felt like a long time when you were waiting—the air moved. We could feel it as it rushed past us. We could see it as it lifted our clothes and hair. Then we saw it move that four-hundred-pound weight. At first it rocked and then it moved forward slowly and then more swiftly until it had moved maybe thirty feet. Costa was panting as if she'd pushed it herself. She probably felt as if she had because she'd externalized the movement physically instead of keeping it in her mind's eye. She raised her right hand as she bent over, bracing her left hand on her knee, and waited for the Nus to measure the distance.

This physical behavior would certainly prove to the Alpha that a healthy body was important to the use of magic, but physical movement really wasn't necessary. I rarely used more than a gesture, but I had to behave like the others or there would be questions.

"Twenty-nine feet, ten inches," the one measuring called out.

"Very good. At ease, Costa. Sit on the ground behind the group."

She straightened up and trudged back to the end of the line and sat down.

The other two four-hundred-pound weight mages took their turns. They didn't move it as far as Costa, but both moved it over twenty feet. She wasn't one of the three mages with allies I'd observed originally, but she might be the best Air mage among us.

The next group began. It was less weight so they should have been able to move it farther if their skills were equal to the first group. The best one in this group moved it over twenty-seven feet. Kappa Benjamin said she should have been in the four-hundred-pound group. The rest moved it under fifteen feet. I noticed one of the three mages with an entourage was in this group. Her name was Lee. She had shiny, blue-black hair, sienna skin, light brown eyes, and symmetrical features.

The third group—mine—did the worst, of course. We had judged ourselves limited in Air for good reason. Averaging the group, we moved the two-hundred-pound weight barely two feet. I allowed myself to do well in this group and moved it three feet, making me the best of the worst.

When we were all seated on the ground again, Kappa Benjamin loomed before us. "This was a very good first test, but I want you all to stop underestimating your abilities. I don't want to see what's easy for you to do. I want to see what you might be capable of. I want the first two groups to move up to the next higher weight and try again."

They did as they were told and repeated their performances. Only one person changed as far as ranking. None of them moved the next higher weights as far as the lower one, but they all could move the weights some distance. Before we were finished, he had us all try moving the five-hundred-pound weight. Everyone moved it a little. Even the mages with the lowest expectations of their Air abilities could rock it a bit.

There must be something psychological in the idea of moving such heavy weights. If you thought about the physical lifting of the weight, it seemed impossible. But if you thought about storm force winds hitting the weight instead of you moving it, then it was possible, if Air was your skill. This seemed as much an exercise in confidence as it was in ability.

When we were all finished, the Kappa told us, "Not all of you will pass these tests this time around, but if you are released, you can practice your skills and apply again in the future if you meet the age requirements. Tomorrow, for your next trial, you will return to this spot at the same time you arrived at the Administration building this morning. You will not enter the lobby, but the door outside the building revealing the hallway that leads to this area. It is to the right of the main door. There will be guards stationed there. Now, you will follow the Nus back out to Alpha's Way. Recruits, dismissed!"

Chapter 7

"Of all the unsatisfactory—(she repeated this aloud, as it was a great comfort to have such a long word to say) of all the unsatisfactory people I ever met—"

NONE OF THE MAGES waited for their friends from the other teams to show up. We might have been the first to finish our trial, because I saw no one else waiting around. I managed to be last again by staying seated until everyone else passed me by. I didn't interact with anyone yet. I was supposed to observe and study before anything else. The only thing I'd said today was my name. I don't think my Jardvari realized how difficult it would be to stay silent. There were so many questions I wanted to ask.

As I followed the last girl and mulled over what I'd learned so far, I was still aware of the man with two different-colored eyes walking behind me. He'd waited outside the first barracks. He stayed far enough back to not crowd me, but I still felt his eyes on me. He had watched me more than anyone else today, but I'd tried not to let him know I was aware of it. That intense watching was still a puzzle to me. I didn't think I'd done anything to deserve it. I thought I'd successfully made myself average enough not to be singled out.

When we finally reached the street and everyone before us had dispersed to wherever, I finally turned and frowned at him. "Are you following me?" I asked.

He had an oval-shaped face that ended in a more square than tapered jaw, wide-set eyes, and a nose that was a little too long and wide to cause him to be labeled pretty. I'd noticed that most shifters were clean-shaven in their human form, perhaps as a reaction to their completely hairy animal form. Both his eyes were pretty in their own way. The green one was a mix of light and dark green pigments. The blue one was a mix of light and dark blue pigments with a burst of yellow around the pupil.

"This is the way out, so yes, I appear to be following you." His voice was a pleasant baritone. He spoke without inflection. He didn't smile, but his face seemed more relaxed.

"Fine." I turned and walked down the street. He was still behind me.

I stopped and turned again. "You're still following me."

"Correct. Appearances are not deceiving," he told me solemnly, but with a twinkle in his eyes. Did he find me funny?

"Why? Don't you have someplace else you need to be? Something else you need to be doing?" I asked brusquely. I was very aware of rule number four. (*Avoid shifters. Mages are your concern.*)

"I do have someplace to be and something to do. I'm walking you home."

My mouth fell open in surprise, but I quickly closed it and frowned again, folding my arms over my chest. "Why? I don't need an escort. I know the way. Maybe I don't want some strange shifter knowing where I live."

He stood relaxed and tilted his head slightly to study me. "Kappa Benjamin told me that when he assigned me this job."

"Terrific," I grumbled. I couldn't hide my situation from the military leaders, but I didn't want every Tom, Dick, and this guy to know. "I didn't realize I required a babysitter."

"You're a stranger to Wolf Trap. An outsider. You're more vulnerable than those born here. No one else will tell you, but I think there are a few things you should know about the Mage Corps before you get in any deeper. You won't hear anything officially, but it's only fair that you should know."

I thought about this for a moment and decided to listen to him. He might have something important to tell me.

"What's your name?" I asked.

"Aryk Saltwyck. I'm a Zeta." He pointed to his red armband with one yellow and one white stripe. "My brother and I will be the only Zetas involved in your training. And I know you to be Rain Dare. Unusual name." He got some points for not making a reindeer remark.

"Are you related to Alpha Saltwyck?"

"His son."

"Your eyes are different colors." There I went, stating the obvious. My social skills could certainly use some work, but since I wasn't supposed to socialize with shifters, it didn't matter.

"Correct."

"You're a twin."

"Correct."

"But your brother's eyes are the same color. That should make you fraternal twins, but you appear to be identical."

He shrugged. "Fraternal, identical—who knows? Does it bother you—my different-colored eyes?"

"No. Heterochromia iridum is rare, but not a dangerous abnormality."

"Hetero—what did you call it?"

"Heterochromia iridum," I enounced slowly. "It's Greek and just means different-colored irises."

"That term has never been mentioned by our healers. They have no soothing explanation for my eyes. You seem to know more about it than anyone here."

"Reading was encouraged where I come from. I've read everything I could get my hands on. Isn't it encouraged here?"

"Practical knowledge is encouraged. Too bad you weren't here when I was born and could reassure everyone that I wasn't dangerous."

"Is that what people think? Are you dangerous?"

"Only to my enemies."

Maybe this was a good time to address my other concern. "Why have you been watching me?"

"What makes you think I've been watching you?"

I stopped walking and stared into his two-colored eyes. "Whenever I look at you, you're looking back. You don't have strabismus, so I know you're looking at me."

"What's strabismus?"

"Crossed eyes or eyes looking in different directions."

"Ummm. That would have generated even more negative attention my way than there is now. I guess I'm grateful to have heterochromia iridum instead." He said it correctly this time. "Maybe I watch you because you watch me."

"You were watching me first," I insisted.

"Maybe I watch you because you aren't like the others."

"What do you mean? I'm exactly like the others. I'm average—very, very average," I insisted.

He shook his head. "No, I don't think you are, but you will have to do something dramatic to catch my brother's eye."

"Why would I want to do that?" Catching anyone's eye was the last thing I wanted to do. Having Aryk Saltwyck's unwanted attention was bad enough.

He nodded his head decisively. "I thought you might not realize there is a secondary purpose for this Mage Corps. It's a theory my father has professed frequently and has given my brother the opportunity to employ. It's not as important a reason as creating a fighting corps of mages, but the others probably know why two Zetas have been assigned to this Corps."

"Explain," I commanded. "Please," I added as an afterthought.

"My father believes besides a powerful father, a mother strong in magic is also necessary for a powerful son. Part of the purpose of this Mage Corps is to gather the strongest appropriately aged mages from which my brother can vet and possibly choose a wife."

"Unbelievable," I laughed. "This is like a fairy story in reverse. Women fighting it out to win the prince instead of the other way around."

"You could win his attention if you wanted to," he said once I'd stopped snickering.

I recoiled. "No, I couldn't. I don't stand out. I'm just average in every way."

He shook his head. "I don't think so."

"What do you know about it?"

He was quiet for a long moment. "I was watching you during the trial."

"I know that. Everyone was watching every testee."

He nodded his head. "True, but I might have been the only one to make the right comparisons. I think you were holding back."

My heart skipped a beat as I felt a stab of alarm. "Why would you think that? I worked my magic the same way every other mage did." I thought I'd mimicked the other mages' movements exactly. Did two different-colored eyes give him some advantage others didn't have?

He shrugged. "I've seen mages work. I see the physical effort they put into their magic. All twelve mages worked their magic before you. They strained, sweated, and grunted so much I wanted to step in and help."

"I did all that, too," I said hotly. He was making me mad. I did everything right.

He shook his head. "You didn't sweat or strain or groan like they did. At one point, you didn't move your arms much at all. And you didn't speak as much."

"What?" I thought back but couldn't remember exactly what I did. My eidetic memory served me well for written words, but not as well for other things. I had to pay close attention to commit everyday actions to memory. I didn't want just anything cluttering up my synapses.

He expounded. "All the others looked as if they were moving the object themselves, not with magic. Their entire body tensed and strained. Their legs were braced. Their arms were taut. They were sweating heavily from the effort. They were constantly muttering. You went through all the motions, but you weren't sweating from anything but the heat. You worked faster and smoother, too. Not by a lot, but I noticed. You were acting the part."

Damn! Why was he more observant than anyone else?

"Is that all you've got? Maybe I just don't sweat much. Some people don't. I worked just as hard as everyone else to move those objects." Maybe harder because faking being weak was more difficult than I'd thought it would be. "I didn't even move it as far as half the girls."

"So it would seem," he agreed politely.

It was time to change the subject again. Being put on the defensive was dangerous. I could inadvertently reveal too much.

"I'm not the only stranger to Wolf Trap. There are three other mages. Are you going to share this bride-for-your-brother information with them, too?"

"Of course. I'll look for an opportunity to inform them. It's only fair."

"Do you think they need that added incentive to do their best? I would think being a member of a new and unique Mage Corps would be incentive enough."

"It depends on their ambition. Wife to the Alpha is the highest mage position in town. Being an Omega will still be second best. They should know what every mage in Wolf Trap knows. It will be important knowledge when the competition gets ugly."

"What do you mean—*ugly*?"

He looked at me with pity. "I've seen mages fight over something they both want. It can get ugly and dangerous very fast with uncontrolled magic being thrown around. Mages can get just as aggressive as shifters when the stakes are high enough. That's one reason my father thought mages could develop offensive skills."

We were nearing the boardinghouse. There was a lot more I wanted to know, but now wasn't the time. I had to think about all this.

"Don't worry. I'm no threat. I'm not interested in being Mrs. Future Alpha." I very much doubted I would seem a threat to any of the other mages in this regard. I would work harder to prove I was only average. Aryk Saltwyck noticing me was surely an aberration. Maybe I'd already been described to him as the fifty-second candidate. That had seemed to excite the officers at the Administration building when I'd signed up.

"That won't matter. You're an outsider. You'll be one of the first they'll try to eliminate."

"We'll see. Thanks for walking me home. I'll let you get on with whatever it is you do when you're not babysitting mages."

"I'll see you tomorrow. My brother and I will be observing every day."

"And reporting to the Alpha?"

"As is everyone else, so watch yourself."

"Warning heeded. Goodbye." I left him and went through the front door. I turned to observe him before shutting the door, but he didn't linger.

I wasn't sure what to make of him, but I didn't think he was being totally honest with me. There was no reason he should be, but now I was curious. I wondered what our landladies knew about this new wrinkle in the Mage Corps. I intended to find out.

"You're invited to dinner," Dorrie greeted me when I turned from shutting the door.

It was more like an ambush than a greeting. I started when I heard her voice. Audrey and Tara were right behind her.

"I helped," Tara said excitedly. She seemed happy today.

"Thank you, but I don't remember if I told you—I don't eat meat," I warned apologetically. I hadn't figured out yet how to explain that to the military unless they didn't plan to feed us during the day. It had taken us until afternoon to get through the introductions and first test, and they'd only offered us water.

"I told them. We made a vegetable and nut pie for you. I told them you can eat eggs."

"That sounds good. I can't wait."

"Will it bother you if the rest of us eat meat?" Dorrie asked.

"No. I know I'm the odd one out with whomever I eat."

"Good. We can eat now. Audrey and I usually have our main meal in the afternoon and a snack in the evening. We usually go to bed with the sun until it sets too early. There's no point wasting precious candles just to sit up late, and neither of us has enough Fire magic to burn a fuel-less flame. Come on out to the kitchen."

I followed behind the others, with Tara leading the way. Audrey had allowed her sister to do all the talking, but she was not one to resist speaking her mind. I assumed she had nothing to say—yet.

Once we sat down and food was distributed, Dorrie began the questioning. "Now tell us all about your day. Will the Mage Corps be a success? Is it difficult? This is a first for all of us. Tell us everything."

I wasn't told to keep anything a secret. I assumed all the other girls would detail our tests to their families. I saw no reason not to reveal almost everything. If I seemed open and straightforward, maybe they'd be the same with me. I described my day from the beginning. When I got to the Air trials, I began my dissembling by praising the other girls' abilities.

"I recognize the names of several of the girls in your trials," Dorrie said.

"I know the Lee family. They have a Gamma and Zeta in the army," added Audrey.

"This is *so* exciting. Imagine *us* housing an Omega!" Dorrie exclaimed.

"I haven't made it through the trials yet. I didn't fare too well with Air," I warned. Part of me wanted to fail completely and get out of this fledgling corps. My Jardvari would prefer that. But the other part of me—the one who drove this mission when my Jardvari wanted me to wait—was curious and excited to witness mages achieve more in life than the overprotected existence the shifters had granted them up to now.

"Then Air's not your skill. That's all. You'll do better tomorrow. What is tomorrow's trial?"

"I don't know. They didn't tell us."

"I wonder if Stone knows," Dorrie mused.

"Why would he know?"

"He has many friends active in the military and they frequent his tavern. He hears lots of things," Dorrie explained.

"And he tells us all the gossip," Audrey said with satisfaction.

Is that so? "Did he tell you the secondary reason for the Mage Corps?"

They exchanged surprised glances. "What secondary reason?"

"The Alpha wants to find a strong mage mate for his son."

"Oh, that. We may have heard such a thing, but it's not like Ayden wouldn't be able to find a suitable bride. He's a strong one. He's bound to become Alpha one day, not too far off."

"He's handsome, too. What girl could resist such a combination?" Dorrie sighed.

"You might have warned me. I'm not in the market for a husband, no matter how strong or handsome he is."

"You'd be lucky as an outsider to win the Alpha's son," Audrey sneered.

"What about his other son?"

"Aryk? He's not as popular as Ayden."

"They're twins. They're exactly alike," I argued.

"Not exactly," Audrey demurred.

"Those strange different-colored eyes," Dorrie added, shuddering a little. "Was he there? Have you seen him?"

"Yes, I have. Why can't his eyes be two different colors?"

"It's not right. There must be something wrong with him," Audrey stated.

Here too was that idea that different meant wrong. Maybe Aryk was one of my anomalies. He wasn't one I was expecting because I didn't think his different-colored eyes were magically induced, but maybe there was more to it. I would definitely keep a close eye on him, which would be no hardship, but I wouldn't let him or anyone else know that.

"If you've read history, you'd find that different-colored eyes were not an uncommon trait in the past. It's called heterochromia iridum." I fibbed a little. No need to encourage the landladies' xenophobia.

"Is that really true?" Audrey asked suspiciously.

"It doesn't mean anything bad? How do you know?" Dorrie asked doubtfully.

"No, it doesn't," I said firmly. "It just means one eye has more pigmentation in the iris than the other. I read about it in a book once. I enjoy collecting odd facts."

"Everyone thought twins were a good sign, but then the youngest had two different-color-eyed eyes. It just didn't seem natural."

"Nobody has two live twin births anymore. The second rarely thrives," Audrey agreed. "That was different enough. The youngest, having different-colored eyes, was *too* different."

"It should have been considered a fortuitous event," I admonished.

"I don't know about that," Audrey said darkly. "Sometimes children are born wrong, and you have to do something about it. The Alpha was strong enough even as a new Alpha to protect his son. His mother was a strong, protective mage as well. The two of them wouldn't let anyone harm him."

"What do you mean sometimes children are born wrong?" Maybe the anomalies had been appearing for a while. Maybe I wasn't catching the first one in Tara. I glanced over at her to see her reaction. She kept her eyes down, but I could see her mouth trembling slightly.

"Never you mind," Audrey snapped.

"It doesn't happen often," Dorrie said. "Only twice that I've known about. Three times if you count Aryk Saltwyck."

"Shut up, Dorrie."

Dorrie was the weak link here, but I wouldn't get anything out of her with Audrey around—and Audrey always seemed to be around. I'd have to look for opportunities to find out more. I was finished pumping the sisters for information today.

Tara and I helped clean up after dinner, then we went upstairs. The days were growing shorter, but we still had a couple hours of sunlight left in the day.

Once we were in our room, Tara asked, "Do they kill kids who are different here, too?"

"It sounds like they might."

"But they let this Aryk guy live? Why *him*? Why not *me*?"

"I don't know, Tara. A female shifter may just be harder to accept than two different-colored eyes."

"I haven't felt like shifting since I was in the hole. I got caught because I couldn't stop shifting. Why don't I feel like it now?"

"I'm glad you don't feel like it now. Don't worry about it. The first day I have off we'll go outside the town and give you some shifting time."

"Okay."

"What did you do today?"

"Dorrie and Audrey make yarn and knit stuff. Dorrie tried to teach me a knitting spell, but I couldn't get it to work right. I'll keep trying."

"Do you have the knitting here? I can help you."

"Yeah."

She pulled some knitting needles and messy-looking knitting from behind her bed. "They told me to practice on my own, but their spell doesn't work for me."

"What's it supposed to be?" I kept my face solemn although I wanted to laugh at the sad-looking little knitting project.

"A washcloth."

"That should be pretty easy to do once you get the hang of the stitches." I took her knitting and, with a little magic, easily unknotted and rewound the yarn. "Have you ever knitted before?"

She shook her head. "My mother was a weaver. She said I would learn that when I was older."

"Weaving is for larger projects like cloth to make clothes. It would require more magic to complete significant work without machines."

"Machines?"

"There used to be factories that wove material in no time. But those factories required a lot of electricity to power them. Today, our power is magic. Magic is less harmful to the environment than machinery."

"Huh?"

I shook my head. "Never mind." I had to stay off my soapbox on the evils of technology or I'd face nothing but tough questions, derision, or open opposition. Instead of words, I needed actions. If I could train the mages today in the full use of their magic, destructive technology should never again get a foothold on the planet. That was an enormous task that I wasn't sure how to accomplish, but I was the only one I knew who could possibly do it.

"What kind of charm did Dorrie try to teach you? Does she use magic to do the knitting?"

"Not exactly. Miss Dorrie said she could never get magic to really knit for her. She just used a charm to keep her knitting look nice and even. She says knitting doesn't seem to fit into any of the elemental categories she's strong in—Water and Air. She said knitting by hand is fun and relaxing even if it isn't magic. When I get enough practice on this washcloth, she said I could learn to knit socks. They're harder to do."

I thought knitting might be an Earth skill. At home I'd learned to knit by hand because it was considered an excellent exercise to develop motor and dexterity skills. Plus, it was nice to make some things oneself and not rely on magic for everything. But knitting using magic was useful in training magic itself to do fine work. Raw power was one thing, but performing intricate work with magic was just as powerful. I wondered if the Alpha saw magic that way—or was he only interested in raw power? The Air trials today had been designed to use a brute strength mass of power quickly and bluntly.

"Did she charm her yarn or her needles?"

"I don't know. She just said 'Make my stitches strong and tight. Make my knitting look just right.'"

A rhyming charm. Rhyming wasn't necessary for commanding magic, but a singsong rhyme was more memorable. I was more straightforward and detailed in my charms. It wasn't worth the trouble to develop rhymes when any words could do the trick.

"I think I can help you with that. You can't always use someone else's charms. Sometimes you have to use your own words. Close your eyes."

"Okay."

"Picture the finished washcloth in your hands. Dorrie showed you a finished washcloth—didn't she?"

"Yeah. I know the stitches. Cast on thirty stitches. First row knit. Next row purl."

"Good. You watched Dorrie knit. Can you picture it in your head?"

"I guess so."

"What would you tell magic to do to help you knit?"

"I don't know. I kinda like what she said."

"Okay, say what she said, but tell your needles, not your yarn, to do the work." It would work better for the tools to have the magic rather than the material because when the charm wore off, the knitted work shouldn't be affected.

She repeated Dorrie's charm, prefacing it with the word needles. I told her to repeat it a few more times. I could feel the magic stir around her.

"Now open your eyes and start."

She opened her eyes and slowly cast on the first thirty stitches. She continued to mumble the charm, treating it like a chant. I watched until the thirty-by-thirty wash cloth was finished.

The yarn was a large ply. It would be a rough washcloth, good at exfoliating. It only took about thirty minutes for her to finish. I could see that her needles never faltered, and her knitting was tighter and more even.

"Good job. I think the magic really worked for you this time. Don't cast off. Let Dorrie see it first."

"I don't know how to cast off. I was just supposed to practice this part first."

"I think you might be ready to learn to knit socks now." I studied the off-white washcloth. "It's awfully plain."

"Miss Dorrie said we can send it to a dyer. I can pick any color I want. She said I could keep this one."

I thought I could color it with magic. I could almost feel a color word on the tip of my tongue. But if that wasn't something anyone else could do, I shouldn't do it either. It was another Earth skill that could come easily to a skilled Earth-dominant mage. I couldn't tell which elements were Tara's strengths. She would show equally in all four elements until she hit puberty, then her two dominant elements would pull ahead—unless her shifting ability used up most of her magic. Then she might continue equally weak in all elements.

Tara looked happy with her small use of magic. Magic had been good to Tara tonight. I was glad it worked. I would ask greater and greater things of magic in the future. I only hoped it cooperated as nicely with me.

Chapter 8

"That's very curious," she thought. "But everything's curious today."

THE NEXT DAY, WE had our Earth test. I didn't think the order of the elements had any significance, but since I didn't know the Alpha's mind, I couldn't be sure. I couldn't help but wonder what he could have seen mages do with Earth magic that he thought would be useful in battle.

Earth mages were good at concocting potions, but how would they get an enemy army to drink one? You could taint their water supply, but when it was the same one as your own (the lake) that would be stupid.

They could dig a moat around the town, but I didn't think that was a good defense unless you could stock it with monsters, because shapeshifters were excellent swimmers and climbers. Plus, it would take a lot of water to moat a town the size of Wolf Trap.

They could attract lightning. An Earth mage could draw lightning any time from a cumulonimbus cloud. But without decent control, this would be dangerous. Hitting the wrong targets and starting fires were just two hazards. I wasn't even certain today's mages could do it or that anyone would think to try.

Anticipating the Alpha was futile at this point, but a pastime I couldn't seem to stop. He must have something in mind for each element, or what was the point of all this? Now that I'd involved myself in his Mage Corps, I was very curious about it. I would witness, up close and personal, mages try to work greater magic. That was the best justification I could imagine for me to be involved. I don't think I could find this situation anyplace else in town.

I arrived behind the barracks to find thirteen squares marked off with ropes and colored spikes for boundary markers. They were approximately six feet apart and four feet by four feet in dimension. I deduced our trial was to dig a hole. I could see no tools available to us like shovels, picks, or spades. Although tools were made of metal and therefore more attuned to Earth magic, mages strong in other elements could magically manipulate tools. The right charm wouldn't discriminate and would use any available magic.

Digging a hole with magic alone was, I suppose, one way to test the potency of an Earth mage. I doubted any of these mages had ever dug a hole with magic alone, or if they had, then never one so big. The gardening they would do wouldn't require holes so large. And I would bet any largely physical tasks were done by shifters. They were stronger than mages because they would retain some of their shifting strength in human form.

Kappa Benjamin began his introduction to today's trial when we all finally stood quietly before him. "Today you will dig a hole. It will be as wide as the dimensions marked out and it will be as deep as you can make it. There are no tools to help you. We are not here to measure your physical prowess in digging a hole. We are here to measure your magical ability to dig a hole. To be precise—your Earth magic ability. When you begin, you will have approximately one hour to dig as deep a hole as you can. I say approximately because without a sundial we will use a rough and ready measurement. Do you see that man over there?" He pointed to a man at least five hundred feet away.

It was Qzyx. He waved at us as if he could hear the Kappa. He hadn't lied. He was working for the Alpha. My doubts about him were slowly eroding.

"He will swiftly walk the perimeter of this training field. It should take him about an hour, probably more, because he's also the measurement for the other three groups, who are also being tested in Earth magic today. When I see him again, I will call on you to stop. We will then measure the width, length, and depth of your hole. Questions?" he asked, in a way that suggested we shouldn't have any. "Move to your places. It doesn't matter which area you choose. The holes are all numbered, and the Nus will mark down your positions before we begin."

I couldn't see the advantage of being able to dig a hole within an hour. This must be another test of gross power. The bigger and deeper the hole, the more powerful the mage. I stationed myself at a marked area on the perimeter where I could watch most of the other girls work. Some looked defeated before even starting. I don't think this test was any more difficult than the Air test, but it might seem just as daunting if never done before, or if one was a weak Earth mage.

Once the Nus had finished and joined the Kappa, he held up his hand then brought it down, shouting, "Begin!"

Several mages were still standing and looking down, as if planning a strategy. Several others were already holding out their arms, moving their hands over the hole, and chanting their charms. I'd decided Earth would be my secondary magic, and I needed to perform behind the top five girls. But keeping the same pace as these girls was slow and tedious work. They all had some trouble when they came to rocks. The bigger the rock, the more trouble it caused them. Many simply pushed them aside rather than magic them out of the hole. I witnessed this best in the girls working closest to me.

I could tell by her ability a good Earth mage was next to me. I patterned my work to hers, ensuring my pile of removed dirt was always lower than hers. I made sure to sweat, grunt, and strain significantly for Aryk's benefit, especially. He couldn't accuse me again of hardly trying.

By the time Qzyx reappeared, the top Earth magic users and I had managed nearly four feet in our hour's work. I thought that was pretty good for mages who barely knew their magic. However, if they wanted a deep hole dug magically during a battle, the battle could be over before the hole was completed.

"Stop!" the Kappa called out. "Step back, sit down, and give the Nus room to measure."

We all stepped away while the Nus brought out their measuring sticks. They measured the depth, width, and evenness of the holes. They diligently wrote everything down while we sat and watched. Qzyx had moved on already. I guess we weren't the last group of the four to finish our test.

I'd been aware of Aryk covertly watching me during the trial. He would circle around the entire group occasionally, but always ended up behind me. The hairs on the back of my neck seemed to tingle whenever he was back. I continued the pretense of ignoring him while he oversaw the Nus and their measuring. It was a pretense, because how could anyone ignore someone watching them?

When the measuring was complete, the Kappa told us, "Recruits! You are dismissed. Return here tomorrow at the same time."

We all stood up to leave. I lagged behind everyone as usual, but I wasn't alone for long. Aryk was right behind me. I wanted to hear what he had to tell me today about the trials, so I looked back at him, acknowledging his presence for the first time that morning.

"How am I doing?" I asked him before we'd even begun walking together.

"Fine, I guess."

"You've seen the results. Don't you know?"

"They haven't been analyzed yet."

"Some speculation must have been raised," I persisted.

"Not by anyone in authority."

"Who is speculating?"

"The Nus taking the measurements. The Nus always have opinions." He rolled his eyes.

"Where do I stand with the Nus?" I wondered if the Nus were just as observant as Aryk. I was more aware of his scrutiny than the others. Maybe because he was talking to me. Nobody else had said as much as "good morning" to me yet.

"Somewhere in the middle."

"I think I did better than middle in the Earth test. I think I was near the top. What do you think? You saw the measurements."

"That's about right," he conceded.

"Good." That's where I wanted to be.

"But I didn't need to confirm that. You know exactly how you did."

"What do you mean?" I gave him a swift glance. I didn't find two different-colored eyes scrutinizing me disconcerting at all. I found their discernment annoying.

"I was watching you."

"So what? You've been watching me from the start." Without a satisfactory reason.

"I watched you watching the others."

"So, what, again? I'm an outsider. Of course I'm going to watch the others to see how I fit in."

"I think there's more to it than that."

"What do you know about it? I performed the exact same way the others did." I'd mimicked them carefully. There should superficially be no difference.

"Are you going home for lunch?" he asked, suddenly avoiding my question.

I stopped walking to absorb this change of subject. "I don't know. No." I didn't want to get back too early. I wasn't ready for the onslaught of questions. Dorrie and Audrey were insatiably curious about the Mage Corps. "Maybe I'll get something from a street vendor. Since I'm not going home, you're off duty, Zeta."

"I'll continue to accompany you."

"Why? Surely, I'm not in any danger in broad daylight."

"Not yet, perhaps. You haven't demonstrated superior magic skills yet. But if I'm around, that will ward off any harassment."

"I have my doubts about anyone attacking me just because I have good mage skills."

"You haven't witnessed how competitive things have been even before this new Mage Corps was announced. My brother has been unrelentingly courted since he turned eighteen. Eliminating rivals early is good strategy."

"Won't it look strange—you following me around this way? If I pass the trials and stay in the Corps, I won't be staying in the barracks. I need to come and go every day."

"No problem. I already look strange. I can't do anything without drawing attention."

"But you're drawing attention to *me*."

"It won't matter. You're an outsider. That in itself will garner attention."

"But won't the two of us together garner even more attention?"

"I'll walk behind you if that makes you feel better."

"I'd feel better if you didn't find it necessary to walk me home at all."

"I'm under orders. I don't have a choice."

I almost sighed. This was a complication I hadn't anticipated. Why couldn't this just be a simple task? Get in, observe the other mages, gauge their magic skills, and get out. It would take months of training to whip these mages into a cohesive Corps—at least all fall and winter. That's all the time I planned to stay in Wolf Trap. It was the perfect setup for me. If only the Alpha hadn't assigned his sons to the Corps, it would have stayed uncomplicated.

I could almost hear my Jardvari yelling in my head to get out now. Don't break any more rules. Fail the trials. Fake an injury. Leave town. Anything to avoid engaging, conflict, or singular attention. I'd lived my whole life without a lot of rules and now I was expected to follow twenty-one of them, all designed to keep me safely outside, distant, and uninvolved from others. They never considered the possibility I might need to be involved—that observation from a distance wasn't enough. I'd go along with the requirements of the Mage Corps for now and see what happened. I could always leave if I got in over my head. It wasn't like I was imprisoned. I only had one guard to deal with and he just walked me home, nothing more.

"Are the other outsiders getting escorts?"

"Yes, until they're stationed in the barracks."

"Will my not staying in the barracks be a deal-breaker for me with this Mage Corps?"

"Tell the Kappa in charge when you get through the trials. I'm sure that can be worked out."

"Does that mean I'll always have an escort home?"

"Correct."

In that case, maybe I could pick his brains for more information about life in Wolf Trap. It wasn't like I could ignore all shifters any longer. I would be training with several of them as well. My Jardvari should understand the bending I had to make in the rules. At this point, shifters weren't an obvious threat to me.

"Once the other mages are attached to the barracks, I doubt whether anything dire will happen to me on my way home. I can take Mart Street most of the way. It's only a twenty-minute walk."

"No point in taking chances. Once my brother notices you, all bets are off."

"Look at me. I'm average. Average height, average weight, average hair, average everything. I'll blend right in with the others." Why didn't he get that?

He looked at me just as I'd asked. Why did that make me want to squirm? "The Nus had an opinion about that, too. You're in the top half of their attractiveness rankings."

"The Nus are ranking our looks, too? Is that really necessary?"

He shrugged. "My brother can't be everywhere. He's enlisted help. The Nus will be with you every day. He doesn't want to overlook anyone."

"Are you helping him, too? Is that why this has become more than an escort service? The outsiders are an unknown quantity. You're watching and chatting me up for information," I accused. That would explain his intense attention.

He shook his head. "I won't report anything you tell me unless you want me to. I'm only interested in what's best for the Corps, not my brother. My father thought assigning me to the Mage Corps along with my brother would deflect some attention from him. My opinion is not required or desired by my brother."

"You're twins. Doesn't that make you closer?"

"Not since he realized I was different in a way other people couldn't accept. He doesn't hate me, but he wishes he were an only child. Abnormalities make him uncomfortable."

Why was he telling me this? Was it true? Was he just trying to get me to trust him with this sad story? Was he as much of an outsider as I was despite being an Alpha's son, or was he playing me? I couldn't trust my instincts on this. Growing up an only child, I didn't think I had any instincts where others my age were concerned. And reading old psychology books only got you so far.

As we walked down Mart Street we approached a street vendor. They sold savory meat pies and fruit. I wasn't sure if they had anything besides fruit that I could eat.

"What would you like?" Aryk asked me.

"I don't eat meat," I confessed.

"Okay. Do you eat eggs?"

"As long as they were never fertilized—yes."

Aryk talked to the vendors, one male and one female. They had a vegetarian pie with scrambled eggs, spinach, and zucchini. He bought one for me and two beef pies for himself. They were about the size of one of his hands. One pie was enough for me. He also bought a small jug of water and a couple of apples. They were half the size of the ones from home.

We ate our pies as we meandered down the street toward the west gate. There was a large oak tree nearby with a wooden bench surrounding it. We sat down to finish eating on the side hidden from the gate guards. They couldn't watch us behind the wide oak from their post. We shared the water jug.

This was unexpected. I hadn't intended to get this comfortable with a shifter. I could learn things from him, but there was the danger that he would learn things about me, too. He'd just learned I was a vegetarian by my allowing him to eat with me. I didn't think it was important information, but it was something he'd learned because I let down my guard a little. What more would I reveal just being in his company? I needed to control the conversation, not him.

"What do you think about today's test? I want your opinion, not the Nus. You watched everyone, not just me."

"You may want to be average, but you aren't. If you fail in the next two trials, you could still be chosen for the Earth group."

"Even with the other groups added in?"

"So far, the groups are fairly evenly matched, with less than a handful of top mages in each trial. You tied for third in the Earth trial, the differences being negligible."

I had to do better than fourth in Fire if I wanted that to be my strongest element. Fire was the most dangerous of the elements. I wanted to witness personally how it was handled by the other mages. "Which group is your brother watching?"

"He intends to move to a different group every day."

"What trial do we have tomorrow?"

He shook his finger at me. "No inside information. You'll learn tomorrow along with everyone else."

"As if knowing in advance can really prepare you. You can't increase your abilities in one day."

"We're testing your nerves, too. You're being watched all the time. Two girls went home crying yesterday. One threw up before entering the training ground. One fainted during the trial."

"Are those things worth disqualification?"

"Not yet, but we'll be looking for signs of confidence and stability before the end of training. It's not all about powerful magic. You will be trained just as diligently in other fighting skills. It's a dangerous assignment. It requires courage, confidence, quick thinking, a strong body, and powerful magic."

"Why not set the minimum age higher? Maturity can add to confidence."

He gave me a considering look. "You're only a year off the minimum age and you seem fairly confident and mature."

"What do you mean? I don't swagger and strut." I was thinking of the last girl to arrive on the first day. She'd done the female equivalent on the first day. That was a sign of confidence.

"No, you don't, but you size up the room confidently. You probably see as much as I do when you watch the others."

"Self-preservation. I don't have the security of parents to take care of me if I fail. I'm responsible for a young cousin as well as myself. I need a good-paying job."

"I know. We checked out the four outsiders carefully. You're the newest to Wolf Trap. The others have been here less than four years."

"And they're still considered outsiders?"

"It can take a while. Depends on how old you are to start and who you make friends with."

"You didn't have time to do much checking. I was only given a day's notice before the first trial."

"You were the only one we didn't have much time to research. We still don't know very much about you. However, Qzyx vouched for you. He's been selling his finds here for over thirty years. He's trusted."

I wouldn't mention that Qzyx and I had just met four days ago or reveal that he sells to Clan Cat as well. Giving up his secrets would only put me in a bad light, and I didn't object to his selling wherever he wanted to. He could be my way into a Clan Cat village when I wanted to check them out more closely.

We got up and Aryk completed his job, walking me home. I still needed to be certain why he'd singled me out before he'd even seen me use magic. The Kappa's orders didn't quite ring true. Had I done something unusual to draw his attention, or was he simply more acutely observant than anyone else? Maybe his different-colored eyes meant more than a genetic condition. Maybe it was caused by magic and gave him some greater acuity. I could speculate endlessly, but my only option was to watch him as closely as he watched me. If he continued with my group and walked me home, I'd have plenty of opportunities.

This was a challenge I found strangely stimulating.

Chapter 9

She generally gave herself very good advice (though she very seldom followed it)

TODAY WAS THE WATER magic trial.

As I stood with the others looking around, I saw that all of yesterday's holes had been dug out to the depth of approximately six feet and were nearly uniform. Many somebodies had completed all the work we'd begun in one night. The Alpha must want these trials concluded in a hurry.

As we waited, a Nu brought out an old-time alarm clock with a two-bell ringer and a windup key. It could function without electricity. I wondered why they hadn't used it for yesterday's trial, but then I heard it. Its ticktock was loud—irritatingly loud.

If these mages were to become battle mages, they would need to concentrate with chaos and distraction all around. But I couldn't imagine anything in battle being as tediously annoying as that clock. This could be another kind of test. I would consider it one.

I looked at all those uniform holes and could only think of one use for them in this trial—fill them with water. And I knew immediately that this trial had a particular issue not inherent in the previous ones.

The surrounding land was dry. It had last rained a week ago. A Water mage was like a dousing rod and would pull water from the nearest source. Except for the water in use in Wolf Trap through pipes and wells, I could sense no closer major water source than the lake, two miles away. That meant all fifty-two mages were also drawing on the same water sources. Four by four by six feet would be ninety-six cubic feet. Seven and a half gallons in a cubic foot meant approximately 720 gallons per hole or 37,440 gallons total. That was a lot of water moving underground, with some of it lost, saturating the ground during travel.

This trial would become more than who could fill up their hole first. This would become a battle for any close water, which meant Wolf Trap water as well. It would get worse the closer the water got to us, and the mages began to steal from one another. This contest would deplete energy and power quickly, with no one filling their hole. The stronger mages would tire out pulling it from so far away, while the weaker mages stole it as it neared them. Their struggles wouldn't be noticed for a while by the Kappa or Nus watching. On the outside, it would look like any other trial.

I could just let this play out and let this trial fail, or I could try to salvage it.

I didn't give myself any time to debate the pros and cons. If I wanted to witness the progress of this fledgling Mage Corps, now wasn't the time for a fail, especially when I could do something about it. Doing something meant me alone bringing water close enough for all the mages to use while protecting Wolf Trap's water sources. This would require juggling several charms and some powerful magic. The last big thing I'd done was my three-leagues-a-step walk to get here. I was sure I had enough power, but would magic cooperate with me? I'd had no good opportunity to test it until now. I guess I'd find out one charm at a time.

As we waited for the Kappa to announce today's trial, I planned my charms, dividing the work into segments in anticipation of the mages' own charms working against me. This was the closest I'd ever come to a magic duel. It was kind of exciting if I thought of it that way.

After calling for quiet, the Kappa told us to find our places from yesterday. After we were all in place, he began his introductory speech. "Today, you will fill these holes with Water magic as quickly as you can. They've been deepened to six feet. As you see, you will be timed during this trial. When the water reaches the top of the hole, ground level, raise your hand. I will come over to check your work. Once approved, you will sit against the barracks wall until I declare the test ended. I'm not waiting all day on the lot of you. Once six of you have successfully completed the test, it's over for everyone. Now wait until I say *begin*."

We all stood quietly, waiting. Only the ticking of the clock could be heard over the field. It seemed even louder and more insistent in the tension of waiting. Most of us had no real sense of time. When we gave estimates without having a clock to check, we were often wrong. And waiting always seemed longer than it was. My internal clock was very accurate. If I let myself focus on time, I could feel every second pass, just like the ticking of the clock. I chanted my first charm silently in my head.

The Kappa kept us waiting until the large hand on the clock reached the twelve before he called, "Begin!"

I first cut the training area off from the town by placing a ward beneath us between Wolf Trap and the training ground to keep the pipes underground from being disturbed by our Water magic. I used another charm to create an Earth ward, changing the porous dirt between the training ground and the lake into something less conductive to water. This would keep the water where I wanted it to go without losing any along the way. I shouldn't need 37,440 gallons because only a quarter of the mages would be strong enough to come close to filling their holes, but I'd plan for almost the entire amount.

Next, I created four underground channels from the lake to the training field, creating four underground reservoirs. I pushed the excess soil backward, and I tied each tunnel to a particular group by using my heat source charm to locate them. Then I pushed water through to fill up the reservoirs—the easiest of the charms. There would still be some stealing, but the stronger mages should be able to get water first. To prevent stealing from each hole or natural leaching into the soil, I added another Earth blocking and retention charm for any water collected.

I could feel the magic coursing through me, willingly following my charms. My meditations were paying off. I felt stronger and closer to magic than I had since leaving home. My magic use, except for the two trials and suppressing Tara's ability to shift, had been small since I entered Wolf Trap. Today magic seemed to want to be used, as if it missed me. In fact, it rushed out of me in a torrent as if it were a flash flood. Could I possibly run out of magic? That had seemed inconceivable before today. I would definitely need food and rest when I finished here to replenish my reserves.

Once all my charms were in place, I had to monitor everything constantly and reinforce when necessary. This was cheating, but it was cheating for everyone's benefit. Otherwise, we could be here into the night stealing water back and forth.

It should have taken some time for the water to travel a respectable proximity for the mages to begin siphoning, but my magic pushed it out quickly, taking only about fifteen minutes to travel two miles. It took over an hour after that for the strongest mage to fill her hole. I felt myself growing weaker as my magic continued to deplete itself. It was good I hadn't chosen Water as one of my elemental strengths because my magic had slowed to a trickle by the time the fifth-best mage had filled her hole. I managed to divert about a foot of water into my hole before the Kappa called a halt to our work.

Once six mages had finished, the last seven—me included—were told to stop. Our times were listed as the same and our water level was measured.

Then we were all dismissed and told to return—same place, same time, tomorrow.

I finished third to last, which surprised me, considering the trouble I had toward the end of my magic spree. This had been the hardest I'd ever had to work for so little visible effort. No one would know how hard I'd worked to salvage this flawed trial. That thought was surprisingly deflating. I had to keep my secrets, but I missed the praise and encouragement my Jardvari would give me when I'd successfully passed one of their tests. Now that this was over, I felt an emptiness I'd never felt before, not only of magic, but that glow of acknowledged success. I'd never felt so alone in the four weeks since I left home.

Aryk and I trailed last out of the training area as usual. But I was slower and more measured in my steps than ever before. I was afraid I would trip and fall, or just fall—I felt that weak. We didn't speak until we were well away from everyone else. He came closer and took my arm. I leaned against him for the support I seemed to need. He led me down Alpha's Way instead of Mart Street. There was a tiny park at the end with three trees, ten square feet of grass, and a bench. He sat me down and said, "Wait here."

I watched him walk into a large house across from me on the same side of the street as the Administration building. It was the only house down this way. When he came out, he carried some bread, cheese, apples, and a tall mug of water. He handed them to me. "Here. Eat. Drink."

I drank down the water in one long gulp. He took the mug and went back to the house for more. I ate the bread and cheese while he was gone. I was feeling better already.

"What is this place?" I asked when he returned, gesturing to the house.

"I live there."

"The Alpha's house?" I shouldn't be here. I didn't want to draw any attention from the Alpha.

"Don't worry. He's not there during the day. He has an office in the Administration building. He stays there all day."

"What about the rest of your family?"

"They're out and about all day, too. You won't meet any of them here."

We were quiet while I finished eating. He took all the detritus from my meal back to the house. I got up and started walking when I saw Aryk come back out. He reached me quickly since my steps were still a little faltering.

Now I needed to sleep, but I felt somewhat revived. I don't think I'd ever used that much magic at one time before. It had been a ridiculous amount for what I'd wanted to do. Magic had rushed out of me with no control. What was that all about?

"How are you feeling now?" he asked.

"Better. After a good night's sleep, I'll be fine." That was how it usually worked, anyway.

"What happened back there at the trial?" he asked. "I think you might have worked harder than everyone else. You looked exhausted—like you'd run for miles. I thought you were going to collapse on me."

"It was a hard trial," I told him. "Water's not one of my strengths. The lake was at least two miles away. That's a long way for the water to travel," I lied. I was grateful for his help, but not enough to tell him anything important.

"That's the closest water? Isn't there water in the ground beneath us?"

There was now. "Not close enough. You draw your water from the lake. So did the mages."

"Two miles," he said thoughtfully. "It didn't take much more than an hour for the first mage to fill her hole. Water moving from the lake through the ground—you'd think it would've taken longer."

Without my help, it would've taken—never. "Just an hour? It seemed longer."

"Kappa Benjamin thought it would take longer. He left and said he'd be in his office for a while. You might have noticed that I had to send a Nu to fetch him. He thought it would take at least a couple of hours for one of you to finish. I sent for him when two of you were done."

"I hadn't noticed," I lied again. Of course I noticed what was going on around me. I'd taken that time to rest a little. I didn't work some water into my own hole until I saw the Nu returning with the Kappa at his heels. It had come sluggishly, as if I hadn't much magic left, but I didn't think it would look right to have no water in my hole. Even the weakest mages had pulled up some water. I could look weak, but not entirely lacking.

"Why couldn't the mages conjure water from thin air?" he asked. "Isn't that how it works?"

"No, it doesn't." I had some energy left for exasperation. "Something doesn't come from nothing. A Water mage can harvest water from the air, but there isn't a lot there unless it's raining."

"What about a cloud?"

"Sure, but the clouds float anywhere from two to three miles high. Not any closer than the lake."

"I guess we don't know much about how magic works."

"It's hard to get to know. Allowing mages to try new things is a good start."

I said nothing more about the workings of elemental magic. There were no books written about today's magic, only the fantasies of magic from the past. I couldn't use the excuse that I read a lot to convince him that was where I got my knowledge. It would just reinforce his belief in my difference from the others. I wouldn't validate that belief. He'd been fairly light on the questions so far, but that could change, and I had weeks or months to go in his presence. My Jardvari would think it much too soon to trust anyone with that kind of knowledge, especially a shifter.

He said nothing more, and we continued the walk home in silence. I'd read about that trick people used where, if they're silent, the other person would fill the gap. I was never told to be quiet when I was a child. My Jardvari never got impatient or irritated with my questions. Just being an observer did not come naturally to me. I wanted to fill in the silence with information, especially because Aryk seemed interested. Reciting the important to Wolf Trap rules in my head helped me keep my mouth shut. *(1) Trust no one; (2) Hide what you can do. Need to know only; (3) Take only smart risks. (4) Avoid shifters. Mages are your concern; (6) Access any situation before acting; (7) Act only if absolutely necessary; (8) Interact without engaging; (9) Allies and friends will come when you are more powerful ...*

Tara showed off her knitting that evening. She was still knitting squares, but she told me they were for a blanket, not washcloths. She was practicing other stitch patterns besides stockinette, like the rib stitch. She was also using pre-dyed yarn. She had red, blue, and purple yarn. She seemed to be enjoying herself and didn't need my help. I was glad of that. Of course, I couldn't abandon her, but the more self-sufficient she became, the better.

She didn't question me about my day. She heard it all when Dorrie and Audrey asked me questions, anyway. So, she chattered about hers. Dorrie had taken her under her wing nicely, relieving me of any anxiety I might have felt at leaving her alone all day. Tara reported everywhere they went, what they did, and what they said. I half-listened, making comments whenever she stopped for breath. She reminded me of myself as a child. Maybe all children were like this, and I wasn't as unusual as I thought I was.

When bedtime came, Tara finally settled down. I decided to reinforce her back story and shifter suppression a few days early. If she chattered away like this with me, what might she let slip with Dorrie? I couldn't take any chances. If I thought it necessary, I would do this every evening to keep us both safe from exposure.

Once Tara fell asleep, I had time to think about the Water trial and how drained I'd felt of magic afterward. I'd never reached that point at home, and I'd practiced a lot of magic there. Maybe I'd been feeling too secure in the thought that I had more magic than anyone else. It was still finite, and I had to be careful.

I almost wished I had left well enough alone today. It would have been amusing to see the Kappas' reaction if no mage had attracted water. Like Aryk, they must have thought mages would create the water from nothing. An elemental mage drew their element to them and utilized all its possibilities but didn't create it. A higher-level mage could teleport water in an instant, transform something else like dirt into water, or create the illusion of water, but higher-level magic would be rare.

This type of magic wouldn't just come from experience and maturity, as my abilities were destined to develop. It could come unexpectedly, to anyone, for no apparent reason. The appearance of anomalies would be the precursor to the completion of magic in penetrating to the Earth's core. I was looking for those anomalies in my travels. The more I found, the closer the world would be to a seismic shift in magic. It would mean a greater adaptation to magic, more available power, different kinds of power, and new creatures to share the world.

When I was sixteen and on the cusp of adulthood, my Jardvari told me I was an anomaly—a planned one. I was born when magic had saturated seventy-five percent of the planet. As I matured, along with magic, I would develop and exhibit new magical powers. I would become a beacon and leader for these new powers. It took almost a hundred years for the seeded magic to reach seventy-five percent saturation, which had been unexpected. It was originally thought this would take less than a decade. There was no certainty for how long the last twenty-five percent of the saturation would take. I didn't want to wait for some nebulous future; I wanted to look over the world as soon as possible. I gave my Jardvari a year, and they developed the rules.

I wasn't supposed to collect or protect the anomalies I found, only catalog and record the changes. I don't think my Jardvari realized how hard it would be not to protect them now when an anomaly had a face, a personality, and a doomed fate. Or maybe they had. Maybe that's why they'd wanted me to wait until I was older to travel and why they weighed me down with rules.

I didn't break or bend these rules lightly. I had justifications for what I did. However, helping the mages in the Water trial might have bent the rules too much. Maybe I'd been selfish using my powers so rashly. It had seemed like solving a puzzle. I felt great satisfaction in my accomplishment, but I could tell no one. And it was so tempting to tell Aryk just how hard I'd worked to make the Water trial a success. I could almost see his face express his admiration. But I could also almost feel the intense scrutiny, pressure, and lack of freedom I'd be under when he told his father and the Kappas of my abilities. I wasn't nearly ready for that. Those chains would be worse than my current rules.

Chapter 10

Never imagine yourself not to be otherwise than what it might appear to others that what you were or might have been was not otherwise than what you had been would have appeared to them to be otherwise.

FIRE.

That was the last trial. That was the element I'd chosen as my specialty, but I wasn't certain I was up to it. That had me worried.

I'd slept nearly eight hours, and I still didn't feel completely recovered from yesterday's magic drain. I'd gotten in less than two hours of meditation time. My connection to magic felt fractured, like a bone that needed time to heal properly. What if I didn't have enough magic to be in the top three?

I assured myself it wouldn't be disastrous if I was accepted in the Mage Corps in another element. But I thought Fire to be the most important element for offensive magic and the most dangerous. If this Mage Corps fell apart, or destroyed more than the enemy, it would be because of Fire. I wasn't even close to any kind of leadership role, but I had more control over the elements than the others. I believed, surreptitiously, that I could stop disaster if the other mages lost control, even if my magic reserve wasn't completely recovered.

On the walk to the training grounds, I wondered what form our challenge would take today. There were so many dangerous possibilities. Thus far, the trials had involved unsubtle demonstrations of our command of the elements. Although power was the key, we were expected to use that power quickly. If only I could read the Alpha's mind. I was curious to see his vision of the future Mage Corps. Would they simply throw their power element at the enemy, or did he have something more strategic in mind?

My group met once again behind the barracks. None of the holes from yesterday filled with water had completely drained for several reasons. First, the skies had been overcast all afternoon, blocking the sun from doing its evaporation work. Second, it had rained last night. And third, the ground wasn't porous enough to quickly absorb all the water. However, none of that mattered to today's trial. We were led around that wet, pocked area to another completely altered section of the training ground.

Looking beyond the holes, I would have been blind not to notice thirteen very tall metal poles anchored to the ground about five hundred feet apart. Each pole was tapered and thicker at the bottom, where it was anchored by metal chains to heavy boulders. As we approached, I could see little metal flags fringing one side of each pole. There were eleven of them.

A massive amount of work had been done overnight to prepare for this trial. Every single soldier in the Alpha's army must have been working all night to get fifty-two of these things erected by morning. Everyone was rushing to get this new Corps launched.

Kappa Benjamin stood before us and explained our next trial.

"These metal poles are thirty feet high. At ten feet, and every two feet, there is a metal flag approximately six inches wide, six inches long, and half an inch thick. You each have a pole to work on, but you will work one at a time. Today we're going to measure the duration and length of your ability to build a fire—a powerful fire. There's nothing to burn around the pole. You will start your fire on the rocks beneath the flagged side, raise it one flag at a time, hold it, melt the flag, and move to the next one. At a high enough heat, the metal flag should melt completely in a few minutes. You will stop when you can't maintain the height and heat of your fire, or you've burned off all the flags. You will be timed. I've brought the same annoying clock again but try to ignore the ticking. You will stay and watch each other. The order of your trial is determined by how you ranked in the Water trial."

Fire and Water were opposites just as Earth and Air were. A mage rarely held the two opposites as their strengths. I thought rarely, only because I hadn't met every mage yet, and that ability could be another anomaly. Therefore, those strong in Water would not be strong in Fire. Surprisingly, two mages did worse than me in Water, so there was no telling how strong they might be in Fire. I couldn't be average here, but I couldn't be stellar, or I'd stand out too much. I needed to see the other top mages work first. I needed to be last.

Kappa Benjamin called out the name "Lee!" and we began.

Before the end of Lee's trial, I raised my hand, and the Kappa came over. I knew the top Fire mages would be up in close succession.

"What is it, Recruit?"

"May I talk to you in private?"

He motioned for me to stand and step over several feet behind the line of mages.

"I'm sorry, but I'm, ah—menstruating. I need to use a washroom." I didn't know if there was a more modern term in use. My readings of the past had offered many euphemisms and slang, but I thought medical terminology would be the most likely common descriptor. What I did understand was that it would be an embarrassing fact of life to the Kappa, and I would be granted the time I wanted. Any other malady would have gotten me some aphorism like "Recruits must push through pain. Grin and bear it."

His mouth tightened in a grim line, but otherwise he showed no other sign of discomfort or distaste. Before he could respond, Aryk had walked over to us and asked, "Can I be of assistance, Kappa?"

"Will you accompany Recruit Dare to the barracks, wait, and accompany her back? Her trial will be moved to last."

"Of course, Kappa."

He turned back to me. "If you find you can't continue today, we can hold your trial tomorrow."

"Thank you, Kappa. I think I can manage as the last one."

The Kappa turned away to watch the end of the first trial.

I walked quickly, so I could get back quickly. I'd gotten what I wanted—the coveted last position—but I needed to witness how the others performed. When I came out of the restroom, Aryk was waiting just inside the back entrance of the barracks.

"Was that a ploy?" he asked as we walked out.

"What?"

"You don't smell like you're menstruating."

I hadn't thought about that. The Kappa must have known, too. I wondered why he let me leave.

"Ah, you've caught me. I guess I didn't fool anyone."

"The Kappa probably thinks you're nervous and may have needed to throw up and didn't want anyone to know."

"Why would he think that?"

"There have been similar issues with some others, especially the outsiders. They know less of what to expect and it ratchets up the stress."

"The Nus of the other groups are comparing those kinds of notes as well?"

"Of course. Why did you want to come in here if not to throw up?"

"I didn't want to come here especially. I just wanted to be last."

"Why?"

"I'm competitive. I wanted to see what everyone else can do first. I guess we should get back."

"Okay."

Interrogation over. But it wasn't really. He'd only superficially accepted my answers to his questions. He had plenty of time walking me home to ask more. And I think he was getting more information out of me than I intended. I hadn't realized how gratifying it was to have someone show an interest in me despite my efforts to appear average. I also hadn't realized how affecting the attention of an interesting male would be. I'd read all about male-female interactions, but I thought I was immune to that. My Jardvari had fully instilled in me the dangers to my secrets should I engage in intimacy of any kind. I hadn't understood the warnings until now.

It took over four hours to get to the end of the line and me. The best Fire mage in the group, Lee, raised her stream of fire to twenty-seven feet in fifteen minutes. She held it for another fifteen minutes, burning off all but the top two metal flags. The next highest only managed twenty-six feet for fifteen minutes in total. The third highest managed just over twenty-two feet for twenty-three minutes in total. After that, the height and duration diminished dramatically. Number three was the one I needed to beat, to, well, be in third place.

The extra time I had was good, but not enough to give me complete confidence in making third place. Today my magic came out slowly. My fire sat in the rocks with only a small flame for a good minute. I kept mumbling my charm, appealing to magic by adding new flattering adjectives each time like pretty magic, great magic, powerful magic. I'd always thought magic could understand my tone and words, along with my intent. But that could just have been anthropomorphism—the way people gave human characteristics to nonhuman things. I didn't know if flattery was the key, but after a rocky start, magic suddenly burst forth in a powerful, steady stream.

In less time than I feared, I raised my flame to a little under twenty-six feet and held it for thirteen minutes, not completely melting that third to last flag. My total time was twenty-eight minutes to give me the third spot. If they took the top three from all the groups, I should be in the top thirteen, but then again, I might not be. There could be more and powerful Fire mages in the other groups. Maybe I should have gone for second place. I wanted to be in Fire, but I didn't want to be close to the best. There would be too much attention on me. I wanted to be average. It was wait and see now and hope I'd guessed the best spot correctly to appear average.

The results weren't announced to us, but anyone paying attention had a good idea which of us was best in Fire. I got some dark looks from the other mages after almost besting number two. I hadn't been approached by any of the other mages in a gesture of friendship. My guess was that nobody really wanted outsiders to be better than insiders.

When my trial was complete, the Kappa told me to sit down with the others. He gave us his closing statement.

"The trials for a place in the Mage Corps are complete. Your scores will be compared to the other three groups. You will be ranked and divided into your strongest elemental group. Some of you will not make the cut. All of you have three days free. After the third day, if you haven't heard otherwise, report back to the mess hall after daybreak. We don't expect you to walk here in the dark, but be here as soon after daybreak as possible. We will expect most of you to live in the barracks all week with weekends off. Don't worry about what to wear. On your return, you will be given training clothes and shoes to change into, and lockers to store all your clothes. That will be all today. Recruits! Dismissed!"

Of course, Aryk trailed behind me as I trailed behind the other mages. A three-day gap would be enough time for the insiders to learn everything they wanted to know from the other groups. Many of them would probably learn the results before I did, since I had no friends or family in the military. I didn't think I could count Aryk as a friend, and I didn't think to see him during the three-day break. The results would come as a surprise to me. I just hoped they went my way.

When I reached the street, Aryk strode forward to walk beside me.

"Good job," he said.

"Maybe. It depends on how the other groups do."

"You don't need to worry. You're in the upper half of each test except Water."

"Compared to the other fifty-one?"

"That's right. You won't get cut from the Corps—*yet*."

"How many will they cut after tallying all the trials?"

"Probably eight for the first cut. Thirteen in a group is too large a number to manage for a trial Corps. The Alpha wants it pared down to no more than ten and no less than eight per group, eventually. We don't expect everyone to make it through the physical training either."

"Why? Will it be that hard?"

"It will be grueling on those who have never done much athletically. Mages aren't expected to be athletic."

"But they work. Everybody works."

"True, but some of them do less strenuous work than others do. You're one of the best toned of the bunch."

"I am?"

"You move more agilely than many of the others. You have quicker, smoother movements. You didn't really strain physically in any of the trials. You made the appropriate facial expressions, but you didn't look like you were lifting something heavy. Magic comes easier for you than the others, but you still move as if you exercise every day."

"You can tell all that just be watching me?"

"I'm very observant. I'm one of the best trackers in the village."

Maybe it would be better if I said nothing in my defense. Aryk was questing and dogged, but he knew when to restrain and withdraw. That didn't mean he didn't engage at the next opportunity. He'd decided I was a mystery that he needed to solve, and that put me on the defensive.

"I still don't understand why I should attract your attention. I'm not that different from the others. You haven't adequately explained to me why you've singled me out."

"I was told to watch the outsiders. You were pointed out to me."

That made sense, but I didn't think that was the whole truth. Something else was going on that I needed to know.

"What else have you learned about me?"

"You have a secret."

"Everyone has secrets," I scoffed.

Before he could challenge that statement, I heard Qzyx call my name.

I stopped and turned my head to see him hurrying toward us.

"Hey, Zeta Saltwyck." He greeted Aryk with a grin. "I didn't expect to see you out here. Aren't you part of the big meetin' to divide the recruits?"

"I am. I'm just on my way there now."

"You're headin' in the wrong direction."

Aryk turned back to me. "What will you be doing on your free days?"

I didn't know where he was going with that question but decided it wouldn't be a good idea to spend any more time in the sharp-eyed Zeta's presence. He was too good at getting information out of me.

"I'll spend time with my cousin. Maybe we'll go outside the village on a picnic in the woods."

"You need to be careful if you leave the protection of the town walls. There are bands of unsavory shifters out there. They prey on travelers who don't have the sense to travel with a caravan."

"They prey on caravans, too. Sometimes travelin' quietly alone is the best way to travel," Qzyx argued good-naturedly. I could have debated that point considering how I found him, but he was arguing on my side, so it wouldn't be in my best interests.

"We'll be fine. We won't go far. We need a break from all these strange people." Tara needed a chance to shift and run free for a few hours. "If you're still monitoring the mages, I guess I'll see you in three days."

He looked at me for a moment, then accepted his dismissal by abruptly turning and striding off. I had the feeling I hadn't seen the last of him on my free days.

"You need to stay away from him," Qzyx warned.

"Why?" I asked just to be contrary. I already knew that. "You sounded as if you liked him."

"He may be the Alpha's son and a Zeta, but he's not to be trusted. Them different-colored eyes has got people worried. Not me, but lotsa other people."

I ignored this advice. "All these Greek letters. Why didn't they just go back to old military ranks?"

Qzyx shrugged. "All shifters are ranked. All shifters have some position in the military. Alpha was already a thing—why not use 'em all? How does it feel to be an Omega?"

"I haven't passed training yet. Today I'm still just a recruit. You're working for the military. What's your rank?"

"No rank. I'm jest a general dogsbody. Last night, I got to fill in some of the holes you mages dug up. Once the water disappears, I get to fill in some more."

"I'm sure you'll fill them in more quickly than we did emptying them."

"You'll get better. It takes practice. Everythin' takes practice."

He was right. Magic didn't come naturally here. It would still take more than the almost hundred years it had been here for us to fully adapt to its use.

"Where are you going?" I asked as he continued to walk by my side.

"I've been invited to dinner by your charmin' landladies."

"You're an outrageous flirt—you know that? I would never have suspected it."

"I'm jest a really friendly guy. Besides, there's somethin' you may not know about your landladies."

"What's that?"

"They're not really sisters. They're a couple. That don't bother you—*does it*?"

My eyes widened in surprise. "It doesn't bother me at all. Not Stone's sisters?"

"Audrey is. She was married once and had a son. Both left her and Wolf Trap."

"I would have thought Dorrie to be the married one."

"So would I, but it never happened. I think she jest likes to flirt."

"Okay. C'mon. You can hear about today's trials firsthand."

Interesting information, but nothing changed. I still liked Dorrie better than Audrey. I now had a better understanding of the phrase "opposites attract" in a context other than magnets. That thought made me smile, but I didn't share my thoughts with Qzyx. One male getting too close to understanding me was already one male too many. Since I saw him less often, Qzyx could remain a distant acquaintance. I may have saved his life, but I didn't feel at all responsible for him like I did Tara. I wouldn't be adding him to my collection of anomalies.

Chapter 11

"It's all about as curious as it can be," said the Gryphon.

THREE WHOLE DAYS OFF.

I didn't need three. I was sure one more day would see me completely recovered, but the powers-that-be seemed to be careful not to overuse the mages. It might be good strategy for a test, but it was the wrong strategy for developing stronger mages. Magic was like an additional muscle. The more you worked it, the stronger it got. Today's mages needed to use their magic all the time—and meditation would accelerate the growth of their power. I don't know how I would get this idea across or even if I should. I really didn't want the Alpha to use mages to fight Clan Cat. I wanted mages to be more powerful magically for other things, like running their electrical grid without fossil fuel. That was a better use of their magic.

Tara was awake early. I'd told her of today's plans last night. Young shifters ordinarily shifted every day because the need was overwhelming in the beginning. Controlling her need to shift the way I did wouldn't harm her, but the longer she went without shifting, the harder it would be for her and me to control it. I didn't want her to shift spontaneously at an inconvenient moment. I had to make sure she shifted regularly under my watch.

"Let's go now. You can eat your breakfast and lunch in the woods," I said after she was dressed.

"What about you?"

"I've got some food in my backpack. And don't worry about Audrey and Dorrie. I told them last night we would be out most of the day." It seemed polite to give them a heads-up since they were usually minding Tara when I was gone all day.

We left the house before Audrey or Dorrie could intercept us with any last-minute objections. They hadn't approved of my picnic plans but had no authority to stop us. That didn't mean they wouldn't try.

We were using the west gate today, not the main one. I didn't want to be that close to the main road and potential visitors. Two guards also manned this gate. They gave us the usual caveats about leaving.

"It's not safe out there."

"Gate closes at sundown."

"We only patrol the outskirts of our settlement, includin' the farms."

"There's no huntin' party scheduled for today. You'll be out there on your own."

"I understand. We won't go far. We're just having a picnic," I lied.

Tara and I walked through the gate with a cheerful wave to the guards. She was nervous about leaving the protection of town, but eager to shift. Once we were far enough away from the gate and the shifters' sharp hearing, I told her, "Don't be afraid to hunt as far as you want. If you sense danger, return to me. Otherwise, I figure we can spend half the day here."

"Won't you get bored?"

"I have a book to read."

"What if there are Wolves hunting out here?"

"Remember, the guards said there aren't any hunting parties out today. The patrol shouldn't patrol where we'll go," I assured her. After the practice I had during the Water trial, I was fairly certain I could make a short-term ward over an area that would keep out anyone but us. Wards were my specialty. Unless someone was looking for a particular spot in my warded area, they wouldn't even notice that a square mile or two was missing.

Once we were about a mile into the woods. I stopped and used a charm to scan the area for topographical details. This gave me only a thousand feet of enhanced vision. It wouldn't be enough room for Tara to explore. As a Cat, she could easily run several miles before stopping. I would have to walk the perimeter I wanted her contained to make certain the ward covered the desired area.

There were no heat signatures for anything bigger than a rabbit or squirrel this close to the west of Wolf Trap. Tara was small. A few rabbits, squirrels, or mice should be enough for her meals. She didn't need to take down a deer. She'd leave too much meat behind, and that would be too suspicious a kill for the Wolves not to get worked up about. I didn't want to start a large-scale investigation that would preclude more Tara shifting visits into these woods.

As per our hypnosis sessions, she would wait for me to give her the go-ahead to change. I wanted to get my ward started first. I'd have her follow me as I set up the ward. I found a log that I could sit upon on my return. That would be where I began the ward.

Warding could be a major drain on one's magic reserve. You didn't just set a ward and be done. You had to regularly pump it with magic depending on the amount of time required, size, and scope of the ward, or it developed weak spots. My blood rocks took care of much of this for me when I made my smaller wards. I didn't need a permanent long-term ward here, just a large, completely shielded one. I wouldn't leave myself vulnerable by depleting my magic reserves for this, but it would require a lot of magic. Although I was a magical powerhouse, I still had limits, as I'd discovered during the Water trial.

"Okay. You can change now," I told her when I'd outlined the basic shape of the ward. "I'm going to set a ward to protect a space for you to hunt. For a ward this big, I'll have magic follow me and set the boundaries as I walk the perimeter. You can follow me, too."

Tara started to remove her clothes, but I reminded her she could shift with them on now. She'd done it once with my help, but she had a lot of pent-up magic to help her this time. It took about fifteen minutes for her to change without my help. Fifteen minutes was a long time to be vulnerable in a shift. Teenagers could take as long as five minutes, while adults could shift in a minute or two because they had more magic and more practice shifting. Anything she carried or wore went into and out of her shift, which helped add to her bulk as an animal and reduced vulnerable time getting naked.

I watched her shift before I began my ward charm. I'd seen adults shift from afar. It wasn't pretty. This was my first up close and personal view.

Her skin rippled with the elongation of bone and muscle. Her face distorted to accommodate larger feral features. Her skin stretched, losing color as it first thinned to cover larger bones and sinews, then thickened to an anemic yellow, only forming fur when all the other shifting was complete. Her body as an Ocelot was larger and heavier than her human form or a normal ocelot. It wasn't painful—magic hid the growing pains—but it looked terrible. Shifting back to human would be less traumatic visually and would take less time.

When she had completed her shift, Tara lay still, recovering. It only took a moment before something caught her attention. She shook off the alien feeling of the shift and bounded away. I started my boundary walk, chanting my ward charm to follow my steps and keeping my scanning ward active. I would set a one square mile ward.

Tara returned to stalk me before I'd finished the last side of the square. It took me about an hour. I used Air and Earth to fix the ward, hiding us from view. When I was finished, I returned to sit on the log I'd found to wait for Tara to explore her large cage.

I took one of my juicy apples out of my backpack and a book.

My education had consisted of the world's literature on any and every subject written. Previous generations had stored caches of books all around the country, and I'd had access to several. I'd gobbled up knowledge like nuts and stored much of it with my eidetic memory. I was chock-full of how the world used to work. Now I was amusing myself with fiction while waiting for personal experience to show me how the world presently worked.

I'd found several old lists of what was considered the best fiction, and I had worked my way through them—not in any particular order. I preferred children's books now. I never had a normal childhood, so I was discovering childhood in books. I liked to reread my favorites. Today I was reading an annotated version of *Alice's Adventures in Wonderland* and *Through the Looking Glass*—not the same edition I'd given Tara. She had begun the book while I was away all day. She wasn't used to nonsense, and it often confused her. I sought more explanations for the nonsense in today's reading.

I stopped my reading when I reached the "Jabberwocky" poem and thought about the monsters mentioned there.

It was good there wasn't a detailed description of the Jabberwock, Jubjub bird, or Bandersnatch, or we might see those creatures walk the earth one day. Magic could be a very valuable asset, but it also had a dire side. Along with the anomalies I was hoping to discover, I was prepared to find monsters. Magic had already made one monster—shifters, the stuff of legends, folktales, and fantasies. But they were still more human than monster. Where magic created one monster from Earth's old legends, it would create others. I didn't know if it would use humans again, animals, or create them from earth and clay. My Jardvari had warned me that magic was chaotic, and creation was one of its properties. Those chaotic creatures wouldn't all be friendly to humans, and they were the creatures mages should be training to fight.

I finally got up and stretched my legs. I kept Tara always in my awareness as she explored her large cage. She wouldn't realize it was a cage. I'd added an avoidance charm to the ward that would cause her to turn away from the borders. I wanted her to feel free without actually being free. I felt no guilt about my lies. They were a necessary protection, much like my wards.

Tara spent about four hours exploring, chasing, and killing her breakfast and then lunch. She came back afterward and lay down on the grass full and contented. Killing didn't bother her at all in her animal form, and once more in human form, I don't think she gave it a thought. Children could easily separate their two selves. It was only when they matured that shifters gained a sense of wrongness in their shifting and tried to keep tight human control over the animal. Even after three generations, many had trouble accepting their dual natures. People had still been in survival mode when magic had taken hold. It had taken decades for temperatures to begin to cool, rain to become more predictable, and the population to stabilize. But people were adaptable. It just sometimes took them longer than was wise to realize that.

I let Tara laze for another hour in her Ocelot form before asking, "Are you ready to head back? It's about time we return, before the guards at the gate worry about us."

She stood up, shook herself, then began to return to human form. It was much less disorienting than the reverse. Once finished, she sighed, stretched, and announced, "I feel much better now."

"I'm glad. We'll make time every week for you to shift. I wish you could shift more often, but while I'm in this Mage Corps, it's better for you to wait until I can be with you." I couldn't let her shift back in our room because she might do so when she was alone and unmonitored. I had to instill the idea that this was the only safe place.

She looked down at her feet and kicked a stone out of her way. "I know that. I hate being a shifter. It's not right."

"It's not wrong, Tara. Don't ever think that. There will be others like you. I promise."

I carefully released the ward, allowing it to slowly contract to nothing rather than take it down all at once. That should make it virtually unnoticeable to anyone nearby.

We strolled back to the west gate rather than hurry. Again, I did what I could to not draw attention. There were two new guards at the gate. They'd been appraised that we were outside.

"You've been gone a long time. What did ya do out there?"

"You're outsiders. We wouldn't a sent out a search party if you didn't come back."

"We had a picnic," was the only explanation I offered.

"You'll get yourself killed if you keep that up."

"Doesn't anyone else here have picnics?" I asked reasonably.

"Not so I've seen."

"Mages and such don't go out the gates without a shifter along."

It looked like they wanted to argue further, but suddenly, Aryk was there.

"That's enough, Rho. You've done your duty by giving warning. This isn't a prison. Anyone can go outside the gates. Let up."

"Sir!" they both said abruptly and stood at attention, then turned back to face the gate. They weren't facing Aryk any longer, and I could see one of them make a moue of distaste. You would think soldiers would be more accepting of one of their own, even one with strangely colored eyes.

"Please, follow me," he said to me and walked away.

Tara and I followed Aryk to a nearby tree with a bench surrounding it. It was the one Aryk and I had eaten at before. There sat a girl not much older than Tara. A man about Aryk's age stood beside her.

"What are you doing here?" I asked, looking from the girl to Aryk. "Were you waiting for me?"

The young girl spoke up. "We've been waiting for you such a long time."

Aryk shook his head. "We've been here five minutes."

She ignored his comment and looked me over. I did the same. She had fairer hair than Aryk's. She wore it in a short braid. She was the palest person I'd seen in Wolf Trap, with only the lightest tan and a sprinkling of freckles shielding her skin. Her eyes were round, wide, and appeared a grayer green than Aryk's one green eye. She had a snub nose and a small rosebud mouth. Her face had a triangular shape with a pointed little chin. She had a small, thin figure. She was neither pretty nor plain. But she was arresting.

"My sister Valery told me this morning she wanted to meet you—today. Valery Saltwyck, meet Rain Dare. Also, Valery's bodyguard, Machi Jones."

"And my cousin, Tara Jansen," I added, gesturing Tara forward.

Valery's bodyguard was taller than my five foot six by about three inches. He had short blue-black hair, medium brown skin, astute hazel eyes, and a broad nose and thin mouth in a square face. He appeared lithe, quick, and alert. He must be a good fighter to be chosen as a bodyguard for the Alpha's daughter. But why would she need a bodyguard?

"We need Rain," Valery said, looking solemnly at me.

I took her literally and looked up at the sky. "I think it will rain tonight." It was early fall and the beginning of a rainier season. There had been no significant rainfall in the almost week I'd been in Wolf Trap. It was time for a good, soaking rain.

"Are you a prophet as well?" Aryk asked.

"As well as what?" I brought my gaze back to him.

"My sister speaks prophecy. It's why she needs a bodyguard. She scares people, maybe more than I do."

I turned my eyes sharply back to his sister. I hadn't noticed before; I hadn't looked beyond the superficial. There was something different about her. I fully met her eyes. This time I didn't see a reflection of what she looked upon—myself—instead, I saw a swirl of green and gray like the ripples on a mossy stream surrounding a small black pupil. Her gaze was difficult to hold but also difficult to look away from. An interesting paradox.

Prophecy was a higher-level magic. It wasn't related to the elements. I thought to find it eventually as another anomaly, but not so soon after finding Tara. Attracting the anomalies would be convenient since that was part of my quest, but I couldn't go around collecting people yet. I wasn't ready to protect a large group, and I wasn't sure I could safely leave them be. My Jardvari may have anticipated this with their rules.

"Is she accurate?" It didn't feel odd talking about her while she sat there. She wasn't looking at me anymore but was staring off into the distance.

He shrugged. "If you understand her meaning. She isn't always clear. Sometimes she sounds crazy."

"We're all mad here," Valery said.

I looked at her sharply. That was a quote from *Alice in Wonderland*. How did she know I was reading it? Was it a coincidence, or was she reading my mind? That would be two higher-level magics in one person.

"That's a curious thing to say."

"Curiouser and curiouser."

Curiouser, indeed. "What if I should say to you, 'Twas brillig, and the slithy toves did gyre and gimble in the wabe?"

Everyone except Valery and Tara looked at me in puzzlement.

"O frabjous day! Callooh! Callay!" Valery said in a singsong voice.

"What language is that? Can anyone play?" Aryk asked, looking back and forth between us.

Valery smiled absently and fiddled with the hem of her tunic. At least she wasn't dressed in a pinafore like the illustrations of Alice in my book.

"It's just a nonsense poem. Your sister and I must read the same books."

"That's not possible. She can't read."

I looked at him in surprise. "Why not? I would think all girls are taught to read these days."

"They are, but Valery wouldn't learn. She can't write either. She didn't start talking until she was five. Like me, she owes her life to the fact that her father is the Alpha."

"You speak of it so matter-of-factly—and in front of your sister."

"My sister knows it is what it is." He paused and looked at me sharply. "She often talks of rain these days. I wonder now if she was speaking of you and not actual rainfall."

What could I say to that? If Valery spoke prophecy, she might well have been speaking of me. I hoped she wouldn't reveal any of my secrets.

"I feel rain in my big toe. Is that prophecy?"

Valery giggled. "Rain feels rain. When will it snow?"

"You're the prophet. You tell me."

"When Rain breaks the curse, winter will return to the land."

That sounded like a prophecy. What curse could she be speaking of? Blessing and cursing were higher-level magics. The climate was dry and warm from the actions of humans in the past, not from a curse. But prophecy often spoke in riddles.

"I have no answer to that. Why did you tell your sister about me?" I asked Aryk.

"I didn't. She told me. 'Rain has come. Bring me to her,' she said this morning. So, I did."

"How did you know I was outside the gates?"

"I asked your landladies where you were."

Oh, great. I wouldn't hear the end of that. I'd tried very hard to keep my acquaintance with him quiet. The ladies were such gossips.

I must have looked dismayed because he added, "I was very official. I told them I had an urgent message for Recruit Dare."

"Couldn't Valery tell you where I was?"

He shrugged. "I didn't ask, and she didn't tell."

While we'd been talking, Tara had been staring at Valery. She didn't look scared or horrified by her. I don't think she understood Valery was as abnormal as she was. Valery suddenly looked at her and said, "Here, kitty, kitty."

"Stop that!" I said sharply. "Her name is Tara."

"I know. Have no fear. She is the first. There will not be another until you wish to find one."

Aryk looked at Tara with interest, but he asked nothing.

"You are too clever for words, Miss Valery. How did you get them to believe you couldn't read or write?"

She smiled. "I know many things. Machi helps me. He promised my mother he would take care of me. I am sorry he will die in my service."

Machi looked stoic, as if he'd heard this before.

"That only means he will never stop serving you."

She looked at me in delight. "Of course it does. You are clever too, Miss Rain. We shall deal well together."

"Shall we?"

"For a long, long, long time. I'm tired now. I want to go home."

Machi came forward and took her hand, placed it in the crook of his arm, and led her away.

"Goodbye until next time," she said and waved before walking away with her bodyguard.

We watched until they were gone.

"That's the most I've ever heard her talk to anyone in other than prophecy," Aryk remarked. "Mostly she just stares, smiles, and nods her head, making everyone feel uncomfortable."

"Her bodyguard never said a word—not even hello or goodbye."

"He's much stingier with words than my sister. I never know what he's thinking. But he goes wherever Valery goes. For a Fox, he's a mean fighter, and he's the only shifter I know who can shift only part of his body. If you engage him in a fight, he can shift his hands to claws before you can blink an eye. Despite what Valery said, he's only been her official bodyguard for two years."

Rats! Another anomaly?! Maybe Valery was right about not finding another female shifter until I was ready, but she hadn't promised I wouldn't find other anomalies. Tara and Valery were more than enough. Now I might have to add Machi to the group. I didn't count Qzyx. I wasn't sure if he was an anomaly. He might just be an interesting old man. I didn't count Aryk yet either. He might just be an interesting young man.

I must have been quiet too long because Aryk suddenly said, "Why don't I walk you two home?"

"Okay," I agreed.

"We haven't been formally introduced, Tara. I'm Aryk Saltwyck. I help the mage recruits in the Mage Corps."

"Hello," she said shyly and shook the hand he held out to her.

Tara and I fell into step on either side of Aryk as he escorted us home. "What did you think of my sister?" he asked me.

"She's not mad, but she is scary. It's good she has a bodyguard."

"Nobody willingly talks to her. Only my father seeks out her counsel. He waited for fifty-two mages to begin the Mage Corps at her insistence."

"I wondered how he came up with that specific number. She didn't prophesize the war with Clan Cat, did she?"

"No. It was always a possibility. For too long, they've been a burr in our sides. We've fought over the woods to the east for years. But there's a part of it neither of us can use anymore. It's become—I don't know—strange, creepy. We blame the Cats for it. They probably blame us."

I glanced at Tara, but she looked down at the ground with her lips tightly pressed together. Time for a subject change. "Strange, creepy how?"

"In the past, shifters going in didn't always come out. Now nobody wants to go near it anymore except fools on a dare—and it might be growing closer to the lake. We worry about what it could do to the lake—our main water supply."

I remembered the landladies and Qzyx talking about weird woods. Shifters going in and not coming out—could this be the first appearance of the monsters I was expecting? "I'd like to take a look at those woods." I looked over at him and met his eyes to let him know I was serious.

"Didn't you hear me? If you go in, you might not come out."

"I don't plan to go in. I just want to have a look. That's all." Rule number five: *Beware of monsters*, I reminded myself. How would I know exactly what to be wary of if I couldn't observe one? I was calling them monsters because my Jardvari had, but creatures might be a better word. They would be nonhuman creations, but they wouldn't necessarily be frightening or ugly.

He contemplated me in silence for a long moment. "It's about a two-hour walk from the east gate at the end of the training grounds. Next time you're off, I can take you there."

"What about tomorrow?" I persisted. Why wait when I was available now?

He thought about it for a few seconds, then shrugged. "If that's how you want to spend your day off—sure. Don't bring Tara. It isn't safe for adults, let alone children." He glanced at her with an apologetic smile, but she wasn't looking at either of us.

"Okay. We can go early in the morning—if you're free, that is."

"I am. Tomorrow it is."

He walked us home and said he'd be back after breakfast in the morning.

Tara waited until we were in our room to ask, "Should you go to those woods? *He* said it was dangerous."

"I just want to have a look. I don't plan to do anything dangerous. Don't worry. I will be back by the afternoon," I assured her. Just a look. That was my only plan.

"You shouldn't go with him. I don't like him."

"Forget what he said about Cats. He doesn't know any better. I'll be fine," I assured her.

Tara couldn't help but worry when I did worrisome things. I was her lifeline. Whatever happened tomorrow, I would make sure I got back home safely—and bring Aryk with me. He was a big, bad wolf and able to take care of himself, but I wouldn't let him be a sacrifice to my curiosity. Neither one of us would be going into those creepy woods, no matter how curiouser and curiouser things got.

Chapter 12

Ono, two! One, two! And through and through The vorpal blade
went snicker-snack!

ARYK WAS AT MY door before the sun had completely risen into the sky. It was early, but I was up before the sun myself and munching a hunk of banana-walnut bread I'd pulled from my backpack.

"What're you eating?"

"Just bread," I told him vaguely, quickly wolfing down the last bite. "You know I'm a vegetarian." I deflected him away from my muffin. He wouldn't be familiar with bananas. They'd never grown on this part of the continent.

"I won't tell you what I had for breakfast. You wouldn't approve."

"I don't care if other people eat meat. It's just not for me."

"Meat is the most plentiful foodstuff available," he argued.

"Then you must not be farming properly." I didn't argue the case against meat being foodstuff. Shifters needed more protein for shifting. Mages could be choosier in their nutrition preferences, but protein was still a necessary part of one's diet. I selected mine from nuts, soy, beans, and peas.

"I'm not farming at all, but we have farms. You might speak to that rain you predicted. It takes lots of water to grow vegetables and grains. Much more than we had last night."

"You notice my prediction came true. I didn't specify the amount," I couldn't help pointing out.

He looked down at his muddy shoes. "So it appears."

"Ha! I may not be a prophet, but I can sense rain in the air."

"With your big toe?"

"That was just a joke. My big toe doesn't do much talking."

"Valery was always telling me to watch out for rain. I didn't realize before I heard your name that she might be talking about you. I'd taken to wearing a very broad-brimmed hat and carting around a waxed poncho in case the sky suddenly poured down on me."

I grinned at the picture that made in my head. "It could still happen. Don't let your guard down yet."

"Hanging around two prophets ought to gain me some advance warning—don't you think?"

"I'll keep you informed if I get any dire weather premonitions."

"If you please."

Seeing I was accompanied by Aryk, the guards at the east gate didn't issue any ominous warnings about leaving town. They didn't warn or acknowledge me at all. I guess they figured he knew better than to leave town without taking precautions, and I was his problem.

"How far is this strange, creepy forest?" I asked after we were well outside of Wolf Trap.

"Technically, it's called a wood because it doesn't cover as much ground as a forest. But it's much denser than any forest hereabouts. I told you it was about a two-hour walk—a brisk walk," he warned.

"I think I can handle that. Does this wood have a name?"

"It *was* called Little Wood because it was only about a quarter of a mile in area. Now it's called Weird Wood. You'll understand why when you see it."

"It can't be that close to Clan Cat if it's only about twelve miles away from Wolf Trap. What made this wood so important? There's plenty of forest on the other sides of Wolf Trap for hunting."

He shrugged. "It was ours. We claimed it decades ago. We marked our boundary trees up to ten miles from Clan Cat. They should have left it alone."

"When was the last fight you had there?"

"I think the last actual battle we had in and around Weird Wood was about ten years ago. It was one of the best hunting grounds back then."

"How big a fight?"

"Two hunting parties clashed inside Weird Wood. Five or six were killed on each side. A lot of shifters came back with permanent scars. Cats are no-holds-barred fighters."

I thought of Stone, the bartender at the Tooth and Claw. That must have been the battle where he'd gotten his scars.

I stopped talking soon after that. I needed my breath for the rapid pace Aryk set. It took us over two hours to hike to Weird Little Wood—which was what I was now calling it in my head. It didn't take me long to realize how out of shape I'd gotten in my travels using magical league steps instead of my quadriceps, calf muscles, and glutes.

I could see the lake clearly once we left the heavily forested area. The trees petered out completely as we hiked through rougher terrain. The ground sloped gently up and down in a rocky scrubland. In another mile, when we reached the top of another rise, I saw what must be Weird Little Wood.

The wood was darker and denser than anything we'd passed earlier, and I could see a murky gray miasma hovering over the top of its canopy of dark leaves. We stopped walking at a clearly delineated clearing surrounding the wood. I bent over and breathed deeply. My lack of significant exercise to get to Wolf Trap had caught up to me. Bending over wasn't helping my recovery enough, so I plopped down to rest more comfortably.

"No one in their right minds will go in there now," Aryk said as he stood next to me and studied the wood. He didn't relax his guard.

"Can you see that gray fog over the top?"

"Of course. It's been there a while."

"When was the last time you know that someone went inside?"

"A couple of years ago. A few shifters were chasing a wild horse. They didn't shift because they thought they'd scare the horse. It ran right into the wood. One guy went in after it. He didn't come out. The others circled the wood, calling his name, but they didn't go inside. They went back to town and got a patrol to follow them. Six went in together. They stayed together while searching through the wood, but when they came out, there were only five of them. They said you could barely see in front of you inside. The Alpha sent a unit of twenty next. They found no one in the wood, but when they came out another was missing. The Alpha declared the wood off-limits. We tend the clearing every spring, digging up any fresh growth, but the wood is still expanding. Children are warned off this place from toddler age. It's the bogeyman of their childhood."

"You know about the bogeyman?"

"I might have read a book of old folklore once or twice and shared it with Valery. The Alpha banned it when Valery started having nightmares."

Perhaps that book had kick-started her prophetic abilities. She might have been dreaming of the future. "That wasn't very nice of you."

"I was twelve. I thought the stories were cool. I wanted to share. I wasn't thinking about the sensibilities of six-year-old girls."

"Unfortunately, I think the bogeyman may be real."

"I was afraid you'd say that."

I stared into the dense gloom of Weird Little Wood. If there was a monster in this wood, it wouldn't be nice and friendly. Many monsters of legend ate people. If people were staying away, what was it eating now? "What happened to the horse?" I asked, as I thought about his story.

He looked at me blankly for a moment. "The last patrol found it outside the wood. It was ready to be caught."

I stood up and walked near to peer as closely into the wood as I could without going in, but Aryk grabbed my arm.

"Don't go in there."

"I wasn't. I just wanted a closer look."

"Don't. One guy said if you stand too close, there was a pull that made you want to go inside. He said it took all he had to move away. Even the young idiots who should know better but are up for a dare usually stay away from here."

"Usually?"

"There was one incident, but they were stopped before they reached the wood. They were publicly punished as a deterrent for future idiots."

"If we can't go in, let's walk around it," I suggested.

We walked around the wood, keeping a careful distance. Once we reached the lake side, Aryk remarked, "Look how close it's come to the marsh. It used to be over five hundred feet away. Let's turn around and walk the other way. I don't need any more mud on my shoes."

The wood was maybe three hundred yards from the edge of the marsh. The edge trees were oddly not new young sprigs but fully grown, as if the existing trees had moved to fill the gap between the wood and the lake.

"What do you think?" he asked me after we'd walked around to the marsh point on the other side, then back where we started. It only took about fifteen minutes. I'd learned nothing except it was strange, creepy, and weird on all sides.

"I don't think anything good. I haven't seen anything like this before." Which wasn't saying much since I'd only been out in the world for about a month now. In our walk around, I couldn't see or hear anything moving within the dense, twisted tree trunks and branches. Even if the creature was living in the center of the wood, there should have been sounds of other types of wildlife. That there weren't even the sounds of insects was sinister.

I was certain that whatever was in there was a manifestation of the darker side of magic. My purpose here was only to collect data. But while this wood seemed to contain whatever it was now, it could leave or, worse, multiply and leave. I couldn't simply allow this—whatever it was—to fester and grow further. If there was any possibility I could stop it now—shouldn't I at least try?

"If something came out of the wood, do you think you could kill it?" I asked. If I messed with it, what would come out? Was it something the two of us could handle? I'd killed nothing bigger than a mosquito before. I was trained to protect, not kill. But I thought this thing should be destroyed.

"I'd give it my best shot. The biggest thing I've ever killed was a moose. It was six feet tall and maybe a thousand pounds. We don't see many moose as a rule. This one surprised me when I was out hunting. I could have called for help, but I was in a life-and-death battle before I knew it."

"Don't moose have antlers? Isn't that dangerous? Couldn't you have run away?"

"Males do. It was a male I fought. Being stomped on by hooves heavier than me is dangerous, too. Instead of trying to fight him from the front, I jumped around and attacked his haunches. It's the most vulnerable part of his body. Tearing there causes massive blood loss. I only had to stay clear of his antlers and wait for him to exsanguinate to finish him off."

"Eww! Thanks for the visual," I said, grimacing. I was already feeling an adrenaline rush from the anticipation of a fight I didn't want. Aryk would do most of the fighting, but I had to be ready to use magic if the thing proved wilier and more dangerous than I expected. Fire was the best offensive magic I could control.

"You asked. How do you plan to lure the thing or things out of the wood without going in there yourself? Because you are *not* going in. I won't let you." He gave me a steely-eyed look. He seemed pretty determined to keep me safe, and I was happy to let him.

"I hadn't thought about there being more than one creature in the wood," I confessed. "If there are more, I don't think they're fully grown. Once you stopped people from going inside, I don't think enough game approached the wood to fully feed whatever is there. I'll use some magic to chase it out."

"If I can handle a moose, I think I can handle whatever this is," he told me confidently. "What's your plan?"

I looked up at the sky. There were always clouds, sometimes plentiful and sometimes sparse. All clouds held moisture, but not all clouds became saturated enough with droplets, ice crystals, dirty air, and clashing temperatures for gravity to return the condensation to earth. In today's drought-ridden climate, clouds selfishly held onto their moisture. There was enough rain for wildlife and today's small settlements to thrive, just not enough to support the massive populations of centuries ago. But I was named Rain for good reason.

"I think it's going to rain. Maybe a nice healing rain will flush it out."

Aryk looked doubtfully into the sky. "Those clouds don't look like rain clouds to me."

"You're thinking of nimbostratus or cumulonimbus clouds. We don't need hours of rain or thunder and lightning. We just need a short, steady cloud burst. All clouds contain moisture. Those cumulus clouds will give us a nice bit of rain." I looked back up at the sky and began moving clouds.

I'd moved and sculpted clouds from childhood. That part of my plan
would be child's play.

"Why would rain drive it out?"

"I don't know that it will. It's just an idea. You might want to shift now
if you plan to fight as a wolf."

Magic came easily for this task and allowed me to combine condensed
clouds into a single large saturated one, move it over Weird Little Wood,
and hold it stationary. I wanted whatever was inside driven to our side of
the wood, so I stationed the enlarged cloud formation over the far side.
I could feel the moisture inside become heavier as the cloud increased in
mass. It still wasn't close enough to dropping water on its own yet, which
was good because I needed something more than the plain water and dirty
air found in those clouds.

First, I purified the water, then I blessed the moisture inside. I had
studied all the past religions of the world. I blessed the moisture invoking
a generic divine creator. Intention was as important in a blessing as it was
in magic.

Last, I created conditions in the cloud to cause the droplets to descend:
convergence, convection, frontal lifting, and physical lifting to cool and
expand the droplets. Once the healing rain began its drenching, I moved
the cloud slowly toward our side of the wood. As it moved, the gray miasma
hovering overhead shrank as the blessed water fell onto and through it.
I kept most of my attention on the cloud while Aryk, in his wolf form
beside me, stared at the wood, waiting. I could hear nothing until the trees
before me began to move. It only took about ten minutes before something
erupted from within.

I say *something* because it was not a normal-looking creature. It was
squat but still big and wide, with hulking arms and legs. It had mottled
pinkish-gray skin. Blisters were beginning to form where the rain had

touched. It had no recognizable head but a face in the middle of its torso with tiny, red eyes, a bulbous nose, and a large wide mouth with sharp, pointed teeth. It also had long, sharp claws on its hands and feet.

Aryk snarled, growled, and menaced the creature, not yet coming within striking distance. He had shifted into a quite large, possibly three-hundred-pound wolf with a black and silver coat. His eyes were the same dual color as his human form. His teeth weren't as serrated as the monster's, but they looked sharp and dangerous enough. However, the monster appeared much bigger and heavier. That had me a little concerned, despite his moose story.

I kept the rain cloud directly over the woods. I didn't want the creature to hide again. He obviously didn't like the blessed and purified rain but might feel that was the lesser danger if it stopped raining. I knew this was a fight that had to happen. This was a dangerous creature that had eaten people and would continue to do so. I needed to help Aryk in this fight. I couldn't wield a sword, but I could wield magic.

The least dangerous aid I could think of was a charm to vanish the monster's teeth and claws. I didn't like thinking about those predatory appendages scoring Aryk. Without those, the monster was only half as threatening.

Unfortunately, magic decided to work too well for me once again. It couldn't decide which one was the monster and took away Aryk's teeth and claws as well. Aryk startled and looked down at his paws. His claws were not retractable. They should have been evident. He backed away from the monster and threw me a look. Apparently, even a wolf could look concerned and confused.

I'm sorry, I mouthed at him and opened out my hands apologetically.

Before I could think of a way to charm his sharp features back and not the monster's, Aryk shifted again, took out his sword, moved forward suddenly, and stabbed the monster before it moved toward him. It had been standing hunched, looking menacing and growling even without sharp teeth and claws. I hadn't noticed what effect my charm had on it. I'd only been concerned about Aryk.

The monster swung its arms, trying to swipe at Aryk, but it was too slow and probably not used to this sort of fight. I imagined when it came across people in his wood, it would simply wrap its arms around them from behind, squeeze, and bite down on their neck. That would be the most efficient method of killing unsuspecting trespassers. I wondered if there was a poison or numbing agent in its saliva as well. That could explain why strong, healthy shifters could be quietly subdued. It surprised me to find these thoughts crossing my mind without the usual squeamishness. I was more engaged in this fight than I'd realized.

Aryk was well trained in using his short sword. He cut the monster methodically and efficiently to shreds while dancing out of reach of its meaty, forceful arms. Only once did the monster catch him with a sweeping swing of one arm. I winced as Aryk flew off his feet, but he rolled with the punch. He was up and stabbing before the monster could grab or knock him down again.

At one point it tried to run, but Aryk was too fast for it, and he stabbed it several times in the back. Between his cuts to the front and back, he must have cut into vital organs and arteries, because the monster bled profusely and finally fell to the ground. There was no rise and fall of his chest, movement of his mouth, or opening of his eyes. It lay unmoving except for the blood oozing more and more slowly from its wounds.

I approached carefully while Aryk stood over the creature, waiting for it to move again. He held out his arm to keep me back. I stayed far enough back not to be caught if the creature should suddenly jump to its feet. I was feeling my aversion to blood and gore return, making me suddenly feel sick to my stomach. I turned away and spat out the acid taste in my mouth again and again to stem the urge to vomit.

"What should we do with it?" Aryk asked when I seemed to recover. "I'd like to take it back to Wolf Trap to show the Alpha, but that thing looks heavy and smells bad. I don't want it on my back for hours on the return trip."

That was a horrible idea. "I don't think we should bring it back. It might reanimate or metamorphosis into something else. I've never seen anything like it. I have no idea what properties it may have."

"Can we bury it?"

"We can burn it, then salt it, then bury the ashes," I said firmly. My Jardvari had considered the possibility of my confronting creatures created by magic before I stepped one foot away from home. There were contingency plans in case being wary wasn't good enough. Finding workable ideas for their safe disposal was one of those discussions.

"Salt?"

"Salt will neutralize any residual magic in the ashes. For all we know, this creature can regenerate from ashes."

"Okay. We're not taking any chances. Where do we get the salt? There's no salt mine this close to the lake."

"I have some in my backpack."

"Seriously? Why would you carry around salt?"

"I told you, it neutralizes magic. Who knows if or when it might be useful? If I poured salt on you, you'd have trouble shifting." I hadn't tested that on a shifter, but I thought it would work.

"Okay. I would cut its head off first, but it doesn't seem to have one."

"Just cut it into pieces. Separate the arms and legs. Quarter the torso. We'll burn and bury those separately. " I winced. Wow, did I sound bloodthirsty. I never thought I'd hear those words come from my mouth. But it was a monster. I had to remember that. Alive, it would continue to kill and eat people. It might also spawn somehow—it did have dangling genitalia hidden under the only place on its body with some hair. The *eww* factor just increased exponentially.

"I can sharpen your sword for this work with a spell," I offered.

"Sure," he agreed and held out his sword. "Just don't sharpen my teeth."

"Ha, ha," I said, but was very specific in my charm casting.

I was careful in my burn charm as well. I didn't accidentally include Aryk again. I canceled the remove-teeth-and-claws charm first and watched them grow back on the monster's hands and feet. They would have returned eventually, but I wanted all its parts burned.

Magic seemed to differentiate between Aryk's human and animal selves. His teeth and nails had returned when he'd shifted once again to human. I should never have thought of shifters as monsters. I had confused magic with my thoughts. Maybe a lack of understanding, not recalcitrance, made magic seem less effective. I'd have to think about that.

"Losing my teeth and claws was a shock. What happened there?" he asked me as he noticed their return on the monster.

"Magic got confused and took all the sharp teeth and claws. If I ever use that charm again, I'll have to word it more carefully," I explained honestly. The truth here shouldn't hurt me.

I didn't watch him dismember the creature. Instead, I looked up at my rain cloud still saturating Weird Little Wood. The gray miasma was completely gone, and I'd watered every inch of the wood. It already looked less dank and dark. I was fairly certain this was the only monster. Once Aryk had finished his job, I thought it safe to stop the rain and allowed the cloud to float away.

"That's probably the best watered patch of ground in the area. That's a nice piece of magic to have," he remarked. "I didn't think Water was your element."

Oops. Of course, he would notice that. "I just nudged the cloud over the wood. The rain was already there."

"Why would a little rain send that creature outside the safety of the wood?"

I shrugged. "It was just an idea. I didn't know if it would work."

He gave me a measured look, then returned to his hacking. When he was finished, he asked, "How will we bury the ashes? I'm not going to use my sword as a shovel. I won't risk nicking the blade or breaking it on a buried rock. Swords aren't easy to make. And I won't shift for the job—I really don't want smelly ashes embedded under my claws. Plus, I don't know if I could shift a third time today without food and rest."

"Don't worry. I'll take care of it. You know I can dig a hole with magic. You've seen me do it." I didn't plan to dig holes. I planned to sink the ashes, which would unfortunately reveal more of my abilities to him.

"That's right. You are a proven Earth mage."

I had Aryk drag all the body parts about ten feet apart and away from the wood. I thought that would be space enough to keep them forever apart.

I burned each body part separately and thoroughly with a high heat—I wanted no chunks remaining that could regenerate. I also burned all traces of blood soaked in the ground. I wanted no trace of the creature left above ground.

The creature did smell, and worse when burning. I steered a breeze to blow over the fire and away from where we stood. It helped, but not enough. I thought about magicking the smell to something flowery, but that would display too many new magic skills. I'd just continue to breathe through my mouth.

After I was finished with the burning, I took a bag of salt from my backpack, poured it over each pile of ashes, then I magically mixed each one separately. After that was done, I charmed the earth to bury each pile deeply in the ground. I took the ashes down to different levels, the last at least three thousand feet, before I thought it safe to leave them.

Aryk just stood stoically by watching the long process. I performed my magic behind barely audible muttering and waving of arms, just not as exaggerated as the other mages did. He already sensed that I had faked all that, but I didn't want him to realize the entire performance was fake. That would be too revealing.

"Is it safe now?" Aryk asked as he watched me stretch out my arms to release the tension. I'd felt working my magic. I was never sure when or if it would falter. That last bit of moving the ashes underground had seemed to take longer than it should. Perhaps after a two-hour hike, moving clouds, purifying rain, and the adrenaline of the fight, I was more tired than I'd realized. My physical condition would affect my magic abilities.

"I hope so. We've taken every precaution we can."

He nodded his head. "We should head back."

"Yes. I'm getting hungry. Would you like an apple?" I pulled two from my backpack and gave one to him.

Before we headed back, he gave one more look to Little Wood, no longer weird. "I won't mention any of this to the Alpha. It would be difficult to explain and leave out your part. I don't believe you want that kind of attention. I think this wood should remain out-of-bounds yet a while—at least until we know if the change is permanent."

"That might be wise. What was spawned once could spawn again under the right conditions. If that gray cloud doesn't return, it should be all right." At least from this particular kind of creature.

We began our trek home, munching on whatever I pulled out of my backpack. We didn't talk much. We'd said all we needed to about the creature and the fight. It would be good to get back to a town of friendly monsters.

Chapter 13

"It's really dreadful," she murmured to herself, "the way all the creatures argue. It's enough to drive one crazy!"

"DARE. FIRE." KAPPA JŌTARŌ ended his division of the groups with Fire and me.

I was exactly in the group I'd intended to be. Ten girls had been excused. There were now forty-two of us. Twelve were in Water, twelve in Earth, ten in Air, and eight in Fire. Although igniting a spark was one of the easiest first magics, sustaining and controlling one needed the strongest power and skill. I wasn't surprised to find fewer mages in this group.

The benches in the mess hall had been divided and positioned to accommodate each group separately. As we sat in our new groups awaiting instructions, Kappa Jōtarō continued with his introductory remarks. "Every morning from today onwards, you will dress in your training clothes, eat breakfast here in the mess hall, and then gather outside to run laps. Following laps, you will perform strength, aerobic, balance, and stretch exercises. All four groups will train together in the mornings. We have a special area set up for that purpose. After a break, you will begin martial arts drills until lunchtime. After lunch, you will reform into your elemental groups and practice your magic in separate selected areas."

"Now for the remainder of the time this morning that you would normally run laps, I want you to stand with your elemental group and introduce yourselves to your new teammates. These are the mages you will work closely with for the next few months."

We followed the Kappa's instructions and stood up. Cabello, who was the dramatic mage I'd noticed at our first gathering, moved away from the benches to an open area. Two of the girls followed her. She stood with her hands on her hips, waiting pointedly for the rest of us to move along. Another girl and I did so, then the last three came over once they were a minority. Lee, the leader of that group, stomped purposefully to us, and once there, put her hands on her hips to imitate Cabello. They were like chickens establishing a pecking order. Unlike mages, shifters can usually tell who's dominant unless it's too close to call, then they fight. Luckily, Cabello ignored Lee's mimicry and began her introduction.

In my mind, I referred to everyone by their last names, since that's how we'd be addressed in the Mage Corps. The others introduced themselves, alternating between Cabello and Lee allies with the outsiders last.

RUBY CABELLO: Seventeen, long, curly, dark brown hair, dark brown eyes, plush mouth, average height, hourglass figure, tawny skin tone.

JADE LEE: Seventeen, straight, short black hair, slightly slanted hazel eyes, delicate features, a little taller than average, less curvy figure, sienna skin tone.

PEPPER SMITH: Eighteen, medium brown hair, pale blue eyes, slightly pear-shaped figure, bronze skin tone.

SUNNY RUSSO: Sixteen, average height, broad shoulders, narrow hips, blond hair, light brown eyes, open friendly face, gold skin tone.

APRIL NOVAK: Eighteen, streaky blond hair, hazel eyes, lanky, long neck and hands, sienna skin tone.

DAISY EVEREST: Nineteen, short curly black hair, dark brown eyes, heart-shaped face, medium features, triangular figure with a tiny waist, umber skin tone.

MAYA REDWING: Sixteen, long blue-black hair, gray eyes, symmetrical features, taller than average, graceful figure, sand skin tone.

I observed the girls in the Fire group critically. I had studied books discussing feminine beauty throughout history. I wasn't certain what today's standards would be, but symmetrical facial features, a healthy appearance, and good grooming were always an attraction. We had a variety of girls all attractive in their own way, but some were standouts. Cabello was the most striking beauty of our group, with Lee a close second. Confidence was an alluring quality. Cabello and Lee fit perfectly in that category. They were both strong mages and would be noticed by Ayden Saltwyck, if only for that reason.

Smith and Novak were Cabello allies, while Russo and Everest were Lee allies. Redwing was an outsider like me. I thought she could be a real contender for Mrs. Alpha if she had more confidence. She hunched her shoulders slightly, never made eye contact, braced her legs, and looked ready to run at any moment.

Once the introductions were complete, Cabello took control, not unexpectedly. "I think we need a leader. I nominate myself for the position."

Lee immediately took exception. "I've been running my father's house since I was fourteen. I think I have more leadership experience."

"You know my father's a Gamma. He raised us like a military unit from birth. I know how to lead and give orders," Cabello retaliated.

"So what? My father's also a Gamma. I understand military life just as well as you do."

"If we take this to a vote and the two outsiders split, there will be no decision. Let's come to an agreement. I'm older than you are. I should be the leader."

"You're only a few months older. That doesn't count."

"I'm also the best Fire mage in this group," she bragged.

"Who said?"

"The scores don't lie. I beat yours by a good inch."

"You probably cheated somehow. You were always good at that."

Before this could get into a real fight, I offered my opinion. "I think we should wait for the Kappa to assign leadership roles. Isn't higher rank based on merit? Nobody here has earned a promotion yet. We've only just started."

They both stopped talking and looked at me as if a rock had just spoken. As an outsider, I gather I was supposed to sit quietly while the insiders made all the decisions. I should have done that, but I was tired of sitting on the sidelines. I blamed Aryk for making me chattier. That thought made me wonder where he was today. I'd noticed immediately he was not in the mess hall with his brother.

"You're right." Lee capitulated first. "It's the Kappa's decision."

"Whatever," Cabello said, flipping her hair. "I'm sure the Kappa will be able to recognize my superior leadership abilities."

"There's nothing superior about you except your attitude," Lee retorted. "I wouldn't follow you unless I was forced to."

Cabello's eyes flashed angrily. "You'll have to when I'm promoted."

"When pigs fly."

Before this got nastier, Kappa Jōtarō called us to order, and we all stood at attention. He was frowning. Caught up in our own drama, I wondered if the other groups were having the same problem identifying as a team.

"I don't like what I've witnessed here, recruits. No one today is deemed higher or lower than anyone else in any facet of this training. Your ability to work as a team will be evaluated during your training, along with other qualities we deem essential to the Corps. Promotion will be decided by leadership potential. *Leadership is action, not position.* Leadership will not be proven by argument, disrespect, or force. *A leader knows the way, goes the way, and shows the way.* I want to see more cooperation, collaboration, and solidarity in your teams and in this group as a whole."

I recognized a couple quotes in that rebuke. I wondered if Qzyx had shared his book of quotations in Wolf Trap. You could find an apt quote for any situation.

He looked around the room before continuing, his eyes lingering on the ones I assumed needed the most direction. Cabello and Lee certainly fell into that group, but I got a looking-at myself. It made me aware that I had violated rule number seven (*Act only if necessary*) when I interrupted a possible fight.

"To continue with the next order of business: You will call me Master Jōtarō during training and Kappa at all other times. You will learn hand-to-hand unarmed combat, armed combat, and melee combat taught in turn by each of the Kappas you met on your first day. This instruction will take place after your morning exercises." He paused and looked at us sternly. "Those of you who can't keep up will be on the chopping block for the next round of cuts. The success of the Alpha's Mage Corps depends on your performance. Always be aware that the Alpha is relying on you to do your best." He took a deep breath.

"This training may seem excessive when you will not be on the front lines of battle. You will never be expected to be a foot soldier, but battle is unpredictable. Your expertise is magic. However, if you are forced into a situation where you must defend yourself, we want you to have all the tools necessary for survival. This means you must be in top physical condition. You will not only be expected to work every muscle in your body every day, strengthening and stretching your body to its limits, you will be expected to learn the movements of many forms of martial arts. You will know these martial arts movements so well you could fight in your sleep." He paused and let his eyes travel over each one of us, as if assessing our weaknesses.

"Before we begin, there are other conditions to be met. We would prefer that you stay in the barracks during the week and return home on the weekend. This will give you the opportunity to become better acquainted with your team. If this isn't possible, please know that you will remain in training from sunup to sunset, five days a week. I'll need names of those not able to stay in barracks by end of day. Those staying will bring their belongings tomorrow. Today, everyone will be assigned lockers. We will provide your training gear. In the barracks, you will select two best fit items from those made available, change, place the spare and your regular clothes in a locker and form a line outside the barracks. Your training gear will be cleaned over the weekend and replaced in your lockers. You will not take them home. You will not share them. They will be labeled by week's end. Am I clear?"

"Yes, sir," some of us said.

"Yes, Master Jōtarō," he said in a commanding voice.

"Yes, Master Jōtarō," we all responded loudly.

He nodded. "Follow me to the barracks for your locker assignments and to choose training gear."

The lockers were numbered but misnamed because they were unlockable. They were made of wood, not the metal of old-time lockers. I placed my backpack inside my assigned locker, glad that I'd reinforced its charms last night. If opened, it would contain only a spare set of clothes. If taken, it would return on its own. If cut, torn, or burned, it would heal itself. I was taking no chances. It was my lifeline to my home base.

The gear we chose from was all a light gray—the natural color of the material. There were no colorful dyes wasted on the training gear. Unfortunately, I had to wear leather shoes. The synthetic materials and rubber that shoes were made from in the past were no longer available. Leather was the most durable material today. I would have to try to forget that I had dead animals on my feet until I could acquire a facsimile of this footwear from my other source. I usually wore finely woven hemp shoes with a wood sole.

All hats had brims today to protect the face and neck from the scorching sun. Our new ones were also gray, with flexible brims and under-the-chin straps to keep them on our heads.

After we were changed and assembled outside, Master Jōtarō led us away from the barracks to a central part of the training grounds I hadn't seen before. A large tent had been erected there. It was open on the sides, with a pole in the center that gave the roof a pointed top. It would protect us from the rays of the sun, but not the heat. I was prepared to conjure up a breeze whenever the heat proved too stifling.

"Tomorrow, by daybreak, you will arrive, change into your training gear, eat breakfast in the mess, and report to this area. Everyone will gather here to run laps. As your assigned Kappa this week, I will tell you when to begin. It's best to do the run as early as possible in the mornings before the heat becomes oppressive. Once you've moved in, breakfast and lunch will be served every training day for all. Breakfast will be no longer than thirty minutes, lunch no longer than forty-five. Those not staying overnight can choose to eat breakfast before arriving. Dinner will be available only to those staying in the barracks. Today, we will begin and end our training with exercises."

The rest of the day, we trained physically. Sit-ups, push-ups, jumping jacks, jumping rope, chin-ups, weight lifting—the works. Since I seemed to be in better shape than most of the other girls, I had to fake my breathlessness and exhaustion. I collapsed when a majority of the girls did. Cabello and Lee were stubborn and tried to outdo everyone—especially each other. They were determined to show who was the best. I think they misinterpreted Master Jōtarō's points about leadership.

An older mage and Qzyx passed among us, handing out some special drink during our first exhausted break. He just nodded and winked at me, not drawing attention to our acquaintance. I don't know if he was protecting me or himself. I didn't see any advantage either way. The powers-that-be knew he'd vouched for me, and I was fine with that.

I sniffed the drink before I tasted it. It was a healing potion that contained plants I identified as having natural analgesic and inflammatory properties mixed with some Water magic. It worked as well as the medicines technology provided in the past, but with no side effects. I wondered if the recruits would be given another potion at bedtime, because its healing properties would work better while sleeping. That was a perk the go-homers would miss. Was that a subtle punishment for not being a complete part of the team? I wouldn't put it past the Kappa to add some kind of pressure. Teamwork seemed to be an important element of the Mage Corps.

Once we were semi-restored, we performed a series of stretches, then were told to follow Master Jōtarō to the mess hall.

We had lunch with meat, bread, raw vegetables, and fruit. I passed on the meat. The girls mixed and mingled to sit with their own friends rather than by teams. Cabello had the biggest following, with Lee close behind. There were two other girls who seemed to lead a group of allies. That would mean four obvious contenders for Ayden Saltwyck's attentions. Popularity would be a decided appeal.

We four outsiders sat at our own table. Besides Maya Redwing, I could now add Rose Sacheri and Mona Rivard to the outsider contingent. Both girls were above average height. Rivard was two inches taller than me, one inch taller than Sacheri and two inches shorter than Redwing. Sacheri had russet-colored hair and hazel eyes. Rivard had sable-colored hair and dark blue eyes. Both had medium-tanned skin: Rivard, a sand skin tone and

Sacheri, a sienna skin tone. Rivard was eighteen and an Earth mage. Sacheri was nineteen and a Water mage.

I started the conversational ball, rolling with what Aryk had told me about his brother. I could verify his veracity with these girls.

"I heard a rumor—I wonder if it's true," I said casually after we'd quietly begun to eat.

"What is it?"

"The Alpha's oldest son is going to use the Mage Corps to find a mate. That's why he's helping with the Corps."

"Which son?" Rivard asked.

"Ayden Saltwyck."

Rivard and Sacheri exchanged a glance.

"Where did you hear that?" Sacheri asked.

"I don't know—maybe my landladies said something." I wouldn't admit to knowing Aryk. It wasn't exactly a secret. Plenty of people had seen us together, but I would explain him away as protective detail, not a source of information.

Sacheri shrugged. "Nothing's been said about that, but we've all heard the Alpha's theory about strong mages mothering strong shifters."

"Yeah, he visits the school at year's end and says it in his graduation speech. We've all heard it," Rivard agreed. "I wondered why Ayden was here."

"I suppose this could be his chance to view the strongest mages," I suggested.

"He watched my group two days of the trials," Rivard admitted.

"Did he watch anyone in particular?"

"Cabello," Rivard grinned and glanced over at her table.

"She's very attractive. Is she a strong mage?" I could already tell she was by her confidence, but since I hadn't interacted with her during the trials, and I was a new outsider—as evidenced by the *S* still marking my hand—therefore I shouldn't actually know.

"Yeah. She was the best Fire mage. She's the one they call on when they need a controlled burn. She's a good Earth mage, too. I think she was one of the top finishers along with me," Rivard verified.

"Lee was the best Fire mage in my group. I think she did well in Air, too," I said.

"That sounds right. She's good at moving heavy objects," Sacheri agreed.

"How good is she?"

"I've seen her move stuff just for fun, but usually, the shifters can do most of the heavy work."

"I guess there isn't much opportunity to show off magic except this Mage Corps," I criticized.

"We're tested at school. We're offered jobs that use our particular magic skills," Rivard explained.

"It must be harder to find a job if you didn't grow up here. I'm too old for school. If there wasn't this Mage Corps, I don't know what I would do."

"There are jobs that don't require a lot of magic ability. Not everyone gets beyond the basics. My older sister works as a clerk in a shop because her magic skills are weak," Sacheri volunteered.

As I asked questions about them and offered my backstory, Redwing began to relax and talk more about herself. I learned that all three of the other outsiders had been in Wolf Trap for less than four years. They'd all come from smaller settlements originally. Their families had traveled here for better opportunities. The bigger the settlement, the more prosperous.

While I was thinking about their stories, the conversation moved on. Even the reserved Redwing was speaking readily as lunch wound down.

"Dare practically challenged Cabello and Lee when they were about to have a knockdown drag-out fight over who would lead our group," Redwing told the others with a shy smile to me.

"No way!"

"That's brave."

"I just thought it was stupid to fight about something we had no control over," I explained. "I don't know about Redwing, but I wasn't about to vote for either of them. I told them to let the Kappas decide who's leadership material."

"You've made a couple of enemies now."

"Especially with Cabello. She doesn't like to back down."

"I'll handle it. She doesn't scare me," I scoffed. I was acting braver than I should, but it was drawing out these girls. I had a better chance of making friends with this group than any other.

"You should be. Half the girls here are her allies. You don't know what bullying's like until you get in her bad books. I've heard stories," Rivard said.

"I can see teamwork will be an issue in the Fire group," I responded dryly.

"Oh, it will. Cabello and Lee hate each other."

"Why?"

"Some incident when they were younger. I never got the details, but I heard Lee crossed Cabello, who never forgave her," Sacheri said.

"Have they fought Fire to Fire?"

"I heard they did once in school, and a Water mage teacher doused them with cold water before it got too ugly."

"Lee's eyebrows were singed off and the ends of Cabello's hair burned. That was the shortest I've ever seen her hair."

"They must have known they'd be on the same team here."

"They probably thought this Corps would involve individual challenges, not working as a team."

"I wasn't sure what to expect until the Kappa talked about teamwork and the Alpha depending on us. Where did he even come up with this Mage Corps idea?" I could guess, but I wouldn't. I didn't think Valery's prophecies would be well-received.

"I've heard talk about it since I've been here."

"I never heard about mages in battle until I came here."

"My old village would never have thought of such a thing."

"It's different, all right," I agreed.

We seemed to get along well, but there were only four of us against thirty-eight other girls. I wondered how many of the girls were serious about attracting Ayden Saltwyck's attention. That would surely contribute to the contention between Cabello and Lee. How many other girls would clash over this same contest? If they wanted us to work as a team, why set up such a stupid situation? What was the Alpha thinking?

The day proved arduous, even for those of us in fairly good shape. A second round of potion was delivered in the afternoon, but it seemed less effective. Everyone was groaning by day's end.

I was last in line to report to Kappa Jōtarō that I needed to remain at home rather than stay in the barracks. There were only four of us, and I was the only outsider. He emphasized the importance of becoming a part of the team, and that this decision would impede my progress, but he understood my reasons. He hinted at fostering, but I told him our trauma was too recent. My cousin had terrible nightmares, and I was her only family. He dropped the idea, but I could tell it would come up again. I planned to be gone before it became an actual issue.

My new friend Redwing volunteered to wait for me, but I told her to go on. She would stay in the barracks after today and wished I'd be there, too. She said the outsiders needed to stick together. I agreed and explained my reasons for not staying in the barracks. She was reluctantly satisfied with that.

I was surprised to find Aryk waiting for me in the street outside the alley next to the Administration building since he hadn't been at today's practice.

"How'd your first day go?" he greeted me.

"Grueling. I didn't see you today. Have you finished watching us?"

"No. I had another task to accomplish today. I've volunteered to help with the martial arts training. Master Jōtarō can't monitor you all, although he's very sharp. There will be more of us around than before, correcting your form and being used as practice dummies. Even Ayden will do more than watch. He needs every opportunity to interact with his future bride—whoever she may be."

"The girls I talked to today had heard about the Alpha's strong-mothers-make-strong-sons theory, but not that it was a secondary reason for the Mage Corps."

"It hasn't been stated aloud, but they must wonder why Ayden is part of it. He and I are the only Zetas participating."

"You're not looking for a bride as well—*are you*?" None of the outsiders had mentioned him in this respect.

He shook his head. "No. My father assigned me here because my brother's here."

"You're reporting to your brother, too? What have you told him about me?"

"Nothing. You haven't demonstrated any superior abilities that he needs to be aware of."

"I don't plan to. There's nothing to report. I still don't know why you noticed me."

"I told you I was tasked with studying the outsiders. There are only four of you. You're easy to spot. You all stay outside the main group."

I still wasn't satisfied with his answer. There was something more to his first noticing me other than my outsider status. Unless he knew every mage in Wolf Trap, a town of over five thousand people, he'd noticed me before he knew I was an outsider—and in the very back row.

If he continued to walk me home, I was sure to get it out of him eventually. He could use an ally as much as I could. I had to admit to myself—I didn't mind having Aryk as an ally—not one little bit.

Chapter 14

"The rule is: jam tomorrow and jam yesterday—but never jam today."

ALTHOUGH I PRESENTED LIKE an average teenage girl, I was not average. I was an only child. I learned to read by age three. I was set no arbitrary limits on anything, even bedtimes, only advice and models of best practice. I was given the freedom to use my magic however I wished. I was encouraged, praised, or gently guided in my choices. It was not a learning experience everyone could thrive under, but it was ideal for me. Now that I shared my life with a bevy of teenage mages, I realized how atypical I truly was.

I should have been delighted to meet and get to know girls my age. If I were the average person I pretended to be, this would be the happiest time of my life. But I was not, and it was not. Unlike them, I wasn't worried about a bloom of acne, if I smelled too sweaty after a workout, if I looked fat in the ugly workout gear, or whether one of the cute Nus might notice me if Ayden Saltwyck didn't. I had nothing to share because I didn't care about any of those things. I had to fake sympathy for their woes when I really wanted to scream "Who cares!? None of that's important! Your magic and protecting yourself is all that matters! Focus!"

It wasn't just listening to constant teenage angst, gossip, and complaining that wore on my good humor, it was faking ignorance in martial arts and trying to appear average every second of every day. It was the most tedious time of my brief existence, and that included reading manuals on appliance maintenance and repair. I didn't think *not* being myself would be the hardest job I would have.

More every day, I thought it unfortunate that the Alpha had tied his Mage Corps to his son's matrimonial prospects, because that idea intensified the mages' ordinary dramas. Even the girls who thought they hadn't a chance fanned the flames of rivalry with Ayden talk. How handsome he was. How muscular he was. How charming he was. Ad nauseum. Everyone preened when Ayden looked at them, sighed when he smiled, and jostled for a place near him.

Maya was the only one besides me who wanted the opposite results. She hunched more, made mistakes, and kept her eyes down when Ayden was near. She said nothing when Rivard and Sacheri sang his praises as much as the others. They didn't believe me when I said I wasn't interested and to knock it off with the Ayden talk. How could anyone not be interested in the golden boy?

I wished he would choose someone already, then leave us in peace. At least I did until I thought about Aryk. If Ayden finished with the Mage Corps, then Aryk might leave, too. I didn't want that. He was my only source of reliable information—at least, that's what I told myself.

The few hours a day we spent in magic practice were the most tedious. All we did was perform the same magic we'd done in trials—making and sustaining a tall column of intense fire. I couldn't see the advantage of that in battle. It was impressive but wouldn't do anything to an enemy it wouldn't also do to the surrounding countryside—burning and destroying until everything was ashes. I wished I could read the Alpha's mind and know what he was thinking, but that was a higher-level magic I didn't yet possess. He must have some plan for a column of fire, or why did we practice it every day? I just couldn't imagine what it was.

I was regretting my involvement with the Mage Corps, especially when a sudden escalation in the contest for Ayden involved me directly in the wrangle.

The bullying tactics of mean stares, unexplained laughs, accidental bumps, and sotto voce insults grew from mild to constant in our second week. The outsiders were the primary target, but anyone making clumsy mistakes or getting noticed by Ayden could garner laughs or derisive comments. It was annoying, not dire—then the instigators upped their game. The first serious instance of harassment came toward the end of the third week during lunch. The four of us outsiders were, as usual, at our own table. The first one to discover the problem was Rivard when she took a big bite of her meat and noodle entrée.

"Ack! This is way too salty." She hastily drank some water to drown the taste, but quickly spat it back out and put down her glass. "Damn! Even the water's salty."

The others tentatively tried theirs and quickly put down their forks. I was only eating raw vegetables, but they'd also been drenched in salt. I'd noticed the massive amount of salt crystals before Rivard had taken her first bite. I'd waited to see if I was the only one affected before acting.

"What should we do?" Redwing asked me. Somehow, she'd gotten the idea that I had some leadership ability and thrust me into the role at every opportunity. I in no way wanted to be the de facto leader of our little group. Too much limelight. But she made it difficult for me to back away.

"Not eat," I said unhelpfully.

"I can't get through the rest of today's training without some food," Sacheri said. "I'll pass out."

"Yeah, and suppose they do the same thing at dinner. What'll we do then?" Rivard added.

They looked at each other in consternation and helplessness. It was obvious they'd never faced a challenge or given a thought to their magic to solve one.

"Tell the Kappa," I suggested. That would be a sure way of stopping the harassment without using magic.

Everyone looked at me in horror. "We can't take this to the Kappa," Sacheri hissed.

"Why not?"

"It's ratting. You just don't do it," Rivard hissed as well.

"Ratting?"

"Snitching, tattling—you know. It's just as bad as doing something wrong yourself," Sacheri explained. "We'd get punished, too."

Interesting dilemma. One had to solve this problem without official action or sanction. Was that typical military behavior or a mage thing? "Okay. We can't not eat, and we can't rat out the ones who sabotaged our meal. What do we do?"

They continued to look at each other helplessly. I could tell without looking directly that girls from the other tables were surreptitiously watching us and smirking. It was a mixed group from all the main contender camps. I doubted they worked together, but somehow word had gotten out.

I almost sighed. I shouldn't have to be the one to offer a solution. Magic should be the go-to for any mage with a problem. "Rivard, aren't you a good Earth mage—even one of the best ones? That's what you've told me."

"Yeah. Not the best, but one of them," she said matter-of-factly.

"Isn't salt a mineral?"

"Yeah. We have a salt mine. I've been there."

"Well, use your magic and mine the salt from our food. That's an Earth magic skill you should be able to perform."

Her mouth rounded in surprise. This idea had never occurred to her. "How?"

"Start with Sacheri's food. Look at it. Picture the salt in your mind. Imagine the way it looks and tastes. Think of a charm to tell magic to transfer the salt and only the salt from the food. Pile it on the table."

She began siphoning the salt from each of our plates and water. Her magic was sluggish. I gave her a boost of magic to speed up the process. I didn't want to spend the afternoon hungry if she didn't finish in time for us to eat.

"Won't the food taste just as bad if she removes all the salt?" Redwing asked as she watched the tiny pile of salt build on the table.

"We can sprinkle back whatever we want for taste."

"What made you think to do this?" Sacheri asked, also fascinated as Rivard finished her food and started on Redwing's.

"We had an Earth mage in our village who could bring metals out of the earth. Removing the salt from our food is the same kind of work," I lied.

There was a nice little mound of salt when she was finished. We all took pinches to add some back since she'd removed even the naturally occurring salt. It wasn't quite the same, but it was edible.

"We'd better eat fast. Lunchtime is almost over," I said.

We continued to be watched but with puzzlement, not smirks. I wondered what fresh surprises we'd find in our food in future. I don't think they'd actually poison us—that would too severely undermine the Alpha's Corps—but there were plenty of plants that could cause nausea, vomiting, and diarrhea. I'd scan our lunches from here on, but the others were on their own for breakfast and dinner. I'd have to warn Rivard to check their food every meal. As an Earth mage, she should be familiar enough with noxious plants to identify them even partially sprinkled on food.

Next day I learned pepper had been liberally added to their dinner. Rivard had mined it out like the salt and accepted the accolades of the other two for her prowess. She was excited about this new use for her magic and wondered if she too could pull metals and other things from the earth. I told her I wouldn't be surprised at what she could do if she practiced.

That seemed to be the end of the food sabotage and any other serious harassment that week. But the following week, the other bullying tactics still in play were stepped up. The best place for pushing and shoving was when we did our laps in the morning. Although our training Nus were stationed around the course, there were stretches where they were farther apart. Some girls were faster than others. Maya was always out in the lead, with Sacheri not far behind, while Rivard and I were toward the end. Three days we suffered through the indignities, the scrapes, and bruises of being tripped and falling before the incidents culminated in an official sanction.

The last morning of laps before our weekend off, Redwing was in the lead as usual when she was suddenly shoved hard from behind by Cabello. She fell sprawling on her hands and knees, just grazing her chin. About twelve girls running behind them veered sharply around this mishap before they tripped over it themselves. They kept running but slowed down to watch.

Cabello kicked out at Redwing, who curled up on her side to protect herself. Sacheri, one of those running behind, tackled Cabello, knocking her down. The next group of girls caught up and three of them stopped, including Smith and Novak from Fire, who helped Cabello to her feet. The third one, Varma, shoved Sacheri away from Cabello, knocking her down. Cabello began kicking Redwing as she curled up tighter. Sacheri was on her feet again, swinging her fists while Smith, Novak, and Varma tried to knock her down again. The rest of us came to a stop to watch two Nus attempt to pull them all apart without hurting anyone. I saw our Kappa for the week, Master Benjamin, running toward them shouting orders, Qzyx running from the opposite direction, and four more Nus coming from their posts behind and in front of the fray.

"Recruits! Attention! Now!" Master Benjamin barked.

They paid no attention until a Nu held on to each attacker. Redwing was still lying on the ground, groaning. I could see she had hit her chin and her knees and scraped her hands in the fall. I couldn't see the internal injuries from the kicks, but she wasn't making any attempt to sit up. Cabello had some nice bruises on her own face and knees where she'd hit the ground when Sacheri tackled her. Sacheri had her own injuries as well as landing some good punches on the girls who had attacked her. There were plenty of cuts and bruises to go around.

"I want to know what happened here. Nus, what did you witness?"

Shifters had sharp eyes, even in their human form. Two of the Nus had seen most of it. They described the sequence of shoves, kicks, and punches. Qzyx corroborated and added to their report. He'd been walking back from inspecting the wall around the training area for damage when he'd witnessed the first takedown. He seemed to have eyes as sharp as any shifter, even if he couldn't shift anymore.

There were about twenty of us who hadn't continued the run. Rivard and I had stopped out of concern for our friends. A couple were part of the Cabello alliance, and the rest were just plain curious. Lee and some of her cohorts were in that category. We watched while four more Nus arrived on the scene from other parts of the course, making that almost the full complement of Nu helpers. I noticed neither Aryk nor Ayden were there. They didn't usually show up until we'd finished laps.

When Qzyx and the Nus had finished talking, the Kappa looked with narrowed eyes at the transgressors. "I don't know what the provocation was for this incident, but it will *not* happen again. This is unbecoming behavior for any unit under the Alpha's command. Recruit Redwing will be escorted to the infirmary. Nus Dusku and Banta, help her up and take care of that. Recruits Cabello, Sacheri, Varma, Smith, and Novak, you will report to me at the end of the day for punishment detail. There are no extenuating circumstances for attacking a fellow recruit. You are a team. You will behave as one. Do you all understand me?" He encompassed the entire group with his gaze.

"Yes, Master Benjamin," we all intoned.

"All of you, continue your run. *Now!* No excuses."

Sixteen girls immediately resumed their run. Two more Cabello allies stayed with her and the other minions. The Kappa stood watching them flank Cabello as she limped back onto the course. He waited until they were some distance away before turning his gaze to us. Rivard and I had stayed back with Sacheri, waiting for everyone else to leave. The Kappa gave us a nod before heading back to our training area.

We were more walking than running now ourselves as we kept pace with an also limping Sacheri.

"How are you feeling?" I looked Sacheri over but didn't see any serious damage. Once knocked down, she hadn't stayed down to suffer the same damage Redwing had. Three on one had been an unfair fight that the Kappa should have acknowledged. Maybe he'd reflect the difference in the fights with the punishment details. Everyone involved in the fracas had been technically at fault, except for Redwing.

"I don't know. I hit my knee when Varma pushed me. Smith punched me in the stomach. That still hurts. And I feel like my hair hurts. I think Novak pulled some out." She kept her arm around her stomach and one hand on her head where her hair had been pulled.

"You're walking—by yourself. That's good," I assured her. "Cabello's minions have to practically carry her."

"Minions. That's a good one. Don't make me laugh," she groaned.

"We've only got another lap to go," Rivard said consolingly. "Sorry, I don't run fast enough to have been there to help you."

"Redwing got the worst of it. She was totally taken by surprise."

"I'm amazed Cabello hadn't gotten one of her minions to do the dirty work for her," I continued the minion tag, since it amused Sacheri.

"Yeah. What got into her?"

"Redwing is up there with Lee and Cabello in power. She must be a bigger threat than the rest of us," I suggested. "That is, if you're interested in being the future Alpha's mate."

"That *is* the highest position a mage can achieve in this village," Sacheri agreed. "He hasn't looked at me once."

"Me neither," Rivard said. "But I didn't think he would. I thought it was just fun to think about."

"That's presupposing he achieves the position of Alpha," I said dryly.

"Why wouldn't he? Everyone says he's the best."

"He's the only one who can claim challenge on the Alpha."

"He has a brother with an equal opportunity of challenge," I suggested.

"He doesn't count," Sacheri said.

"No one would follow him if he tried," Rivard added.

"Why not?"

"It's creepy the way he has different-colored eyes. I don't like him looking at me."

"That brown eye is really weird. It doesn't look like anyone else's brown eyes," Sacheri added. "It's all wrong."

"Yeah," Rivard agreed. "He's all wrong."

"Nonsense. Except for the one eye color, he looks exactly like his brother," I defended him.

"I think the eyes look in different directions. It's not normal."

"That's not true. His eyes are perfectly normal. Different eye colors are a completely natural condition," I explained. I don't know why I was trying so hard to convince them that there was nothing wrong with Aryk. It suited my purpose to have him sort of ostracized. He was more willing to give me information than if he'd been a fully accepted member of the Clan.

"How do you know?"

I shrugged. "I read it somewhere. It has an official name. It just happens sometimes." I didn't get technical this time. Too much knowledge made me more of an oddity.

They still didn't believe me. This teaching people to accept change was going to be more difficult than I thought. Aryk had lived in this village all his life, and they still wouldn't fully accept him. I didn't have the gravitas or wisdom of age to influence anyone into thinking otherwise. Maybe I should have done more to my appearance than make myself average. Maybe I should have made myself look much older, but then I wouldn't be in this unique position getting to know other mages.

This lack of taking me seriously did not bode well for the changes coming in the future. Right now, no one would believe me if I told them mages needed to learn offensive magic to fight not Clan Cat but monsters; Clan Wolf and Clan Cat should be allies because of the monsters; and changes were coming, the least of which was someone with two different-colored eyes. These were Valery-type warnings that could get me ostracized as well.

I hadn't told Aryk anything about the harassment last week as he walked me home every evening. I hadn't really taken it seriously. We outsiders were all tough mages. Once the insiders realized it wasn't working, I thought it would die down. I hadn't anticipated today's attack. Aryk hadn't been on the field when it happened, but I should have known he'd hear about it.

"What happened today?" he asked as soon as we were out of earshot of the Administration building.

"What did you hear?"

"There was a fight during the morning run. Several girls were hurt. One seriously. I heard the Nus talking about it. I noticed Redwing was missing from training today. I noticed several mages sporting various bruises and cuts. I noticed Cabello and Sacheri wincing during exercises."

"You have excellent observational skills. Do you know how Redwing is doing?"

"Besides the multiple contusions from her fall and the kicks, she has two cracked ribs. She'll have to take it easy for a while. No running or strenuous exercise. No martial arts training. Unless it gives her trouble breathing, she can practice her magic in the afternoons."

"That's good to hear. I'm glad she won't be dismissed." And maybe I could speed her healing.

"I take it you weren't directly involved in the altercation since you don't have punishment detail."

"You heard about that too? What kind of punishment will they have?"

"I spoke with Kappa Benjamin about that. I knew you'd be interested. Novak, Smith, and Varma will each take two six-hour night patrols of the training ground with a Rho. Cabello will take three nights. Sacheri will get up an hour before everyone else and help serve breakfast next training day."

I thought about those punishments. They were fair enough, I guess. Each received a punishment equal to their involvement except Cabello. She should have had a week of patrol as the instigator and a poor example for her allies.

"Your turn. How and why did it happen?"

"I don't really know why or why now. I was near the end of the run. The fight started at the top. You were right to give me a warning. The harassment could be because of your brother, or it could be that nobody likes outsiders, since we're the ones being targeted."

"I told you mages were competitive. What else has happened that you haven't told me?"

"What makes you think there have been other things?"

"Experience. And you said harassment, which suggests more than one incident. Go on. Tell me all."

I told him about the meal tampering and the week of trips and falls. I told him about my poisoning theory.

"I agree. I don't think they'll escalate the food contamination with something more lethal. That could end the Corps. They want to make you uncomfortable, not dead or sick enough to be noticed. But today's fight got completely out of hand."

I shook my head. "I don't know what Cabello could have been thinking."

"That Redwing is a serious contender?" he suggested.

"I think she might be. I don't know how the other groups stack up—I haven't seen them work magic—but Redwing is up there with Lee and Cabello in power and looks. She's not as obvious as they are, but I think she's noticeable."

"There's at least one other my brother has his eye on, McGuire. She's a strong Water mage. She's the opposite in looks from the Fire team three. She has strawberry blond hair and extraordinary blue eyes. She's also just as confident as Lee and Cabello."

"I've noticed her in our group training. Extraordinary blue eyes, eh?" I knew the girl he was talking about. Dervla McGuire. She had a smaller group of minions than either Lee or Cabello, but still enough minions to be a threat.

He shrugged. "They're an unusual color. It may not surprise you, but I happen to notice eyes."

It didn't surprise me, and I didn't ask him what he thought of my eyes. I made sure mine were not remarkable and would remain that way for the foreseeable future. "I'll have to ask Sacheri about her. She's a Water mage as well."

"What you *must* be is careful. Despite the Kappa's warning, this isn't over. They're just going to be more subtle in their harassment in the future," he warned.

"If they harass Redwing and I right out of the Corps, the Fire group will be down to six. What would the Alpha think about that?"

"He thinks eight is too small. He would have preferred ten in each group. He won't easily give you up."

"Which means whatever Cabello does, he won't oust her from the Corps either."

"No, but she will continue to be punished until she learns teamwork. The threat of promoting Lee over her might be enough incentive for her to be more cooperative. The Kappas will use any tactic to achieve cooperation."

"What makes you think promotion is that important to her?"

"Her father's a Gamma—"

"As she often tells us," I interrupted, rolling my eyes.

"It wouldn't reflect well on him if his daughter were passed over for promotion. She knows that. Capturing Ayden won't release her from the Corps."

"Then Lee is the next best threat."

"Possibly, but there's room for more than one promotion in your Corps."

"Then why pick on the outsiders? Why not each other?"

"All four of you outsiders are strong mages. Ayden will eventually check out the top mages in every group."

"Not me. I'm just barely in the top four of the Fire group. I don't stand out."

"You impressed Kappa Jōtarō. He thinks you're one to watch."

"Why? How? I don't *want* to be watched," I said in dismay. I tried so hard not to stand out.

"The Kappas work with recruits all the time. They're excellent judges of character. You're calm, confident, and calculated. Besides power, those are admirable qualities, especially for promotion to a higher rank."

"Drat. I'll have to screw something up. I don't want a promotion."

"You'd be safer promoted. You'd have the authority to stop the harassment."

"I'd be a bigger target. How do I avoid it?"

"It won't happen until the end of training. That's months away. You have plenty of time to do something stupid. I'm sure the right opportunity will present itself in no time."

I glared at him, which made him grin. I don't care what the other girls gushed about Ayden. Aryk had the more disturbing smile. That they were identical twins made that thought a paradox and not at all ridiculous.

Chapter 15

"I don't think they play at all fairly," Alice began, in rather a
complaining tone.

I'D HAVE LIKED TO say that was the end of the harassment, but I guess
it wasn't over until someone could hound us out of the Corps.

During the three weeks before Redwing returned to minimal duty,
they subjected the three of us outsiders to a daily round of hissed
oblique threats and ridiculous insults rather than physical assaults.
The threats weren't very specific. Mostly they consisted of different
versions of "You better quit the Corps or else." The cursing used
various derogatory and inflammatory invectives from the past. I wasn't
surprised to hear them still in use, but surprised to hear the mages use
the female-specific ones like bitch (and worse). I would have thought
newer terms would be in use, but these words from the past did the job
very well.

I think minions from all three of the top factions—Cabello, Lee,
and McGuire—were involved. I heard them most often during the
morning runs and exercise when the Nus weren't as close to us as they
were during martial arts training. I'm sure the other outsiders received
more verbal abuse than I did since they were trapped all night with the
other recruits. There was an older mage who stayed in the barracks as
a chaperone, but she had no rank. She was one against thirty-nine. She
couldn't witness everything.

Cabello may have done our team out of regular visits from the future Alpha with her overtly aggressive behavior, but she didn't keep her minions in check. They were targeting the ones they perceived as the weakest first, just like any predator, but they were underestimating our little group. I would see that we weren't the weakest ones.

The first day Redwing returned, the harassment elevated to a higher level. It was at the end of her first day back that they ambushed us.

There were only four shower heads in a single large shower. Nobody enjoyed showering with others, but there was no choice. It would take too long for all forty-two girls to shower one at a time, even allowing for less than three minutes per shower. Groups of four were necessary to arrive at the mess hall on time for dinner. Of course, they pushed aside the four of us outsiders to the last, no matter how quickly we arrived in line.

I was expected to shower and change into my regular clothes, even if I could easily have waited to shower at the boardinghouse. Everyone except me seemed discomfited by stripping down naked with others. They didn't all crowd into the shower room but stayed outside until their turn. Only the four in the shower had an intimate view. It didn't bother me as much as the others, but I guess I had to suffer the same indignities as everyone else. Just like misery, discomfort enjoyed company. I think this was part of the team-building experience.

I didn't have to worry about being on time because I and two others would go home after the showers. Everyone else would go to the mess for dinner, then back to the barracks. Besides the locker room and showers, the barracks contained a large room with forty-three single cots. Three were empty awaiting those of us who went home to change our minds and join the team. One of the original four already had, and I was sure the other two would give in soon. Then the pressure would intensify for me to capitulate as well.

I felt a little guilty that I was never there at night to support my fellow outsiders, but I would have felt guiltier leaving Tara alone all week. The needs of a child came before the needs of adults or practically adults. Tara required the reassurance of my presence, if only at night. She had recently started school, and I was worried that as an outsider her experiences would mirror mine. I had to be there for her.

The shower began as usual. The soap was just soap, although there was little enough of it after the thirty-eight showering before us. The water was sun-warmed only, but plentiful enough for the last four three-minute showers. We cleaned ourselves quietly and quickly, not lingering over the wonderful feeling of shedding our sweaty, oily outer layer.

When we got out of the shower, we found our towels and clothes had been removed. Only our shoes were left. We stood there dripping with Redwing, Rivard, and Sacheri hugging themselves to hide their exposure to the expected prying eyes. A prank like this would need to be witnessed at some point to give satisfaction. I thought we might find gawkers when one or more of us left the showers in search of something to wear. I said as much, which ratcheted up the embarrassment factor of the others. Wearing clothes was more than protection from the elements. They hid perceived imperfections. Females were still being judged and judged others by their appearance. Maybe that was a facet of females that would never change, but maybe it would change when mages finally came into their own.

"Wait here," I told them. "I'll check out the locker area." I heard no protests.

I walked into the locker room. No one was there. That might have been too suspicious. If anyone were waiting around to witness our naked escape, they'd be in the barracks with some Nus around to add to the embarrassment. Maybe Ayden himself was still hanging around. That would be the icing on the cake of this stunt.

I briefly wondered where they'd hidden our clothes and towels but decided not to waste time searching a hundred lockers. I had other resources to fix this.

I went to my locker. There was nothing there but my backpack. Whatever they tried to do, I knew my backpack would be there waiting for me. It would seem empty and useless to anyone else. I reached inside and pulled out some clothes that looked exactly like the clothes I'd taken off earlier. I'd sent my second pair through weeks ago to be copied. I was no prophet, but I'd intuited a need for extra clothes.

I'd already dried myself with warm air, whisking off the water on my way to the lockers. Once I was dressed, I pulled out clothes in the approximate sizes of my comrades. Hopefully, they were close enough not to be noticed. After all our training, we were all close to the same width, if not height.

I walked back into the shower room to find Rivard on the ground and Sacheri panicking over her. Redwing paced beside them.

I dropped everything outside the door so it wouldn't get wet and kneeled beside Rivard. "What happened?"

"I tried to remove the water like she'd done with the salt and pepper from our food. She collapsed. What do we do?" Sacheri pleaded tearfully.

"You can't treat a person like a plate of food!" I scolded, then immediately calmed my voice. This was no time for recriminations. Sacheri had tried to be enterprising. That should be encouraged—along with common sense.

"You probably took water from inside and outside. You need to be very careful if you try to remove the water rather than dry off with air or heat. If you completely dehydrate her, she'll die." I placed my hands on her to scan her. Just as I thought, Sacheri had taken water from inside her body, too. Luckily, she'd stopped as soon as Rivard had fallen. I saw nearby the puddle of bloody water Sacheri had removed. I had to return it to Rivard—*quickly*.

"Sacheri, Redwing, I brought some clothes. Go get dressed in the locker room. I'll take care of Rivard," I ordered. I needed them out of the way while I worked my magic.

Once they were gone, I quickly siphoned the fluid back into Rivard, removing any impurities but leaving all the vital blood and minerals. It was easier than I thought it would be. Just like the dirt I'd returned to Tara's oubliette, magic knew where Rivard's blood belonged and put up no barriers to its return. I think most of the fluid had been taken from the stomach, bladder, and kidneys, where most of it had been stored. If the brain and heart had been involved, she might not recover completely. I made sure her blood flowed evenly through her major organs before I stopped my tweaking. I'd studied anatomy from medical books. This was the first time I'd used my knowledge when it really counted.

Rivard's eyelids fluttered open. "What—what—what happened?"

"How do you feel?" I'd healed the bruises from her fall while I was at it. Healing without the aid of potions was a higher-level magic. I'd always had the ability to scan a body for injuries, but I could usually heal only simple breaks, sprains, and contusions with a few carefully worded charms. This had been a little more intricate, but still not what I considered higher-level healing.

"Tired." She sat up with my help.

"I've brought you all some clothes. You should be dry enough now."

Redwing and Sacheri had sorted through the clothes and found something to fit them. They brought Rivard the leftovers and helped her dress. This incident had thrown us several minutes off schedule. Someone would come looking for us before too long.

"Where did you find our clothes?" Sacheri asked.

"The lockers," I said. Good, they hadn't noticed the clothes weren't theirs. One simple gray outfit must look like any other. They must have forgotten to look for the tiny last names sewn into our clothes. That explanation could wait for another time.

"I would think they'd hide them somewhere else. That way we'd be more embarrassed having to walk through the barracks naked."

I shrugged. "Not this time. How would they carry out extra clothes and towels without looking suspicious? Laundry isn't done until the weekend."

"This time? You mean this could happen again?" Rivard's voice rose shrilly.

"This plan wasn't well thought out. They could make improvements and try again."

"What can we do?"

"I'll teach you a simple warding charm for the lockers, so they can't take all your clothes."

"Okay." They docilely agreed after their brush with humiliation. It could have been very embarrassing if our harassers had enticed Ayden into the locker room.

We went over to the lockers.

"Stand in front of your locker."

I reached into my backpack and pulled out a small dagger.

"Whoa! What are you going to do with that?"

"The best and most lasting wards are made with blood. Your blood is as powerful as you are. When it's your turn, I want you to prick your finger, place a small drop of blood on the door of your locker—somewhere you'll remember so you can refresh the ward regularly—like once a week. Then say a charm that allows only you to open the locker."

I did mine first as an example, speaking my charm aloud. It was a simple "Locker, open only to me," so it didn't need to rhyme. They all punctured their finger, more squeamishly than I had, repeated my charm, and warded their lockers. Then they had to test the charms by trying to open each other's lockers.

"How do you know how to do that?" Rivard asked.

"From a mage in my village. She was good at wards."

"How can your small village know things we don't?" Sacheri asked. "I don't remember this kind of magic from my village."

"Me neither," Rivard agreed.

"Neither do I," Redwing added.

"Because we were small, each person had to know more things. We didn't have the luxury of assigning one task per person. I assumed every small village functioned the same way." That sounded logical to me, but I don't think small villages were really as capable as I made them out to be. I think they did without if they didn't have people knowledgeable enough to provide the skills needed.

"What else do you know how to do that we don't know?" Sacheri demanded.

"I can't possibly know that. I guess we'll find out on a case-by-case basis."

We went through to the cot-filled room and then parted ways, me for home and the rest for the mess. I was surprised to find no one waiting inside or outside the barracks. The cot sheets would have been our next best source for coverings. I had expected the perpetrators of our dilemma to want to witness our embarrassment. None of the shifters would go into our barracks without incentive—usually by order from the Kappa. Maybe their plot hadn't worked as expected or had been foiled early. Lucky for us.

I didn't see Aryk anywhere on my long way out of the training grounds and then out to Alpha's Way. He usually made his presence known before I reached the street. Maybe he thought I no longer needed an escort. I didn't think I needed one, but a companion on the journey home was always a welcome relief from the day's tedious workings.

It was fully dark by the time I started down Mart Street. The days had been gradually getting shorter as we moved closer to winter. Today we'd trained until nearly sunset. After the showers, even if we'd been on time, it would have gotten dark by the time I reached home. There were lit lamps attached to some buildings periodically, but a lot of darkness in between. I would guess few mages walked about at night unless they were accompanied by a night-visioned shifter or could create flameless light. It should have been a simple charm, but I hadn't seen any mage so far produce it. Fortunately, I had extraordinary night vision myself. I wouldn't need to use a magic no one else could.

Although Mart Street held most of the shops, there were no taverns along this route. Everyone closed by light's end so as not to waste candles, oil, or other fuels for light. Many lived above their shops, so there was some light from second stories, but this added little to the light at street level. I expected Rhos to be patrolling the streets but passed no one. It wasn't until I was about a block away from the Administration building that I realized I was being followed.

Was it Aryk or someone else? I didn't stop. I didn't speed up. But I listened more sharply. I also had exceptional hearing for a mage.

There were three of them—all shifters, quiet and moving fast. There wasn't anyone on the street now except the four of us. Did Aryk send them to accompany me home because he couldn't? Why weren't they identifying themselves? Was this just a coincidence, or should I be worried?

After another block, I stopped and turned. "Who's there? What do you want?"

They came up more quickly now. One ran faster to outflank me. He grabbed me from behind and pulled my arms back to hold me in place. The other two came up in front of me. One pounded his fist into his hand—a definite threat. The last one answered me.

"We're here to teach you your place."

"What place is that?"

"Away from the Mage Corps. Outsiders aren't welcome."

Okay, then. They were after me in particular. It had probably been stupid to stop and confront. My Jardvari would have thought so, but I'd practiced some self-defense magic before taking this journey. I thought I could protect myself.

I opened my mouth to respond and the one behind me stuffed a cloth in my mouth. The one with the pounded fist stepped forward to punch me. He wouldn't hit me in the face. Questions would arise from that. I tensed my stomach muscles in anticipation of the blow and began a charm to layer a dense pad of air between my stomach and his fist. Unfortunately, I wasn't given the time to complete the charm before the first punch.

He didn't punch once, but three hard jabs. "This'll teach ya," he said between punches.

That really hurt, but I didn't think he damaged any organs. However, I was having trouble breathing, and I felt nauseous. I groaned and slumped, causing the one behind to let me drop. I fell to the ground and chanted my air charm more quickly to shroud myself with the air ward as protection from the kicks I was sure they'd all deliver now that I was down. The mages kicking Redwing when she was down had to get the idea from somewhere.

"That was too easy," one said.

"Naw. Mages aren't used to getting punched. They'd go down that easy."

"It ain't enough."

"We're not through. Step on her hands. Hard. She can't train with broken fingers. A few kicks after that should keep her out of the Corps—forever if she knows what's good for her."

I had my hands clutched around my stomach. One of them tried to pry up my arm. The Air ward prevented him from touching me. Seeming to struggle, I swung out my leg and knocked him down. I wasn't completely helpless yet.

"Hey!" the one knocked down yelled. He sat there watching his companions.

The other two reached down to grab my arms just as I sensed someone else running up to us. I hoped it was help. I could keep my ward up, but I didn't want to lie here forever. The attackers were mumbling angrily and fumbling, trying to get a hold on me. I looked around them to see Aryk swiftly approach. They were too busy paying attention to me to realize they needed to protect themselves.

Aryk grabbed the two trying to grab me and slammed their heads together while pushing them away from me. The one I'd knocked down was up and moving toward him. Aryk hunched over and rammed him, knocking him off his feet. The other two had scrambled to their feet and came toward him. He used a flying kick to send one into a wall and punched the other in the nose. The third one was up and coming at him again. Aryk used his momentum to throw him over his head. The other two came at Aryk again. He punched and kicked before they could even react. It was like he could anticipate their moves. He was in motion to block and attack before they could barely form an action in their head.

It wasn't long before the three attackers decided this was a losing battle. Once they were all on two feet together, they turned and ran back the way they'd come. Aryk didn't attempt to chase them. He turned to me.

"Are you all right?" He reached down to give me a hand up.

I let him heave me up. Until now I had stayed on the ground, but I'd rolled out of the way of the fight and scooted into a doorway. I'd charmed the pain to my abdomen away along with the bruises. I didn't think they'd done any lasting damage.

"Yes. You came just in time. They were going to break my fingers." It wouldn't have happened even without his rescue. I would have made it an impossible task for them to achieve. Setting one or more on fire would have done the trick. Someone in the Mage Corps must have told them I was a good Fire mage.

"Did they hurt you?"

"Just a couple of punches in the stomach. I'm okay, I think."

"Those bastards got off lightly. I know who they are," he said ominously. "Did they say anything?"

"They called me an outsider and wanted me to leave the Mage Corps. Who are they?" I asked as we started walking for home. He'd wound his arm around mine for support.

"A few Rhos in Zeta Lee's unit."

"Recruit Lee's brother?"

"Correct."

"I wondered when Lee would begin her harassment. I thought she'd taken her turn earlier." I described the shower incident.

"I think it might be best if I spoke to the Kappas about this."

"What can they really do? They won't dismiss any Fire mages or that will be the weakest elemental group in the Corps."

"Punishment details are an excellent motivator. Walking patrol isn't the only arrow in their quiver. We're responsible for some really nasty jobs like cleaning septic tanks, foraging ruins, skinning kills—to name a few. The Rhos usually handle the dirtier jobs, but we can make an exception and include recruits."

"What if that isn't enough? They seem really determined to get rid of the outsiders."

"Do you think you mages are the only ones to buck authority and discipline? There are ways to coerce obedience."

"By breaking the spirit. Is that the best way to run an army?"

"If you can't follow orders, you're a danger to everyone. There are always a few shifters who can't be molded into regular soldiers."

"What happens to them? Are they ostracized?"

"A few leave us no choice, but there are niches even in the military for more independent-minded shifters."

"What niches?"

"Reconnaissance for one. Scouts and spies naturally work alone."

"What else?"

"Bodyguarding. That's what Machi does. His rank is Xi. It's outside the general ranking system, somewhere between a Nu and Kappa."

"Are you *my* bodyguard?"

"I'm too high a rank to be a bodyguard. As the Alpha's son, I was given an officer rank after my basic training. All the sons of the highest-ranking officers from Alpha to Delta are awarded the rank of Zeta after training."

"How do you get promoted from there?"

"We have to distinguish ourselves in battle or move up through attrition. That's one reason the Alpha wants a war with the Cats. The military has remained virtually status quo for years. Every soldier wants to see glory at least once in their lifetime."

"That's a poor reason to start a war."

"I'm only presenting the Alpha's reasoning. I have no true military ambitions. Once my father is ousted as Alpha and my brother takes over, my rank will increase to Beta or Gamma. I don't have to do a thing." His tone was bitter.

"What would you have done if your father hadn't been Alpha?"

"I'll never know. There was no other choice offered but the military. It didn't matter that I liked to read and learn. I could never be allowed to apprentice to anything else. My only purpose is to serve the Alphas of my family."

"That's sad."

"Maybe. But if I hadn't been born into the Alpha's family, once my two eye colors became apparent, I probably would have been left in the woods to die. Living, even in the military, is better than not living at all."

That was far too close to Tara's story. How many children had been abandoned because of some unique difference? I didn't want to think about it. That was the past. I had to present an alternative for the future.

Aryk had a last word about tonight's incident before he left me at the boardinghouse.

"You should have waited for me before heading home."

"How did I know you'd be coming and not off on some other mission? Where were you? I thought maybe you didn't think I needed an escort home anymore."

"I was detained for what I now think to be a spurious reason. I won't let it happen again."

"How will you stop it if a higher-ranking officer gives you an order?"

"I'll pull the Alpha card and tell them I have to run an errand for the Alpha before all else."

"Won't you eventually be caught in a lie?"

"The Alpha will support me. He wants this Mage Corps to be successful. He'll see my escort of you as supportive."

"If you say so."

"Not just me, Valery. You were number fifty-two. That was the applicant he waited for to begin the training of the Corps because Valery told him to."

"How do you know I was the fifty-second applicant?"

"It was reported to the Alpha. We all knew your name, and that you were a newly arrived outsider."

"Is that why you've been guarding me in particular?" If this was the reason he'd noticed me, I could relax. Valery had predicted it. There was nothing I did specifically that drew his attention.

"You could say that."

That was a nonanswer. He was still being cagey about something. Until I knew what, he'd remain on my do-not-trust-completely-yet list. It was a short list. He, Tara, Maya, and Qzyx were on that list . No one had made my trust list yet.

The next day, after our run and before our calisthenics, the Kappa of the week, Idris, had an official word with us.

"Attention, recruits."

"Yes, Master Idris."

"Yesterday there was an incident." He paused and looked around the room. Several girls looked down, not meeting his eyes.

"You are a team and I expect you to behave as a team. Each of you has been selected for this unique Corps because you've demonstrated superior magic abilities. No one will be dismissed from this Corps unless I deem them unworthy. The four outsider candidates have demonstrated their value to this team, and they will be accepted as equal team members. I will not tolerate any more incidents. If I hear of another such incident, I will isolate the instigators. That person or persons will live alone, eat alone, and train alone. They will have no weekend privileges but will be confined on their own under guard. I have no more tolerance for a lack of respect for a fellow recruit. This is your last warning." He stared at each one of us again during another long pause.

"Recruit Lee, you will report to me at the end of day. Recruits, continue with your training."

Lee's face flushed. I guess Aryk had reported both incidents to the Kappa. I wondered how long it would take for that feeling of *team* to kick in. Maybe longer than I'd be here in Wolf Trap. I had no intention of fighting, so my time was done when the training was done. I still wanted to find out exactly what use the Alpha intended to make of mages. There had to be more to it than using up all our magic every day with a long power burst. I hoped he'd get to it soon. I wanted to know what he had planned sooner rather than later. I had my own plans to make.

Chapter 16

As THE DAYS GREW shorter and winter approached, storms grew more
frequent and violent. Winter was the wettest season, with spring running
a close second. Some storms had hail, some had snow that melted within
hours of the storm passing, and often storms were accompanied by lightning and fierce winds. There were some days now that we just stayed in the
barracks all day.

The canopied area we practiced martial arts in was taken down before
every severe storm so it wouldn't blow away or tear. It wasn't a simple
piece of equipment to manufacture, and they took good care of it. I'm sure
Valery had a hand in warning which storms would be severe.

Snow days were the most joyous. Everyone wanted to play in the snow.
It was colder than anything except hail, and it didn't hurt when it touched
you. Even the military indulged in the novelty of cold and allowed us the
freedom of being outdoors when it snowed. It wasn't my first experience
with snow, but after the days of unrelenting heat, I, too, enjoyed the
all-too-brief bout of cold.

Those stormy days could be incredibly boring even when we would still
do exercises in other empty barracks farther out, but no martial arts training was attempted to forestall damaging the building. In the afternoons,
in close and closed quarters, we Fire mages could only sit and think about

our magic, which we were told to do. There were some fears of us burning down the barracks if we unleased even the smallest amount of fire. The Kappas hadn't seen us do anything but expend huge amounts of power and didn't want any barracks damaged or destroyed in our practice.

I found the time that would have been devoted to martial arts training to be my best opportunity to teach my little crew of outsiders about reaching their magic through meditation. It wasn't the most conducive atmosphere for quiet contemplation, but I thought it was the best chance I'd get.

Meditation wasn't the easiest thing to learn, especially with all the surrounding sounds. I emphasized the importance of practicing without all the noises of awake people about. I suggested doing it after lights out or early, before anyone else was awake. These suggestions were met with skepticism, but since there was nothing else to do, they practiced on the rainy afternoons with me.

Rivard struggled the hardest with meditation. Her mind didn't want to quiet. She complained she couldn't find that place deep inside her where magic dwelled. In what I thought was a nice way, I told her to be quiet and try anyway. Redwing and Sacheri meekly obeyed my instructions. Sacheri also struggled, though not as mightily as Rivard. Redwing showed the most promise.

I waited hopefully for one of them to have an epiphany. Surely, one of them was practicing outside our cacophonous rainy afternoons. If meditation couldn't be universally accepted, I couldn't think of any easier method to reach magic. It would take generations for mages to come into their power without it. This was their best chance.

I observed other girls watching us and some imitating. Cabello and Lee sneered and kept their groups whispering during the entire process of quiet, thinking time. It was too bad they scorned my methods. It would have made them far superior mages. Their loss.

The only highlight of my dull days was walking home with Aryk. He was there to walk me home even on the darkest, wettest, windiest days. He provided me with my own wide-brimmed hat and waxed poncho. Of course, that didn't keep my legs or feet dry, nor did it help much if it were particularly windy, but I appreciated the effort he made and the fact that he would have a return trip to slog through. He waved aside my concerns and said he'd often patrolled under worse conditions. This short walk was nothing in comparison.

It bothered me a bit that I looked forward to that walk home every day. I'd told him more about myself than anyone else. It was still only a smidgen of who I was, but it was nice to have someone know even a small part of me and want to know more. I didn't have that same one-on-one opportunity with anyone else except Tara, and I was more interested in getting her to talk about her day than sharing much about myself.

I couldn't help thinking Aryk had some ulterior motive in his escort duty besides watching out for number fifty-two or reporting to the Alpha, his brother, or the Kappas. That didn't mean I wanted it to stop. I wanted and needed a friend, even a temporary, convenient sort of friend. Eventually, he'd reveal his motivation. I just had to wait him out.

Of course, his sister Valery the prophet knew a lot more about me without me having to say a word. She was the other person who kept my life from becoming humongously boring. I usually ran into her, Aryk, and her bodyguard, Machi, accidentally on purpose on the weekends after Tara and I spent a few hours in the woods. I had to keep on my toes around her, so she didn't reveal too much about me or Tara. Luckily, the statements she made were vague and confusing enough that I was the only one who had a chance of understanding her meaning.

I saw Qzyx often, but not always to talk to. He helped move equipment and fetch supplies during our training. When he showed up for dinner sometimes on the weekends, he spent most of his time entertaining Audrey and Dorrie. They'd stopped asking me questions about training since every day had become the same dull practices.

Qzyx himself still puzzled me. There was something different about him I just couldn't put my finger on. He'd sometimes show up at my impromptu meetings with Valery, Aryk, and Machi, too. We'd all somehow become a group. Maybe it wasn't surprising for Aryk and Valery to hang out with an outsider; they were almost considered outsiders themselves. I was surprised no one in the Mage Corps asked me about any of them, but I rarely saw any of the other recruits during our two days off.

While I might consider our ragtag group the most unusual people in Wolf Trap, I wasn't sure the other three outsiders belonged in my collection of anomalies. I didn't choose them; circumstances did. But I knew fate to be a tricky thing. It might be more than fate that I'd become attached to this group. I didn't find anything unusual in Rivard or Sacheri, but Redwing had possibilities. I'd continue to observe everyone—and meditate.

Magic still didn't completely understand my will, and had some trouble with my words, but it was always there when I wanted it now. We were definitely forming a relationship that worked. The next time I wanted to do something huge, I was confident it would be there. This would be important as I navigated magic's dark side. I knew there would be more monsters out there than the one in Weird Little Wood. I needed to protect myself and Tara from everyone and everything we encountered once we left Wolf Trap, which was inevitable. This was only a place to visit, not to stay.

By December, due I'm sure to the Kappas' warnings, I could happily report there had been no new or obvious harassment; only our mock fights in martial arts training were sometimes more ferocious than necessary. Redwing and I received this special attention more than Sacheri and Rivard. We were the only two in Cabello and Lee's faces every day as part of the Fire group. Cabello had the more volatile temper and trouble controlling it, while Lee simply took advantage of any opportunity afforded to trounce us. This usually happened when we were paired in a mock fight.

Unexpectedly, Redwing held her own even against Cabello. In another life, in another world, I thought she could have been a dancer. She was fluid and graceful in her movements, unlike Cabello, who was fast, jerky, and tired more easily because she put everything into her speed. If you could avoid her punches and wait her out, she almost defeated herself.

Despite all this muscle building and training to punch, kick, and throw an opponent, we were no match for the physicality of a shifter. Even with a sword, we'd need more than a few months' training to hurt anyone but each other. I think learning to fight was just a pretext to get us strong for magic use. It couldn't hurt, but it was wrong to make these mages feel they stood a real chance in a physical fight. We needed to be more creative with offensive magic to survive in battle.

We still didn't know what we would do with all the power we were drawing down during magic practice. Rather than fake weakness, I longed to demonstrate just what a powerful, skilled Fire mage could do with fire. How one could juggle fire balls like apples; set flames dancing about like little human figures; or flash burn something as small as a pea while burning nothing under or around it. Those were not useful fighting skills, but they could be the basis for something offensive.

Magic wanted to be used. It needed to be used, and not just in the passive way every living creature contained magic. Magic didn't initiate any of its uses except to maintain the well-being of its vessel—good health, longer life, and the quicker healing of minor injuries—but I could feel joy when I used it skillfully. I'm sure other mages would feel the same once they'd made a more intense and personal contact with it.

Of the three I was teaching to do so, only one really seemed to get value from meditating and getting in touch with her inner magic. That was Redwing. I knew she was a good mage not just from the trials, but from the magical connection I felt with her. Already a quiet, introspective girl, I think even without my guidance she would have developed better magically than many of the others.

Like any teacher or parent, I tried not to show favoritism, but I was very pleased with Redwing's progress and rewarded her with praise. This made Sacheri sometimes try harder for her share of approval, but Rivard continued to be stubbornly frustrated. She couldn't or wouldn't maintain the quiet mind needed for this exercise. These rainy afternoons, when we couldn't get outside to power up, our elemental skills put her in a bad temper, too impatient and curt for meditation. I was afraid I was alienating her with scolding, however mild.

This idea bore fruit when she suddenly joined another table for lunch without giving us so much as a backward glance. Her face flushed under our gaze, but I could tell she'd had enough of being an outsider. She longed for acceptance, and her seeming resistance to my way of training magic didn't make her feel a part of our group, either. There was one group that would make her feel comfortable.

"Rivard's joined an enemy camp," Sacheri said wistfully.

"They aren't our enemies. They're our teammates," Redwing said firmly.

"She chose the Earth mages, her comfort zone. Who would you join if asked?" I asked Sacheri.

She started guiltily. "I wouldn't leave you guys. There are few enough of us as it is."

"It's okay if you want to. Our group is just an arbitrary collection of those who haven't lived in Wolf Trap long enough to be considered an insider. It isn't a life sentence. I suspect eventually we'll all be approached by one of the contender groups. It's best to divide in order to conquer," I told them pragmatically.

"I think McGuire needs more friends than Lee or Cabello. She's a Water mage like me." Sacheri would find Water, her own strength, the more attractive choice for a partnership.

"Have you already been approached?"

"Maybe," Sacheri admitted guiltily.

"What about you, Redwing?"

"Yes," she said reluctantly.

"Well, go ahead and join them. I don't mind." I did, actually, but that was my problem. They had to do what was best for them. I was the temporary person here, not them.

"You really don't mind?" Sacheri asked eagerly.

"No. You need to fit in. Not being here at night keeps me viewed as an outsider."

"I won't join a group until you do," Redwing said loyally.

"I'm not sure I'll join any group, but you do what makes you feel comfortable."

Sacheri made no promises, but the next day, she sat at one of McGuire's tables. Redwing made no comment but continued to sit with me at lunch every day. She shot disapproving looks at both Rivard and Sacheri when she caught their eyes. I voiced my concern about her sitting alone when I wasn't here, but she said she sat with Lee's group for breakfast and dinner. They made no demands on her lunchtime situation, thinking she was trying to win me over. Her behavior brought Sacheri back to join us at lunch and showers, but not Rivard. She clung to the Earth group even during shower time. I may have been too impatient with her lack of progress in meditation. I'd alienated her. This was a learning experience for us both. I didn't realize teaching could be such a frustrating experience. I had to remember not everyone was motivated and willing to learn new things, especially when the instruction didn't come from someone in authority. I had to take this experience as a partial loss.

Redwing and I continued our meditation on rainy days. I could see that Sacheri had explained what I was doing to her new group and some of them were trying it. I noticed McGuire was especially interested. She'd soon out-magic Lee and Cabello if she persisted. I wasn't sure if Rivard shared since she didn't like meditation, but some in her group seemed to be trying it as well. There wasn't much else to do on rainy days.

One rainy day toward the end of December while we stood at the back of the line for the showers, Redwing turned to me with bright eyes and whispered, "I felt it at the end. Finally, I really felt it."

"Magic?" I asked with a smile.

"Yes. It felt light and happy—*with me*. It was so nice—like finding a friend."

"That's exactly what it is. The more you connect, the better your use of magic will be. The next time we practice our magic outside, I bet your fire stream could be the tallest and strongest," I praised.

She smiled at the idea.

When I encouraged her, I wasn't thinking about the effect a demonstration of her increased power would have on Cabello and Lee or Ayden Saltwyck. I didn't think about it until I watched her outshine the top mages. I assumed the Kappas' orders would deter them from more harassment. I'd retreated to my stupid rules again and gave her no warning or advice. I just let things play out.

I couldn't help feeling guilty even thinking about bad things happening. Apparently, once you had a friend, you felt a responsibility toward them. I hadn't anticipated that. I thought my feelings of responsibility for Tara were different because she was a child. Human relationships were more complicated than I'd originally determined. Who knew?

I wasn't surprised when Redwing outperformed Lee and Cabello at our next outside practice. Her column of fire was higher, broader, and lasted while theirs sputtered out. She was given plenty of dirty looks after that, but she seemed oblivious. I worried about her staying in the barracks, but it was Friday, and everyone was going home for the weekend. Next week would be the time for worry.

"Congratulations," I said as we waited for the showers. "Your meditations are really paying off. You'll become even better if you keep at it."

She practically glowed. "It was glorious. I felt more energy than ever before. I felt I could still keep going and going. I only stopped when everyone else did."

"That's great, but you don't have to put on a grand display every time we practice. You know you have the power. Everyone knows you have the power now. You should just show enough to keep up with the leaders, not show all you've got." I finally gave her the direct warning I should have given originally.

She frowned. "But isn't that what we're supposed to do—use it all up?"

"That's just the Alpha's idea of increasing our power. He thinks using it up every day will increase it. He's on the right track, but his way's the slow way."

"How do you know what the Alpha thinks?"

"I don't really, but that's the only reason I can think of that makes any sense."

"Are we really going to simply burn a fire before the enemy?"

"I think he has something more elaborate in mind. I have no idea what it could be, but I hope we find out soon. This making a big fire every day for hours is boring. I want to do something more interesting."

Redwing looked doubtful. "I still have magic to burn. Maybe I should have kept going."

"So, you *do* want to win the attention of the Alpha's son?"

"What?" She blushed. "No, no. I never thought—*No!* Absolutely not! I'm in the Corps to be self-supporting. It pays better than any other job. And it has prestige."

I wanted to ask what she meant by both reasons. Why did she need to be self-supporting? Normally, she would live with her family until she was married. If she didn't marry, it was still expected that she would live with her family. There wasn't enough planned or repurposed housing for single-people dwellings. Audrey and Dorrie's boardinghouse wasn't a typical situation, hence only one permanent resident.

Redwing also didn't strike me as someone out to win accolades. I think she would have been perfectly happy using her magic for more practical purposes. But what did I know? My knowledge of people was from old books in a time before magic. I was learning as I went along.

"Well, if you don't want to be noticed, I'd tone it down. If you want to practice full out, wait until the weekends."

She nodded her head and said nothing more, so I dropped the subject. We parted ways after our shower. It was early enough for the sun to still light my way home. Since it was Friday, she hurried off, mumbling about getting home before dinner. I waited for Aryk to join me as usual. I had questions for him today.

"How's your brother's mate search going? Who's in the lead?" I asked as soon as we hit the street.

"Are you asking for yourself or a friend?"

"I'm asking out of curiosity. I see him during our martial arts training, but he's making himself scarce during our mage training."

"He's been staying away from the Fire group. He'll be interested to hear of Redwing's improvement."

"Don't tell him."

"Why not?"

"She's not interested in your brother. She's not going to shine as brightly in the future. Why has your brother been avoiding us?"

"After the harassment, he was told to spend equal time with all the groups, even those with no mage that interests him. He's observing Earth now."

"What's wrong with the Earth mages?"

"Let's see. How can I word this that won't be offensive? Pleasant girls, but as a group, they are the least exciting of the mages—personally and physically."

So, Aryk had noticed the tendency for mages with similar elemental strengths to have similar characteristics. It wasn't just me. Still, I shouldn't encourage him to stereotype the mages.

"Women are always judged on their appearance. I've been doing it myself because of this stupid bride contest."

"Everybody is to some degree. Attraction is subjective."

"There's nothing wrong with Earth mages," I defended.

"I didn't say there was. Earth is solid, fixed, and unexciting. So are their mages."

"What's wrong with that? They're dependable and constant. Your brother would be lucky to have an Earth mage mate." I couldn't picture a real standout in Earth magic if Ayden was looking for the best-looking bride. Just as Aryk said, they were pleasant, average girls. If I hadn't wanted to be right there for the most dangerous element, I would have chosen Earth. And if one of them had the power to draw lightning, that would draw his attention pretty quickly.

"Maybe, but none of the Earth mages attract my brother."

"Well, they should. Earth mages tend to be more successful breeders, to put it as delicately as I can. If he wants to continue the Saltwyck dynasty, he should at least choose a mage with Earth as her secondary strength."

"Is that so? How do you know?"

"It's basic logic. Earth is the elemental magic of growth and nurturing. It shouldn't be surprising that those qualities would be a part of the mage wielding it. Your mother had three children, which is rare today. Was her element Earth?"

"Water was her strongest element. She looked and acted like many of the Water mages—tall, athletic, strong, serene, confident."

"You've given this some thought."

"I'm observant. I can tell you I wouldn't want an Air mage mate. They're attractive enough, but too flighty."

"If they had wings, they would fly."

"I was talking about their personality. Erratic, impulsive, whimsical."

"I know. Flighty just seemed fitting in more ways than one." I wanted to ask him which element I looked like since I was strong in all four. I knew he couldn't read my mind, but he told me what I wanted to know without my asking.

"You're more difficult to categorize. You move gracefully, like an Air or Water mage. Your temperament is calm and stable, like an Earth or Water mage. Your appearance fits in with the Fire mages, but you don't have the Fire mage volatility or drama."

"What about my appearance?" I shouldn't ask, but I really wanted to know what he thought of me.

"Most of the Fire mages are about average height and weight. They all have attractive figures and pleasing features," he said matter-of-factly. I had my answer. It pleased me, but I wouldn't show it. I reminded myself I wasn't like the other mages. I wasn't looking for a husband, boyfriend, or any other male attachment. I had loftier goals than that.

However, he really had been studying me more carefully than I'd thought. But he'd been studying everyone. He was incredibly observant. I wondered if he'd shared these observations with his father or brother. "I don't think you can make any inferences from the small test group of the Mage Corps. It may simply be coincidence that makes the physical and personality similarities of the groups magnified."

"You sound like a scientist."

"I've read a lot of science books. Learning was encouraged in my village."

"It's encouraged here, too, but more practical skills take precedence. Manuals and handbooks of useful skills are the encouraged reading material. If you don't like reading and learning or don't find a skill you like, then you join the military."

"That's all well and good for shifters, but mages have far fewer choices."

"And now the military is one of your choices."

I didn't want the Mage Corps to fight the Cats, and I didn't want the mages to fail. They needed this opportunity to shine. I wanted to see what the Alpha had planned for them, but I didn't want to be here for the endgame. Did I have only weeks or months before I had to take Tara and leave? I didn't want to go yet. I was still learning, observing, and interacting. I was still enjoying my walks home with Aryk.

"You still haven't told me who's in the running for your brother's mate."

"He has his eye on the same few as before. He's in no great hurry. This is his opportunity to look over the strong mages as a group. He'd never get a chance like this otherwise. Rest assured, he'll be back watching the Fire group soon enough. Most of the mages he has his eye on are in that group."

"I'm not worried unless the harassment starts up again."

"It shouldn't. They were warned."

We parted ways at the boardinghouse. I didn't ask Aryk if he had his eye on anyone in particular. If eyes were his thing, my brown eyes didn't stand out like extraordinary blue eyes. Plus, it wasn't any of my business. I didn't want to know. He was helping me, and I didn't want to become too intimate with his affairs. There was no future in it. I was meant to have friends and allies, but no family. To effectively lead, I should remain above the throng. That's what I was told anyway. I was beginning to wonder if my progenitors had it right. They didn't predict I'd meet someone like Aryk. I wondered what else they might have gotten wrong.

Chapter 17

"The more there is of mine, the less there is of yours."

ON THE PENULTIMATE MONDAY afternoon of December, we were introduced to a new magic initiative. As we arrived at our designated Fire practice area far behind the barracks, our Kappa, Master Wójcik, was there before us and ordered, "Quiet! Attention!" He then gave us a further glimpse into the Alpha's eventual plan for the Mage Corps.

"Recruits, henceforth, your magic practice sessions will be a little different. No longer will you work alone; you will be partnered with another mage to combine your magic to create higher and stronger fire columns. We have observed your practice sessions for three months and have a clear idea of the strengths and weaknesses of this group. We have determined the best partnerships to make this work. You will be paired as follows ..." The Kappa read from a list in his hand, and we regrouped accordingly.

Immediately, I perceived the pairings were designed to separate friends or allies. Redwing was paired with a Cabello and I with a Lee minion. Lee and Cabello were paired with each other's minions as well. This did not bode well for our practice.

"I want you to spread out. Give each other space to work intense magic. At least twenty paces between each group. That's right. Now begin," Master Wójcik instructed.

And that was all the instruction we were given.

Immediately, I knew the Alpha had no idea how magic and mages fundamentally worked. He was treating the process like any other job. Working together to accomplish a goal succeeded in most cases, but not for magic. Mages were instinctively possessive and protective of their magic. They might share spells, but not their magic. In order to combine their magic, giving control of their magic to another was exactly what they would have to do.

Before magic became a reality, all the literature I read in the past about magic was fantasy or wishful thinking. In this reality, the number thirteen had no significance beyond being a prime number. Any prime or odd number was acceptable to magic. Covens were impractical. The devil was a Christian construct that had nothing to do with magic. The concepts of good and evil were based on a society's system of ethics, not magic. Magic was neutral. But mages were not.

In order for the Alpha's partnership idea to be successful, there had to be one who controlled the magic and one who submitted voluntarily to that control. Just as with shifters, the strongest should be the one in charge. If one person tried to take over without consent, the other one would consciously or unconsciously fight for control. Without that partnership agreement, you'd have what was happening now—everyone sitting with a partner but working alone.

I looked over at my partner as we worked on our separate flame streams.

Her name was Daisy Everest. She was one of Lee's minions. She had short, curly black hair, dark brown eyes, umber skin, and a triangular fig-ure. Her facial features were medium-sized, but nicely fit her heart-shaped face. In general, I'd found features too small or large for face size were unattractive, but hers were just right. She was older than most of the others in the group and hadn't stood out as one of our major harassers in those first weeks of training.

She distorted her attractive face into a frown of displeasure when she found herself paired with me. She looked at Lee for guidance but only received a curt shake of the head. It wouldn't be in Lee's best interests to buck the Kappas' decision. She didn't need more black marks against her.

I thought my chances of winning Everest's cooperation through charm or guile were nil. I had no skills in either, and she was too wary to be easily swayed. Everest was as stuck with me as I was with her. I could see the other groups also struggling with this idea of collaborating with a rival. There was a far better chance for success if we worked with a friend.

The Kappa wouldn't listen to me, but I could give Aryk a heads-up—or not. I was against furthering the Alpha's ambitions for a war with Clan Cat, but I still thought the mages would need better offensive skills in the future. This Corps would help them with that, and so could I if I disregarded my Jardvari's rules again. A famous general once said, "Rules are mostly made to be broken." I learned that more every day.

I was too quiet when I met up with Aryk at the end of day. He immediately picked up on it.

"What's wrong?"

I was still debating whether or not to interfere with our new directive. I knew what my Jardvari would say, but despite all the contention in the group, I wanted them to feel success, not failure, in their first major magical undertaking. I guess I felt more a part of the team than I'd realized. "Nothing."

"It's something. I can tell."

"How?"

"You don't have that relieved *I'm finally free from practice* look."

"What look do I have?"

"The concerned *I don't like what's going on* look."

"I didn't think my face was that expressive."

"It is. Right now, you have the scornful *He thinks he's so smart* look."

I laughed. "You nailed that one. Okay. You're right. I don't like what's going on. This pairing is ridiculous. How can they expect us to work magic with our enemies?"

"Not enemies—teammates."

"Calling us a team doesn't make us one. Even without the prize of winning the Alpha's son, there are rivalries in place that have intensified with the promise of promotion. If you want this exercise to work, team us with friends and allies, not enemies."

"I don't think anyone realized just how competitive the mages could be under these circumstances. It was thought you'd develop a sense of unity by now. Considering the time needed for magic practice, you weren't expected to engage in the team-building exercises shifters do. Shifters would have mock battles to capture the opponent team's standard, team rope pulls, blind obstacle course challenges, and scavenger hunts."

I continued to voice my objections. "Working magic together is a whole other dynamic to working it alone. There must be an element of trust to work together. That's why we should be doing this with someone who is a friend or ally. Most of the mages are fairly young. Their established friendship circles from childhood are still alive and functioning." I didn't use the term clique because I didn't think it was a well-known term today. I'd read about cliques. They formed in adolescence and were considered a normal social development. Commitment to an already established clique was interfering with the formation of team Mage Corps.

"That won't always be possible in the heat of battle. There are too few of you. That's why you must think of yourselves as a team. You must be able to work with anyone in your unit."

"That will be difficult to impossible. If you want a successful combining of power, one person must be in control, which means the other person must agree to being controlled. You can't do that with just anyone. It especially won't work if the two mages are of equal power, and neither will back down to a subordinate position."

"I? I don't want anything. This isn't my plan. I'm just along for the ride," he protested mildly.

"You're a representative of the military. Therefore, the plan belongs to you, too."

"If shifters had magic, there wouldn't be a control issue. Shifters naturally follow the most dominant."

"Shifters do have magic. They just use it all for the ability to shift. That takes a great deal of magic."

"What if a shifter had magic outside of shifting?"

"That shifter would be unique. Do you have more than shifting magic?" That would explain my attraction to him outside of his being the only person in the military to really care about my welfare. He would be another anomaly.

"I don't make that claim. I was simply speculating, since you seem *so* knowledgeable about magic."

"I am not *so* knowledgeable. I just seem to know more about it than you or anyone else in Wolf Trap."

"Well, Miss Know-It-Most, what do you want me to tell the Kappa? I assume since you're telling me all this, you want me to pass it on."

"Do you think I only use you as a conduit? Do you repeat everything I say to you?" I assumed as much, but it was still disappointing to have confirmation.

"No, not everything, only those things that make the Mage Corps run more smoothly. And I don't think you're just using me to get to the Kappa in charge. I think we have a give and take here that works to our mutual benefit."

"I don't see how any of this benefits you. What do you get out of the Mage Corps or walking me home every evening?"

"I get to learn a lot about magic and other things I didn't know before. I get to walk a pretty girl home every evening who doesn't look at me as if I might curse her if she meets my eyes. And I get to oversee a group of attractive mages instead of surly guards patrolling the boundaries of town."

I ignored the compliments because I wasn't prepared to deal with them. "Was that your job before the Mage Corps?"

"Someone has to see that the guards are doing their duty. It gets tedious walking a patrol. Shifters have been known to fall asleep or zone out. Most of the Zetas have their own units to drill. No one wanted to be in my unit, so I'm in charge of the patrols."

He said that so matter-of-factly, but I found it sad. I wished I could make everyone understand how stupid it was to ostracize him for his eye colors. Like Tara and Valery, he was another victim of the *you're different so you must be bad* school of thought. I wanted to help them all, but I didn't know how yet.

"You must do a lot of walking," I said instead of voicing my outrage and sympathy.

"I usually shift when I do my rounds and howl at them to keep them alert."

"Are they allowed to shift on patrol?"

"Yes, if they don't get distracted and give chase to whatever they see or hear. There are severe punishments for deserting one's post."

"I would think walking a patrol would be punishment enough."

"We have plenty of other punishment opportunities, like clearing out more ruins for future growth."

"Is your population growing that fast?"

"From every passing caravan, we receive more outsiders wanting to relocate to a larger town. We received twelve new residents this year by caravan."

"How often do caravans come through?" When Tara and I left Wolf Trap, traveling by caravan would be a consideration.

"We see maybe six a year. There is one that travels from one coast to the other, but that one takes over a year to come back through. Crossing the country must take a few thousand miles."

I must have been quiet too long again because Aryk asked, "What are you thinking? Why are you asking about caravans? Are you planning to leave?"

It was safer to not answer that one. Who knew what expression he'd read that I didn't want revealed? "Don't tell the Kappa about my reservations regarding this new mage partnership. I'll deal with it on my own."

"Okay."

"That's it? No protests? No arguments?"

"I'm not one for quarreling. You can handle it however you want. Magic's your thing, not mine," he said artlessly.

I gave him a suspicious look, and he amended his statement.

"Except for shifting. I don't think of that as magic. It's just something I do."

"Even when magic shifts everything you carry into and out of your shift?"

"I never thought about it that way. That is rather fantastic."

"It's magic," I said drily, and our conversation ended at the boarding-house.

Tara was in a sullen mood when I got home, but I didn't confront her until we were safely in our room. I didn't want Audrey or Dorrie privy to our conversation in case Tara's problems were of the shifting variety.

"What's wrong?" I asked once the door was closed.

She tensed and scowled. "Nothing."

I jumped to my own conclusions. "I'm sorry I can't be with you more than a couple days a week. I know how hard it must be to live in the center of what you've always thought of as the enemy camp. You've been very good and uncomplaining."

She slumped down on her bed, looking down at her feet. "I know all that. It's not that."

Nothing more was forthcoming. "Then what is it?" I prompted.

She kicked her feet against the bed a few times, then looked up at me defiantly. "I hate school!"

She'd been going to school since October. She hadn't said a word about it in those almost three months except "okay" when asked. Now it was suddenly hateful. I should have figured it out, but I'd been more concerned with the goings-on in the Mage Corps than what was happening here.

I sat down on the bed beside her and nudged her shoulder. "What happened to change okay to hate?"

"None of the other kids like me."

"Do you think they sense you're a cat?" I thought my weekly magic reinforcements were doing well. She didn't seem to want to shift until I told her she could, and I detected no cat musk smell anywhere on her.

"No. It's because I'm an outsider. They don't like outsiders." She looked at her hand, but the *S* had been dissolved away months ago.

"I've got the same problem in the Mage Corps. There's nothing I can do about that. We'll be outsiders no matter where we go."

"Why do I have to go to school? Why can't I just stay here with Dorrie and Audrey? They like me."

"Sorry, but you have to go to school. There's a lot for you to learn. It's only three more months. Surely you can manage three more little months?"

"That's a long time!" she protested.

"You're halfway through. It's downhill from here."

"Until next year," she said glumly.

"We probably won't be here next year."

"Can we go to a Cat village next? I'd like that better."

"We'd still be outsiders, and from what I understand Clan Cat dislikes outsiders more than Clan Wolf does."

Her face fell. "Yeah. They don't like them. I can't live anywhere with anyone. Nobody will ever like me."

"I like you. You can always live with me."

"But we can't live by ourselves," she declared.

"Sure, we can, but I don't think we will be by ourselves for long."

"Why not?"

"I want you to learn everything you can. Not now and not soon, but someday we'll start our own village, and we'll welcome people like you."

"Girl shifters?"

"And boys who can't shift and anyone else who's different."

"Are there boys who can't shift?"

"If there aren't, I think there will be. Anything's possible. I've already met a couple people here in Wolf Trap who are different from the others."

"Why didn't their families try to kill them like me?"

"You've met two of them. They're the children of the Alpha. If they'd been anyone else's children, they could have been killed."

"Are they going to come with us?"

"I don't think so. I'm not ready to start that new village yet. That's why you have to get along here, learn everything you can, and be ready to move on."

"When? Why can't we leave now?" she asked eagerly.

"I haven't learned everything I need to here. But I can promise you we aren't going to be here when Clan Wolf starts a war with Clan Cat. I won't be a part of that."

She sighed hugely. "Okay. I'll try to get along in school, but I don't like it."

"Getting along is all I ask. I'm sorry you can't make any friends, but a friend can get too close. You might reveal something. It really is better that we keep our distance. You understand that—don't you?" Those were the Jardvari's rules. I didn't like them, yet here I was telling Tara to follow them. If she were the rebel I was turning out to be, we were definitely going to have problems.

"Sure," she agreed, but she didn't sound convinced.

I hadn't realized how difficult it would be for a ten-year-old in a strange village. I didn't much care if I made friends or not. I was here to interact and learn. That I seemed to have made a couple of friends was strange. Redwing was sticking with me during the day despite her alliance in the evening with the Lee coterie, and Aryk was sticking with me every evening after training.

That they couldn't be real friends because I couldn't tell them the truth about myself was strangely disheartening. I was surprised how much so. Wanting connection must be a universal human trait. Maybe that was one reason I'd so easily accepted a ten-year-old companion. I hadn't thought of that before since I'd been raised to be self-sufficient. I didn't like the idea of depending on anyone. That way could lead to mistakes, and mistakes could lead to being found out before I was ready. That would be disastrous for me and any companions I took on.

I'd been warned that breaking or bending the rules I'd been given could have dire consequences. Yet those rules hampered my ability to learn about others. Plus, there was no way I could have left Tara alone to die in a hole. I know my Jardvari had traveled around the country many times, breaking no rules. Was I too young to be traveling the world alone, as they'd feared? Was I a more social creature than they'd considered? Or was there some other reason I found certain rules so difficult to follow?

Whatever the reasons, I would do what I could to keep myself and Tara safe, even leaving Wolf Trap as abruptly as I'd entered. Despite the rules, I wouldn't leave her behind.

I waited silently, but impatiently, an entire week to see if anyone would figure out on their own how to work their magic with another. They had to overcome their antipathy for their partner first. That was the hardest hurdle to success.

I couldn't see how the other elemental groups were doing with the partnership problem. I assumed partnership work was being forced on the other groups as well. I thought if someone had figured out the best way to work together, it would be noticeable. The Kappas would share and instruct all groups to copy that method. That was an assumption, but I thought it a reasonable one.

On the third day of the second week of the new year, I'd had enough of this useless practice and decided if my partner was willing, we'd be the ones to show them the way. I didn't think they'd get there on their own anytime soon, and I couldn't stand the sense of failure in the air.

As we sat down, getting ready to begin our flame session, I looked at Everest. I thought she might be the weakest mage of the eight in our group. That didn't mean she wasn't a strong mage. The truly weakest ones had been released from service early on. To me, her weakness and the fact that she was a minion meant she might not have an inherent sense of her own superiority. It would be nigh on impossible to convince a mage the caliber of Cabello or Lee that they were weaker than me without revealing just how powerful I was. Some intrinsic understanding of magic or mages had led the Kappas to pair the strongest mages with the weaker ones. Cabello, Lee, Redwing, and I were the strongest of the group. We were the natural leaders of this exercise in teamwork.

"Do you want the Alpha's idea of the Mage Corps to succeed?" I asked Everest abruptly, before she started her fire column.

She looked at me with surprise at first, then quickly frowned. "Of course I do. I'm loyal to the Alpha."

"Do you admit we have to work together to achieve his goals?"

She hesitated, as if examining the question for a trap. "I guess so. That's what the Kappa told us to do."

"Do you think that's what we're doing here?" I waved a hand at the others.

She looked around at what she could see of the others working their flames. "I guess. Sure."

"Well, we aren't. We're just sitting together, not working together."

She looked confused. "What's the difference?"

I moved on. "Do you think you're a better mage than I am?"

Her frown grew deeper, and she glanced over at Lee, who was staring intently at the flame of fire she had magicked into existence in the pit four feet in front of her. There was no help there. "I don't know," she said cautiously.

"Let's find out. Fire up as high as you can."

She concentrated on the pit in front of us and started her fire. It rose steadily and stopped at my estimate of almost twenty-four feet. I started my flame and changed the color slightly to a brighter, more orange flame, with highlights of blue. I grew my flame to twenty-seven feet. I could go much higher, but three feet higher than hers proved my point.

"Look," I said. "Whose flame is higher? Whose flame is brighter?"

She knew. She clenched her teeth and concentrated harder, but her flame grew only a little higher. She'd reached her limit. She might not want to admit it, but it was obvious my flame burned higher, brighter, and stronger than hers. She extinguished her flame and looked at me sullenly.

"So what? What are you getting at?"

"Do you agree that I'm the stronger mage of our partnership?"

"I guess so," she said grudgingly.

"Do you want this partnership to succeed?"

"Sure. But how?"

"By a successful merging of our flames, of course."

"Duh. That's what we're all trying to do now."

"That's what we're all not trying to do now. We can't do this separately. We'll only succeed together. Instead of creating your own flame, I want you to feed your magic to me. I'm strongest, so I must be the one to control our merged powers," I explained logically.

"You want to take my magic!" she exclaimed in alarm.

Those closest to us looked over. I'd been talking quietly and getting quiet responses in return—until now. Luckily, the crackling and rushing noise of all the fires covered up most of the sounds of our talking. I wanted to keep this new dynamic a surprise until we were successful. It all depended on Everest's ability to trust me.

"Hush. Don't disturb the others. I won't take away your magic. What we work here will be temporary. You'll still have your magic. You're simply funneling it to me for this exercise alone. I will only use what you give me. You're still in control of your magic."

She gave this some thought. "What do I have to do?"

"Come sit beside me. It will be easier at first if you touch my arm as you give me magic. Once we've practiced this enough, you won't have to touch me to feed me magic."

She scooted over to sit beside me. No one was watching us except the Nus standing around as guards and Aryk. The Kappa had been called away, but he should be back soon. He had to be present to report our progress accurately to the Alpha. The Nus weren't trusted to be objective observers. Aryk was trusted in his observations, but not in his constant presence. As a higher rank than Kappa, he could come and go as he pleased. Most afternoons, it pleased him to stay in the Fire group.

Everest gingerly put her hand on my arm. "Now what do I do?"

"Close your eyes and tell your magic to help me create the flame. You don't need to talk loudly. Magic can respond to even a whisper. You can open your eyes if you can keep your magic flowing to me without distraction."

She followed my instructions, and I felt her power slowly added to mine. I didn't need it, but the others would if they wanted the biggest, broadest flame they could create. We were the example of how to achieve that. There was power in shared magic, but it wouldn't be long before Everest would want to wrest that power away from me. It could be days or weeks from now, but it would happen. Sharing would always come down to a power struggle. Working well together was just a temporary condition without complete trust.

I matched the power I received from Everest to support the illusion that my power was within the same range as hers. Our column of flame would still grow and broaden to more than what each of us could do individually.

We were noticed almost immediately. The other mages stopped their practice and scrambled away from us. We were well apart from the other mages, and my fire wasn't moving. They were safe enough. The Nus woke up from their lazy stroll around our practice grounds, and Aryk sent one to get the Kappa. Master Jōtarō was the Kappa in charge of us today. He came running and stopped short at a safe distance from our giant flame.

I fancy our column was high enough to be seen beyond the government building if anyone looked up. I kept the heat away from us, but four feet was too close for comfort. Next time, I'd have us sit at least six feet back. For now, I had to decide how long to keep it going. Everest was usually good for almost an hour on her own without a break, whereas I was sure I could go all day.

"Everest, keep going until you run out of power. Let's really show them how it's done."

"Okay," she agreed, but I could feel the distraction of everyone watching already affecting her magic flow. She'd never be able to sustain a long-term stream in the midst of battle if she allowed even this small amount of attention to distract her.

Distance from the flame would be an important factor for these mages to stay away from the battle and stay alive. I'd been imagining them stationed on the outskirts of the battle, not in the center. I could be as far away as I wanted to be, but how close did these mages need to be to keep the flame going? I had to do everything I could to see that the Mage Corps stayed alive if they made it to that future battle. I couldn't stop the war, but right now I could foster mage power. That was just as important.

Why not run a distance test here and now?

I told Everest to stand up while still feeding me magic.

Chapter 18

"Now I can do no more, whatever happens."

"Recruits Dare, Everest! What are you doing? Where are you going?" Master Idris demanded as everyone backed up to give us plenty of room.

"Testing our limits," I told him.

Everest had scrambled up beside me, awkwardly keeping her hand attached to my arm. She couldn't maintain her magic feed without touching me. I slowly backed away from our flame column with Everest one step behind. Her eyes were open now, and the flow of magic from her to me fluctuated as her attention wildly swung between the flame column, walking backward, the others watching, and me. But I kept the magic pouring consistently into the flame column regulating it to what her contribution should be. In a battle I expected the flame column to move, not the mage. I'd reveal that knowledge later if someone else didn't beat me to it. I was hoping Lee or Cabello would start thinking of improvements, so I didn't have to take the lead permanently. I was already regretting throwing myself into the limelight.

We kept the flames surging for another twenty minutes or so as we backed very slowly away from it. We halted every few steps for Everest to recover her magic flow. I wasn't about to give anyone the idea that I could effect this power alone. I'd never escape if they thought me too valuable.

We reached about a hundred yards before I felt the flame begin to weaken significantly and I let it die out. That was enough to prove that mages didn't need to stand close to keep the flame going. I was pretty sure that Cabello, Lee, or Redwing could keep it going for at least that distance away. It all depended on what the Alpha's plans were for columns of fire.

When the flame was completely quenched, Kappa Idris approached us.

"What happened? None of you have been able to combine your flames since you started the practice. How did you do that?"

I shrugged. What could I say that sounded like a lucky guess and not insider knowledge?

"That's no answer, recruit. I want to know what happened here," he commanded.

I took a breath, ordered my thoughts, and began a reasonable if not truthful explanation. "I could see that no matter how close we placed our flames, they wouldn't combine. It was frustrating. I thought about it and remembered in my old village one time two Earth mages worked a healing charm together for a serious illness. One mage wasn't powerful enough. The stronger mage enlisted the help of another, and they stood together holding hands. Both chanted different charms but one put her free hand on the wounded person."

"Was that it? Do you remember the charms?"

"No, but I was told one charm funneled magic from one mage to the other. The strongest of the two used a healing charm. I wondered if that could be done for this kind of magic, too. The strongest mage between the two of us would control the flame, and the other would funnel her magic. Everest and I tested our magic against each other, and I had the stronger flame. She sat beside me, touched my arm, and charmed her magic to flow into me through our connection. It seemed to work," I said modestly. This was a real test of my acting abilities. Aryk wouldn't buy it—I had already let him see too much of my magic—but I hoped the others did. I didn't need any more scrutiny than I'd already brought down on myself.

"Why did you decide to walk away from the flame?"

That might have been a mistake. I should have waited a few weeks for that additional inspiration to occur to me. Somehow the closer we came to the end of our training, the more impatient I became to get it finished. "Well, I thought—did we have to sit or stand right beside the flame to keep it going? That would be hard to do in the middle of a battle. Why not test that out right now? I asked Everest to stand up and walk with me away from our flame column. That seemed to work, too." I hoped I sounded just as surprised as they did that it worked.

The Kappa rubbed his chin thoughtfully. "Good work, Dare. This is an excellent breakthrough. Recruits—did everyone hear Dare's description of how this should work?"

The Kappa, Nus, and Aryk had walked to the sides of us. The other mages had stayed well outside that flanking. No one had wanted to get between us and the column of flame, but everyone was curious about what I was doing.

I'd spoken loudly enough for all to hear, projecting my voice a tiny bit with a little magical assistance. I don't think anyone noticed that except maybe Aryk. He always seemed to notice my magic performances.

There was some shaking of heads, and "No" and "Repeat" comments. The mages were told to move in more closely and listen up.

"Dare, repeat what you told me about how this new procedure should work."

I paraphrased my earlier explanation of what had to be done. I emphasized that only the strongest mage should control the fire and that the other had to feed her magic by touch at first. I told them it would be best to sit farther from their fire than the original four feet, so as not to acciden-tally singe themselves. I think I had all the precautions covered.

Many of the mages looked distrustfully at me. They didn't like taking direction from an outsider. Nor did they like the directions given. Determining the strongest should be easy enough. The other three minions should be used to submitting their will to a stronger mage. They'd been doing it with Lee and Cabello for years. However, having to give magic over to an adversary would not be easy to do. Since I'd already talked too much for one day, I decided to let someone else solve that problem. I'd done enough. I turned the explanations over to Everest so she could tell them the charm she used to funnel her magic.

Cabello looked angry. She didn't like that she hadn't thought of this herself. She wanted to walk away with all the honors in this Mage Corps. Lee probably felt the same way, but she hid it better with a thoughtful expression. She was wilier than Cabello. After all, she'd got-ten her brother to perform her dirty work while Cabello had joined in as well as instigated her own dirty deeds. Neither would be happy being shown up, but I didn't think they'd risk sabotaging my procedure. If Everest and I could do it, they'd have to prove they could too, and even better if possible.

We returned to our fire pits. I suggested that they be placed farther apart in case the others had trouble controlling their fire. The Kappa said he would have us stationed one hundred feet apart instead of twen-ty the next time we met. For the rest of today, he suggested everyone simply practice working the new way of creating fires but keep them small and stationary. Moving away from the fires would be tried after we'd successfully practiced long-lasting, bigger, and better fire columns.

We'd already been working for almost two hours. Many of the mages were nearly tapped out, the weaker mages especially since their magic reserve was smaller. Testing their powers against one another was an easy win today. I expected new challenges tomorrow.

After about twenty minutes with little to show for this new procedure, the Kappa announced an end to the practice session. He told us to rest up because he expected great things tomorrow. He'd have Everest and I demonstrate our achievement again first thing, while Everest and I explained what we were doing during each step. He expected to see everyone perform this partnership successfully.

On the way home, of course, Aryk wanted to discuss my reveal.

"I see you didn't need my help talking to the Kappa. You handled it in your own way just as you said you would. I'm surprised at your solution."

"I hope I did the right thing. I didn't expect the Kappa to get so excited about it."

"As far as he's concerned you've made a singular breakthrough. The other groups were faring no better in their partnerships. The Kappas were in a quandary on how to improve the situation. Even the Alpha could offer no solution except more practice."

"I wondered if all the groups were being paired off to work magic. It didn't seem likely that our group would be unique."

"You are unique in many ways, Rain Dare."

I ignored this implied compliment and didn't look at him, but I could feel my face warm. "Two separate streams close together were still an impressive force. But I assume not what the Alpha was expecting from the partnership?"

"Correct. The Alpha wants enough power to overwhelm and alarm the enemy. This new way accomplishes that very nicely."

"Of course, if two can work together why not four?" I suggested drily. That wouldn't be awkward at all.

He took me seriously. "Why not? Maybe all eight could work together for a wall of flame."

"Why not enlist a few more mages, even weaker ones, to round out the number to thirteen and form covens again?" I continued my sarcasm. I thought I might be able to control that much magic flowing to me. I would be a conduit, not the final destination of all that magic, but I was certain the others wouldn't be able to control a huge influx of magic. It would be dangerous at their level of skill.

"What's a coven?"

"A large group of witches—ideally thirteen—who work magic together."

He stopped in his tracks, looked around then turned to me urgently. "*Never ever* mention or talk about witches. There are no witches. Witches are evil creatures who must be destroyed. The word has been stricken from our everyday vocabulary." That Old Testament exhortation against witches was still in force even if organized religion had yet to make a comeback.

"I know all about that. 'Thou shalt not suffer a witch to live.' But it's just semantics. What mages do would have been considered witchcraft in the past. Magic isn't evil. Intention is what makes magic use good or evil. Call them what you will—witches, wizards, sorcerers, enchanters, or mages—they source the same magic."

"Your logical argument doesn't matter—don't use any term but mage, even lightly. Don't discuss your theories with anyone else. They won't be tolerated. They might even be considered subversive."

"Fine. You're the only one I really talk to anyway." I knew all this. I was just being tetchy after my magic exposure. "I don't suppose you plan to turn me in."

"I have no intention of repeating any of this to anyone. It's best if you keep it to yourself. *Please!*"

I agreed with his urgency. I had no wish to be arrested and imprisoned or worse for saying the unspeakable. I would never say the word *witch* again, even to him. "I won't mention covens again either. They're too closely associated with those who must not be named."

"That's an excellent plan. Your knowledge is a dangerous thing."

"There's a quote close to that—'A little knowledge is a dangerous thing'—I think that's the real problem," I said stubbornly.

"Your village must have had access to a very fine library."

"It did. Several, in fact. I read everything I could get my hands on," I admitted.

I could feel his eyes studying me. "You were very chatty today. I don't think I've ever heard you talk so much in one day."

"I'm working all this out myself. It helps me to talk it out. Besides the Kappa wouldn't have been happy with a briefer explanation for my epiphany."

"You know, I recognize sarcasm when I hear it. You really don't think we should have more than two mages working together—do you?"

"Two is enough for these mages. Any more would require someone very powerful to control the group."

"Like you."

"Not me. I've never made that claim."

"But you are more powerful than the others," he insisted.

"A little bit, I think," I conceded. I wouldn't validate what he thought he knew. I still wasn't completely certain what he would do with the information.

"I've been watching you. None of the other mages could have pushed that creature out of Weird Woods with a rain cloud. None of them could have removed its teeth and claws. None of them control their magic the way you do."

I gave him a hard stare. I doubt whether I could really intimidate him with a look, but I'd give it a try. "I've just learned a few useful things from my village. That's all."

"I'd like to see this village of yours. They seem to know things the rest of us don't."

"You don't know that. All you know is that they do things differently from Wolf Trap. You don't know every town or village in the world."

"What's the name of this village of yours?"

Name? I thought back to my original story. I had named my fictitious village initially, but perhaps it would be better if it didn't have a name. I didn't want anyone looking for it and not finding it. "We just called it the Village. We weren't on the caravan routes. We had to travel to other towns to trade."

"How did you get to Wolf Trap if you didn't travel by caravan? Traveling the roads alone would have attracted outlaws."

"I walked through the forests, away from the roads."

"With your cousin, Tara?"

"Of course. I didn't just pull her out of my backpack. She wouldn't fit," I joked.

"And Qzyx?"

"We picked him up along the way."

"He claims you rescued him, along with the claim he's known you since you were a child."

"We did rescue him." That was enough with the questions. It was time to redirect. "Why all these questions suddenly? I preferred your uncurious acceptance."

"They're not sudden. I may not have been asking but I've been thinking them since I met you."

"Now suddenly you decide to ask?"

"Since you're in such a chatty mood, I thought I might get some answers."

"Well, my chattiness is at an end. No more questions and no more answers."

"Okay," he said agreeably.

We said no more on the way home, but it wasn't an uncomfortable silence. It was companionable. I sensed no disquiet in Aryk. He'd taken his chance to learn more about me and taken no offense at being stymied. I'd have to watch my step around him in the future. He knew far too much about me as it was.

As the stars of the Mage Corps, Everest and I went around to the other three groups to explain our methods after we'd gotten our own group successfully started. Everest had worked on her charm, and it had a nice singsong rhyme to it. I'd offered some improvements that she'd taken seriously. I didn't like rhyming charms myself. They weren't as accurate when choosing words to force a rhyme instead of crystal clear directions.

Everest had become particularly loquacious in her descriptions of what she did and how it felt. I found her more imaginative than I'd first thought her. To be frank, I hadn't given her much thought at all in the beginning. She had just been a useful tool. But now I saw her with a will and mind of her own. She was pleased to be singled out for this attention, and I allowed her to shine once I'd set forth the original idea.

If she thought this attention gave her a leg up in the marriage stakes, she was mistaken. She might not realize it yet, but she had as good as confessed to being a weaker mage. That wouldn't recommend her to the Alpha or his son. Only one mage could win the prize since polygamy wasn't an accepted practice. She also wasn't a real standout except that she'd partnered with me, and I'd forced her into the public eye. If Ayden Saltwyck were looking for the exceptional, Everest wasn't it, but she'd make some shifter an excellent mate.

We stayed with each group until they caught on. These other groups had more members but fewer adversarial relationships than the Fire group. Some partnerships had more difficulty than others in determining the strongest member, but less unwillingness to share magic. I had to emphasize what an integral part of the equation the funneling magic member was. I stressed further that the magic couldn't be forced or appropriated but had to be offered willingly. That wasn't exactly true, but besides being unethical and immoral, there were inherent problems with attempting to coerce power. These mages didn't have that kind of power—yet—but it was best to get the prohibitions set down early in their training.

We spent a few afternoons in this way and only returned to the Fire group when all the other groups had a good understanding of our method. Everest was more confident than ever, and I could see she had half a mind to challenge me for leadership again. It was the nature of power to always test it against others. I didn't mind. I would always best her. She'd eventually come to that realization. I just hoped it wouldn't rock her newfound confidence. That was the one thing that would improve her magic as surely as practice and meditation.

Aryk was impressed by everyone's improvement.

"I can't believe such a little thing would bring on such a marked increase in power."

"What little thing is that?"

"Giving your magic to another."

"But that isn't such a little thing! A mage has to work so much harder to reach her magic than a shifter. Shifting is almost instinctive whereas manipulating magic takes more thought and practice. It can be frustrating unless you can make the leap to true communion. Asking them to give what little they can manage to someone else is a huge demand."

"It's not like it's permanent. What's the big deal?"

"When you're not the one in control, you feel impotent. Plus, you're admitting to the world that you're the weak link in the partnership."

"After all the tests and practice wouldn't they already know who the strongest and weakest are?"

"They were all treated as stars before. Now they're relegated to sidekick."

"I don't see the difference. Everyone has an important part to play. The controller can't succeed without the controllee."

"Mages don't have a sense of who has more magic until they're put to the test, and then they believe if they only try harder, they can eventually be the best. Shifters can sense dominance from their animal side, which is why Wolves tend to lead villages. I know you don't choose your Alpha based on real challenges, but I don't think you would allow an incompetent or weak shifter to lead."

"Challenges can become real. We have a rule: If the heir isn't powerful enough or the Alpha is deemed incompetent or too weak by a quorum of

Betas and Gammas, then real challenges can be issued until that Alpha is overthrown."

"Has this rule ever been enacted?"

"Of course not. My father is only the third Alpha this town has had. My great-grandfather was the original leader. We're still a long way from incompetence."

"Your brother is to be the next Alpha—correct?"

"He's the oldest. That's what's expected."

"Would you be able to challenge the Alpha as well, since you're twins?" I already knew the answer, but I wanted his take on it.

"Any son of the Alpha can offer challenge when the time is right. A brother can challenge a brother within the first year of his rule."

"When would that be?"

"When the Alpha has served thirty years or reaches the age of fifty-five. My father is forty-five and has served twenty-four years."

"Fifty-five is rather young to be forced out of power."

"Average life span for a shifter is seventy. A decline in strength and power begins at about age fifty. There is an advisory board of older shifters from the higher ranks of the military. They can serve until age seventy. They meet once a month."

"Will you challenge the Alpha, or your brother if he wins Alpha?"

He shook his head. "No. My brother will make a decent Alpha. He's the strongest of his age group, and he's my father's choice."

"What about you? Where is your place when your brother becomes Alpha?" He spoke so dispassionately about the future. For some reason, this worried me. He was an anomaly because of his two-colored eyes. I didn't know if it had any significance beyond an accident of birth, but he wasn't as accepted in this town as he should be. What would become of him?

"Uncertain. Ayden may not be as vested in protecting his siblings as the Alpha is in protecting his children. The Alpha thinks Valery and I can be useful to my brother. But my brother is uncomfortable with our flaws. He sees us as liabilities, not assets."

"But you're family. Your animal nature values family even more than your human nature. Why wouldn't he follow your father's lead?"

"Ayden doesn't always agree with the Alpha. When we were children and became aware of our differences, he was always testing himself against me. When I stopped letting him win, things changed for the worse. We stopped being brothers and became at best rivals. When Valery manifested her abilities, he lumped her in with me as someone to be endured, not embraced."

"I'm sorry for that. Neither of you should be shunned for your differences." Families should be the first bastion against outside attack. How awful it must be to be aware every day that you couldn't count on your family to support you. I didn't have any family except my Jardvari, yet I knew they had my back.

He shrugged. "It is what it is."

"What other ways does your brother disagree with the Alpha?"

"He thinks the Mage Corps is a waste of time. He has no problem using it as a marriage mart, but once that objective has been accomplished, if it hasn't proven itself, he'd just as soon disband it."

"Do you believe in the Mage Corps?"

"I believe in the mages. You're helping them achieve wonders they never thought to. I'd like to see their powers used in better ways than battling the Cats."

"So would I, but this is a first step toward recognition. Mages were meant to do more than kitchen tasks, knitting, and gardening."

"What more do you see them doing?"

"Any number of useful things. All your machinery can run on magic instead of oil and gas. You wouldn't need sewage systems. A mage could transform waste into something else. You don't need miners. A mage can bring up the gifts of the earth with magic, not earthmoving machinery. There are endless ways mages can make life easier for everyone."

"Then of what use are shifters?"

"Protection and policing. That creature you fought in Weird Wood is only the first of many to come. Magic is creating them even as we speak. Many will have their own magic and they won't follow any rules. Their only limitations will be those designed by magic itself in their creation." This was what I had been told before leaving home. It was one downside of magic.

"How do you know all this?"

"I just do. You'll have to take my word for it." There I went again revealing more than I should, but at least when I left Wolf Trap someone would be forewarned of future dangers.

"What else do you know that we don't?"

Oh boy, I could write an encyclopedia there, but I'd give him the condensed version. "Nothing is static, everything changes. Some changes will be good, some bad, but there will always be change. Your sister is one of those changes. Prophecy is a higher-level magic few possess. There will be others."

"You sound like Valery—like a prophet."

"I may seem prophetic, but I'm nothing like Valery. She's unique for now."

"I feel like I should tell someone about all this."

"Don't do that!" I said in alarm. "No one's ready to hear it, and the mages aren't ready to do any of it."

"Why not? You've shown them how to work as a team. Teach them the rest."

"It's not that easy. Magic's not that easy. I'm still working out the kinks myself."

"Why isn't it that easy? Either you have it, or you don't."

"Magic's in everything, organic and inorganic, but it's inert until you stir it up. To use it, magic must be courted. It doesn't just appear at your command, perfectly catering to your every whim. You must teach it to come to you, obey you, and understand your intentions." I was digging myself a deep hole here. Aryk would soon know all my secrets. "No more questions. You have all I know."

"I don't think so. You wouldn't tell all your secrets."

"I don't know about that. It's very flattering to have someone ask me questions as if they're interested in what I say."

"I enjoy that, too, and I am interested. You're different. I noticed that the first time I saw you."

"How am I different in a way that's immediately noticeable?" He'd yet to answer that question to my satisfaction.

He shrugged. "You just are."

"That's no answer. Now who has secrets?"

"You said it before yourself—doesn't everyone? No one's an open book. You're not the only one who's noticeably different."

"Who else?"

"Qzyx. He's the only nonmilitary or nonmage we have working for us. He's never stayed in town this long. I never interacted with him much before, but now that he's working with the Mage Corps, I see him all the time."

"Qzyx. Yes, there is something different about him. I sense it, too, but I don't know what it is." I didn't mention his seeming inability to shift. Even Aryk might find that too odd not to mention to someone.

"He came to town with you. He's always around when you are. I bet he leaves when you do."

"What makes you think I'm leaving town?"

"You don't like the purpose of the Mage Corps. I don't think you'll stick around for the end results."

"We'll see," was all I told him. He was figuring me out better than I was him. He was more dangerous than I'd ever imagined—because I liked him. Not just him—I liked Redwing, too—but I interacted with him more than anyone else. I would miss them all when Tara and I left, but him most of all. For the first time in my short life, I felt a weighty sadness. How strange.

Chapter 19

"I know something interesting is sure to happen," she said to herself.

We didn't spend long happily creating massive columns of flame before the Alpha added a new twist—and twist it was.

"Listen up, recruits. Today, we want you to make your column of fire twist and rotate like a tornado in a continuous spin," Master Jōtarō told us on the first Monday of the third week of January.

I wasn't the only one to stare at the Kappa in disbelief. This new directive would take a simple display of Fire power and completely complicate it.

"This is the next part of the Alpha's plan for the Fire group," he said, watching us sit still, silent, and stunned after his big pronouncement. "Carry on, recruits."

Where was the Alpha going with this? Did he really believe a twisting, turning fire looked more threatening than a vast wall of flame? Was it supposed to deflect rather than absorb projectiles like arrows? Was this one of Valery's prophecies? Too bad I couldn't get a straight answer from her to find out. She only said what she wanted to say, and past predictions were just that.

Although twisting by itself or turning by itself was haphazardly successful, twisting and turning together appeared impossible. The mages couldn't do all three things at once—burn, twist, and turn—no matter what sort of rhyming charm they put together. Mainly because they all needed arm and body movements added to the charms as if to show magic how to do the twists and turns. This required standing up to aid in their movements. Cabello and Lee led the way, embracing the fallacy that they had to physically involve themselves in their charm. It was how they and the mages before them had always worked magic. I thought they'd gotten over that need to move with their fire columns. They used their hands at the start of making their flames, but then relaxed once their flames grew to their maximum height. I thought they'd figure out eventually that they didn't need all the movements. I was wrong. It had become a ritual or superstition now. They'd shake it off over time, experience, and an increase in their power. But not yet.

Of course, I watched them before making any genuine attempts myself. But I had to do the same stupid dance the others did, and it made me angry. I felt like an idiot spinning and twisting my body, waving my arms around chaotically. Everest had to feed me magic without touch, which was difficult for her. That was everyone's problem and added to the lack of success. It was too much and too soon to incorporate this extra dimension into our magic. And there was nothing I could, would, or should do about it this time. I'd done enough toward a goal I wanted no part of.

We weren't going to be the stars this time, no matter how much Everest grumbled and forcefully suggested that she take over the flame. I told her to try it with her own flame first, just to shut her up. She did even worse on her own. Her flame, reduced to its old stream, became much smaller when she twisted it. Turning was impossible without dropping the twist and knocking herself over with all the hand movements and gyrations. She was dizzy from the effort and sullen when she ultimately admitted defeat. Her "Fine. You do it," was grudging at best.

These pathetic practice sessions gave me more time to think about how disastrous it would be to unleash fire into a battle, and the part I was playing in this stupidity. How had I let myself get sucked in this far? I couldn't just leave well enough alone and let them fail in the Fire pairing. I couldn't just follow the rules and observe only. No, I had allowed myself to show off my superior understanding of magic, giving the Fire mages more power to create a disaster. Maybe my Jardvari had been wise to give me rules, and maybe I'd been a stupid, arrogant idiot to ignore them when it suited me. Maybe I'd be leaving the mages worse off than before I came.

Fire was not a toy. Once loosed, it had a life of its own. Seven barely skilled Fire mages wouldn't be enough to rein in what they'd started. Even a fire without an initial fuel source wouldn't stay that way. Practicing among rocks gave a false assumption of control. Once the fire touched a fuel source, it would flare out of these mages' control. A fire could spread up to fourteen miles an hour, consuming everything in its path. Ceasing to feed it magic wouldn't stop the burning already started, nor would a piddling charm. Even twelve Water mages engaged in the same battle wouldn't be able to bring sufficient water quickly enough to quench the fire. Where did the Alpha think his battle would take place? Did he want to burn the Cats out? Did he realize he could burn down Wolf Trap, too? There was no safe place for the massive fires these mages would create.

I had no true understanding of wars, the desire to annihilate an enemy, or the idea of glory in battle. I'd known in the beginning I wouldn't stick around to see this to the end. I'd only wanted to interact with others, and as a sideline, help the mages achieve some offensive skills. I hadn't seriously thought of the consequences. I'd been reacting to present problems, not future ones. And now I didn't know how to stop it.

Tara and I met up again with Aryk, Valery, and Machi on the weekend. This had become a common practice—so common that they brought lunch with them when they greeted us outside the west gate. They timed their arrival to after Tara had had her five-hour run in the woods. I'd told Aryk never to expect finding us until the afternoon. He took me at my word.

We ate that lunch far enough outside the gates that none of the guards could observe or hear us from their patrol stations. On the second visit, Aryk and Machi had found substantial logs for us to sit comfortably upon, and I'd quietly preserved them with magic. They would remain untouched by animal, vegetable, or mineral as long as my charm lasted, and I renewed the charm every weekend. If anyone except Aryk noticed anything unusual about our log picnic area, they said nothing to me.

Qzyx also joined us today. He didn't every weekend, but often enough that he became a welcome friend. He gained a position of trust by treating everyone as if they were his age and not children. I had thought him overly talkative at first acquaintance, but that had apparently been for Tara's benefit. He didn't seem to need to be the center of attention in our little group.

Valery was particularly talkative herself today. She would quote from *Alice in Wonderland* and *Alice Through the Looking Glass* suddenly and often as we ate. She'd taken an unexpected liking to that book and consistently quoted from it—today more so than any other.

"The time has come the walrus said to talk of many things: of shoes and ships and sealing wax, of cabbages and kings," Valery said after we'd begun to eat. I was given a thick cheese sandwich while the others ate some kind of meat sandwiches. Aryk always remembered that I didn't eat once-living animals. He was good at that—remembering even the most insignificant things. I would miss him for that and many other reasons when I left Wolf Trap.

"And why the sea is boiling hot and whether pigs have wings," I added to hurry things along.

"That's from *Alice Through the Looking Glass*," Tara said knowledgably. Since I'd lent her my combined edition to read, she'd been doing so all fall and winter. "That's a sad poem. Why did the Walrus and Carpenter have to eat the Oysters? They were just little kid Oysters. I didn't like that."

"I've never eaten one myself and probably never will," I told her.

"You could only eat oysters if you lived near the ocean," Machi pointed out prosaically. He was often a silent presence at our lunches but had become a little more talkative over the many weekends we were all together. Aryk and Valery seemed to treat him less as an employee and more as a friend. I followed their lead.

"How do you know about oysters when you live so far away from the coast a caravan couldn't even bring you seafood fresh enough to eat?" I asked.

"Curiouser and curiouser," Valery said.

"We have books. We all become familiar with what may be available in other regions," Machi answered. "I'd like to see the ocean sometime."

"I've seen the ocean. Water as far as the eye can see. 'Water, water everywhere. Nor any drop to drink.' That's from a poem. I can quote, too," Qzyx said.

Everyone laughed.

"The sea was wet as wet could be. The sands were dry as dry. You could not see a cloud, because no cloud was in the sky. No birds were flying overhead—There were no birds to fly," Valery recited again from *Alice*.

"Are there fish in your lake? Of course, you've seen fish," I asked rather than throw out another *Alice* quote at Valery.

"Plenty. We've caught catfish, largemouth bass, and trout in our lake," Aryk contributed.

"No wise fish would go anywhere without a porpoise," Valery remarked.

Aryk laughed at that quote. "What's your porpoise, Valery? You're trying to tell us something. I'm listening."

"I'm afraid I can't explain myself, sir. Because I am not myself, you see."

"I know, sweetheart." Aryk patted her hand.

Valery looked at me then and said, "If you don't know where you are going, any road will take you there."

That wasn't exactly in the book, but it was close enough. "But I don't want to go among mad people," I quoted back anyway.

"Oh, you're sure to do that if you only walk long enough. Begin at the beginning and go on till you come to the end: then stop."

What did that mean? Two quotes this time and not together in the books, but both were about travel. Asking her directly wouldn't work, but feeding her quotes right back wasn't working either. Why had she fixated on Alice? Was it just because I was reading it when we met? Or because it was significant to me? Did she see me as Alice traveling in a strange land? Was she telling me I was soon to return to my travels? I already knew that. It was just a question of when, and she wasn't giving me a time frame.

"If you believe in me, I'll believe in you. Is that a bargain?" I asked.

"Yes, if you like," said Valery. "Come, fetch out the plum-cake, old man."

"Off with her head!" Tara interrupted with her own quote and giggled. "I don't remember as many things as you two do. But I like the Queen of Hearts. She's terrible."

"I've never known Valery to talk this much to anyone, even the Alpha," Aryk observed. "But I can't make heads nor tails of what she's trying to say. Can you?" he asked me. I shook my head.

"It's about as curious as it can be," Valery stated with a smile.

"Take care of the sense, and the sounds will take care of themselves," I replied.

"It would be nice if someone made sense for a change," Aryk complained.

"Now, here, you see, it takes all the running you can do, to keep in the same place. If you want to get somewhere else, you must run at least twice as fast," Valery replied.

I gave her my no-nonsense look. "This has been fun, but I'm not getting your point, Valery. Can you make things clearer—maybe without the *Alice*-isms?"

Valery gave me a beaming smile and nodded her head. "Anon, the quest begins again. The players have been chosen. Roll the dice for attributes. The game has come unfrozen."

She'd spoken in rhyme this time. Like a charm, there was magic in it, but of what kind I couldn't tell. "Is that it?"

"Beware the Jabberwock. Beware the JubJub bird. And shun the frumious Bandersnatch." Valery had her last *Alice* word—I hoped.

"Okay, then. That's a little clearer." But not much. I didn't want to run into any of those imaginary creatures, but I wouldn't have a choice once I left Wolf Trap. She was warning me they or creatures like them would be out there—nothing I didn't already know.

"Curiouser and curiouser," Aryk announced, using the shortest quote. "Can I ask how it's any clearer?"

"You can, but I can't say. I'll just add 'Oh my fur and whiskers.' And that's the last of *Alice* I'll say today."

Tara had been listening wide-eyed and puzzling over the quotes. For this one she laughed. "The White Rabbit! Oh dear. Oh dear. I'm late. I'm late. I liked him, too. I want to find a rabbit hole."

Valery gave her a solemn look. "Beware the Cat. She may have nine lives, but curiosity can kill her."

Tara looked suddenly scared.

"Enough of the Alice and cat talk!" I ordered sharply. "Isn't that a forbidden word?"

"It is in some circles, but I think we can discuss anything among this group," Aryk looked at each of us. Even Machi nodded his head, though I thought he'd be the least likely to care. Then again, he must hear plenty of iffy things from Valery that he's kept quiet about, or Aryk wouldn't trust him.

"Now that that's cleared up, I suppose we'd better head back. I need time to digest all that Valery's told me today." I stood up and brushed my hands off on my pants.

"When you figure it out, will you explain it to me?" Aryk asked.

"Maybe." I was pretty sure she was predicting the end of my stay in Wolf Trap. I had no idea what the rest of it meant. With my head chock-full of everything I'd read about this world since I learned to read at age three, there had to be something filed away that would be useful. Valery seemed able to easily find things in my head. But I really should have a leg up there. It was my head, after all.

Things went along the same into February. No one had much success in twisting and turning their wall of flame. I wasn't sure what made this procedure so difficult. Maybe the idea of juggling three tasks at once was a mental block. They were also probably unused to a charm that had to do three things at the same time. If they had more control of magic to begin with, three tasks would not seem so formidable.

I wondered if anyone here was meditating except Redwing. She'd been taking my advice seriously. She was the only one with a notable twist to her flame and sometimes a true turn, but I thought her partner was holding back. Her partner was one of Cabello's minions. I didn't think Cabello and her faction could handle another successful outsider. She'd rather one of hers looked bad than for Redwing to look good. It was a shame because Redwing could be the next star if she had all the magic her partner could give.

While we struggled with our magic, martial arts training had become a little more interesting. We'd started learning the strategies of armed combat the same week we'd started our twisty fires. We had wooden swords for practice instead of the metal ones we'd be using once it was thought safe to allow us to carry them. But the wooden ones could still do a lot of damage to beginners. We wore chain mail vests to protect our ribcages, metal vambraces to protect our arms, and a visored helmets to protect our faces. This made training hideously hot, even on the wettest days. Instead of running, most mornings, we immediately headed to the practice tent or mess hall for weapons training before the hottest part of the day.

We were two weeks into weapons training and just putting on our armor when we heard two piercing whistles. Everyone immediately stopped to listen. Two more whistles came after a brief interval. The Kappa for the morning, Master Benjamin, ordered, "Everyone to the east gate. *Quickly!* Recruits, bring your swords."

The east gate was the one at the end of the training grounds. It was about a mile from the back of the Administration building. We were about halfway there on the training grounds. After a moment of stunned silence, all forty-two recruits ran after the Kappa, ten Nus, and our two Zetas.

Many of the mages were missing their helmets, either from not putting them on earlier or removing them on the run. I had left mine behind as well, thinking of the minimal field of vision they provided. Even with the visors raised, it was difficult to see anything but what was directly in front of me. I wanted to have my peripheral vision unimpeded if we were about to enter an actual fight.

The walls were only about five and a half feet high. Most shifters were taller than that, so they could easily see over. More than half of the mages were taller as well, but the ground was rolling, and we could see more of the land beyond the walls the farther away we were. Whatever was coming hadn't arrived yet, but as we approached, we could all see a dark wave of something coming closer with a huge shape slithering behind it.

"Rats!" one of the patrol Rhos yelled out. "Huge rats! As soon as I saw 'em I ran back here and gave the signal."

"Just rats. I thought it was something dangerous," a Nu said in disgust.

"*Huge* giant rats, I said. *Hundreds.* And there's a big-ass snake chasing them. I saw them near the lake. I shifted and hightailed it back here as fast as I could." He fell back, exhausted from his double shifts.

"All right, everyone. Stand back and spread out. We'll wait for them to come over the wall. They'll be slower and easier to kill. Don't let one get by you. I don't want any to get into town," the Kappa ordered. "Those who want to shift for this do so now."

We spread out fifty feet back along the length of the wall. The wall itself was easily two miles long. It wasn't expected that the rats would try to run around it. Over would be quicker and give the illusion of a place to hide. All the shifters except the Kappa had shifted. I noticed Aryk and Ayden weren't exactly alike when they shifted. Aryk was black with silver streaks while Ayden was a gray, brown, and black mix. I didn't know what that meant, but I found it interesting that the twins weren't twins as Wolves. By rights, they should have been. I briefly wondered if the different eye colors had something to do with it. Any thought was better than that of the hundred giant rats soon to be invading.

We didn't have long to wait before the rats began to climb and jump over the wall to escape the snake. There weren't hundreds, but there were a lot of them.

They weren't giants, but they were larger than an average rat. Almost three feet long, dark gray to black, with long snouts, sharp teeth, black eyes, and long tails. Even though I didn't like the look of the rats, I wasn't ready to kill one. Up until now, I'd killed nothing bigger than a mosquito. With so many other more experienced fighters around me, and without my life on the line, I didn't think I could kill anything bigger even now.

Instead, I stood farther back from everyone and worked a charm. I created an invisible wall blocking the rats from coming more than about a hundred feet from the wall without having to turn back. I didn't think too hard about the fact that blocking off their exit was almost as bad as actually killing them. I knew these rats weren't normal, that they could easily kill a human, but still I was reluctant to kill them. One day I would have to bloody my hands to save my life or the life of someone else, but not today.

I told the magic to allow the shifters and mages to pass freely in and out of the magic wall. That way they might be puzzled by the rats' behavior but have no idea why it happened. I didn't want to deal with any magic questions. I'd brought enough attention to myself without adding more.

Although I didn't actively kill a rat, I swatted away any that came near me. I noticed some of the other mages were squeamish about getting near them as well. I heard squeals of disgust as they batted their wooden swords and danced out of the way of the approaching rats. A few of them stood still and stared in horror until they were ordered to get out of the way by the Kappa.

The shifters were doing most of the damage. Many were simply biting the rats' heads off. The smell of blood and death was awful. I created a temporary sensory ward around myself to keep it out. Now I wished I'd kept my helmet so I could block out most of the sights as well. I couldn't close my eyes because I didn't want any rats sneaking up on me.

Somehow, it seemed worse when the snake slithered up the wall. It was at least three feet wide, and I couldn't see yet how long it was when it reared up four feet over the top of the stone wall. It had fangs in its wide mouth, so I imagined it was venomous. I wondered if it had constricting ability as well. It was such a monstrous size I couldn't help feeling someone was going to get hurt today—either swallowed, squeezed, or bitten. I braced myself and wondered what I could do to prevent that and still protect the secret of my abilities.

As the snake hovered there on top of the wall examining the scene before him to decide who would be his next meal, the largest raptor I'd ever seen suddenly swept down and plucked the snake right off the wall.

The snake must have been over a hundred pounds on its own, so the raptor had to be over twice as big to carry it. Raptors generally picked up prey they could ingest immediately—mouth sized. The snake was far too big for a one-bite meal even for the enormous raptor. One of the rats would have been a better meal choice. What was the raptor up to?

I watched it fly up into the sky with the snake trailing down, twitching its long, long body and trying to escape. Everyone around me was intent on the rats. I didn't think many of them had noticed the raptor or the snake.

I backed away from the scene of carnage, and most of the other mages followed my lead. The Kappa didn't stop us. He had his sword out and was doing his own damage. I noticed Cabello and Lee had tried to set the rats on fire individually, but the stench and screams were so awful they stopped and continued to bat at any rats coming near them. They had to demonstrate their leadership abilities to the Kappa by staying in the fight. I couldn't see their expressions because both still wore their helmets, but I imagined it was determination mixed with a little fear and disgust.

Two mages fainted from the heat. I dispersed my personal ward and enlisted a few others to help drag them beyond my invisible wall. I didn't want any rats near them, even just running over them. They'd have nightmares as it was without envisioning being a rat's steppingstone. My sensory ward was gone, and the heat and smells were getting to me, too.

Qzyx ran up to us. I hadn't noticed him before. He must have been someplace farther away on the training grounds.

"What can I do? What do you need?" he asked me.

"We need out of the sun, and we need water."

"I'll find some stretchers. The fight is wrapping up."

I looked around. It was true. Some shifters had already shifted back. The others were finishing off the last of the rats. I noticed that when they shifted back, none of the blood and gore came with them. I wondered if that happened to all the dirt and sweat they gained during the day. If so, that would be a cheap way of keeping clean. Had they thought of that or maybe never noticed? If shifting could only be done once or twice in a day, shifting to get clean might seem a waste of power, but it would certainly save water and mages physically doing their laundry, which was still considered women's work.

While we waited for Qzyx to return, I looked back up and saw the raptor hovering high overhead with the snake now a long, unmoving weight in its beak.

"Look out!" I yelled in warning.

Once everyone was looking up, the raptor dropped the snake. It fell in the middle of the slaughter. Its head was almost completely torn from its neck. It was decidedly dead.

The raptor flew down and perched on the wall, turning its head back and forth to watch us with its beady red eyes. In the mess of the almost-decapitated snake amid a mass of huge, dead rats, that ominous black raptor was a major contender for the scariest sight of the day.

Chapter 20

"I'm very brave generally," he went on in a low voice, "only today I happen to have a headache."

THE KAPPA ORDERED FOUR Nus to stand watch near the raptor. He ordered another four to carry the heavy body of the snake to the tannery. Apparently, snakeskin was useful in making belts, shoes, and bags. This amount of snakeskin would make a great number of people happy. I wouldn't be one of them. I was perfectly happy with my hemp belt, backpack, and shoes.

The rest of us he ordered to throw the rats into one enormous pile. This order included all forty-two mages, two Zetas, a couple of Rhos, and the last two Nus not given other duties. The only ones not zealously flinging rats were the forty-two reluctant mages.

Picking up a dead, headless rat by its tail wasn't the worse thing I could imagine doing. I didn't like it, but it was dead. It couldn't hurt me, and I couldn't hurt it. I did it gingerly and without flinging. I walked each body slowly, holding it out as far away from me as possible.

Touching a head, however, with any part of my body, let alone picking it up, was another matter entirely. I couldn't pick it up and I couldn't kick it toward the pile. Whenever I came across a head, I used my Air magic to roll it toward the pile with fake kicking motions. I tried to remain stoic, but I'm sure my face reflected my revulsion. I hadn't learned to school my face from completely indicating my feelings. I'd had no need to do so as a child. As an adult, or almost one, people responded more favorably to me if I was expressive.

My evident distaste for this job was mirrored by most of the other mages, but not one of them thought to use whatever Air power they had to move the heads—not even the Air mages. Although there were more of us than the others, we squeamish recruits did the least rat pick up. We could only manage one body or head at a time. The shifters were picking them up, also by the tails, and holding them in bunches by one hand before taking them over to the pile. The heads they picked up and threw. Some of them aimed at their comrades standing close to the pile. There were some smothered laughs and smirks among the shifters. None of the mages found this amusing. They squealed if a head came too close to them. None of the shifters did this deliberately, but they weren't always careful or exact in their tosses. Aryk gave them a hard look if they got too close to the mages, but Ayden smirked at each squeal.

As we worked, we all kept a watchful eye on the raptor. It sat as still as the stone wall it perched upon. Except for the red eyes, it could have been a black painted stone. Its black beak was hooked like a vulture's, but it was unlike any vulture I'd seen in pictures. Even its talons were black. It was an ominous and oppressive presence looming over our work. The Nus watching it were poised to attack if it pounced.

When we were finished, Kappa Benjamin and the two Zetas discussed what should be done with the carcasses. The Zetas were of a higher rank than the Kappa, but both deferred to his age and experience. There was some talk of burial, but more often they looked our way. I could tell the discussion always returned to burning. It would be the quickest method of disposing of the rats, and the safest, not knowing their magical properties.

I couldn't tell if there was something more magical to the rats besides size. Every living thing carried some magic, but using magic was another matter entirely. There was no telling if the rats could regenerate or meta-morphose. If burning were the next step, I'd have to say something to Aryk about mixing salt with the ashes and burying them away from any inhabited area. These were not the sort of ashes I'd use for compost or making soap. He would know what to do.

Redwing came over to where I stood farthest away from the pile of rats and raptor when we had completed our onerous task. We both avoided looking at the rats and watched the raptor watching all of us. If eyes were the windows of the soul, I would say black-eyed rats were soulless, but the eyes of the raptor seemed intelligent and inquisitive despite their unnatural color. I thought maybe I was being fanciful when Redwing spoke up.

She moved as close to me as she could without touching me and said quietly, "I can sense its thoughts."

"Whose thoughts?" I kept my tone low as well. This was not a conversation others should overhear.

"That bird. I know what it's thinking."

"What does it think?"

"Saved two legs. Killed no legs. Four legs dead. It keeps thinking that over and over."

"How are you getting its thoughts? Do you hear it?" I decided that was the important point, not speculating on the raptor's thoughts.

"I don't know. I've always been able to sense animal thoughts."

"They speak our language?"

"No. All I get are pictures in my head. I think I somehow translate what they're thinking into something I can understand."

"Did you sense the rats' thoughts?"

"Some. Mostly it was just fear and escape." Wow—Redwing, who I'd already considered superior to the others, now turned out to be anoth-er anomaly with her unique ability. Communicating with animals, even one-way, was a higher-level magic. If she could command animals, that would be the height of the ability. In time, she might be capable of that.

"Can you sense what a shifted shifter thinks? Isn't that a tongue twister?"

She smiled at that. "I'm not sure. I've never been that close to a shifted shifter. They usually only shift during patrol, hunts, melee days, or if their job requires it. Even my uncle never shifts at home."

Before we could speculate further, the Kappa called the Fire mage group to join him. "Fire mages, I want you to burn these rats. Incinerate them. I want nothing left but ash," he commanded.

The eight of us slowly approached the large, gruesome pile of rats. I stopped at six feet. The others copied me, even Lee and Cabello, who had seemed so brave and ruthless in their rat swatting. Killing, blood, and death would be new to most of us. Dealing death had been the province of shifters since their inception. Even the meat from hunts was prepped by shifters before presented to a mage for cooking.

I took charge because the de facto leaders just stood looking disdainfully at the pile of rats. "Let's spread out a little around the area," I told them. "We should burn as hot as possible to reduce the rats to complete ash. A high heat will also burn more quickly and reduce the smell. We shouldn't get too close. We don't want to catch fire."

They all listened to what I said since I made sense. Lee and Cabello both grimaced at me and reluctantly followed my instructions. Knowing their resistance, I tried to make them sound more like suggestions than orders.

"Put out your hands as a guide for your flame and focus only on the pile. If you look anywhere else, that's where your fire will go. Now, on the count of three, let's burn. One. Two. Three."

We'd all had plenty of practice burning a flame as high as we could, but we didn't have the practice of burning it hot enough to incinerate. Most of the mages had to back up farther as heat strongly radiated from the diminishing pile. I wasn't sure how hot the others could flame, but I knew I could easily generate incinerator strength, so I spread my flame around. I wanted this awful task finished quickly. This was the second time I'd had to burn a kill. I still didn't like it, but magic made it necessary.

When we were done and moved fully away from the smoldering pile of ashes, I managed to catch Aryk's eye and mouthed *salt* to him. I shook my hand as if shaking a saltshaker. I also motioned and mouthed *away* and hoped he caught on. He nodded his head, but I couldn't be sure he really understood. If he hadn't gotten it right, I'd be certain to tell him to do the job properly for the safety of the town.

Once we'd backed off completely and stopped, the raptor suddenly took off from the wall, flew straight up into the air, and disappeared into the trees. I heard a round of gasps and sighs as it left. I'm sure there would be some discussion on how to combat the creature should it return, but it hadn't harmed anyone. Not all new creatures would be hostile. Thinking about it, none of those creatures had attacked anyone of us. The rats were running from the snake, the snake was chasing the rats, and the raptor took out the biggest threat. That might be why the Kappa hadn't ordered the shifters to attack it. I thought that promising for future benign creatures.

Once the Kappa issued orders for ash disposal to the two Rhos and Qzyx, leaving Aryk in charge, he ordered the recruits to pick up their weapons and head back to practice. The rest of the soldiers walked us back to the training tent.

I touched Redwing's arm and told her to wait until the others had passed us. When they were ahead enough, I gestured for us to follow.

"I wanted to ask you not to mention your ability to hear animal thoughts to anyone else."

"I won't. I haven't. It seemed to me to be dangerous to exhibit any new and different skills."

"Very wise. No one wants the status quo to change anytime soon. They're still getting used to what they have now."

"I get that."

"Can you communicate with animals as well as hear their thoughts?"

"I don't know. I've never tried. I'm not sure I can translate my thoughts into pictures and send them to the animals."

"You should try it. You never know if such a skill might come in handy."

I really liked Redwing. She had a difference that could eventually make her noticeable—not in a good way. She seemed more adaptable than the other mages I interacted with. I thought she would prosper under my training—and she didn't strike me as particularly happy in the Mage Corps. Maybe I could add another member to my little band of travelers.

"Are you happy here?" I asked.

"Here? In Wolf Trap or in the Mage Corps?"

"Both. Either."

She sighed. "I'm not unhappy or happy. I'm resigned."

"You don't have to be. Have you ever thought Wolf Trap might not be the place for you?" I asked.

She sighed again. "Ever since we moved here. We came to Wolf Trap after my father died three years ago. My mother has family here. They took us in, but now my mother wants to remarry—a man with two small children. There's no place for me there. My aunt and uncle didn't like my father and I think would rather not keep me. I'm the odd one out. That's why I joined the Mage Corps. I needed to be independent and make my own place here."

Why not go for it? It couldn't hurt. "You could come with me. I'm not planning to stay in Wolf Trap much longer. I only joined the Mage Corps to see what it could do. Mages don't belong on the battlefield. I think they're all going to get killed."

She stopped walking and looked at me in consternation. "You really believe that?"

"I didn't at first, but I do now. You saw how squeamish they were killing rats and even picking them up. Imagine them killing or fighting shifters in human or animal form."

"You were squeamish, too," Redwing pointed out politely.

"I know. If I can't kill a rat, I won't be able to kill a human being, not even one wearing a Cat shape. Standing farther away and not right on the battlefield wouldn't help because I'd know it was a human and not a cat."

"The Cats are our enemies. They would kill us if they could."

"Would they though? Has anyone tried diplomacy? Have they sent an envoy to talk?"

She frowned. "I don't know. I've never heard of any talk with Clan Cat, but I might not have. Not everything the Alpha and his soldiers do is up for discussion."

"The Cats should be your allies. Cat's Paw is the closest settlement to Wolf Trap. The next Wolf town is almost a hundred miles away. I think huge rats, snakes, and raptors are the least of your future worries. I think there will be other creatures out there who could attack you. The Mage Corps will be needed to ward off those attacks, not fight a potential ally."

"How do you know all that?"

How much to tell her? Would she remain my friend or use any information I gave her against me? I wouldn't be here much longer; I'd take the chance.

"I watched Aryk Saltwyck fight and kill the creature terrorizing Weird Wood. You've heard of that wood—haven't you? If you go in, you don't come out. I think the creature was eating them."

She looked alarmed. "I have heard of Weird Wood. I hadn't heard the creature had been killed. That would have been celebrated."

"He's keeping it quiet for now. He doesn't know if it's the only creature or if the wood will attract another. It's better to let the fear of it continue to exist until time proves it was the last. The wood looks different—better now. If it stays that way, he'll tell the Alpha."

"You and Aryk Saltwyck?" That seemed to surprise her more than the killing of the Weird Wood creature.

I shrugged. "I was attacked once on the way home. He walks me home every evening. He ensures my good health."

"I didn't know that! When? Where?"

"It was during those weeks of harassment. The Kappas took care of it, but it was thought best to keep me under protective detail. Anyway, I want you to think about leaving with me and my cousin Tara. We could use the extra company."

"Will you be allowed to leave?"

"I don't plan to ask. I'll be here one day and gone the next."

"But won't it be obvious when you book a place in a caravan?"

"I won't travel by caravan. I won't take the road. It's too dangerous. Outlaws tend to follow the caravans looking for opportunities to attack. I'll travel far away from the road through the forests."

"Isn't that more dangerous? What about wild animals? Won't the creatures you mentioned be out there—and we'd have no shifter protection?"

"I'm certain I can protect us. I traveled from the west coast to get here with no incidents. I can do the same on the way back." Liar, liar, pants on fire. My swift mode of travel had helped me evade any predators along the way. I thought I could protect the three of us if I stayed alert, but chance was a fine thing. I might be asking her to jump out of the frying pan into the fire, but it might be her only chance to find a life that could make her happy. I didn't think the Alpha's battle plans had that option.

"I'll think about it," she said doubtfully. "That's a big risk."

"Do it fast. I think my days here are numbered," I said, thinking of Valery and her *Alice*-laced predictions. She wouldn't have made them if she didn't think it was happening soon.

We stopped talking as we entered the training tent. The others were already standing at attention. The Kappa told us to get moving, and we immediately joined them.

He began his dressing down as soon as we were in place. "I was embarrassed by your performance today, recruits. I witnessed two members fainting and a shirking of duty from several others. That could have been a fight for your lives, and you would have died. This is not a game we're playing here. When you go into battle, you must be prepared to defend yourselves and your comrades, or you *will* die. I want you to think about that and train as if your life depends on it. The next time you're told to fight, I want to see you fight to kill. If necessary, we'll go to the lake and beat the bushes to find more huge rats to practice on. You must be prepared to kill your enemy. Don't hold back in training against the Nus. They can take it. Now, back to weapons training."

I looked around at the others. Nobody looked happy, but some looked determined. The reality of battle was finally sinking in. I don't think they liked it any better than I did, but they didn't have a choice. It was up to the Alpha to determine if the mages would be an asset or liability. I wondered how set he was on his battle strategy and whether I'd get the entire plan before I left Wolf Trap. I couldn't do anything to change his plans, but I was curious. If nothing else, I could warn Aryk and Valery about whatever dangers I could perceive in his plans. I had no vested interest in his war, just the mages. I wanted them to survive.

Aryk was his same stoic self when discussing the rats, snake, and raptor. Nothing seemed to faze him. He took everything in his stride.

"I noticed you were reluctant to kill the rats," he remarked.

"Of course I was. How could a vegetarian feel otherwise?"

"They weren't food."

"They could be. I don't want to kill or eat any animal. But if you were hungry enough, I'm sure you'd eat a rat."

"I have," he agreed. "But you didn't even want to touch them."

"Dead rats are almost as disgusting as living ones. Of course I didn't want to touch them. Did you mix the ashes with salt and bury them far away from Wolf Trap and the lake?"

"I did. I understood your pantomime." He grinned at me. I noticed his dimples. He didn't smile that broadly very often. A dimple was just an anomaly of muscle that caused a dent in the cheek. It wasn't unusual or unsightly. Why did I find his dimples so attractive?

I just grunted in response.

"I am puzzled how a large swarm of huge rats, giant snake, and enormous bird of prey could have passed unnoticed by our best hunters, let alone our patrols," he continued. "We patrol out as far as the lake every day."

"When was your last hunt?"

"We hunt twice a month—a week ago."

"Do you hunt all around the town and farms, or do you have a favorite hunting spot?"

"We have enough shifters wanting to take part to hunt everywhere. The lake is a favored spot. It's the biggest watering hole around. There is no way a Wolf or Coyote missed any of those creatures. Even if we don't bring rats back to share with the mages, it would have been irresistible not to chase them down."

That seemed to rule out the rats' long-term existence in the area. Maybe they were born fully grown from the bowels of the earth with the snake and raptor not far behind. As far-fetched as that sounded, magic knew no natural boundaries. It could easily defy science. However, that was a preferable scenario to a sudden migration of the creatures to this area. That would mean something bigger or a gang of something forcing them to migrate.

"Then they must be new to the area. Something caused them to migrate here. You should give your patrols a heads-up."

"Are we to beware of strange creatures all the time now?"

I shrugged. "How would I know? Magic has gotten a foothold on the world. Who knows what it can stir up?"

"You know something more than you've told me. When we fought the creature in Weird Wood, you said something then about the appearance of more creatures. I was expecting something more monstrous than rats, snakes, and raptors, no matter how big they'd gotten."

"I told you to be prepared. I don't know what magic has brewing. I just know things will be shaken up. Not everything will be a threat. Some will be friendly or benign. Some may be useful. That raptor seemed more helpful than threatening."

"Perhaps, but we would have challenged it anyway if it had stuck around."

"Because it looked threatening?"

"Correct."

"That would be a mistake. You need all the allies you can get. No matter how fantastical or incredible a creature looks, it can still be an ally."

"How do we fight against the fantastical and incredible?"

"Your Mage Corps is a start, but defensive and offensive tactics should be taught to every mage, not just an elite few. Everyone should know how to protect themselves. Tell that to your Alpha."

"I'd like to, but he doesn't always listen to me. He'll listen to Valery. He's the only one in a position of power who listens to her. I'll have a word with her."

"She can guide her predictions?"

He grinned. "She can fake a prediction when she wants to. That's how she got Machi to be her bodyguard. He was planning to leave Wolf Trap. He doesn't like being the only Fox in town. He wanted to find others of his kind. Once he was assigned to protect Valery, he stopped making leaving noises."

"How long ago was that?"

"Two years ago. He's only a year younger than me. He was teased unmercifully as a child and called the runt of the litter. We're mostly Wolves here in Wolf Trap. We have a group of Coyotes, but once Machi's father left, only one Fox."

"There could well be a Fox or Coyote town. Not every town is found along the east–west road. There are other roads, but the most populous towns like Wolf Trap are on that road. I would think most caravans coming out this far from the west coast travel the east–west road," I remarked thoughtfully.

"They do. We have good trade agreements with lots of towns along that route to supply what we don't produce and vice versa."

"Caravans are useful and profitable. I hope they have plenty of guards in case of monsters."

"They do to ward off outlaw attacks. You seem to be fixated on caravans. Just don't forget to tell me when you plan to take this journey of yours."

"What journey?" I asked innocently.

"I haven't lived with Valery all these years without noticing the hints in her prophecies. Despite her insistence on quoting from your favorite book, most of what she said hinted at a journey. I want to know when and where once you know."

"That sounds like an order."

"I *am* your superior officer, but it's not an order. It's a heavily stressed request."

"I'll keep that in mind. Now you see me, now you don't is how I usually operate." There was nothing usual about my visit. It was my first, but he didn't need to know that. I imagined all my future comings and goings would be more spontaneous than planned.

"You're too important to the Mage Corps to simply disappear. Every shifter will be out looking for you."

"Thanks for the warning. I'll be sure to take precautions."

"*Please* keep me informed."

"Since you said please, I'll try."

Because of Valery's warnings and predictions, I wasn't sure how much control I'd have over my leaving. I got the impression it would surprise me as much as everyone else. I always had my backpack with me, so I was ready to leave at any time. It was Tara who would need notice. Except at night and on the weekends, we were at different ends of town. But I wouldn't leave her behind. That could be her death sentence. She was my responsibility now, and I wouldn't shirk it.

I wondered what circumstances would occur to make leaving immediately necessary. Searching for rat nests might do it. I really didn't want to do that. And I didn't want to meet that raptor again. No matter what Redwing said it was thinking today, that didn't mean it would always look kindly on two-legged creatures. I wasn't ready to confront monsters on my own. I could sanction the killing of one, but I couldn't discharge that assignment personally. I wasn't nearly ready to be a killer and might never be, and that could be the death of me.

Chapter 21

"Take care of yourself!" screamed the White Queen, seizing Alice's hair with both her hands. "Something's going to happen!"

As WE MOVED INTO the third week of February, I was given the final piece of the puzzle for the Alpha's battle mage offensive. On Monday during our afternoon magic training, we were joined by the Air group. Master Wójcik was our Kappa for the week. Master Jōtarō led the Air group into our practice area.

As we stood at attention, Master Wójcik addressed the two groups first. Of the four Kappas who took turns with each magic group, he was the most encouraging. He offered praise and support to everyone, no matter how lame their performance. The other three were less enthusiastic and often sounded like they were reading from a script when they addressed us.

"Good afternoon, recruits."

"Good afternoon, Master Wójcik."

He had his hands behind his back and his legs braced apart as he stood, surveying us with a kindly smile. "When I look at you, I see capable, sturdy, fine young mages. You all have come a long way since your first day as new recruits. Your martial arts training has gone well. Weapons training is moving along nicely. You have more endurance and physical strength than when you started. I know it hasn't been easy, but I want to commend you all for your good, hard work. Fire and Air, you especially have shown significant improvements. Your potential is promising." He paused, meeting eyes, and nodding at many mages.

"However," he continued, now not looking at any of us, "I don't think any of us realized how difficult it would be to harness and improve your magic skills. I admit we assumed the charms you learned at school were all that were necessary for you to work and live a comfortable life. Witnessing that some mages seemed to have greater abilities than others led us to think our expectations had been too low, that some of you could do more. Like any other skill, patience, practice, and determination should lead to greater magical feats. It has become apparent that magic will take more time than physical skills to develop along envisioned lines. The Alpha has great faith in you and your abilities." Another pause as he looked up as if to gather his thoughts.

"I know the Fire mages haven't fully instituted the Alpha's vision of a twisting, turning column of flame. I know the Air mages have had trouble maintaining a cohesive, moving spiral of Air. Both these tasks have proven to be difficult magic but must be done in tandem during battle. Your two groups together will fulfill the Alpha's vision. The question we've asked ourselves is—why not work the problem out together rather than separately when you will be required to work your magic together during battle?"

He stepped back and allowed Master Jōtarō to define the new directive. Master Jōtarō had always been more direct and critical in his addresses. "From this point forward, the Fire and Air groups will work together to create their offensive hazard for our ultimate battle with Clan Cat. Fire, you will flame and twist only. Air, you will revolve and steer the flame around the training grounds. You will work together to move the flame column quickly and accurately. We want the flame column to act like the tail of a tornado, spiraling in a seemingly unpredictable but totally

controlled pathway. You will practice this technique here on the training ground first and later under simulated battle conditions. Am I
clear, recruits?"

"Yes, Master Jōtarō," we intoned obediently.

We now added ten new mages, all with alliances, jealousies, and prej-
udices, to our edgy eight. There were no new outsiders, but there was
a new strong candidate for Mrs. Future Alpha Ayden Saltwyck. Her
name was Mila Volkova, which was too perfect. Volkova was derived
from the Russian word for wolf, *volk*. Her family had undoubtedly
changed their name to fit their new station in life. There were no
longer current genealogical records leading to the history of family
names. There would always be a sizable gap between what had been
and what was now. Too many deaths, too much migration, and too
many lost records. "O brave new world that has such people in't!"—an
apt quote from Shakespeare. I wondered what Valery would do with
Shakespeare. His body of work could allow her a vast number of
relevant quotes.

Volkova looked the part of a candidate. Her hair was a lighter shade
of brown than Cabello's or Lee's and had red undertones. It was a
color most often described as chestnut. Her eyes were hazel green. She
had high cheekbones and a narrow, fine-boned face. She had tawny
colored skin. She was tall and thin. She didn't have defined curves, but
she moved with sinewy grace. She was a nice counterpoint to the fiery
beauty of Lee and Cabello.

She inspected our four teams and chose my team to award her Air
magic. I guess she wasn't ready to challenge Cabello or Lee directly,
and she'd already seen me in action when I'd gone around with Everest
to demonstrate our partnership. She must have decided mine was the
best team to meet all her challenges. Lucky me.

She brought two other mages with her. Since the Air group had ten while we only had eight, there were two extra mages. She sent the other extra mage to Redwing. She wasn't giving Cabello or Lee any possible advantage.

Neither Master Wójcik nor Master Jōtarō made comments or suggestions on the distribution of the Air mages. They allowed Volkova to decide. I could see she had her group fully under her thumb. None challenged her authority by look or by word. If any of the Air group had been a Cabello, Lee, or McGuire minion, they'd obviously switched allegiance. I was certain by the end of the day if three Air mages proved a better working group than two, Cabello and Lee would be disputing this distribution. But for now, nobody protested—aloud anyway.

"Let's get this thing started," Volkova commanded as she attempted to take over my partnership.

I could see Everest gearing up to challenge Volkova, but I jumped in first. One, because her arrogance rubbed me the wrong way. Two, because Everest would back down too easily. And three, because I wanted to finally make a stand, even a little one. "Introduce yourselves first," I demanded with a sweet smile. I assumed it was sweet, but it wasn't something I'd practiced.

Volkova frowned and narrowed her eyes. Mean wasn't a good expression for her face. She gave in quickly and said brusquely, pointing first to herself, "Volkova, Asher, Park." She pointed to each of the others. The other two were a little taller than Volkova, but less substantial in appearance. Asher had dirty blond hair, blue eyes, and amber skin. Park had dark brown hair and eyes and sienna skin. There was nothing remarkable about their appearance. They were pretty enough girls and probably excellent minions. I assumed their magic power to be less than Volkova's.

I crossed my arms over my chest. "Can't they talk for themselves?"

"It's best to have one spokesperson for a group," she said pointedly. "I speak for the Air mages. I will speak for this new group as well."

"I can speak for myself. My partner, Everest, is also a good speaker. We don't need a mouthpiece."

"That's right," Everest agreed aggressively, surprising me by backing me up.

"There are three of us and two of you. It's best if I lead our new group."

"We're a team. There's no I in team," I argued. I'd thought that a funny phrase when I'd first read it, but I found it apt for this occasion.

She looked surprised at my resistance. "Every team has a leader. They're necessary to accomplish a group task. It's a heavy responsibility I will gladly take on," she persisted with her argument.

"Fire is the dominant element of this enterprise. Without Fire there is no team. Fire should take point." I don't know why I was challenging her, but I was tired of yielding meekly in these dominance games. They were so unnecessary. I didn't want to win a mate. I didn't want a higher rank. I just wanted to successfully interact with people and influence mages to better magic. Maybe I was just angry that I was failing in both these goals.

She gritted her teeth. "Air is controlling the movement. Air should be in control." She put her hands on her hips to exert her dominance.

I could see the other groups were having similar discussions on precedence and procedure. No one wanted to give ground to another group. Instead of team building from the beginning, we'd been set up to compete. First, testing us in a way that demonstrated who was strongest or weakest. Second, not addressing the issue of Ayden Saltwyck sizing us up for his mate. Third, dividing us by element, which separated rather than united the entire group. And fourth, not successfully integrating the outsiders. We were few, but strong mages. Our presence still felt more exclusive than inclusive. Surely by now mage recruits were proving far different from shifter recruits? Why hadn't the Kappas thought to refine their approach for training mages?

I dropped my arms from their defensive position across my chest and widened my stance to appear more confident. "Let's compromise. We have two separate forces here. We don't need to work together. We'll do our part. You do yours. Separate but equal," I suggested.

She narrowed her eyes again, and gave my suggestion a moment's thought, then nodded her head grudgingly and relaxed her stance. "I can work with that for now. Let's get started." She had to have the last word.

Everest and I began feeding our flame to forty feet in height and fifteen feet in width. No group was yet successful in giving it a pretty twist, so I only gave it the hint of a curve. The Air mages stood to the right of us, with mages bookending Volkova and feeding her magic by grasping her shoulders. She began to mumble and gesticulate at the flame, her hands moving to reflect the movement she wanted to achieve. She didn't dance around like the Fire mages did, but her arms were just as lively. Her two minions had trouble maintaining contact.

I could feel the pressure of the air building up between Volkova and the fire. The flame stretched forward, thinning, and almost touched the ground, but didn't move from its grounding. It was a flame fueled by magic and should have been easy to move by magic. Why wasn't magic allowing it to move?

The other three groups had no more success than we did. The only thing that the Alpha had asked for in our months of magic training was an all-out drain of power. There was no creativity, subtlety, or inspiration in that. If he'd laid out his ideas from the beginning and allowed the mages to problem-solve themselves, the results might have been far different. Instead, he told everyone exactly what he wanted, expecting cookie-cutter results.

Belief and imagination were important mental tools in the wielding of magic. These mages hadn't been encouraged to use their imagination to shape their magic. They were hampered by their inability to see this fire as anything but a large, strong, immovable column. They needed to learn to play with magic. Playful words in their charms might help. Telling the fire to dance, frolic, hop, or skip might work if they would think of movement that way. Given more time, more freedom, and less scrutiny, they could develop something impressive on their own. I knew they were capable of great things. Convincing themselves and everyone else was the hurdle.

The Air mages seemed even more frustrated by their day's work than we Fire mages. If we hadn't been feeding magic to the flame, the Air mages would have blown it out with their strong wind surges. I'm sure they'd all used the proper words, but magic hadn't come completely at their call. It only gave them part of what they asked in their charms. The rest would take the coaxing meditation I used added to the mix. On the next rainy day, I would somehow have to be more convincing when sharing my methods. Maybe Volkova had more sense than Cabello or Lee and would listen to me. Since my experience with dominant mages was a resounding no on that, I would be pleasantly surprised if she did.

"What do you think of today's magic work?" I asked Aryk as we walked home after that first day of double teamwork.

"I was worried there in the beginning. I thought you might get into a fight." He grinned.

"It wouldn't have come to that. We were just establishing boundaries. I noticed you didn't hang around after we finally got started."

"Kappa Jōtarō asked me to check on the Earth/Water group. Their partnership isn't as exciting as Fire/Air, but they're having similar problems getting magic to cooperate."

"Cooperate. That's the right word for it. What are Earth and Water expected to do?"

"Make holes and fill them with water—fast."

"Are they supposed to create quicksand?"

"That's the idea. Cats don't like water. Stepping into a deep hole filled with sludgy glop should keep them immobilized. But the Earth mages can't dig holes quick enough, and the Water mages can't fill them just as quickly while keeping the water from draining out."

"A certain type of soil is necessary for creating a quicksand effect. It should be the right combination of sand, silt, or clay. The soil here is too sandy for natural quicksand," I explained knowledgeably. I was sure Aryk would appreciate the information.

"Now you tell me," he joked.

I shrugged. "If I'd known the Alpha's plans in advance, I could have been more helpful."

"I didn't know the Alpha's complete plans until today. The Kappas kept their ultimate goals close to the chest."

"I don't know which job is harder, but they all seem to be impossible." For everyone but me.

"Can't you at least show the Water mages how to move a cloud over the battlefield for a rain burst like you did at Weird Wood?"

I shook my head. "It takes a lot of skill and practice to move a cloud and make it rain."

"Skills that *you* have," he stated with certainty.

I shook my head. "It doesn't matter what I have. I should never have done it. I should have thought of another way to drive the creature out of the woods. It's not a good idea to fool around with the weather. More rain in one place means less rain in another. It was selfish of me to tamper with the natural order of things," I explained. Of course, I hadn't thought of this until afterward. My problem-solving skills were excellent for immediate fixes, but not the future problems those fixes could cause.

"Was that creature part of the natural order of things? Wasn't it better dead than alive, preying on innocent victims?"

"I still should have thought of a different way to force it out of the Wood. I didn't give myself time to think about the problem. That was a onetime solution."

"I'm glad we took care of it right away. It could have left those woods at any time. Without your help, I think more people could have gotten killed."

"I didn't do very much."

"I know you did more than just cause the rainfall. Something in that rain damaged the creature before it left the Wood. That gave me an edge. That charm to remove all teeth and claws was good, too. It made me shift back to human to fight. My wolf is fast but doesn't have the reach a sword at the end of my arm has. Several Wolves could have taken it down, distracting its attention, but on my own, I think I would have gotten badly clawed. You said there was poison in its claws. I heal quickly, but I don't know if I would have survived that."

He'd never talked about our experience at Weird Little Wood before. I thought he'd taken it in stride like he did everything else. He must have been analyzing the fight for future reference. Now I felt an *aw-shucks* moment coming on at his praise even though he'd done most of the work.

"The teeth-and-claws charm was another fortunate event that could have been disastrous. I'm not used to thinking on my feet."

"You do okay. Once you get over your no-killing problem you'll be even better."

"I'm not sure I can."

He gave me a studied look. "I think the Kappas should take the mages out on a hunt with everyone expected to bring back a kill."

"Don't you dare suggest that! I want to postpone the inevitable as long as possible."

"I'll hold off a little, but it's necessary to accustom the mages to killing. Too many of you were hesitant even killing rats. You have to get over that or you'll be useless in battle. You *will* die."

I winced. "I understand that. I'm just not ready to face that reality yet. Now, back to your mage problem," I insisted briskly. "What's the Alpha going to do if the mages can't deliver?"

He gave me a quick grin, letting me know my unsubtle change of subject was not lost on him. "I don't think the Mage Corps is designed to be the decisive factor to victory. It's designed to add advantage and surprise, offering something the Cats would never have thought of. Whatever the mages can do will be a welcome addition."

"Whatever they can do will definitely be a surprise. I don't expect it to be much of an advantage."

"Do you have any better suggestions? I'd be happy to pass them on."

"I'll give it some thought. Practice would be more exciting if we were doing possible, not impossible, things. It's rather frustrating as it is."

"I imagine it must get boring to contain your power every day instead of showing it off," he suggested slyly.

"It would be if that were true," I denied. I quickly changed the subject—again. "This whole situation is ridiculous. I don't know why I even try to offer any help. The Cats are not your enemy."

"I don't know a time when they haven't been thought of as our enemy."

"Well, they aren't. You need each other. Your real enemies are coming, and they are *not* the Cats. The rats were only a foretaste of things to come."

"Now that sounds like a prophecy worthy of Valery. Is it?"

"There are more things in heaven and earth than are dreamt of in your philosophy, Horatio."

"Is that another quote from that *Alice* book?"

"No. It's from a play called *Hamlet*."

"I wish you and Valery would knock off the quotes. Some of us aren't as well read as others."

"I don't know about Valery, but I can't help it. There have been some wonderful writings in the past. I would hate to have them lost. Your ancestors have preserved much of their literature, but some of it is in a technological format currently not available. It will be a long time before it can be accessed."

"My ancestors? Aren't they your ancestors as well?"

Me and my big mouth. What was it about Aryk that gave me lips loose enough to sink ships? Maybe it was simply his interest. I'd have to remember how dangerous it was to attract someone's interest. That might help me keep my mouth shut in the future, but it was too late to help me now.

"Once you start asking questions, you can't stop—can you?"

"I may not be a Cat, but I'm always curious. I don't expect you to satisfy my curiosity, but I have to ask—and hope for answers."

"You've gotten enough answers out of me for today. Warn the others or don't. Pass on my advice about the mages or don't. I won't be here to see the results."

"You *are* leaving soon, then?"

"I don't know when the urge will take me. It could be soon, or it could be a few weeks or months from now. I only know I won't be here for your battle. That fight is not mine. Just have a care for the mages. They still don't appreciate what they're getting into. I think some of them could die."

"I'll do my best to apprise the Kappas. But I think they have a pretty good understanding of what the mages can and can't do."

"Even though Kappa Jōtarō gave the I'm-disappointed-in-you speech after the rat fiasco?"

"What choice did he have? His job is to get you fighting ready. Some of you will respond to that tactic and perform better. It's the Alpha that needs convincing. So far, he's only heard reports shaded to the positive."

"This might be the time for Valery to step in."

"She hasn't seen the future you have. She sees this as a step forward for mages."

"It's a good start. I only wish it weren't all about fighting Clan Cat. Maybe something will happen to prevent a showdown with the Cats."

"Like more giant rats?"

"Something like that. Maybe I'm worried for nothing. I'm not really a prophet. Mine is more hypotheses based on known facts."

"Known only to you?"

"Some of them, maybe. What is your assessment based on what you now know?"

"Five months is not enough time to create a soldier out of a protected mage. Not even every shifter enjoys the hunt. There are some that hate the animal within them. Your idea of training the mages in self-defense from childhood has merit. But in this reality, we must make these particular mages battle ready."

"By Alpha decree, there's only this reality. If more time is needed, he needs to make more. Can't Valery at least give the mages another year?"

"I'll ask her."

We left it at that. I didn't have an answer except *don't fight the Cats.* Maybe fate would intervene and create a new target. The mages would have to figure things out for themselves. I would mention visualization and meditation whenever I could. That was all the help I was willing to give to this enterprise any longer.

We continued into another week with no changes in our routine except a day of rain that allowed me to mention my getting-to-know-magic ideas. The Air mages were receptive and gave it a try, which seemed to galvanize Lee and Cabello. They wouldn't be outclassed by Air Mages.

It was on Thursday winding up weapons practice that we heard not a whistle this time but the loud, constant clang of a bell. I remembered seeing a bell tower in the center of town. I'd forgotten to ask its purpose. I was about to find out.

"Cat!" the Nus around us all shouted at once.

"Everyone into town. Recruits, bring your weapons. Let's find out what's happening," yelled the Kappa.

All I could think of was Tara. I'd been reinforcing the suppressing charm every weekend, but I hadn't erased her knowledge of being a Cat. I hadn't wanted to tamper with her memory or identity too much. I wasn't certain what the psychological consequences would be. She was psychologically damaged enough without me heaping on more.

If Tara was the Cat the alarm tolled for—how could I save her?

Chapter 22

"Our family always hated cats: nasty, low, vulgar things!"

WE RAN TOWARD THE bell tower in the center of town as it continued to ring. It was over a mile from our training area. I tried to be one of the leaders, but the shifters were all faster than me, and I only outran the other mages. I was glad of all the running practice we'd had. It kept me in better shape than I'd realized for a run like this. I was barely winded when I arrived.

The ringing bell stopped just before I reached the convergence of shifters, which had to be the hub of the emergency. Besides our group of forty-two mages, ten Nus, two Zetas, and one Kappa, there were ten Rhos, eight Nus, two Zetas, and a Delta already there. Other unranked shifters had gathered from the businesses fronting Mart Street and beyond. I didn't try to count them since they didn't wear armbands and didn't stand still.

There were no other mages to be seen. All other mages had probably barricaded themselves in their homes or businesses until the Cat issue had been resolved. Only the Mage Corps had any formalized combat training, so we were the only mages expected on the field.

For a moment, after the last toll of the bell died out, there was absolute silence; then it was broken by everyone talking and questioning at once.

"What's going on?" the Delta's deep voice seemed to amplify as he pitched it over the babble of the shifters all clamoring to know what was happening.

"Someone saw a Cat."

Various versions of this same message were spoken at the same time by several nonmilitary shifters. None of them claimed the Cat sighting.

"Who rang the warning?" the Delta spoke loudly again.

Everyone looked around. One man raised his hand and came forward.

"I rang the warning," he said uneasily. "I heard the cries of Cat. I'm in charge of the tower today. I thought it better to chance being wrong than let a Cat run around."

"Who saw the Cat?" the Delta continued his questioning. Fewer shifters could answer this question.

"Some boys."

"A couple of kids comin' home from school yelled *Cat*," someone more knowledgeable said.

"Did they really see a Cat or was this some juvenile game they were playing?"

"They said there was a Cat."

"Where are these boys now?"

Only a couple shifters could answer this one. "We've got 'em over at the bakery over there. We were holdin' 'em to answer questions."

"Have you conducted a search yet?"

"No, Delta. We were awaitin' instructions."

He nodded his head and turned to the military leaders around him. Aryk was one of them. "I want you Zetas to take charge of the search teams. There are four of you. We'll divide the search area into four quadrants." He designated the boundaries of the quadrants and assigned the Zetas to numbered teams, then issued further orders. "Rhos and Nus, half of you shift. Your senses will be more acute. Search systematically. Knock on doors if you deem it necessary. I want that Cat taken alive. I want to know what the Cats have planned to send someone into Wolf Trap."

The Rhos and Nus chosen began to shift.

Kappa Idris spoke up, "Sir, I'd like the mage recruits to take part in the search."

The Delta turned to look at us. I stood in the back of the group now. "Agreed. Give them their orders, Kappa."

He swiftly divided us by our element and assigned us to the four teams. I was lucky enough to be assigned to the sector that included the boardinghouse, but I didn't intend to leave with the others. I wanted to hear what the boys had to say first. "Keep your eyes sharp. Beat bushes with your swords. Let the Rhos and Nus search backyards. Don't put yourselves in jeopardy. Report back to training when you're finished."

In the meantime, the Delta told the unranked shifters to return to their jobs and asked to be shown to the boys.

There were grumblings from those told to leave. Everyone wanted to be the first one to find the Cat, but the military had authority over the situation. Most reluctantly returned to their previous locations, but some slowly followed the Delta and Kappa. The one who'd spoken up about the boys guided them to the bakery.

I waited to follow behind all those heading to the bakery. I hoped Kappa Idris wouldn't notice me. Once I heard the boys' story, I would go home and check on Tara before joining the search. She would have been walking home from school at the same time as the boys. I sincerely hoped she wasn't the named Cat, but I couldn't believe that another would be foolish enough to shift in the middle of a Wolf town.

The boys in question were three scruffy schoolboys of about eleven or twelve. They didn't look scared, but excited. All the attention was on them. That seemed to gratify the biggest one in the group.

"Which one of you saw the Cat?" the Delta asked.

"I did," they all said at once, but the biggest boy jostled ahead of the other two. He threw his chest out importantly.

"What did this Cat look like?"

All the boys chimed in on this description.

"He was brown and white with squiggly black circles on his back."

"He wasn't nearly as big as a Wolf, but he was bigger than us."

"He jumped on me and knocked me down," the bigger one bragged. "I saw him clear as day. He had yellow eyes and black spots on his head."

"Why didn't any of you shift when you saw the Cat?"

"'Cause we already shifted once today at school."

"Yeah, we practice shifted at school."

"I can't shift more than twice in a day."

"Okay. I understand. He knocked you down. Why did he knock you down? Was that all he did?"

"I don't know. He grabbed my—he just stood on me a minute. He wasn't that heavy. I wasn't scared." It was still the biggest one doing most of the talking.

"He grabbed your what?"

"Just something," he muttered, suddenly looking down at the ground.

"It was that outsider's necklace you took," one of the other boys said.

"Yeah. You shouldn't a took it," the other one agreed.

The bigger boy glared at them and hissed, "Shut up."

The Delta homed in on this. "You stole another child's necklace?"

The boy looked down and mumbled, "My sister liked it. I wanted to see it up close. It wasn't very much. Just a shiny butterfly thing. I don't even think it's real gold. That outsider didn't need it. It didn't even look good on her."

The Delta said sternly, "I don't care if the necklace belonged to an outsider or insider, that's stealing. Stealing is not tolerated in Wolf Trap. There are severe punishments for stealing."

"I didn't steal it. It broke, and I picked it up. I wasn't gonna keep it. I just wanted to look at it, but the outsider ran away," he whined, definitely lying.

"She wouldn't give it to you," one of the smaller boys mumbled.

"You tore it off her neck," the other small boy mumbled. "You shouldn't a done that."

"Assault as well? You're racking up the punishments, young shifter. Was that when the Cat jumped you?"

"Not long after."

"He wanted the necklace?"

"I don't know. He knocked me down first and growled in my face."

"That's when he showed his big teeth," another boy said.

"But he didn't bite you?"

He shook his head. "I thought he was gonna, and I yelled *Cat*."

"You screamed," another boy corrected. "Harry and I yelled *Cat*. Then he—the Cat—turned his head and took the necklace in his mouth that Tommy dropped and took off."

The bigger boy glared at him. I could tell there would be a reckoning once this was over. The bigger boy had to prove his superiority once more. He couldn't do it facing a Cat, but he could lord it over his smaller companions.

"Where exactly did he confront you?"

"We was walking down Elm Street from school. We turned on Third Street thinkin' of goin' to the bakery afore goin' home. There were other kids walkin' the same way goin' home. We saw the outsider first. We waited for her to get even with us. After we started walkin' again. We saw the Cat 'afore we got to Pine Street."

Pine Street was the street before Oak Street, where our boarding-house was located. The bakery was two streets down from Oak on Mart Street, which was where we were now. The tree-named streets were parallel to Mart Street and perpendicular to the numbered streets. Tara could have gone that same way to walk home. Ocelots had dark linked spots. The Cat this kid saw could very well have been Tara.

Who was I kidding? It had to be Tara. The butterfly necklace was hers. What other Cat would risk coming into Wolf Trap to grab that necklace? I had to get home to see if she'd gone there when she left Pine Street. I couldn't allow her to be captured by the Wolf Trap shifters. I had to find her first.

I slipped away before the Kappa noticed my presence— I hoped. I didn't stay to hear the boy's punishment or the Delta's conclusions about the whole affair. He was bound to confront Tara, the outsider with the necklace, to get her side of the story.

I walked fast but didn't run. Running would draw unwanted atten-tion to me and my efforts to get as far away as possible from Mart Street and the sharp-eyed Kappas. There was no reason for him to suspect Tara of being a Cat. There were no female shifters as far as anyone in this town was concerned. That wouldn't be the obvious conclusion to any shifter, except maybe Aryk. I didn't think anything connected to me would surprise him. He might not have my full measure, but he was closer to it than anyone else.

I entered the boardinghouse quietly. I couldn't hear Audrey or Dorrie, but they could be anywhere behind the closed doors of their living space.

And I hadn't seen the search party on my way here. I didn't know if that was a good thing or bad.

I walked upstairs, stepping only on the sides of the stairs. I'd discovered early on that the center sections squeaked and learned how to walk upstairs without making too much noise. I slowly turned the knob on my door and gently pushed, but it didn't budge. Tara didn't have a key, so she must have locked it from the inside. The door had a deadbolt lock, but the door itself was flimsier than an outside door and would be easy enough for a shifter to kick in.

When I unlocked the door with the only key we had, I quickly slipped inside. Tara was pacing the floor as an Ocelot, and to my alarm, Qzyx was there, sitting in one of our two chairs.

"What are you doing here?" I asked him urgently.

"I was on my way to the laundry, and I was coming up Third Street. I saw what was happenin'. I saw Tara run away. I was just comin' toward those boys to tell 'em off when the Cat came out of the shrubbery and pounced on that big boy. When the Cat ran off, I followed. It ran here and crouched in the bushes in back. I took my laundry out of the basket and told the Cat to get inside, and she did. I covered her up and brought her up here. I didn't see or hear Audrey or Dorrie. I don't think they're home."

"How did you know the Cat was Tara?"

"I could tell when I looked in her eyes," he said simply.

"How? They're Cat eyes, not human eyes, when she shifts." They weren't even the same color brown. They were a reddish brown when she was an Ocelot.

He shrugged. "I don't know. I just did. Eyes are the windows of the soul, they say. I guess I saw her soul."

That was very poetic, but highly improbable. Although I'd had that same thought about those giant rats—that their eyes were soulless. "Doesn't it shock you—a female shifter?"

"At my age, nothin' shocks me anymore. Let me tell you, I seen stuff you wouldn't believe. A female shifter is just one more thing to add to that unbelievable list."

I sat down on one bed. "I've been trying to suppress her urge to shift until the weekends. That's why I take her out of town and away from everyone for a few hours. She's able to shift and hunt. That should have been enough to assuage her instincts. I thought she knew better than to shift in town. She knows the danger if anyone sees her. She deliberately shifted when that should have been her last recourse, no matter the situation." I shook my head. I should have realized I was asking too much of her when she told me how much she hated school. She never mentioned bullies, but I should have guessed. Along with cliques, contending with bullies seemed to be a rite of passage for adolescents today just as in the past. Human socialization had not changed radically despite the advent of magic.

"Maybe she was provoked enough to override whatever magic you used on her." He held out his hand. The broken necklace was in his palm. "She was holdin' this in her mouth. She dropped it at my feet when we got safely in her room."

I sighed. "I knew that necklace was a bad idea. I told her to keep it hidden. I shouldn't have allowed her to wear it. There were three boys involved. One of them took her necklace. They were the ones to shout *Cat*."

"What child is gonna hide somethin' so pretty? I'm right sorry to have given it to her. I never woulda if I'd thought about the trouble it would cause. I shoulda come up with somethin' else to reward her for my rescue," he said regretfully.

"You and me both," I said. "Tara and I need to get out of town—the sooner, the better. They'll easily be able to trace the start of this to Tara. They might not suspect her of being a Cat, but they'll be watching and questioning her. At worst, those bullies won't leave her alone." It was Thursday. One more day of mage training and I would be free for two days. No one would miss me until after that.

I looked at Tara. She was slowing down her pacing now that I was here. As I watched, she finally came over to me, put her head on my knee, and sat down. I stroked her soft fur.

"I want to go with you," Qzyx suddenly announced.

"What?" I turned my gaze to him. I hadn't expected this. "Why?"

"I only stuck around this long to keep an eye on you two. I usually only stay in town weeks, not months. I might be gettin' too old for a scavengin' life. I would never a been caught in that mantrap when I was younger. You two gals shouldn't be travelin' alone."

"That's not necessary. My next stop is hundreds of miles away. It'll take weeks if not months to get there on foot. You're safer here," I protested.

He shook his head. "You'll need my help. There are monsters out there. I seen a few. I might not be able to shift, but I can still fight."

Stubborn old man. I didn't think I could easily shake him. I could make sure he didn't follow us, but should I? I wouldn't mind having another traveling companion. He'd certainly help relieve the boredom of a long trip. Plus, an extra pair of eyes and hands to protect Tara wouldn't go amiss. He now knew one of our secrets, but if he came with us, he was bound to learn more. Should I trust him further?

As I continued to watch him, silently thinking, he spoke up again. "Saturday mornin' will be the best time to leave. You always go outside town on Saturday. You won't be changin' your routine. The gate guards will change before you'd usually come back. No one will miss you until Monday mornin' when you don't show up for training."

"I know." Those were exactly my thoughts.

"You can manage one more day of trainin' without anyone gettin' suspicious."

"What about Tara? She'd have to go back to school or that would look suspicious considering she'd been at the center of today's incident. Can she handle facing those bullies one more day?"

"Cats ain't cowards," Qzyx declared fiercely. "No matter what the Wolves think."

Tara lifted her head and snarled her agreement.

Qzyx was very good with Tara. He would be an asset on our travels. I was decided. "All right. I should get back to the search. I wouldn't know what happened today if I'd followed orders."

"I need to get back to my laundry. I should be gone before your landladies check in." He picked up the laundry basket I'd noticed in the corner.

I concentrated on the basket and said a charm to remove any Cat evidence from the basket and sheets. There was no point in bringing suspicion down on Qzyx. A light breeze came through the room and fluttered through the basket, taking the Cat musk, hair, dander, and prints from the sheets and basket to carry high in the sky and outside the town.

"It's time to shift back now, Tara." I gave her a little power for the shift while continuing to remove Cat evidence from her and the room. I'd already removed evidence of Cat on my way here.

"Rain," she almost cried after shifting. She clutched her neck. I could see the faint marks on her neck where the necklace had been torn off. It wouldn't take long for them to disappear. Shifters healed fast. "That bully broke my necklace when he took it. I hate him!"

"You were brave. You didn't hurt him when you could have," I soothed.

"I have your necklace now." Qzyx again held out his hand with the necklace before putting it back in his pocket. "I'll fix it. You shouldn't have it, anyway. They'll be lookin' for that."

She reluctantly nodded her head. "I'll go to school tomorrow, but I don't want to. I might shift again."

"No, you won't—not if you want to stay alive. You can cry and look sad, but don't get angry. It won't help. Bullies like that get their comeuppance, eventually."

"I'll remember them," she said darkly.

"You do that. Now we must go. Stay in your room. If you hear knocking at the door downstairs, don't answer it. Lie down on the bed and pretend to be napping. If they get into the house and knock on this door, then answer it. Let them come in. They won't find anything wrong with our room. They know what happened with the necklace and the bullies. You can verify that, but tell them you ran home. You never saw a Cat. When Audrey and Dorrie come back, you can tell them about the necklace. You can cry. They'll be sympathetic."

"Okay," she said dismally.

"Don't be afraid. Remember, this is all the bullies' fault, not yours. You are the victim here."

"Okay," she said, more determined this time. I hated leaving her alone to face them all, but I had no choice. I had to get back to find out what was going on officially.

Qzyx and I parted company outside, going in different directions. I still didn't see any search party on this street. I looked around for a little bit but didn't find the other Fire mages.

Somehow, I was the last one to return to training. The mages must have been released after the ground search. The Kappas and Zetas hadn't returned, but the Nus had. They were all in the mess hall eating lunch. A few snide remarks were made about my prolonged absence, but nobody questioned me—not even Redwing. I ate quickly to catch up.

Only the Kappas should know that the involved outsider was my cousin. No one else should have the entire story yet. And Kappa Idris didn't return by the end of training.

Aryk returned from his quadrant search in time to walk me home.

"What took you so long? Why did the mages return early?"

"The mages weren't as useful as the Kappa thought they'd be. I don't think any of them wanted to meet up with a Cat. They were excused back to training early on."

"Did anyone find anything?" I asked with what I hoped was proper curiosity.

"No. Not even a scent past Pine Street. I should say there wasn't a scent there either, but we knew he'd been there. A few other kids walking home from school had seen him, too, so the boys weren't making up a story."

Good. I was happy to hear my charms had worked. It was just good luck that the search party hadn't reached the boardinghouse before I did. "How is that possible?"

"You tell me."

"Me? How would I know? What do I have to do with it?" I feigned surprise.

Aryk gave me a bland *I don't believe you* look. "The outsider girl has been identified as your cousin, Tara. She was questioned. She knew nothing about a Cat. The room you share was searched thoroughly."

"Did you scare her? She's not used to rough handling."

"We searched the room. Your landladies searched her."

"What were you hoping to find?"

"The necklace."

"Oh, that stupid thing. I told her not to wear it where it could be noticed. I knew it would cause trouble."

"She told us Qzyx gave it to her."

"He gave it to her as a reward when we rescued him."

"I've never heard of him being caught in a trap. To hear him talk, he's managed many dire escapes all by wit and cunning."

"You know how people exaggerate. A good story doesn't end in defeat or being rescued by two weak females."

"You're not weak. Even before the martial arts training, you looked like you could take care of yourself, even against an average-sized shifter."

"You flatter me. I might have been taught enough to take one down by surprise and quick moves, but I'd have trouble against a determined one. I've never fought a shifter except in practice. I didn't even try to fight when those three shifters attacked me. I thought resistance would get me more hurt."

"Not if you used magic. That's one thing we haven't practiced. Your magic has been saved solely for your magic practices. The Alpha knows how quickly it can be used up before you need to eat and rest."

"Just like your magic. We all have limited reserves."

"You can't distract me by changing the subject. It's a complete mystery how a Cat came to be in the village, why he should want your cousin's necklace, and where he went afterward. We requestioned the boys, but they're adamant about the Cat. That's when we looked for other witness-es."

"Maybe it was a real cat of some kind. They do exist just like real wolves, foxes, and coyotes exist in the wild."

"That may be, but then why couldn't we smell one around town? Could it be an illusion of some kind? Can mages do that?"

Illusions were a higher-level magic I wasn't able to perform yet. "I don't think so. That would be some good magic if it could be done. But could an illusion pick up an object? That's even better magic."

"It's an idea being generated. Everyone is on the watch for that necklace. If a young mage has developed such a skill, the Alpha would be interested."

"I would imagine so."

I said nothing to Aryk about leaving. I felt guilty about that. He'd been practically my only friend in Wolf Trap. It was safer for him to be as surprised as everyone else. And most important, I thought I might embarrass myself with tears if I said goodbye to him. Just thinking about it made me feel sad. I didn't regret the choices I'd made to violate rules four and eight (*Avoid shifters* and *Interact without engaging*); but for the first time in my life, I wanted to cry for something other than physical pain. I think this new emotional pain might hurt worse than the broken arm that had caused me some involuntary tears when I was ten. How was that possible?

Chapter 23

Its quaint events were hammered out—And now the tale is done

WE SET OUT AFTER sunrise, an hour earlier than usual.

I'd gotten suspicious looks yesterday from the other mages. Everyone had heard the details about the Cat sighting. I was questioned by Kappa Benjamin during morning exercises and had to verify the part of Tara's story about the necklace. Otherwise, there were no repercussions so far regarding Cat Tara's adventures. There was no evidence that we had any dealings with a Cat. That damned necklace was the only thing connecting us to the Cat.

I was able to tell Redwing my plans during lunch since she and I had a table to ourselves. I told her we'd be leaving the next morning after sunrise, grabbing breakfast from the bakery on the way. I apologized for giving her so little notice. She could take her chances with me and learn more about magic or stick it out with the Mage Corps. I hinted I could do a lot more with magic than I had shown in our training. I promised that she would achieve much greater results if she stuck with me. I was very positive and upbeat. I told her nothing about the dangers. I didn't want to scare her off dwelling on possible perils. I was certain I could protect the three of us by wards alone. Defensive spells were my preference over offensive spells. I didn't want to kill any threats, just protect us from them.

She'd looked worried all day as she mulled over her choice. I could tell nothing from her demeanor about her decision, and she said nothing to me before the end of the day. It wouldn't be a simple choice. It might be the scariest thing she'd ever done. She was another Wolf Trap inhabitant I would want to come back to check on in the future if she chose not to come with us.

Tara said the bullies hadn't been in school to annoy her. "Sometimes I was sad and sometimes I was angry. Some girls talked to me and said they were sorry about my necklace. They didn't like those bullies either. They told me stuff about what those bullies had done to them and other kids. If we stayed here, I think they might have become friends with me," she said wistfully.

"Maybe the next town will be more accepting of outsiders," I said encouragingly. I didn't believe that, but one could always hope.

I left a note and a month's extra rent for our landladies. They had been kind to Tara, and she liked them—even gruff Audrey. I blessed their house before we left and hoped that charm would give them good fortune for however long it lasted. That was the best reward I could offer for their kindnesses.

We picked up some breakfast bread on our way out of town. No one at the gate questioned our leaving. The two guards stationed there were ones that rotated duty on our Saturdays out the west gate. They gave us the usual warnings about leaving the protection of the town. They knew I was in the Mage Corps, so they weren't too worried about me. Aryk had made it clear to each set of guards that I knew what I was doing and had permission to leave the town. Nobody of a higher authority had since countermanded that order.

I told them casually that we may stay out later than usual. We might make a day of it and explore the farms. It had been a long time since either of us had seen a cow or pig. Tara felt bold enough to say she used to have a pet potbellied pig. When one guard said, "Them's good eatin' even if you don't get the fun of chasin' 'em down," Tara lost her smile and shut up. I didn't think she'd thought about all the ramifications of being a shifter.

"That was a mean thing to say," she muttered when we were away from the gate.

"It may be, but *Sus domesticus* has always been an enduring food source."

"What's that sus thing?"

"That's the scientific name for domesticated pigs."

"Why didn't you just say that?" she grumbled. "I would never eat Polly, no matter what."

I didn't say anything, but I doubted her family felt the same way. Polly had probably been included as a dinner entrée not long after Tara had been dropped into her oubliette. If you were a meat eater, it was best not to have edible pets.

Neither Qzyx nor Redwing were near the gate, or just outside the woods when we left. We waited there for one or both to catch up. At least I knew Qzyx planned to show up. I could only hope Redwing would, and wouldn't keep us waiting too long.

We sat down among the trees about thirty yards from the west gate. Tara was quiet and still as a cat hunting prey. I'd told her we were expecting Qzyx to join us. I didn't mention Redwing since her addition was still an unknown variable.

I ruminated on my time spent in Wolf Trap. I'd wanted to interact with people, and I did, but not exactly how I'd imagined. I'd wanted to gain friends and allies, but the Alpha's plans had made that difficult. I'd wanted to find anomalies, and I did, but I hadn't thought about the dangers they faced from being different. I'd violated rule thirteen (*Do not collect anomalies*). But I was only rescuing one, or maybe two if Redwing joined us. I didn't want to find any more until I was in a better position to rescue them all. I couldn't continually add people to my travels, because I couldn't keep them all safe. I had to get stronger and find a permanent home before that happened.

Overall, I hadn't adhered to many of my Jardvari's most important rules. I'd made exceptions many times that would most likely have been unsanctioned. I knew the rules were to keep me safe, but some had been more of a hindrance than a help. I'd chosen to rescue one anomaly, trust, as far as I could, one shifter, and engage with multiple mages because these infractions seemed the right thing to do. My one regret was that now I was more emotionally connected to Wolf Trap than I'd intended. I didn't know if I'd ever see certain people again. It was depressing.

I worried about the mages and the Mage Corps. Would the Alpha disband it when the mages failed to meet his magical expectations? Would he deploy them in battle anyway and surely get them killed? Would the mages burn everything down in their attempts to please the Alpha with moving, twisting columns of flame? Was I abandoning them to a fate I could possibly avert?

I shook my head at this thought. I had no power over the Alpha, the mages, or anything else in Wolf Trap. I was too young and an outsider. They wouldn't listen to me even through Aryk, who wasn't trusted either. I'd done the best I could with the time allotted. Maybe the Alpha would have second thoughts and give the mages more time to improve their skills—years more time. I could only hope and direct blessings to the Mage Corps and Wolf Trap. I would hate to find Wolf Trap burned to the ground or the mages I'd trained with dead or maimed if I should pass through there again one day.

As we sat and watched the gate, expecting to see at least Qzyx—it finally opened.

Qzyx came through first, then Redwing (who I would have to remember to start calling Maya), and then of all things amazing: Aryk, Valery, and Machi. I stood up to greet them.

"What are you all doing here? Have you come to say goodbye? Did Qzyx reveal I was leaving today?" I asked Aryk while looking at all the uninvited. It was then I noticed the full backpacks and bedrolls on each of their backs.

"Yes, Qzyx told me—which you should have done—and we're coming with you," Aryk announced.

I couldn't hide my surprise and perhaps a little delight. I'd repressed my sadness at leaving Aryk. I'd been missing him even as I walked out the door of Acorn's Rest. Now I wouldn't have to. "You can't—can you? Should you? Why would you? This is your home." I felt like I was babbling. "What did the guards say?"

"We don't fit in this place any more than you do. We talked it over. We're willing to take a chance on coming with you," he said firmly. "I told the guards we were practicing survival skills overnight. Alpha sanctioned. We shouldn't be missed until tomorrow."

I looked at him a moment. He seemed confident in his decision. I turned to his sister. "You too, Valery? You really want to leave home? We're going too far away for you to suddenly change your mind."

"All roads lead to Rome," she said with her sweet, sunny smile.

She was quoting again. I'd read that quote somewhere before, but right now I couldn't remember where. Rome itself was in the hot zone of the world, but I think the quote meant that all the ways of doing something will lead to the same result. I wasn't sure how this answered my question, but Valery was sure. I'd have to accept that answer. Questioning her might lead to more *Alice* quotes. I wanted to forget *Alice* before we conjured up a Jabberwock amid the nonsense.

I nodded my head and turned to her bodyguard. "Machi? Are you sure? Once we leave Wolf Trap, you're under no obligation to follow the Alpha's orders."

He shrugged. "I take my job to guard Valery seriously. It doesn't matter if the Alpha's no longer my boss. She is. I can't do that guarding if she leaves Wolf Trap. I go where she goes," he said simply.

That response was acceptable. I didn't sense that he had any dark ulterior motives. His loyalty to Valery seemed genuine and firmly rooted. I turned to the last member of the group joining me.

"Maya? Are you sure? I didn't give you a lot of time to weigh this decision. I don't know what dangers we may face on our journey, but dangers there will be. I should have given you more caveats, but I wanted you to come. I can help you become a better mage." I wouldn't have questioned her if she'd come alone. I should have, but I would have been so grateful she'd chosen to brave the journey, I wouldn't have said anything more to dissuade her. With Aryk and Machi along, the odds of the success for our journey had multiplied a hundredfold, but I still gave her the chance to back out.

She squared her shoulders. "No, I'm not sure, but I'm here to find out. I can always come back if things don't work out."

It wouldn't be that easy, but I'd get her on a caravan if it came to that. I would do my best to improve her magic skills in the meantime. If she went back to Wolf Trap, I would see that she was the strongest mage they'd ever known.

I slowly looked at each determined face one more time. These were my friends and allies. I would do my utmost to see that they survived their time with me. Even if that meant revealing some of my secrets. By throwing in with me, they had the right to know what they were getting into.

"Okay then. My plan is to head east and walk all day away from Wolf Trap toward Wolf Haven, the largest town on the eastern side of this continent. It's at least twice as big as Wolf Trap, but I think it should be our next long-term stop. It will take us weeks, if not months, to get there depending on how fast we can travel. Before any of that happens, tonight when we stop, there are a few things I have to tell you. If after that you have second thoughts, you can change your mind then and still make it back to Wolf Trap in a day. Questions?"

Everyone shook their heads. They would have questions after they'd thought about it over a long day of walking. People always had questions when given time to think.

"Okay then, troupe. Let's hit the road—not literally. The road's too dangerous. We'll be traveling further south of the main road."

I turned and led the way. I hoped none of them changed their minds, even after a day of walking and thinking. I rather liked the idea of having a troupe of stalwart companions on my travels. I just hoped none of them had cause to regret their decision.

This could be the beginning of a most excellent adventure.

Acknowledgements

I always thought authorship to be a solitary occupation most suitable to introverts. While this may be true of the writing portion, there are other aspects of the process that require outside input. As an independent author and publisher, I don't have the workforce advantage of a mainstream publisher, but I have enlisted the services of professionals to help me achieve a quality product.

Thanks to Kharysa Watt of Kaylex Editorial Services for her developmental editing skills.

Thanks to Amie Norris of Words Reworked Editorial Services for her copy editing and proofreading skills.

Thanks to Lewis Carrol for the great quotes found in his two wonderfully imaginative works, *Alice in Wonderland* and *Alice through the Looking Glass*.

Thanks to Wide for the Win and the Allied Alliance of Independent Authors for the collected advice of those who have trailblazed a path for success for the independent author.

And last but certainly not least, thanks to all those readers who choose to read my book, hopefully like it, review it, and continue to read on in the series.

About the author

Dauna Grey is an ex-librarian from the central Florida area. She's a fan of anime, manga, fantasy, and dragons. For several years she wrote Naruto fanfiction on FanFiction.Net before deciding to create her own fantastical worlds.

If you'd like to stay updated about future releases, please sign up for the free newsletter and a bonus story:

https://daunagrey.com

You can also find the occasional art, snippets, and bonus stories in the future.